The Blame Game

Terri Reynolds

This book is a work of fiction. Names, characters, businesses, organisations, places and events are either the product of the author's imagination or are used fictitiously. Any resemblance to actual persons, living or dead, events or locales is entirely accidental.

Text Copyright© Terri Reynolds 2017
The right of Terri Reynolds to be identified as the author of this work has been asserted by her.

For Matty; for believing

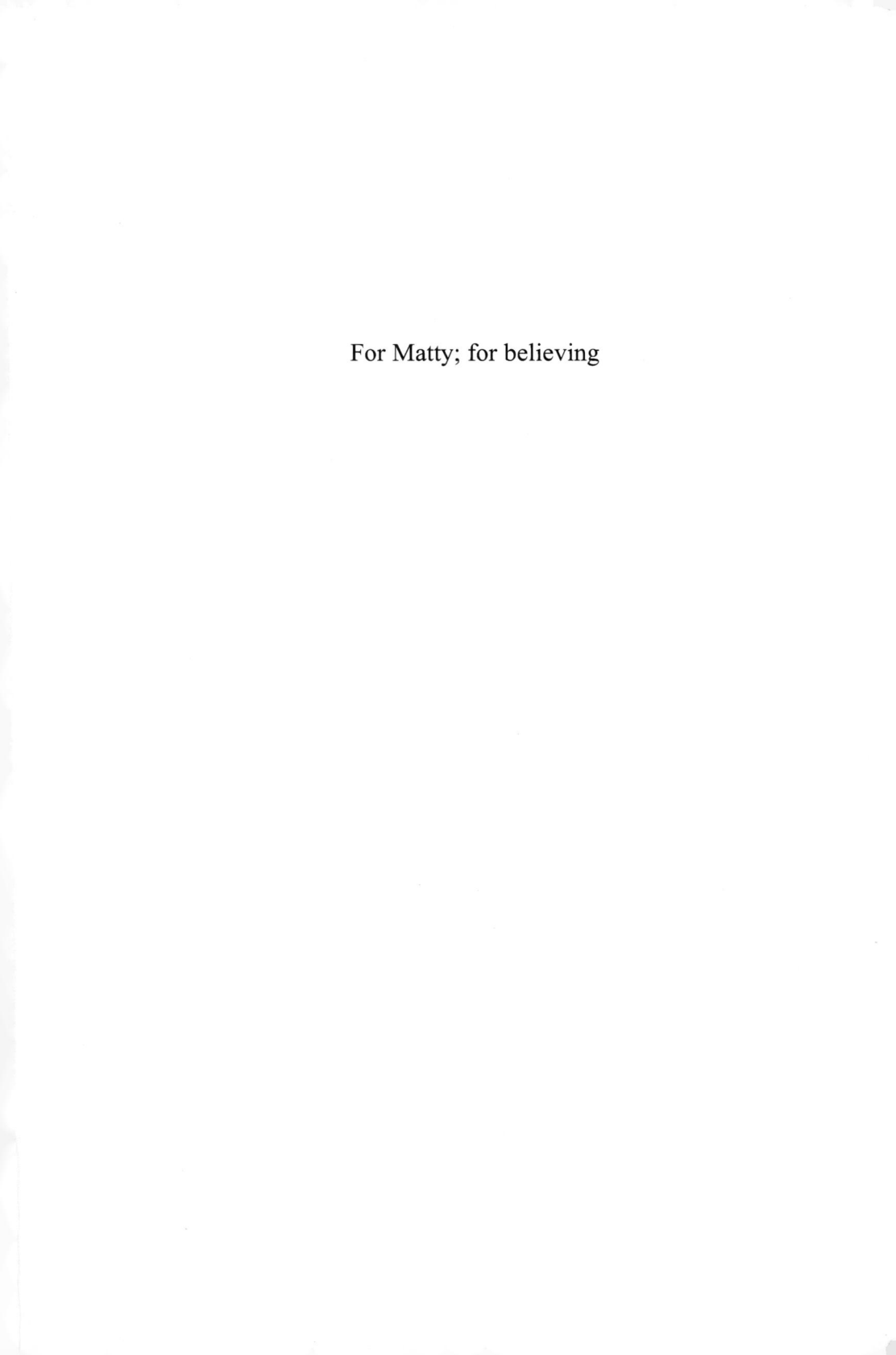

THE BLAME GAME

Introduction

William Thomas Frost, known simply as Will, or Frosty to his closest friends, died on a surprisingly hot afternoon in early May. Other than the glorious weather, there had been nothing exceptional about Will's day. He'd woken early as usual and, taking great care not to disturb his sleeping wife, he had pulled on an old pair of black, lycra shorts and an even older, washed out, pale blue T-shirt. The motif on the shirt had faded long ago and the stitching had come loose around the neck but, as far as Will was concerned, it was totally fit for purpose; Will Frost was not a vain man. Grabbing the backpack he'd prepared the previous evening, he'd made his way quietly down the stairs of his modern, five-bedroomed home, carefully avoiding, as he always did, the two steps half-way down, that groaned with displeasure when any weight was applied to them, even the relatively featherlight weight of Scamp, the small, family dog. In the large, stylish kitchen, Will had made a fuss of Scamp and put on his trainers. In stark contrast to his worn-out shorts and T-shirt, they were in pristine condition, they were his one and only concession to his kit.

A morning run was part of Will's weekday routine, no matter what weather the Gods sent his way. Following the track that hugged the river, he would start cautiously, warming up his muscles as he ran. After half a mile, at the point where both the river and the track narrowed, he would pick up pace and force himself to sprint until he got to the edge of the small industrial estate where his gym was located. Inside the gym, he would methodically complete a short but sustained workout, concentrating mostly on weight training. There was rarely any variation to his routine. On the day he died, he'd seen the usual faces, the men and women who, like him, routinely started off each day this way. The normal pleasantries had been exchanged, along with some banter about the possibilities of the good weather lasting until the weekend. All the men Will saw in the changing room that morning would remark, in the following days, that Will had seemed his usual self; good-natured, funny, upbeat. There had been no sign of his inner turmoil, or the drastic steps this level-headed and popular individual would take before the end of the day.

The outpouring of grief that followed the news of Will's sudden death, would have genuinely surprised and embarrassed him. This wasn't because Will was mean-spirited or disrespectful in any way. On the contrary, he was a generous man, generous with his money, generous with his time and generous with his affection. Ironically, it was his generosity, most notably his generosity of affection, that would lead to his premature death.

Despite an inauspicious start in life, Will Frost had made something of himself. He was considered, in local terms at least, a successful man. Hard graft, dogged determination and a stubborn refusal to conform to stereotype, had paid off handsomely. At the time of his death, Will, the son of the town whore, was a senior partner in a well-established law firm. He'd made it, he was content, he'd come as far as he wanted. To progress any further would have entailed a move to a city firm but this was something Will wasn't prepared to do. He was too loyal to his hometown, to the good friends he'd grown up with and, most of all, to Mary, his erratic and errant mother who had dragged him from one disastrous relationship to another.

Will's success afforded him a very comfortable lifestyle. He had a nice home, a beautiful, if somewhat demanding, wife and two healthy children. The trappings of success, however, didn't sit too comfortably with such a down to earth man so, in return for what he considered to be his good fortune, he supported numerous local initiatives. It's fair to say that Will saw what others didn't, he saw the good in people. In old fashioned terms, he was a pillar of society, decent, hard-working and universally liked, everything his mother wasn't. This reputation would stand him in good stead when, posthumously, less flattering details about his private life became public knowledge.

As the news surrounding his death gradually emerged, shocking though the detail was, Will's saintly image would remain intact. He had been a good man and few were prepared to think otherwise, despite the irrefutable evidence. Behind their own front doors, some people grudgingly accepted that Will had probably been weak, that he'd given into temptation but, by and large, the local community thought as one; Will's death was a tragedy. And, as with most tragedies, those left behind wanted to pin the blame on something, or more specifically, on someone. It wasn't long, therefore, until the finger of blame was pointed squarely at Molly Pope. Justifiably or not, every man and his dog laid the blame at Molly's door. Molly had form, Molly had done this kind of thing before.

Chapter One

The old dog, her black, bushy tail wagging furiously, was pushing her way, relentlessly, through the trees and shrubs that lined the edge of the park. Molly couldn't help but smile, being with Lottie was therapy, cheap therapy. Suddenly, from the depths of her coat pocket, her phone rang. The noise was shrill and intrusive in the peaceful stillness of the park. The number on the screen was unfamiliar and, for just a fraction of a second, she considered ditching the call.

"Hello." She grimaced at the sound of her own voice, the telephone voice, the voice that sounded a little too much like her mother.

"It's me." Just two words. No other introduction necessary.

Instantly fearful, she stopped walking and scanned the park. To her left, at the bottom of the hill, the cricket pavilion, shut for winter, stood tall and square. Its pale, yellow paintwork looked sad in the weak, winter sun. The river behind it flowed slowly and the trees in the distance were still bare of leaves, simultaneously desolate and austere. One other lone dog walker, wearing a bright blue, woolly hat, a flash of colour against a stark, winter background, was throwing balls for two large Spaniels. The dogs rushed eagerly into the river water, undeterred by the cold. Molly's eyes moved quickly over to the children's play area where the small swings moved forlornly in the gentle, winter breeze. She felt vulnerable and exposed.

"Molly?" the voice insisted, a trace of impatience already evident. "Can you hear me? Where are you?"

Molly watched Lottie's fat, black bottom emerge from a hole in a bush, a discarded, water bottle was lodged firmly in her soft mouth. "I'm walking Lottie for Kate," she offered, grimacing. She couldn't help herself, she always gave in. Her resolve not to speak to him was never strong enough. He wasn't really interested in where she was or what she was doing. He merely wanted to be sure he had her attention, that she was focusing on him and nothing else, not even an old dog. "You've got a new number," she said at last, frustrated with herself.

James ignored the comment. "Do you know what day it is Molly?"

She called out to Lottie. She was fighting for time, desperately trying to think of an excuse that would allow her to end the call. "James, I'm sorry but I can't talk just now." He didn't reply and she imagined the look on his face, the set of his jaw. James didn't handle rejection well, she knew that to her cost. "Of course I know what day it is," she added softly. Fifteen love, first point to James as usual.

"Things could have been so very different for us." He could have been speaking to anyone, there was no emotion in his voice. "You shouldn't have done it Molly. Molly ... goddammit woman, are you listening to me?"

Molly cut in quickly, surprising herself. "James, I'm not going to let you do this. Not again. Not now." She had to end the call, had to stop him before he got into his stride. She glanced over at Lottie, the dog was staring back at her as if sensing the tension. "I need to get Lottie back ... and I have an interview about a job," she lied. "Leave it to the solicitors .... please." The line went dead, she had done it, she had cut him off. Exhilarated, she looked around the empty park. Apart from the man with the Spaniels, she was alone but she felt odd, as if someone was watching her. Lottie waddled over, the old girl was ready to go home. "Well Lottie, maybe I'm getting better at this." But as quickly as it had come, the exhilaration was ebbing away. James wouldn't give up that easily.

With Lottie on her lead, Molly headed back up to the wrought iron gates and turned left to follow the tarmac path that ran along the park wall towards Kate's house. After the walk back up the hill, Lottie was a little unsteady on her old legs and their progress was slow. Surprised by the sound of voices behind her, Molly turned abruptly. The man with the Spaniels smiled amiably as he passed, his muddy dogs trotting, obediently, beside him. Molly returned his smile, relieved to see he was wearing earphones, he had merely been talking to someone on his mobile. She mentally chastised herself, she needed to stop being so paranoid.

Outside Kate's house, Lottie, the water bottle still lodged firmly in her mouth, waited patiently as Molly struggled to open the side gate into the garden. "Don't look at me like that. It's not my fault ... ah, there you go, got it," Molly said, as the gate finally yielded. Inside the house, she pulled off Kate's green wellies and placed them under the stairs. Lottie, a creature of habit, hovered by her side, waiting for a treat. "Come on then," Molly laughed. "Follow me." In the kitchen, she filled Lottie's water bowl and gave her a large handful of biscuits from the treat jar Kate kept near the Aga. Under strict instructions not to overfeed Lottie, she placed a kiss on the dog's soft, black head and whispered, "Don't tell Kate." The dog wagged her tail furiously and demolished the biscuits in an instant before climbing, stiffly, into her bed.

Glancing around the familiar room, Molly smiled. Never tidy but always warm, it felt homely. It was so different to the cold kitchen in the tiny cottage she rented on the other side of town. An old, oak table, habitually littered with newspapers and magazines, dominated the room. Heavily scarred by family life, it was surrounded by six wooden chairs, each one a different style to the next. Potted plants and herbs adorned the two window sills and the fridge door revealed a storyboard of Kate's life. Photographs of dogs and children were held in place by a variety of magnets, as were a handful of recipes for dishes that Kate would never cook. Washing her hands at the sink, Molly noticed the battered, old chalkboard hanging on the wall, next to the window. She picked up a tiny piece of white chalk and scribbled a message in large, ornate writing:

Hope you had a nice time
Lottie's fine
Coffee tomorrow?

She smiled to herself as she added two kisses and a heart, Kate was a no-nonsense kind of girl, not given to overt displays of affection.

Leaving the house, she used both hands to shut the gate. She'd have a word with Eddie, the blasted gate was a joke. After the warmth of Kate's house, the wind felt bitterly cold and she lifted her scarf up to her nose. Unable to resist temptation, she headed to the High Street and stopped off at her favourite coffee shop, The Kitchen. The instant blast of heat was welcoming, as was the tantalising smell of ground coffee. She longed to stay, to sink into one of the deep, soft and all too familiar leather sofas and lose herself for a little while but she had promised Jack and Sophie, the new owners of The Crown, that she would do another shift behind the bar. As she waited for her coffee, her thoughts returned to her precarious employment status. Job opportunities had been thin on the ground for some time and she was, sadly, coming to the conclusion that she was almost unemployable in this town. The offer of a few hours a week in the pub had been a godsend, and Jack and Sophie hadn't judged her or asked any awkward questions, although she was sure they must know something. Not the whole sorry story perhaps but some of it at least.

Stepping back outside and walking quickly towards the Market Place, she cupped her gloved hands around the cardboard coffee cup, grateful for the extra warmth. Her thoughts had moved on to the phone call from James. Sorely tempted to hang up on him on many occasions over the years, she'd never been brave enough, the fear of recrimination had always held her back. Now, as she neared the pub, she was filled with a deep sense of foreboding and, despite the warm coffee, she shivered, it wasn't wise to upset James. Her phone pinged in her pocket. Expecting it to be Kate, she read the message. As she did so, the cardboard cup slipped from her fingers and fell to the ground; hot, milky coffee exploded over her boots and up her trouser legs. She didn't move, she couldn't.

Get the feeling you might be up to your old tricks Moll.
Let's hope you don't kill this one
PS Happy Anniversary Darling

Chapter Two

Kate arrived early at The Kitchen the next day. She bought herself a latte and sat on a low, leather sofa near one of the full-length windows, giving herself the best view of the busy street outside. She had sent Molly a text arranging to meet at eleven o'clock and, in the meantime, she was pleased to have some time to herself, happy to do some people watching. She didn't buy a drink for her friend, years of experience had taught her you could never predict how late Molly would be. You could, however, safely assume that she would always be late. Kate's mother, who had been very fond of Molly, had often said 'that young woman will be late for her own funeral' and, as Kate gazed through the steamy, coffee shop window, she could hear her late mother's broad Irish accent and she smiled, fondly, to herself. With the memory came an image of Molly and herself as young students, sitting in Winnie's tiny kitchen, drinking cheap sherry. Disgusting stuff, she remembered, but with fondness nonetheless.

Winnie had been in Kate's thoughts a lot recently. Memories of her mother's appetite for life, her warmth, and even her courage had been percolating, increasingly, in her subconsciousness. She'd love to talk to Winnie, to confide in her, to talk about what was happening to her, to hear her mother say there was nothing to worry about, that everything would be fine. Yesterday, in a quiet bar, in a town she didn't know very well, she had slowly poured her heart out to Eddie. She smiled to herself again, remembering how Eddie had, spontaneously, escorted her off the train and proceeded to get her drunk. She was grateful to him, it had felt so good to offload but, for a reason she'd couldn't quite explain, she longed to confide in another woman and her mother would have been her first choice. There was her sister Patty, of course, but Patty had her own problems, not least a house full of unruly kids and a gorgeous but unreliable husband, who was away on business more often than he was home. The wistful smile faded from Kate's freckled face; a small frown took its place. She would normally confide in Molly, after all Molly was her best friend, her oldest friend. The thought made her feel uneasy, there was so much Molly didn't know.

As she sat sipping her coffee, Kate's thoughts jumped from her mother to Molly and back again. Winnie, a petite, opinionated red-head, had loved an audience. Making people laugh was second nature to her but, to her credit, she was, without fail, always the butt of her own jokes. Molly, pretty, blond and curvaceous, loved being the centre of attention and, like Winnie, she sometimes had a comical way with words but, unlike Winnie, her humour, although quick, could be unnecessarily cruel. And whereas Winnie continually put other people's needs before her own, Molly was entirely self-obsessed, the unfortunate result of a privileged childhood. Oddly though, Molly had never been ashamed of her self-obsession. 'A little self-love goes a long way,' had been Molly's mantra when they were students. Usually followed by, 'You should try it Kate.' Kate, quiet, calm and introspective, was the polar opposite of both her mother and her friend. Only her red hair and pale complexion hinted at her relationship to Winnie, a not so subtle nod to her Irish heritage. Tall, slim and comfortable in her own skin, she spoke her mind but tried hard not to offend. She hoped people knew where they stood with her.

"A penny for your thoughts," Molly said, as she dropped into the seat opposite Kate, carefully placing her own drink on the low table between them.

Kate jumped, a little startled and slightly embarrassed by some of the unflattering thoughts she'd been having about her friend. "Sorry, I didn't see you come in." She looked at her watch and then at the door. "Err, what have you done with the real Molly? You're on time, more or less, Molly's never on time. What's going on?"

"Oh, aren't you the funny one? I was here before you actually, smart-arse," Molly retorted indignantly. "I was in the loo! A girl's allowed to pee, isn't she?"

"Whatever! I don't believe you for one second!" Kate picked up her coffee and smiled affectionately at her friend noticing, with a little concern, how tired she looked. Behind the always perfect make-up and the immaculate hair, there was evident fatigue. "You look knackered Moll. What's the matter? Everything OK?"

Molly reached for her coffee. "I didn't sleep well. I had a call from James yesterday and for the first time ever, I put the phone down on him." She waited for Kate to react.

"About bloody time," Kate laughed. "Go a step further next time and bin the call. Serve the bastard right."

"He didn't try and call back but he sent a message. Look ... he's got a new number." Molly pushed her phone across the table. Kate read the message and frowned. "Say something!" Molly pleaded. "What do you think it means?"

"Have you responded?" Kate countered with her own question.

"No, he sent it just as I got to the pub last night and they were really busy, so it was all hands on deck. I didn't have the time, even if I had wanted to. Kate, he sounds ... like he did, you know .... before ..." She didn't finish her sentence, she didn't have to, Kate knew the back story. "He won't have liked me putting the phone down on him." There was a familiar sad, shakiness to Molly's voice.

"So what!" exclaimed Kate. "Bloody hell Molly! Why do you do this to yourself? You're such a drama queen. You did the right thing." Kate shook her head and took another sip of her coffee. Molly exasperated her, more so recently for some reason. "What exactly did you say to make him send this message though? The 'up to your old tricks' comment is weird." She was probing, Molly had lied to her before.

"I try to say very little, you know that." Molly's voice had risen a little.

"Moll, calm down. I'm trying to help." Kate sensed she'd touched a nerve. "Do you think it means he's back? This new number? It's a UK number."

Molly shook her head. "Yesterday in the park, I did wonder, I had a weird feeling ... like I was being watched but he can't be, can he? Someone would have told me, wouldn't they?" Her voice carried no conviction and she knew instantly, from the way Kate raised an eyebrow, how utterly stupid she sounded. She had been a 'persona non-grata' in this town for a while now. Time, that old cliché, might have healed some of the rifts but there were many people with long memories, many who would never forgive or forget. Some, to this day, went out of their way to avoid her, left rooms or crossed the street. Others, the kind who relished confrontation, were still vocal in demonstrating their contempt for her; Molly avoided these people. Self-preservation, at all costs, was a skill she'd been forced to acquire. She looked nervously around the coffee shop. A loved-up young couple in university hoodies were drinking hot chocolate and sharing an enormous cake, oblivious to the world around them. A harassed looking young mum was trying to feed sandwiches to her fractious little boy. Molly's eyes lingered on these two, the image made her feel sad. Two elderly ladies were putting on their coats, getting ready to leave. One stopped to talk to the young mum; whatever it was she said, she managed to raise a smile on the pretty woman's tired looking face. Her friend whispered something in the little boy's ear, making him smile and giggle. This simple, heart-warming scene, caught Molly off guard. When she looked back at Kate, her eyes were moist.

"Moll ... don't bite my head off for saying this but he's implying you might be seeing someone new, isn't he? What did you say to make him think that?" Kate chose her words carefully. "Why would he say you're up to your old tricks?"

Molly fiddled with her mug. "I didn't say anything! He just jumps to conclusions ... the wrong conclusions. You know what he's like." She looked around at the little boy again. It made her feel so sad but it was easier than looking at her friend, she couldn't look Kate in the eye.

"For God's sake Moll. Don't tell me you'd risk that now? Be honest with me." Kate had lowered her voice to a whisper. "Holy cow! Why would you do that now? Who is it?"

"Bloody hell Kate, you're as bad as him ... jumping to the wrong conclusions. Is it so bloody easy to think the worst of me? Am I so predictable? Such a bad person? Nice to know where I stand, I suppose."

This time Molly looked directly at Kate, playing the victim was familiar territory.

Kate decided to change tack, she didn't want an argument. "Is it possible he's been in contact with Seth?" She felt slightly uncomfortable asking this question. Seth was Molly's son, a quiet, intelligent, but troubled twenty-year-old, now a second-year medic student in Newcastle. Molly saw little of her son, he avoided calling her and had started avoiding trips home. Their relationship was fractured, maybe beyond repair, damaged by the events of the past, by Molly and by the actions of his father.

Molly glanced again at the little boy who was, at last, eating his sandwich. "Seth doesn't talk to James," she said quietly. "He barely talks to me. Like you, he thinks the worst of me."

"Molly, couldn't you call him? Try a little harder?" Kate's tone was sharper than she'd intended but Molly's self-pity riled her. "Sorry, that came out wrong, I'm not saying you don't try. It just seems so sad, this distance between you, I'd hoped it could have been mended. You never know what's around the corner ... life's too short." An image of the Consultant's room she'd visited at the hospital the day before, flashed in front of her. "Isn't it time to put the past behind you?"

"I'm not sure that's possible anymore," Molly said petulantly.

"That's not true at all and you know it." Kate was growing increasingly angry. "He has a home here, friends here. Aren't you concerned he'll turn to James, if you don't maintain contact? Is that what you really want?"

"Kate, he didn't even come home at Christmas remember. And I'm not going to spend my time worrying about what James might do. I've been there, done that, multiple times. We'll burn that bridge when we get to it, if we need to."

Kate laughed, instantly easing the tension that had grown between them. "Cross Molly, cross."

"What?" Molly looked up, a confused expression on her sad face.

"Cross that bridge Molly, not burn! Very different outcome!" Molly smiled, albeit weakly. "Could James just be trying to wind you up?" Kate's tone was a little softer now. "You put the phone down on him, so he sends you a twisted message to provoke you? Sounds like the sort of thing he'd do to me. We all know what a freak his is."

"Oh God, I don't know." Molly pulled nervously at her pony tail. "Do you think I'm over-reacting? Reading more into this than I should? Was he just cross that I didn't give him any time?"

Kate heard the fear in Molly's voice but she wasn't sure it was warranted. It was easy to set James off and he could be thoroughly evil, if pushed, but if Molly had nothing to hide, there was nothing to worry about. "Yesterday would have been your wedding anniversary, wouldn't it?" she asked. "That's why he called you, just like he does every bloody year but yesterday, for the first time in God knows how long, you stopped him from indulging himself in self-pity, from making you feel guilty. By cutting him off, you denied him the opportunity of reminiscing about the good old days." Her tone had grown sarcastic. "The days when you were happy." She raised her fingers to demonstrate inverted commas. "You pissed the bastard off a little. So what? What does your solicitor say?"

"According to him everything should be finalised in a few weeks but he's said that before, hasn't he? Numerous times."

"I don't rate him Moll … you know that." Kate thought Molly's solicitor was lazy at best, incompetent at worst. But he was cheap, Molly had no money. "But you are where you are. So, we can put the call about what would have been your wedding anniversary to one side, can't we? It was just par for the course. Nothing more than that." Molly didn't respond. "Are there any other anniversaries coming up?" Kate knew James used any opportunity to contact Molly, the list was endless but far from obvious. Birthdays and anniversaries gave him the ideal excuse to call of course but, in his twisted mind, so did the dates when bad things had happened. Such as when her father had been fatally struck down by a hit and run driver or when Seth, aged just three, had been admitted to hospital with meningitis. "When would he normally make contact again? When will he try and get his kicks again?"

Molly visibly flinched. Her voice was almost a whisper when she spoke. "Bad choice of words Kate".

"Shit, shit! Sorry Moll." Kate reached across the table and grasped her friend's hand tightly. "I'm sorry." She lowered her voice. "Is that it? Will that be his next call?" To herself she said, "When is that anniversary? When did that evil bastard kick the shit out of you?"

***

Molly stood at the gates of the cemetery, grateful for the winter cold. The freezing weather allowed her to hide, to pull her blond hair inside her black, woolly hat and obscure her face behind the matching scarf. Even after all this time, she had to be careful when coming to visit Will's grave, careful not to be seen by his children or by Fiona, his wife. In the first couple of years following his death, Kate would come with her, most often in the very early mornings, with a much younger Lottie straining on her lead. But Kate hadn't come with her for a long while now, her visits to Will's grave were solitary visits. 'Life is full of anniversaries,' she'd said to Kate, over coffee earlier that morning. 'Yesterday marked the day I married James and today, well today would have been Will's birthday. All my anniversaries seem to be sad ones.'

A solitary figure in the growing dark, Molly made her way, very cautiously, to Will's grave. She hadn't brought flowers, any token left by her had never been welcome, was possibly deemed inappropriate by some people. In the early days, she had tried to leave discreet, anonymous wreaths but they had always ended up in the nearest waste bin. She didn't know how his family knew these things were from her but it seemed their policy was 'if in doubt, bin it'. In the months following Will's death, Kate had gradually talked her into demonstrating her grief in a more positive way. She no longer bought flowers but had set up a small, regular donation to Will's favourite charity. Kate had made her feel it was money better spent, and she knew Will would have approved and, perversely, it gave her the moral high ground over Fiona. The small monthly donation was money she could ill afford but if it meant she went without then so be it, it was one of her few tangible links to Will.

Leaving the gravel path, she walked slowly between two rows of graves. The grass was frosty and firm beneath her feet, the cold snap showed no sign of letting up. As she walked, she constantly scanned the path behind her. This was where she felt most exposed, there were fewer places to hide. She had learnt a few tricks over the years. No matter what the weather, she always wore black clothes, flat shoes and, most importantly a hat; a woolly beanie in the winter and a sunhat or a baseball cap in the summer. And she never, ever, spoke to anyone. On one of the few occasions that she'd seen Fiona, she had tagged on to a group of mourners standing near a freshly dug grave. She'd felt slightly guilty for intruding on their grief but it was a tactic she would use again, if she had to.

Fortunately, there had only ever been one nasty altercation. No matter how hard she tried, she would never forget the screaming, the physical assault, the taste of blood mingled with mud in her mouth and the overwhelming relief when several strangers had, thankfully, dragged Fiona off her. She shuddered now at the memory of that day. She'd been called in to see the headmaster at Seth's school, he was worried about her son's uncharacteristic, bad behaviour. The cooperative, quiet, well-mannered young boy had been replaced, almost overnight, by a mono-syllabic, churlish and slightly malicious adolescent, who was causing trouble at school. The obsequious headmaster had wanted to make her aware of the situation but Molly was well ahead of him. She knew exactly what had caused the change in Seth's behaviour, she just wasn't equipped to deal with it. More than a little flustered by the avalanche of well-intended advice the headmaster had bestowed on her, Molly hadn't realised just how late she was running or, once at the cemetery, how long she'd spent sitting by Will's grave, thoughts of Seth, not her recently departed lover, uppermost in her mind. She was, consequently, an easy target for Fiona who, furious at finding Molly sitting by her husband's grave, had launched herself at her nemesis and pushed her face down into the recently dug, soft mud. Molly's tongue, badly bitten by the impact, bled profusely. Winded and caught off guard, she remained prone until Fiona flipped her over and straddled her. Such was the imbalance of physical strength, Molly had been like a rag doll in Fiona's hands. Incandescent with rage, Fiona had screamed a torrent of incoherent abuse into Molly's face, at the same time lifting her head and, repeatedly, smashing it back to the ground.

Subconsciously, Molly put her gloved hand to her face, as if to wipe away the spittle that had flown from Fiona's mouth that day. The attack, although ferocious, had only lasted a few seconds. Three young women visiting a nearby grave, had heard the commotion and dragged Fiona away but not before a well-aimed kick had connected with Molly's jaw and smashed two of her lower, front teeth. Molly ran her tongue over the implants that now replaced the teeth in question, remembering, with some guilt, that she had never thanked the young women who had come to her aid that day, she simply hadn't had time. Terrified of a fresh onslaught, she had crawled across the mud like an injured animal and escaped from the scene, she'd been too frightened to look back.

Will's grave was festooned with fresh flowers, a riot of colour against a dreary, winter backdrop. A lot of people have been here today Molly thought as she knelt down, some people still cared. She didn't read the cards attached to the flowers, didn't analyse the words. She had made that mistake too many times before. The messages only served to compound her shame, to deepen her guilt, it was easier not to look. She stayed by Will's grave for a long time, occasionally and subconsciously muttering a few, undecipherable words. Her eyes were, as always, constantly drawn to a tiny inscription at the very bottom of Will's headstone. It looked slightly out of place, as if it had been added as an afterthought. 'One in a Million'. She took off her gloves to run her fingers over the words. Will had been a hero to so many people and she'd only had a little part of him, for a painfully small period of time. She was lost, momentarily, in familiar thoughts of what might have been, of the wonderful future she and Will had lost.

She jumped as a shower of large pebbles, mixed with mud, landed on the frozen grass, just a few inches to her left. She glanced over her shoulder, crying out as a second wave of pebbles struck her sharply on her lower back. In the shadows, she could just make out a figure in a long, dark coat, running clumsily towards her. Molly was on her feet in a second, she'd rehearsed this scenario, in her mind, a million or more times. Jumping quickly over the two graves nearest to Will, she gasped as something heavier than a pebble landed on her shoulder but she kept moving, she couldn't risk another confrontation. Turning right, she sprinted down the slope, tripping and stumbling on the uneven grass, thankful for the darkness that enveloped her. Near the bottom of the slope, she veered left heading deep into the cemetery, feeling her way along the headstones with her hands. She was in the older part of the cemetery now; the headstones were larger and ghostlier. Acutely aware of her own heavy panting, she placed her scarf in front of her mouth; only her silence would protect her. The movement caught her off-balance and she tripped, landing heavily on her knees. Her already tender shoulder connected with the corner of a large, irregular shaped headstone, bringing tears to her eyes. Winded, she remained on all fours, listening intently to the noises around her. They were unfamiliar and frightening but she was relieved, she couldn't hear any footsteps. She inched forward slowly and leant against the headstone that had caused her fall. Her chest was heaving and beads of sweat were trickling, slowly, down the back of her neck. An image of Kate came to her, of Kate doing her yoga, breathing slowly in through her nose and out through her mouth. Molly pulled her scarf away from her face and took a deep breath in through her nose, just as she'd seen Kate do on numerous occasions. Seconds later she released the air through her mouth and repeated the process. Gradually, she felt better. It wasn't taking the fear away but it was helping, a minute degree of calm had returned. She carried on, almost losing herself in the concentration until her rapidly cooling body started to shiver. She didn't want to move but she didn't want to freeze to death either. A rustling noise startled her and she pulled herself quickly to her knees to peer over the top of the headstone. Her heart sank, a weak beam of light was being directed towards the graves around her, her attacker had a torch. Something wet touched her face and she gasped. There was more rustling, accompanied by a whining noise and something wet touched her face again. She put her trembling hand out and felt fur. She couldn't contain the scream any longer.

"Lottie, Lottie," a man's voice called. "Lottie, come here."

"Lottie?" Molly whispered with relief. "Lottie? Is that you?" She reached out warily, her hand connecting with one of the dog's soft ears. "Oh my God Lottie ... Lottie." She grabbed the dog and sobbed into the familiar fur. "Lottie."

***

"We need to get you home, young lady." Eddie had steered Molly back up to the gravel path and, together, they had wiped most of the dirt from her knees and her coat. "Thank God Kate sent me ... and thank God for Lottie." He leant down to stroke the dog's head. "She wouldn't come back. She must have known it was you."

"I thought she was a fox." Molly's forced laugh was weak. "Jesus ... I thought a fox was going to attack me."

"Who was it Molly? Who were you hiding from?" Eddie asked.

"Who do you think? There's only one person who'd do that to me Eddie. She caught me at the grave, she started to throw stuff at me… pebbles, rocks. She clearly didn't want me to be there .... not today."

"Moll! You need to go to the police. It's assault. What if she had seriously hurt you?" Eddie's concern was genuine.

"How come you and Lottie were here anyway?" Molly tried to change the subject. Reporting Fiona had never worked before, the police weren't interested. She wasn't going to waste her time again and no harm had really been done, she'd just be more careful in future. "Don't get me wrong, I've never been more happy to see, or rather feel, Lottie's face but you don't usually walk her up here, do you?"

"Kate had a feeling you might still be up here," Eddie explained. "She told me to come and fetch you. She worries. She didn't think you should be up here in the dark and the cold ... she wasn't wrong either, was she? Bloody hell Moll. It makes my blood boil thinking what that crazy bitch might have done to you."

"Well she didn't, did she?" Molly hooked her arm through Eddie's. "Don't worry about what didn't happen Eddie. What's Kate doing tonight?"

Eddie sighed. "She was going to take a long bath. She said to tell you there's a bottle of wine with your name on it at ours and you're to get your sorry arse over there pronto. Her words, not mine. There might be food too."

They had returned to the part of the cemetery where Will was buried. "Eddie ... give me a second. I didn't say goodbye."

"Shit! It's dark ... leave it," Eddie pleaded. He was worried Fiona might still be around.

Molly pulled her phone from her pocket and switched on the torch. "Two seconds."

"Hang on ... I'm coming too." He followed her, reluctantly, down the dark, grassy verge to Will's grave and watched as Molly kissed two fingers and placed them gently on the headstone. It made him feel instantly sad, Will had been his friend.

"I'll be back soon," she whispered, before linking her arm through Eddie's once again.

The streetlights at the entrance to the cemetery flooded Molly with relief. Less edgy with the physical presence of Eddie by her side, the bright lights represented an almost tangible safety. The path outside the gates was busier than it had been earlier, time had moved on and people were walking home from work. She tightened her grip on Eddie's arm and lent closer, irrationally afraid of these strangers. They were just turning left onto the main road with Eddie steering Lottie away from something she wanted to investigate by the side of a bin, when they were both startled by the sound of a booming voice.

"Still stealing husbands then, Molly Pope?" The voice rang out strong and deep, several people turned their heads to see who was shouting. Molly, still holding onto Eddie, froze.

"Keep walking Molly." Eddie pulled her forward forcefully. "Keep walking love."

***

'There'll be three people in your marriage Eddie,' Winnie, his future mother-in-law, had said to him all those years ago. 'With Kate comes Molly. A lot of men wouldn't be able to cope with that, but you, Eddie Lawson, are no ordinary man, you understand those girls. You'll be grand.' And Winnie had been right, there had indeed been three people in his marriage but he certainly didn't resent Molly's constant presence, he simply didn't know any different. But, as he sat on the battered, old sofa in the playroom, watching Molly tell Kate what had happened in the cemetery, he couldn't help but think how his wife's best friend continually lurched from one disaster to another.

The kids had abandoned the playroom, an extension of the kitchen, when they hit their teens, gradually migrating to their bedrooms with their laptops and mobile phones, demanding privacy and shutting tight their bedroom doors. Kate hadn't fretted at this transition, she knew from her own experience of growing up in a noisy family, that her kids needed their own space. Eddie, an only child, had fretted more. He'd struggled with their growing independence but Kate had reassured him. 'We just need to be here Eddie,' she had insisted, refusing to let him try and bribe them out of their rooms with expensive gifts. Presence not presents, was Kate's method and it had worked. They had provided a secure, loving home and he was proud to say that two grounded, sensible kids had emerged at the other end. Unlike poor old Seth, he often thought. They had, of course, experienced their fair share of dramas with their kids, just like any other family. Lucy had been in a rush to grow up and had sneaked into pubs and clubs underage, only to be tracked down by her mother and dragged, unceremoniously, home. Bobby, the younger of the two, had learnt a lot from his sister's mistakes but was no angel either. Eddie thought his son had just been smarter about concealing his misdemeanours. There was, without doubt, plenty he and Kate didn't know about their kids but he was proud of them and missed them, now they were both away at university. In fact, he had a sneaky feeling he missed them more than Kate did, his wife still had Molly.

The playroom, as they would always call it, had fallen back into the hands of the grown-ups. Kate had installed a second, more comfortable sofa under the window and a winged armchair sat to the side. A large, low coffee table, which Eddie seemed to remember had belonged to Winnie, dominated the floor space and a wood burner had been built into the back wall. Kate had kept and framed a selection of the kids' infantile drawings and they were now hanging from the walls, alongside Eddie's favourite photograph of Lottie. Wet through and covered in sand, the dog looked fit and happy.

Eddie and Molly had walked quietly back from the cemetery an hour earlier, Eddie constantly tugging at Lottie's lead, encouraging the dog to walk more quickly. He'd wanted to get Molly home. "Don't think about it Moll," he'd said. "It was a cheap shot, hiding in the dark and calling out insults and then running off. Just cowardly."

"I know Eddie, I've had worse," Molly had replied. She'd kept looking behind her but there had been nothing to see in the dark. "It's been a double whammy day today, hasn't it? I think I'm just a little shocked. I thought it was all finished with, it's been so long since I've had any nasty run-ins and then two things happen, one after the other. I didn't recognise that voice, did you?'"

"No, no I didn't," Eddie had replied. "It sounded like a bloke though. Does that surprise you?"

"People I didn't even know would call out insults in the early days," Molly had said. "Random strangers, men and women ... even school kids. But then, with time, it dwindled, became a core group of people. Fiona's friends mostly I think. I have no idea who that was just then though. I'm glad you were with me Eddie, thanks again for coming to get me."

"She says jump, I ask how high." Eddie had laughed referring to Kate. "Moll, don't let it get to you ... the shouting I mean. You've had enough of a shock tonight. Put this down to some loser. Don't let the dark over dramatise it either, in broad daylight, it wouldn't feel the same. You might have even shouted back." He didn't really know why he had said this but he'd wanted to make Molly feel better. The truth was the whole thing had felt quite sinister to him. He was glad Kate had asked him to find Molly.

"I think you should stay at ours tonight Molly," Eddie said. "Unless you have other plans. Smells like Kate has something good in the oven, and I don't often say that." He winked at his wife and ducked quickly as she threw a cushion at his head.

Molly laughed, Kate was a good cook but she hated the repetitiveness of cooking. Years of putting food on the table, every single day, had worn down her enthusiasm. "Thanks Eddie, but I'm working at the pub again." She looked at her watch. "God, is that the time? I need to go."

"Give Jack a call, surely they can get someone else to cover," Eddie said.

"No, I don't want to let them down, Sophie's been really good to me. She's not judged me on gossip, well not so far anyway and the cash is very handy."

"OK, well I'll walk you up there," offered Eddie. "I might even pop in for a pint."

"Any excuse, eh darling?" Kate laughed. "Well don't be long or your dinner will be in the dog."

"Thanks Eddie." Molly's gratitude was genuine. "That would be good." She looked down at her dirty boots. "Do you guys have anything I can use to clean my boots?"

"Under the sink in the utility room." Eddie started to get up.

"Don't worry ... I'll find it. I need the loo anyway." Molly got up and headed towards the small utility room.

"She's had an eventful evening, hasn't she?" Eddie said quietly to his wife.

"Eventful?" Kate mocked. "I think I might give Fiona a call ... tell her to call off her dogs, once and for all."

"Leave it Kate," Eddie sighed. "She's had enough scenes."

"But that's it Ed. Enough is enough. When will she give it up? When she's run Molly out of town or worse?"

Eddie smiled fondly at his wife. "I see you've already forgotten what we talked about last night," he teased. "No more fighting other people's battles. Remember?"

Kate smiled back weakly. "Sorry Ed, force of habit. Don't say anything to Molly about yesterday ... not yet."

***

Jack was serving a customer when Molly slipped in beside him at the bar. "Am I glad to see you," he said, simultaneously pulling a pint of lager and pouring white wine into two large glasses. "Look at this lot, don't people cook at home anymore? We might need to have a talk, you and me Molly, might need to make this a more permanent arrangement. What do you think?"

"I'm more than ready for that talk Jack." Molly wanted to reach out and hug him. This was the news she had been waiting for and, after the day she'd had, she felt almost tearful but a hug was out of the question. The last few years had taught her that someone was always watching, always ready to start a rumour. "I've brought someone in for a sneaky pint." She nodded over to where Eddie had installed himself on a bar stool.

Jack's face lit up, he and Eddie were old friends. "Be with you in a second Ed. Usual, is it?"

"Yes please mate." Eddie removed his glasses to clean them. "Looks busy in here."

"Yeah, the 'after-work' crowd seems to get bigger and stay longer. I blame my wife, she's been spreading the word." He nodded towards Sophie, who was skillfully explaining the provenance of their food to a group of four people sitting by the open fireplace. He placed Eddie's pint on the bar and pushed Eddie's money away. "On the house Eddie, I owe you."

"You do?" Eddie was genuinely surprised.

"Sure do," confirmed Jack. "You were the one who let me know this place was for sale, lured me here. Personally, I think you couldn't live without me anymore, could you? Hated me moving to the big smoke. Life just hasn't been the same without me."

"Stop, stop," Eddie groaned in mock despair. "We all make mistakes you know. Anyway, I was just doing my job, I thought there was more in it for me, than for you." Eddie was a senior partner in a local firm of Chartered Surveyors and his field of expertise was the hotel and pub trade, a role that suited his temperament and explained the gradual increase in his girth over the years. The previous owners of The Crown had engaged him when they decided to sell up and retire. The pub had been their home for thirty years and, whilst they begrudgingly admitted it needed upgrading, they were keen to find a buyer who would respect its character and retain its dignity. They didn't want to see it transformed into yet another faceless watering hole, there were too many of those in the area already. But they did need to move quite quickly, they both had health problems and the pub had started to drain them financially, as well as physically. If they didn't sell soon, The Crown, like many of its counterparts, might face an uncertain future. Eddie had witnessed too many pub closures, had seen too many communities left without a heart so when it came to finding a new owner, he had been like a dog with a bone. He'd contacted private investors, far and wide, but it hadn't been easy and just when he thought time was running out, Kate had suggested approaching his old friend, Jack. She'd been following him on social media, she knew he and his wife were looking for a new venture.

"Seriously mate. I wouldn't have looked at this." Jack gestured to the room around him. "Not without your advice and that would have been a mistake. Look around you ... it's proving to be a little gem. We've only been open six months and profits are soaring. Like I say though, Sophie has to take most of the credit but don't tell her I said so!"

"I'm chuffed for you Jack. What you and Sophie have done with this place is amazing. I suspect it's been a significant investment for you. To bring it into the 21st century, that is. You've done a nice job. But let's not forget, you do have a secret weapon."

Jack looked at him questioningly, unsure what Eddie meant. "Secret weapon?"

"Kim's cooking!" exclaimed Eddie with an exaggerated wink, referring to Jack's chef. "People speak with their feet Jack, or in this instance with their stomachs. To have this many people in here, spending their hard-earned cash on a cold winter night with no gimmicks, no happy hour, no quiz, means only one thing. Food!"

"I know ... you're right," agreed Jack, laughing. "It took some persuading to get her to come though ... you know, to leave London. Now I need to make sure she stays!"

"By the way, what did you say to put that smile on Molly's face?" Eddie asked. "She's had a tough day, it's nice to see her looking upbeat."

Jack's eyes darkened slightly. "Sophie's been on at me for a while to say something to Molly about a full-time role with us and I've been reticent. I wasn't sure. But we desperately need the staff, so I've suggested we have a chat about making our arrangement more permanent. She's done quite a few shifts now ... by and large she's a good addition to the team." He lowered his voice slightly. "Eddie, I won't lie. I had my reservations at first. Some customers remembered her and weren't very happy to see her behind the bar. One woman even made it very plain she didn't want to be served by her. That shocked me. But Sophie's insistent ... as I'm sure you can imagine. But there's so much Sophie doesn't know, isn't there?"

Eddie took a slow sip of his beer, he was considering what to say. There was so much Jack didn't know either. "Don't believe everything you hear Jack, you were away a long time and there's a lot of Chinese whispers floating around. Molly's not the enemy, not really, not anymore." He looked over at Molly, smiling at her when she caught his eye.

"Believe me, I've tried to do just that Ed, tried to keep an open mind. I know it's complicated. I don't know the full story ... not sure I want to, but I still have reservations." Jack fell silent as Molly walked past them, on her way to the kitchen with a tray of dirty plates. "If I'm to trust her and let her become part of this business, I should really ask for some kind of reference. I know she's your friend and Sophie won't like it at all. She'll think I'm going over the top, but I'm a stickler for the rules ... it's in my DNA."

"Wise words," Eddie nodded. "It's not my place to share the finer details of her past with you, without her consent at least ... but I agree that, if you're going to put her on the payroll or give her any authority behind that bar, you probably need to do your homework. Some of what you've heard has been embellished. I can guarantee that. Like I said, Chinese whispers. My advice is to take what you've heard with a large pinch of salt. She got caught in the middle. To be honest though, she doesn't have much workplace experience, she was a full-time mum for many years and then I think she helped in the school. Best person to talk to might be Kate? She won't sugar coat it but she'll make sure you don't have any nasty surprises."

Jack shook his head. "I'm not sure Ed, they're friends, aren't they? Old friends at that. Don't take this the wrong way but Kate could be biased. It's too close for comfort."

"You don't know Kate very well, do you?" Eddie shook his head in disbelief. "A spade's a spade with my wife. Like I said ... no sugar coating. Anyway, there's no-one else. As you probably know, Molly's seriously upset a lot of people in her time."

Jack sighed. "Ed, it's that kind of comment that worries the hell out of me, as an employer especially. If someone has a go at her for being behind this bar, I have to know what I'm dealing with and all I really know is that a man died and two young kids were left without a father. And from what I can gather, a lot of the blame lies at Molly's door, like it or not." He looked around him and lowered his voice again. "That man was my friend, as he was yours. I'm not taking sides Eddie ... I never met his wife. I feel bad about that too … perhaps I should have made more of an effort. Shit! It's tricky."

"It was, it's less so now. Molly's very close to putting it all behind her and people in this town quickly move on to new gossip." Eddie tried to sound convincing but the image of his torchlight landing on Molly cowering behind a headstone in the cemetery, niggled him. "Molly paid a huge price, physically and emotionally and don't forget Will was equally guilty. It takes two as they say." But Will died, he thought to himself, leaving Molly to cope on her own, to face the consequences alone.

"Yeah, I know. It can't have been pleasant around here when all that was happening," Jack said. "Small communities ... as much as I love them, can be cruel."

"Pleasant?" Eddie let out a sarcastic laugh, almost spilling his beer in the process. "Bloody hell, you've changed mate. It was far from 'pleasant'. This is a small town. Folk can be fucking cruel ... unnecessarily so." Eddie stopped talking and took another sip from his pint glass. He was thinking back. "But it didn't help that Will wasn't the first, did it? That gave those looking to pin the blame somewhere, plenty of ammunition. It's what pushed James over the edge. He lost it ... big style. Bloody hell, some of the tricks he pulled, some of the things he did. There's been spilt blood Jack … lots of it."

Eddie's words rang in Jack's ears. He had no idea who or what his old friend was talking about. "Eddie," he whispered, as Molly walked past. "When can I talk to Kate?"

Chapter Three

Sophie was taking a rare day off and she had plans, girly plans. Jack and Kim, their chef, could handle the lunchtime trade between them and Molly had agreed to do another shift. Sophie didn't plan on being late back but you just never knew how a day in London with Annie might pan out.

'What would we do without Molly?' she'd said to Jack the day before. 'Wasn't she great last night? Did you see how she handled those guys? She had them eating out of her hands.' Jack hadn't replied but that wasn't unusual. He was a quiet man, a man who generally kept his opinions, good or bad, to himself but Sophie knew he still had reservations about Molly. Checking her make-up in the small dressing-table mirror Sophie thought, not for the first time, that Molly was like marmite, you either loved her or you hated her. "Well I love her," Sophie said out loud to her reflection.

She ran downstairs, her booted feet clattering noisily against the wooden steps. In the kitchen, Kim, her dark-skinned arms elbow-deep in flour, was singing loudly along to the radio. She was wearing a pair of blue rimmed glasses which had slipped down to the very bottom of her nose. Her pristine chef's whites emphasised her lean frame and her mass of dark hair was, as usual, held back with a colourful scarf, accentuating her long, slender neck. Even in these mundane surroundings Sophie was struck by Kim's effortless beauty. Long limbed and dark skinned, she was graceful and sensuous. Doris, the elderly kitchen hand they had inherited from the previous owners, was at the sink washing a variety of vegetables. The atmosphere was relaxed, just as Kim liked it; the two women worked well together. Sophie smiled to herself, it was a reassuring sight.

"See you tonight ladies," she called out above the music. "I won't be too late. Jack's bottling up in the bar if you need him."

Doris turned around and smiled at her. "Have a wonderful day. You look lovely."

"Thank you, Doris." Sophie ran her hands down the soft, dark green woollen dress she was wearing. "I love this dress, it's actually one of

Molly's, a gift apparently but totally the wrong size for her." Doris turned back to the sink but not before Sophie saw the smile disappear from her face. There you go, she thought, marmite Molly.

"You look bloody amazing, lovely colour that dress, next time she's giving stuff away send her in my direction please." Kim's voice, like her appearance, was exotic, almost seductive. She pushed her glasses back up her nose with the back of her hand. "Is Jack giving you a lift to the station? Do I need to watch the bar or is Tansy coming in early?" Tansy was one of their regular barmaids who worked a lot of the day shifts.

"No, thanks Kim. I'm going to take my bike, but yes Tansy is coming in a little early today. And Molly will be coming in later." She glanced at Doris to check for a reaction but the old lady didn't move.

"You and that bloody bike," chided Kim, shaking her head. "It's baltic out there. I can take you, you'll freeze, you mad woman."

Sophie giggled. Everyone teased her about her bike but she loved the freedom and flexibility it gave her. It had also helped put the revamped pub on the map locally, admittedly more by fluke than design, but Sophie was more than happy to take the credit. Shortly after moving down from London, she had joined a local cycling club and would sometimes steal away, early on a Sunday morning, to ride through the open countryside with other members of the club. She had, unintentionally, been doing a subtle marketing job whilst out riding and, after a few weeks, her fellow cyclists, 'the lycra lovelies', as Jack referred to them, started coming back to the pub after a ride, lured in by Sophie's description of Kim's home-made pies and Jack's eclectic range of beers. To Jack's surprise, word spread quickly amongst the greater cycling fraternity and it wasn't long before The Crown became a destination pub for local cyclists. Jack had even installed a bike rack in the beer garden. It had shocked and stunned him to learn how much money these people spent on bikes but he valued their custom and offering bike security was a no-brainer.

Sophie made her way through to the bar where Jack was restocking. She stood on tiptoe to drop a kiss on her husband's cheek. "I'll text you when I'm on my way back."

Jack placed his fingers gently under his wife's chin and lifted her face to his. "A proper kiss please," he whispered, wrapping his other arm around her slim waist and lifting her, effortlessly, off the ground. Sophie offered no resistance. Tall and slender, her height had, since her teenage years, made her feel self-conscious. One of the many advantages of falling in love with Jack, was that it had given her the confidence to wear the heels she had spent so many years avoiding, to finally enjoy her femininity. "Let me know if you want a lift home later," Jack said, as Sophie peeled herself away from him. "We can always put the bike in the van. Don't want you drunk in charge, do we?"

"I'm going to meet Annie for some shopping and a civilised lunch, not a piss-up," Sophie retorted.

"Famous last words, I know what you and the Minesweeper are like."

"Oh, you're very funny today, aren't you, Mr. Fox? I've told you not to call her that! In fact, that comment has just cost you. You're going to pay for our lunch. I'll tell Annie it's your treat! Come on, cough up." She held her hand out expectantly.

Jack chuckled, as he reached for his wallet and handed over several twenty-pound notes. "Everything costs me where you're concerned."

"You can't blame me if you have expensive tastes." Sophie quickly took the cash. "Right, I need to go." She double checked the contents of her handbag. "Cash, ticket ... ooh and the credit card, of course. That might take a hit today."

"Yeah, I thought that might be the case. Maybe you should go shopping before you start drinking and not the other way around." Jack was only joking, he was glad that Sophie was having some time to herself. "Here put this on." He picked up Sophie's cycling helmet and placed it firmly on her head, bending down to secure the strap tightly under her chin.

"Jesus Jack, leave room for me to breath." Sophie pushed her husband away. "You don't know your own strength, you brute." She glanced at the clock above the bar. "I need to get a move on if I'm to catch the ten thirty train. I meant to ask though, what did you say to Molly last night? She told me you had mentioned having a chat. She was very excited."

Jack looked down at his lovely wife. She was so positive about Molly, she wasn't going to like his decision. "I did," he said slowly. "But I said I want to do things properly. You won't be happy but I want a reference."

Sophie frowned. "Who's going to do that for her?" As far as she was concerned, a reference wasn't necessary but she knew he wouldn't budge on this. No-one liked things done properly as much as Jack.

"Eddie suggested I speak to Kate, and Molly's OK with that."

"Really? Aren't they mates?" She noticed the slight change in Jack's body language and decided not to push any further. She just wanted Molly on the team, which meant going along with him for now. "Oh well, you're the boss."

"And we both know that's not true!" Jack relaxed. "I dance to your tune Mrs. Fox. Go on go, before I find you something to do."

Sophie blew him a kiss and disappeared quickly through the door. Unlocking her bike, she paused; she'd forgotten her gloves. She glanced at her watch. It was too late to go back inside and find them, she wasn't even sure where they were. Anyway, she had a train to catch, she wasn't going to keep Annie waiting. Determined not to let the cold get to her, she mounted her bike and started pedalling furiously. The faster she went, the warmer she'd feel.

The London train was already sitting at the platform when she arrived at the station fifteen minutes later. Dismounting quickly, she pushed her bike into a space on the bike stand. Forgetting her gloves had been a stupid mistake. Her hands were numb and she couldn't get her fingers to apply any pressure to the lock. Swearing under her breath, she left the bike unsecured and raced up the steps to the station, blowing ineffectually onto her hands as she did so. She was glad she'd worn sensible boots, running in heels was a skill she had yet to master. She consoled herself with the thought that, at this time of day, she wouldn't have to fight through the crowds, she'd made that mistake before and had vowed never to travel by train during rush hour again. In her opinion, if you paid for an expensive ticket you should, at the very least, get a seat. Turning the corner onto the small concourse her heart sank; in front of her, there was a crowd of a different kind.

"Bloody kids," she muttered under her breath, as she pushed her way through the noisy, over excited throng of uniformed children, physically flinching as their high-pitched screams assaulted her eardrums. The barriers to her platform were open which was in her favour, she wouldn't have to try and fish her ticket out of her handbag with fingers that still felt, and looked, like frozen sausages. But her relief was short-lived. The barriers had been opened for a specific reason, they were letting the kids through en-masse. The noisy brats were going to London and they were going to be on her bloody train. She almost felt tearful, her day off wasn't going as planned. Still wearing her helmet, she boarded the train and sat down next to the window in a group of six seats. A smartly dressed man had already occupied the seat opposite her and the remaining four seats were quickly taken by noisy schoolchildren. Inching closer to the window to avoid physical contact, Sophie glanced at the kids. Three girls, two of them caked in cheap make-up and a tall, skinny boy were already sniggering at her expense. She cursed silently as the train pulled away, as far as these kids were concerned, she looked like a freak. She blew on her hands once more and raised them to her chin for another go.

"Do you need some help with that?" It was a man's voice, the man sitting opposite her.

Sophie looked up at him and smiled gratefully. "Would you mind? I forgot my gloves, left it too late to go back and get them and now I can't feel my fingers." She had a slight feeling that she had seen this man before but quickly dismissed the thought. Working in a pub meant you thought you recognised a lot of people.

The man leant forward and swiftly released the catch under her chin. Sophie was aware of his expensive cologne. "There you go," he said, smiling broadly. "You're free."

"Thanks so much!" She took off her helmet and ran her still cold fingers through her dark, naturally curly hair. "I was at risk of being the on-board entertainment." She glanced at the three girls who'd been watching her. The two with the heavy make-up quickly looked away, the third, a pretty girl with long dark hair, quietly clapped her hands together, as if applauding the success of this man's gallant action. Sophie smiled at her, surprising herself, she didn't often smile at kids.

The man smiled too and glanced at the girls and the young boy. "I think you're safe. I didn't see any phones come out. Not likely to find yourself being ridiculed online just yet." He looked down at Sophie's helmet which was now resting on her lap. "I used to do a bit of cycling around here myself and I know, at first hand, no pun intended, the perils of forgetting to wear gloves when it's cold. Fingers any better yet?"

Sophie tried to move her fingers. "Getting better," she said. "I'm really grateful to you. Next time you're in town, pop into The Crown. Do you know it? It's on the Market Place. I run it with my husband. I'd love to buy you a drink as a thank you. I'm Sophie, Sophie Fox." She felt slightly embarrassed, she was talking quickly and the girls were listening in. They probably thought she was chatting this man up but she was doing what she always seemed to do recently, she was promoting her business.

"Thanks Sophie, I might take you up on that offer. I used to know The Crown quite well in a former life. Restrictions on my time mean I don't get back here very often ... there have been a lot of changes." He stopped speaking abruptly and looked out of the window, Sophie followed his gaze. They were approaching the outskirts of the next town. The urban sprawl had taken over from the rural landscape. She thought he wasn't going to say anymore, he seemed lost in thought. "Not all of them for the better," he said finally, his face tense.

Sophie didn't know what to say and, for some reason, she felt slightly uncomfortable. She looked back out of the window. "I can't really comment about the changes I'm afraid ... we've only had the pub a few months. Anyway, thanks again. Sorry, I didn't catch your name."

"That's because I didn't tell you Sophie," the man said, a wry smile on his face. "My friends call me JP. You Sophie ... you can call me JP."

Chapter Four

"You were away a long time Jack," Kate sighed. "I don't really know where to start."

Jack, Kate and Eddie were sitting in the playroom; Eddie had poured coffee for all of them. Kate hadn't understood, at first, why Eddie wanted her to speak to Jack, to explain about Molly. She'd spent the previous two days swinging between the urge to refuse Eddie's request and the desire to be honest, or as honest as possible without scuppering Molly's chances. In the end, she had simply called her friend.

Molly had been positive about the whole idea. 'I trust you Kate, you wouldn't jeopardise things for me and you'll know how to tell him. It's only a matter of time before someone else tells him their version anyway. And Jack trusts you and Eddie. He's a very straight guy from the little I know. So, go ahead, tell him what you need to ... but Kate, can I ask you not to say too much about Seth?' Molly's attitude had surprised Kate, it wasn't like her friend to be so calm. Keeping Seth out of the picture wouldn't be easy though, he was an integral part of the story.

Sitting in the playroom with Lottie by her feet, she felt guilty. "When Eddie mentioned this reference thing, I told him I wasn't sure you need to know about Molly's private life, but I do understand that as her friend ... I hope you will consider her as a friend, even though it's been so long?" She stopped speaking and raised her eyebrows quizzically at Jack but he didn't respond. "Well, as her friend and her employer," Kate continued, "you might find yourself stuck between a rock and a hard place in this town. And I wouldn't want to think of Molly being in a situation where she doesn't get the support she needs, especially in a working environment. She's still fragile and people have been so harsh ... some can still be harsh."

Jack's eyes were serious but he smiled gently. "Thanks Kate. You're right, I have been away a long time. You were just a young mum ... the years have rolled by."

Kate nodded and laughed. "Let's not dwell on numbers Jack. I don't need reminding how old I am."

"You haven't changed," Jack said softly and he meant it. He thought Kate looked good, seemed more comfortable in her own skin than the young, shy woman he remembered. She was also more striking to look at. She'd found her own style and exuded a self-confidence that was attractive. "Look, I appreciate there's probably a shed load of trivial stuff, stuff I don't need to know but I would appreciate you sharing the important things with me. Not just as Molly's employer but as a local landlord. It could affect my business, which I appreciate may sound selfish, but it's the truth. Don't be frightened to tell me to butt out though … if I'm being too nosy." He grinned at her. "Does that make sense?"

"Yes, of course." Kate nodded. "Total sense. Just keep in mind that this is my dearest friend we're talking about. I'm the first to admit she has faults and I've spent many years holding her hand, propping her up during the bad times, but Molly is, ultimately, the product of her childhood. She was spoilt beyond belief Jack, a late baby to a couple who didn't ever think they could have children. They became indulgent parents and she turned into a supreme brat. What Molly wanted, Molly got. Unfortunately, when she married James he took over from her parents. He gave her everything."

"Kate, don't forget James was also a complete control freak," said Eddie. "She might have had everything she wanted and more but he … well, let's just say there were conditions."

"I don't dispute that Eddie but expecting to get her own way all the time was ultimately her downfall."

"Many of us like to get our own way Kate but we don't all do what Molly did, we don't cause so much pain … not to our friends and family," Eddie replied gently.

Jack looked at the palms of his hands as if looking at notes. He was buying a little time, he didn't want to cause a scene between his two old friends. "OK, shall I tell you what I know so far?" he asked diplomatically. Kate pulled her legs onto the sofa beside her and nodded. "So, Molly and

James got married about the same time as you two? I didn't get an invitation to the big day though." He attempted to make a comically sad face. "I knew Molly through you guys but I never met James."

"Molly met James when he moved here to work at Spicers," Eddie explained. "Don't know if you remember them? They've been taken over by another big drugs company now but James was their blue-eyed boy. A real go-getter."

"OK, maybe I did meet him then." Jack frowned slightly. "Was he any good at football? Didn't he come and do some training with us back in the day?"

"Bloody hell, what a memory!" Eddie was impressed. "He did! He was a good six-a-side player. He's a tall guy ... quick on his feet. He didn't carry much weight back then ... probably still doesn't." He looked down at his own protruding stomach and the buttons that were straining on his shirt. He sighed sadly. "Not like me."

"So, he married Molly but they didn't live happily ever after?" Jack asked. "Sorry, I don't mean to sound facetious but I obviously know about Molly's affair with Will."

"At first they did," said Kate. "Molly fell pregnant quickly ... Seth came along." She instantly made a mental note to say very little about Seth. "James was happy, Molly was happy. His career was taking off and he was head-hunted by a French company, inevitably he travelled a lot, was often away from home." Kate caught the look in Jack's eyes, saw the way he raised his eyebrows. "Don't jump to conclusions Jack ... that's too easy," she said sharply. "Nothing happened then. Molly was happy, she had her baby, had no need to go to work. They moved into the old vicarage up on Willow Hill which they totally renovated ... and Molly proved to have an eye for interior design. She worked hard on that house. To be honest we were all a little jealous. The house was amazing ... they even had a pool. It was like a show home, like something you see on TV."

"Unlike ours," grinned Eddie, looking sheepishly around at the clutter of their lives. "Although to be honest their house gave me the creeps ... it was too perfect."

"They had wonderful holidays too. Seth was very well travelled for such a young boy. He went to places I will probably never get to see." Kate cast her mind back to the image of young Seth, lonely, damaged Seth. Jack waited for her to continue, sensing that she was struggling. He knew not to push. "But Molly did get bored, eventually," Kate said at last. "Seth went to school, James was away, I was working and she didn't have a great relationship with her mother." She shifted slightly on the sofa. "Basically Jack, she had too much time on her hands. She joined a gym, took French lessons .... but, ultimately, I think she was bored."

"She wasn't working herself? It would be good to know what kind of work she's done in the past, what responsibilities she's had," Jack interjected.

"James wouldn't hear of her working," Kate said. If Jack was surprised by this he didn't let it show. "It sounds crazy to a lot of people but, looking back, none of us thought it particularly odd. We all knew what James was like, how bossy he was."

"Controlling," muttered Eddie quietly.

"Yeah ... maybe," Kate sighed. "But they could afford for Molly not to work, couldn't they? They were very comfortably off. Anyway, with the amount of travelling James did back then, she would have needed help with Seth but James didn't want anyone else but Molly to be there for his son. He didn't even like Molly's mother collecting Seth from school now and then."

"That's fairly understandable though. Molly's mother has complex issues herself. I wouldn't have felt comfortable leaving her in charge of Lottie, let alone a small boy." Eddie looked at Jack and raised his hand, as if picking up a drink. "Rita is a recovering alcoholic, she relapses regularly," he explained. "In his defence though, when he was home, James made sure that Molly had a good social life. He was always arranging barbecues, dinner parties and even theatre trips. He didn't keep her entirely to himself ... not at that stage."

Kate smiled fondly at her husband. "We had quite a bit of fun back then, didn't we? We'd have all the kids over for sleep-overs, although not much sleeping took place to be fair. But having the kids altogether meant there were no issues with babysitters." She stopped talking and gestured guiltily to Eddie and herself. "Us lot, the adults.... we invariably got pissed downstairs. It was fun, wasn't it Eddie? Well, until she ..."

"Until she what Kate?" Jack asked gently. He was used to this kind of questioning, he knew how to keep someone talking.

"I so wish I had spotted it earlier, I'd like to think I might have stood a chance of nipping it in the bud but she didn't confide in me until it was too late," Kate said sadly. "I had no idea anything was going on. For the first time, in all the years I'd known her, she didn't talk to me. Some friend eh?"

"It was her dirty little secret," said Eddie. "Sorry ... that sounds harsh but she was doing something sordid, wasn't she? She wouldn't have been able to tell you Kate. She looks up to you, or she did anyway. She would have felt guilty about letting you down."

Kate looked thoughtfully down at the dog at her feet. "I'm not so sure she cares about letting me down," she said quietly. "She only bothered to tell me when she thought it might be too late."

"Are you talking about her affair with Will?" asked Jack. Kate shook her head slowly. "Of course, Eddie said there was someone before Will. Who was it?" Jack spoke quickly, he was keen to hear this piece of the puzzle. This was a small town, there was every chance he might know the first man. The playroom was quiet apart from the sound of Lottie's gentle snoring. "Come on guys. Do I know him?"

"Jack ... you did know him," Eddie said eventually. "It was Tim, Molly's first affair was with Tim."

Jack stared at Eddie, his face slowly registering his shock. "Tim? Tim Baxter?" He was struggling to understand. "Tim? Will's step-brother?"

Eddie nodded. "Were they real step-brothers though? Will had a few 'Uncles' during his childhood. He had more than his fair share of 'step-siblings' too. It's to his credit that he stayed in contact with all of them."

For a few seconds, no-one said anything. "But Tim died shortly before Will, didn't he?" Jack was shocked. "What are you saying guys? Molly ... two dead men."

"She didn't kill either of them Jack, remember that for God's sake." Kate's tone was defensive. "Tim had an accident, a car crash and well ... you know about Will."

"Sorry Kate. I didn't mean anything ... really, I didn't. It's just a lot to take in."

"I know, I know," said Kate softly. "Look, I need to explain about Tim. I think he initiated things with Molly. That doesn't redeem her but she was certainly an easy target. The classic bored housewife. Tim shouldn't have been so bloody foolish."

Jack cast his mind back. Tim, the confident, funny, young man who had left home to join the Army. The girls at school had been drawn to Tim, not because he was good looking but because he made them laugh. "How come I never knew?" he asked. "I'm surprised Will didn't tell me."

"You moved away Jack ... it was local gossip. And Tim wasn't married." Kate sighed. "There was no pissed-off wife, no kids got hurt in the fall-out. And to be honest, I don't think Will was that chuffed with Tim's behaviour, he probably didn't want to speak about it. I've always thought that slightly weird really, considering that it would be him and Molly not long after."

"It's also possible that Molly was just one of his many conquests," added Eddie. "Tim's life in the Army meant he came and went ... rarely had a steady girlfriend. There may have been other irate husbands, in other towns. You know what Tim was like."

"It sounds like we're excusing it, belittling it," said Kate. "But we're not, we wouldn't. And we're not blaming Tim entirely. What they both did was wrong. Some might say her guilt was greater. She was married ... had a child. She behaved dreadfully, like no-one else mattered ... not even Seth."

"Seth?" asked Jack.

"Sorry. I shouldn't have said that." Kate spoke quickly. "Let's just say he got hurt too ... inevitably."

Jack nodded slowly, he knew Kate was holding back. "But her marriage survived?" he asked instead.

"James was outraged, naturally," replied Kate. "He was away when he found out and to this day, I don't know who told him. Weird, isn't it? But whoever it was, he ... or she ... had lots of information. You know, intimate stuff, dates, locations, etc. Molly had been sneaking Tim into the old vicarage for several months ... I couldn't believe it." She didn't add that a small Seth, woken by strange noises in the middle of the night, had found his mum and Tim in bed together. She shook her head slightly, the writing had been on the wall where Seth was concerned, even back then.

"But still ... they didn't break up?" Jack insisted. He was surprised by Kate's choice of words. She'd said James had been outraged. No mention of heartbreak or shock. "I feel like this is none of my business but he forgave her?"

"Yes ... no ... well, not straight away," Kate sighed. "Tim took off, made himself very scarce, dropped Molly like the proverbial hot potato and Molly ... well she had to sit and wait for James to come home."

"Come home?" Jack was confused.

"James was in France working when he found out and that's where he stayed, for weeks. He said he couldn't face her, that the sight of her would make him ill," Kate explained.

"He was weird like that," Eddie interjected. "Loved to play the victim."

"He was ringing her all the time though." Kate looked directly at Jack. "At one stage, he was ringing every few hours, checking up on her day and night. It was cruel. She couldn't sleep. In hindsight, it's easy to see that it was all part of his game but, at the time, it was really worrying ... especially for Molly. One minute he was saying he wanted it to work, that he could forgive her, the next he was threatening to come home and take Seth, take him to France."

"You're telling me that he didn't come home as soon as he found out? He didn't have it out with his wife? That's odd, isn't it?"

"It made no sense ... he should have come home," said Kate. "Molly had no idea what his plans were. She was a mess."

"But he must have come home? Molly had to face the music eventually?"

"Of course." Kate tried to choose her words carefully. Jack didn't need to know everything, especially when it involved Seth.

"He turned up and took Seth out of school," Eddie interjected. "Molly went to collect him as normal, only to find out he'd gone. James took off with him."

Kate sighed, she should have warned Eddie to be more careful. "There was a mix up," she said, willing Eddie to keep his mouth shut. "But no harm was done. Molly got a little worried but it was OK. James brought Seth here later that night, didn't he? He wanted to speak to you Ed, do you remember?"

"Oh, yes." Kate was relieved to see the slight nod Eddie gave her. He'd understood. "I think he wanted to see how the land lay. You know, check on who knew what. He seemed preoccupied with his reputation."

"They did work it out then? For a while anyway?" Jack asked. He couldn't help thinking Kate and Eddie weren't telling him something.

"I suppose so but Molly paid a price ...." Kate faltered. There were so many things Jack didn't need to know.

Eddie, thinking Kate was struggling with the memory of what had happened next, took over for her. "Jack, the first night James was home ... he attacked her. He kicked the shit out of her. She ended up in hospital."

Jack was clearly shocked. "Fucking hell! Bastard! Did he get arrested?"

"No," said Kate quickly. "And I'm not too sure we should be telling you this. It's not relevant to a reference, is it? My husband lets his tongue run away with him." She glared at Eddie. "But now you know, please only use it to understand how tough she's had it." She paused to recompose herself, Eddie had seriously annoyed her. "He was too clever Jack. He had spent weeks torturing Molly mentally over the phone, playing on her guilt, threatening to take Seth. When he finally started punching her that night, she said it felt right, that she had driven him to it. She was paying her penance."

Jack snorted and sprang out of his chair. "Bloody bastard."

"I know but there's more," said Eddie. "James let Seth watch all this. Seth saw his Mum get a beating."

Kate closed her eyes and sighed. Bloody Eddie and his big mouth. She'd promised to keep Seth out of things.

"What the fuck?" Jack shouted. "What kind of evil bastard would do that? And Tim? James never went near Tim? There was no altercation? He beats a woman but doesn't go near a bloke?"

The question didn't surprise Kate, most men would react the same way. "No, Tim's accident, the car crash, happened just before James came back. It was a horrid time Jack, James had worn Molly down, physically and mentally. She didn't know where to turn. She was close to having a breakdown." She shot a look at Eddie, a look that said enough had been said. Jack didn't need to know more.

Chapter Five

Jack checked his watch. "I'm just going to call Sophie ... make sure everything is OK back at the ranch. Is that OK?"

"Of course." Kate got up and opened the patio doors that led out into the garden, Lottie dutifully stepped outside. She was glad of the break, she felt drained.

"It's at times like this, I wish I still smoked." Jack said when they reconvened a few minutes later. "That poor kid."

"I know, behind closed doors and all that." Kate was determined not to be drawn further, Eddie had revealed too much already. "Seth's at uni now ... studying medicine." She felt compelled to say something positive, to give the impression of no lasting damage. Jack didn't need to know that Seth was a deeply damaged individual.

"Was it an isolated incident? That attack? The beating?" Jack took a biscuit from a plate Eddie had placed on the coffee table. He softened his voice, Kate wasn't under interrogation.

"Yes, I think so," Kate replied watching Eddie, as he took several biscuits. "I can't be entirely sure but I don't think he ever did anything as bad as that again. In fact, I'd go as far to say that he became more affectionate."

"More controlling, I'd say," Eddie said. "He never let her out of his sight, always had his arm draped over her ... as if he owned her."

Kate was surprised. "You've never said that before but maybe you're right. He did put an end to her social life, didn't he? There were no more dinner parties, no more drunken sleepovers."

"And Molly did as she was told?" Jack asked.

Kate shook her head. "I don't think she saw it like that, not initially anyway. Oh, I don't know ... but we did see less of her for a few months which was hard. I didn't feel there was anything really sinister in it though." She turned to Eddie. "Did you?"

"Not especially." Eddie paused for a moment. "They were rebuilding their family. That's the impression I got."

"He did some radical things though," Kate said. "He insisted they renew their marriage vows although Molly wasn't keen. I suppose he was showing everyone that he was giving her another chance. You know, 'isn't James an understanding guy' kind of thing."

"Did you think he was doing that?" asked Jack.

"A little. It was a strange time. He went the whole hog, fancy wedding dress, new rings. It was a surreal day, quite painful for her I think." Kate cast her mind back, it hadn't just been Molly who had been in pain that lovely summer day.

Jack was asking a lot of questions, questions it wasn't really his place to ask but he couldn't stop himself. Molly had been involved with two of his old friends and both men had died. Instinct was telling him there was more to this. "Did things return to normal after that?" he asked gently.

"Amazingly they did ... for a while anyway," said Kate. "James even allowed Molly to work." She held up her hands defensively. "I know that sounds ridiculous but it's what he was like. He allowed her to work part-time, helping at Seth's old primary school. Maybe he thought it safer? That way he would know where she was at all times, wouldn't he? And of course, it made sense on another level ... most of the staff are female in these places."

Jack nodded. "That's her only work experience?"

"Yes, I'm afraid so," Kate confirmed. "She's had a few jobs since James left but they never last. This is a small town ... mud sticks."

Jack looked at the palms of his hands again, buying himself a little more time. "Within the local community, did people alienate her? I'm sorry I have to ask but some of our customers aren't always chuffed to see her. Some have even been quite vocal when they've had a beer or two."

"Shit ... really?" Kate was visibly concerned. "She hasn't said anything. How can people behave like that?"

"Don't worry too much Kate. I know how to deal with these guys and Molly seems to have a pretty thick skin. She's coped so far," Jack replied softly. He was genuinely touched to see how much Kate cared.

"Molly? A thick skin? Do you really think so?" Kate was surprised. "Maybe she saves all the tears for me then. Lucky me, eh?"

"You don't think she was alienated?" Jack repeated his question.

"No, not really. Not the first time ... not with this affair. That would happen after Will. Some people may have thought she was a bit of a scarlet woman and her mother came off the wagon in spectacular fashion. But no, in general, she was as popular as ever. Unfortunately, more so with some of the men she came across."

Jack didn't need to ask for an explanation, he knew what she was referring to. Molly would have earned herself a warped respect with some men and been regarded as fair game. It was the same the world over. "I'm almost too frightened to ask my next question."

Kate did it for him. "Will?"

"Yes," Jack replied softly. "How on earth? So soon after Tim?"

Kate studied Jack's face, she was searching for the right words to explain but there were no words, nothing made it sound better. Molly had done the unspeakable, there were no excuses.

"She caught us all out, didn't she?" she said more to herself than to Jack. "She did it all over again but she didn't get away lightly the second time. No-one did." If Jack thought she was thinking of Will, he would have been mistaken. Kate's preoccupation centred purely on Seth.

***

Sophie didn't always like Saturdays in the pub, Saturdays often meant kids came in and she didn't do kids. She had little time for their overly indulgent parents either, most of whom exhibited poor and lazy parenting skills. Finding ketchup smeared across her beautiful wallpaper, or cold peas and mangled chips squashed into the crevices of the newly sanded, wooden floor made her want to scream. Selfishly, she hadn't wanted Jack to offer a kids' menu at The Crown. She'd argued that it demeaned their food and weakened the message about locally produced ingredients, kids didn't care where their food came from. Her opinions had, as she knew they would, fallen on deaf ears and Jack had won the argument. A kids' menu was a cash cow, end of story.

On this sunny Saturday morning, Jack had gone to see Kate and Eddie, her husband wanted some reassurance that it was a good idea to bring Molly formally into their team. He was a fair man but he ran a tight ship when it came to his employees. He'd learnt the hard way that a good team was the backbone of a successful small business and was vigilant in taking thorough references. He'd promised not to be too long but Saturday mornings were always busy, so Sophie had asked Molly to come in for a couple of hours, just in case. Fraser and Andy, two young students who helped with food service at weekends would be coming in too.

Kim was singing loudly in the kitchen; Sophie smiled, singing was always a good sign with Kim. She'd been experimenting with different specials, or posh fast-food as Sophie liked to think of it, and sales looked good. She also did a wonderful brunch for the late breakfast crowd which was proving to be a real success, especially at weekends. Some customers were already tucking in this morning, others were reading newspapers and sipping on hot coffee. They all appeared to be relishing the relaxed pace of a Saturday morning.

"Morning Sophie," Molly poked her head in from the corridor. "Just dropping off my stuff … I'll be two minutes."

Sophie waved. "No rush Molly … I'll make you a coffee." A moment later she heard Kim and Molly laugh loudly, it was an infectious sound. "That's what we want Jack," she said softly to herself. Molly emerged from the kitchen a few seconds later, still smiling. "You look good this morning." Sophie handed her a coffee. "New jeans?"

Molly looked down at her dark blue jeans. "No, not really … although this is new." She pulled at a delicate, silk scarf she had tied loosely around her neck.

"It's good to see you treating yourself. It's pretty. Is it silk? Where did you get it? I might buy one for Kim ... she loves to wear scarves like that in her hair."

Molly blushed slightly as she walked over to serve a customer. "Sorry, I don't know where it's from Sophie ... it was a present." The blush coupled with the bashfulness made Sophie smile, instinct told her Molly had a secret. She'd park this conversation for another time. She might not like gossip or tittle-tattle but she loved girly talk, especially when it involved a new romance.

It proved to be a busy morning and Sophie was glad, yet again, that Molly was there to help. "Molly, there's a work rota for you in the kitchen. Take a look and let me know if any shifts are a problem," she said, when the worst of the breakfast rush was over. "I know Jack's getting your reference but it's only a formality so I've made a head start."

"Thanks so much." Molly was touched by Sophie's faith in her. "I'm looking forward to working here ... you know ... officially."

Sophie smiled. "I hope you still feel that way in a few weeks. This kind of work can take over your life."

"I forgot to ask you. Did you have a nice day with your friend in London on Thursday?"

Sophie stopped what she was doing and giggled softly. "Molly it was lovely. Don't get me wrong, I love it here but I do miss the buzz of London. It was home for so long."

"I bet." Molly's smile was slightly forlorn. "I've often thought about leaving here but it takes guts to start again somewhere new, doesn't it? Especially on your own."

"Yes ... I suppose it does." Sophie looked closely at Molly. "I was lucky though, Jack was coming home, wasn't he? Back to his roots? So, meeting people, making friends, was easier. Why would you want to leave though?"

"Oh, you know ... small town, everyone knowing your business." Molly was amazed at how little Sophie knew about her. Hopefully, the reference

Jack was collecting from Kate wouldn't change things. It was time to change the subject. "So, what did you get up to on Thursday?"

Sophie's face broke into a huge grin and she giggled again. "Eating, drinking and shopping ... in a nutshell. My friend Annie is a master at all three and I struggled to keep up. I don't think Jack's seen how much I spent yet." She made a face like a naughty child. "I had too many bags to be able to cycle home though, so he must have guessed I hammered the credit card. You know he had to come and get me and throw my bike in the van, don't you? I couldn't manage all those bags and the bike." She lowered her voice and moved closer to Molly. "Plus, I may have been a tiny bit tipsy ... unavoidable with Annie."

"She sounds like fun." It felt good to be taken into Sophie's confidence. "Have you known her long?"

"Jack introduced us about eight years ago ... they used to work together," Sophie replied. "She's a friend to both of us really but she prefers to take me shopping for obvious reasons. Unfortunately, Jack still treats her like she's one of the blokes, which I try to discourage. You know what men are like ... lots of stupid banter."

"Speaking of banter, can I ask you a question about Annie?"

Sophie nodded. "Ask away."

"Why does Jack call her the minesweeper? When you rang asking for a lift home the other night, he said he was picking you up because the minesweeper had done it again. I wasn't sure what he meant."

Sophie grimaced but her voice was light. "I keep telling him to stop saying that. It's a term of endearment really but it's not very attractive, is it?" Molly shook her head but Sophie could see she was confused. "From the look on your face you never played the minesweeping drinking game when you were younger?" Molly shook her head again. "I'm going to spare you the ghastly details because it makes Annie sound like she's got no class, which isn't true. It's a nickname from years ago that stuck. That's what happens when you work with a bunch of men. Although there's no denying Annie is a party animal, always the last 'man' standing."

"She sounds a bit like me back in the day," Molly said, a little wistfully. "Kate could tell you. I always stayed out too late, had one too many, couldn't bear to leave a room full of people in case I missed something. I put it down to being an only child. I used to drive Kate mad. Lucy, Kate's daughter, says there's a name for it ... something about missing out."

"FOMO, the Fear of Missing Out. Oh my God Molly ... you have to meet Annie ... she's exactly the same," laughed Sophie. "She's pretty hard core ... like I said ... years of being the only female on the team. She always had to hold her own. You know ... show no weakness. I'm going to get her to come and stay soon, when she's got some time off. We'll have a night out... plan?"

"Plan," said Molly, nodding her head vigorously and beaming at Sophie. It felt like an eternity since she'd been invited to join in. Maybe, just maybe, things were looking up at last.

***

"Are you going to tell me how it went today?" Sophie asked Jack on Saturday evening, when their paths crossed in the kitchen. "Do you feel more comfortable about Molly? I take it she's not going to poison someone or empty the safe?" She had been a little surprised at how long Jack had spent with Kate and Eddie and he hadn't said much since his return, she was curious.

"Yes, it went well. Sorry I was so long but it was good to have a catch up with Kate and Eddie. It's years since I've been to their house. We should try and see them more regularly."

"Which is exactly why we need Molly to come and work for us," agreed his wife. "To give us some time for ourselves, to build a social life outside this place." She stood in front of him, her hands on her slim hips, her blue eyes bright; everything about her body language was saying 'I told you so.'

Jack couldn't help but laugh, she was right. Walking back to the pub earlier in the day, he hadn't been entirely sure what he would say to Sophie. He'd learnt a lot about Molly, not all of it good by any means but there was nothing that made her unemployable. Despite her extra marital involvement with two of his oldest friends, Molly wasn't a criminal, she hadn't killed anyone or broken any laws. He couldn't say he'd changed his mind about giving her a job because some customers might remember she'd gone off the rails several years ago. Sophie certainly wouldn't tolerate that. Jack studied his wife's attractive face. "OK," he said, pulling her towards him and brushing her dark hair away from her blue eyes. "We'll take her on. I'll sort out the formal stuff, you work with her on the rotas but don't put her down for any Sunday shifts yet."

"Why? That doesn't make any sense." Sophie pulled away. "Sundays are our busiest days."

"Don't ask ... until you're prepared to listen," Jack replied cryptically.

Sophie wasn't sure how to respond, this wasn't like Jack. He didn't play games. "What do you mean?"

"Sophie, aren't you curious? About her? About why some people have a thing about her? Not even a little bit?"

"No. Not about old gossip anyway. Everyone has a past, has history, baggage ... call it what you want. Even you." Sophie noticed Jack flinch slightly. She didn't intentionally want to hurt him but this was a subject close to her heart. "None of us are perfect Jack."

She didn't have to spell it out, Jack knew it couldn't be one rule for him and another for Molly. He pulled her close again and kissed her gently on the top of her head. "Sophie Fox, who knew you were so clever? You do such a good job of disguising it!"

"I know," Sophie laughed, relieved at his reaction. "I'm wasted here."

"Do I need to ask you two to get a room?" called Kim, from across the kitchen. "We do cooking in here, not canoodling." She exaggerated her Jamaican accent to give the last word comical emphasis, making them all laugh.

"No, he has work to do Kim, he's been skiving today," said Sophie. "Off you go Landlord, go do your stuff." She opened the door for him and bowed, deferentially, as he walked past. She waited for the door to shut before she walked over to stand closer to Kim. "Good news Kim, Molly is coming on board full-time."

"That's really good news ... she's a nice girl. I like her," said Kim. Sophie wondered if their chef knew anything about Molly. Don't be a hypocrite she thought, remember what you just said to Jack. "Although the lovely Doris won't be too impressed I imagine," Kim added. "She's not a fan."

"I thought I had noticed something. Do you know why?"

"I'm not sure Sophie, it's just a feeling I get. She's never said anything, and she's never been rude or disruptive when I'm around but I've worked in lots of kitchens ... I know when there's an atmosphere. I'm an expert."

"Do you think Molly knows?" asked Sophie, marvelling at Kim's ability to multitask.

"I think we all know when somebody doesn't like us, don't we?" said Kim, slicing two large portions of home-made apple pie and placing them on plates with individual pots of cream, all ready to go just as Andy came in to collect them. "Some of us confront it, others let it go. I like to think Molly is a 'let it go' type of girl, she seems to accept that not everyone will like her. Either that or she's given up trying to get people to like her. Anyway, whatever it is, I admire her, too many people are uptight about being popular. I'm sure she'd face up to Doris, if she had to."

"Let's hope it doesn't come to that, they probably won't come across each other too much." Sophie was secretly pleased with Kim's opinion of Molly, it wasn't too dissimilar to her own. "Doris only does a few hours. You will let me know if there's a problem though, won't you Kim?"

"Of course I will," Kim said emphatically. "Don't worry ... I'm sure it's no big deal."

Sophie walked back into the bar, pleased to see the crowd from earlier had thinned out. Now, only a dozen or so people were hanging on for last orders. She liked this time of the day, liked the routine of closing the bar, of putting everything 'to bed'. Jack was serving a tall man in a dark overcoat.

There was something familiar about him, about his well-groomed appearance.

"This one's on the house Jack, this is the lovely man who helped me out of my helmet the other day. This is JP ... JP this is my husband, Jack."

"Ah, Sophie's hero." Jack pushed JP's ten pound note away.

"There's no need ... really." JP frowned slightly and pushed the money forward again.

Jack refused to take it. "I'm afraid I have to insist. You saved Sophie from the one thing she hates most ... kids."

"Well thank you ... both of you." JP smiled nervously at Sophie. "The kids didn't seem too bad though."

"I have a low tolerance, very low."

"That's an understatement," laughed Jack.

"What brings you back here so soon?" Sophie frowned slightly. JP had said he hadn't been in town for a long time and here he was again, within just a few days.

JP smiled awkwardly. "Nothing interesting I'm afraid ... just family stuff." He glanced behind him at the door. "I caught the last train down and fancied a quick nightcap." He lifted his glass to his lips and downed the shot of whisky in one quick gulp. "Thanks again. Sorry I can't stay for more. Goodnight."

Sophie watched, in surprise, as JP turned sharply and walked away; the door banged noisily behind him. "Bloody hell! How weird was that? Didn't that strike you as odd? He couldn't get out of here fast enough."

"He was OK until you showed up," Jack teased.

Sophie ignored the joke. "He wasn't like that on the train ... he was friendly. You didn't recognise him, did you? Maybe he recognised you? He said he knew this place years ago."

Jack looked thoughtfully at the door JP had just gone through. He hadn't really paid much attention, faces started to blur into one at this time of night. "No," he said. "Not someone I know.

***

He'd been a fucking idiot. Sophie had said she was married but he hadn't expected her to be married to Jack Fox, of all people. His fucking ego had got the better of him yet again. He'd taken a risk on a late-night drink because of a pretty face. He was a complete dick.

"Fucking twat," he muttered viciously, as he kicked a stone across the road and watched it connect with the bumper of a parked car. In his mind, he quickly replayed what he could remember of the conversation he'd had with Sophie on the train. She'd said she was new to the area, he'd stupidly assumed that would apply to her bloody husband as well. "Twat," he muttered again, as he lashed out with his fist at an overhead shop canopy. Frailer than it looked, the canopy frame buckled instantly; James didn't notice.

"He didn't recognise you, you fucking idiot. Why would he?" Gradually, the feeling of dread was shifting, the panic was slowly subsiding. There had been absolutely no recognition on Jack's face, James was just another punter. "You're just another late night loser ... he sees hundreds. Don't think you're so special he'd remember you." He was making himself feel a little better but his heart still raced, he couldn't afford to make this kind of mistake.

Walking parallel to the Market Place, James followed a series of small side streets until he arrived at his hotel. The Priory was a local landmark and although now part of a national hotel chain, the exterior of the building had been sympathetically restored; soft light shone from the mullioned windows, casting a welcome glow onto the street. As he walked up the front steps into the empty reception area, James was reassured to see that he could check in electronically. Regardless of his bravado, he was on edge; small talk would only make things worse. As his room key dropped into the tray below the check-in screen, he glanced nervously around him. The bar was still open, and he really wanted another drink, he needed to settle his nerves. Scanning the tables and chairs, he was pleased to see there were just two middle-aged men sitting together in a corner. They showed no interest in James. He ordered a double whisky from the disinterested, bearded barman; he didn't wait for his change. Too agitated to wait for the lift, he walked up the three flights of stairs to his room, listening and watching. On the second floor, a group of girls startled him. Drunk, their high-pitched, excited voices bounced off the walls. His eyes lingered on one of them. Smaller than her friends, she looked fragile and vulnerable, almost childlike. Her bright, blond hair was styled in a shoulder length bob. He stared at her, she reminded him of a young Molly.

Once inside his hotel room, he took off his coat and sat on a dark, wingback chair by the window. Still preoccupied by the near miss in the pub, he cast his mind back to the Jack Fox he'd met over twenty years ago. Jack had been one of the lads, a popular guy, a keen sportsman, he remembered that much. They had done some winter training sessions followed by a few pints of beer. James, Molly's new boyfriend, had been a newcomer to the group. Jack had been friendly, nothing more; he wouldn't remember James. He got up slowly and pulled the heavy curtains open. Across the Market Place, the illuminated church looked stark and imposing against the dark sky. There was little traffic, just a few taxis waiting for a fare, their engines still running. Over at the far corner stood The Crown, its lights still shining brightly. Everything looked so familiar. This town had once been his home. He'd been happy here, he'd had friends here. But Molly had ruined all that, she'd ruined everything. She'd disgraced and emasculated him, not once but twice. Her first affair had caught him off guard, he had no idea she was capable of cheating on him. Alone in France, working hard to maintain the lifestyle she craved so badly, she'd repaid him by messing around with a local playboy, a bloody squaddie of all people. He closed his eyes, the pain was still raw, the shame still intense. She'd made him a laughing stock, reduced him to an inadequate cuckold. It had been a brutal, embarrassing period of his life but, despite everything, he'd managed to forgive her, to be the bigger person. It hadn't been easy, people had belittled him. But he'd done it, he'd tried to move on. He'd swallowed his pride for the sake of his family. It never crossed his mind that the evil cow would do it all again, just a few months later. He'd put his complete faith in her but she'd thrown everything back in his face and the second time had been much worse than the first. Molly had launched a grenade into so many lives, the fallout had been too much for some people.

Forgiveness hadn't come easily the second time. For his own self-preservation, he had decided to take a break from his marriage but, as far as he was concerned, that's all it had been, just a break. He'd needed to lick his wounds, to sort his head out. Molly's petition for divorce had stunned him. He didn't want to be divorced, he wanted to be married, married to Molly. His own erratic parents had divorced when he was a young boy and the ensuing animosity between them had resulted in both him and his younger sister being sent to boarding schools, rarely seeing their parents or each other again. For James, divorce just wasn't an option. He'd repeatedly contested her request and stubbornly drawn out legal proceedings. Being awkward and uncompromising on every little detail, had been a way of getting his own back. It had also been a weird kind of therapy. But time was running out and his solicitor couldn't drag things out much longer. He'd recently told James that he'd have to admit defeat but just like divorce, defeat wasn't an option.

Playing mind games on Molly had always been easy but she had come to know the routine too well and it hadn't worked, she hadn't come back. Following her to the cemetery had been a clever move but the bitch clearly knew her way around every inch of the place and had managed to get away. To add salt into his ever-present wounds, boring old Eddie, Molly's bloody guardian angel, had turned up. How he'd love to ruin that friendship, to cast Molly astray with no support at all. She'd need him then, she'd come running then. The thought amused him and he raised a toast to his reflection in the dark window. The alcohol stung his throat as he swallowed but his anxiety was settling.

He pulled the curtains shut and sat down at the small, round table, pushing away the room-service menu. Taking his tablet from his overnight bag, he fed Jack's name into his search engine. A younger version of Jack's handsome face appeared instantly on the screen and James let out a long, slow whistle. Jack Fox, small town landlord, had previously been a high-ranking police officer. James was instantly intrigued. "What the hell are you doing back in a place like this Jack Fox?" he said aloud, as he clicked open the first of many links.

Chapter Six

James got up early on Sunday morning feeling unexpectedly fresh. He'd slept well which surprised him, given the anxiety he'd experienced the previous evening. He stepped into the small shower cubicle and turned his head upwards to allow the hot water to cascade over his face. Despite the slight hiccup in the pub, he was going to stick to his plan, it was time to find Molly. In theory, he wasn't supposed to go anywhere near his wife, or her home, unless she gave permission. It was a clause she'd insisted on having written into their separation agreement, to her it was of the utmost importance that James keep his distance during their divorce negotiations. Since Seth had left home, she had even refused to let him know where she was living. It was time to rectify that situation.

James smiled at his reflection in the bedroom mirror as he put on his running gear. Molly thought she'd been so clever but she had seriously underestimated him; the terms of their separation agreement were legally unenforceable. Amongst many things, it called for him to pay Molly a few hundred pounds' maintenance every month but he'd never paid her a single penny. He'd set up his own business and an accommodating, if somewhat dishonest, accountant had helped him fudge his accounts ever since. He'd taken great delight in repeatedly informing Molly that he couldn't give her what he didn't have and her own, small town solicitor, wasn't clever or brave enough, to disprove this ridiculous claim. Making her suffer financially was, initially at least, all the reward he needed. Molly had expensive tastes, tastes he had always indulged in the past. For the first time in her life, she'd had to learn to economise. Putting food on the table took precedence over fancy shoes and expensive underwear, hurting her financially had been a cathartic form of revenge.

He studied his reflection in the mirror. Dressed from head to toe in black lycra, he looked like any other Sunday morning runner. A black, woolly hat and a lightweight, dark blue bandana around his neck completed the look, no-one would recognise him. Satisfied with the result, he picked up his running gloves and, as an afterthought, placed a 'Do Not Disturb' sign on the outside of the door. Once again, he avoided the lifts. Outside, he jogged slowly up to the Market Place, it felt good to be out in the cold, crisp air. After a few minutes, he stopped and bent down, seemingly fixing a loose shoelace. A silver-haired, frail looking, elderly lady was walking towards him with a small, white dog. Behind her, a dishevelled, young man with long, black hair looked like he was making his way home after a heavy night. Over by The Crown, he could see a large group of cyclists and, as he watched, he saw Sophie come out of the building and join them. He heard several calls of 'Good morning' and 'How are you?', followed by a chorus of loud laughter. Still fiddling with his shoelace, he continued to watch as Sophie put on her helmet, the same helmet he had helped her with on the train. The group of cyclists started moving towards him, momentarily catching him off guard, he'd been distracted by Sophie's shapely, lycra-clad legs. Not prepared to take any chances, he pulled his hat further down until it skimmed his eyebrows. The cyclists swept past him within seconds. Several men call out a 'Good morning" and he put up his hand in acknowledgement. Nothing to panic about, he reassured himself. This was just polite, small town interaction.

James was a good runner and could, comfortably, manage long distances. This morning, however, he didn't intend to venture far. He had one goal, he was going to hunt Molly down. Running away from the Market Place towards the river, he was continually reminded what a small town this was. The few people he saw all greeted him, or nodded amiably at him. The friendliness unnerved him, he wasn't used to it. He preferred the anonymity that living in a big city afforded, people didn't even look you in the eye in the city, he liked it that way. Surprised at how well he still knew his way around, James headed for Western Drive, fearful for an instant that Kate and Eddie may have moved home. He slowed his pace to a jog, as he approached what he thought was their house. There was no sign of life, the inhabitants were clearly taking advantage of a lazy Sunday morning. He circled the block and ran slowly past the house again, still no movement. He stopped further up the road and leant against a garden wall, seemingly stretching his hamstrings. To the untrained eye, he looked like a runner coping with cramp. The sound of a gate banging loudly made him jump and he turned cautiously. Someone was emerging from what he thought was Kate and Eddie's garden. He jogged across to the other side of the road and acted out yet another stretching routine. A man dressed in a scruffy, dark anorak, was heading towards the park with his dog. James moved forward slowly, using the cover offered by the parked cars. The man and the dog turned right towards the main park entrance but James couldn't risk running any closer. Thinking quickly, he followed the street parallel with the park and headed for a different entrance. This way, if it was Eddie, he should be able to run towards him. He increased his pace and ran along the river, only turning back towards the hill at the cricket pavilion. He was relieved to see two people talking at the top, near the gates. This was good, it afforded him some flexibility. If he got it right, he could be upon them before they really noticed. He pulled the bandana up over his mouth and increased his speed again. It was tough going. The hill was at its steepest on the way back up to the gates and both his legs and his lungs were working hard.

As he came close to the two men, a voice called out. "Careful … watch out for the dogs in the bushes." James was elated, it was Eddie's voice, his hunch had paid off. He put his hand up to acknowledge the warning, just as he had put up his hand to acknowledge the cyclists earlier on. As he did so, he caught a glimpse of a small, moving object hurtling rapidly towards him. He tried to step out of the way but he wasn't quick enough. Something hard and weighty connected solidly with his lower legs, his fall was inevitable. Landing heavily on all fours, he felt an instant, intense pain in his right knee. He gasped and tears stung his eyes. A fat Staffordshire Bull Terrier sniffed his face and barked excitedly before running back into the bushes followed, less quickly, by the old dog, Eddie's dog.

"Are you OK mate?" It was Eddie and he was getting closer.

James got shakily to his feet, grimacing at the pain. "Fine … no problem." He tried to disguise his voice. It wasn't hard, the shock had taken control of his vocal chords. He sounded croaky, like an old man. "My fault entirely." He tried to run but his legs wouldn't co-operate, they'd turned to jelly. He stumbled a few paces forward.

"Are you sure you're OK?" It was Eddie again, he was too close.

"Just a bit of cramp." James laughed shakily. "No harm done." Intent on putting some distance between him and Eddie, he jogged awkwardly towards the iron gates. His running tights were badly torn and blood was seeping profusely from his right knee. But he couldn't stop, he had to keep moving. He glanced briefly behind him, Eddie was still talking to the other man. "Fucking dogs," he said through clenched teeth. "Fucking, fucking dogs."

***

James lowered himself gently into the bath, grimacing and swearing as the hot water splashed over his wounds. His sweaty running gear lay, discarded, on the tiled floor. Removing his lycra tights had been excruciating. Congealed blood had glued the thin material to his damaged skin and each pull of the fabric had sent shock waves through his entire body. He closed his eyes and submerged his head under the water for a few seconds. He felt beaten up and shaken but, despite the pain, he was pleased with himself. Predictably, boring old Eddie and Kate were still living in the same house, even after all this time but the middle-class rut they were stuck in, was going to work to his advantage. He had absolutely no doubt that Molly would show up at Kate's house sooner or later and if the two women were still as close as they had been back when he and Molly were happy, he'd wager they would be seeing each other today; Molly and Kate were joined at the hip. His stomach groaned loudly, informing him that he needed food. It was still relatively early, he'd be able to order some breakfast from room service, along with a bucket of ice to ease the swelling on his knee. Then he was going to go back, he was going to find Molly.

At half past eleven James left his hotel room for the second time. The bath and the large breakfast had made him feel slightly better but the ice had done little to improve the movement in his knee. He was walking with a discernible limp, which was not only painful but hugely frustrating, he didn't want to stand out in any way. Wearing his long, dark overcoat over a light grey, cashmere sweater and dark blue jeans, he grimaced as the denim rubbed, uncomfortably, against his bloodied knee. The wound needed dressing, fresh blood threatened to trickle down his shin with each step. Outside on the street, he lifted the collar of his coat and made his way up to the Market Place where he knew there was a small shop. He bought paracetamol, a bottle of water, some antiseptic lotion, a pack of plasters, a black pen and a newspaper, and headed back to the hotel. He didn't go up to his room, opting for the toilets near Reception instead. Inside one of the three cubicles, he quickly swallowed two tablets and applied the lotion to his knee, swearing out loud as the cold cream made contact with the torn skin. He then covered the wounds with several of the larger plasters before, gingerly, pulling his jeans back on.

It was just past midday when James paid his second visit to Western Drive. There were more people around now and he felt uncomfortably exposed but he'd spotted a bench earlier, where he might be able to rest and keep an eye on the house at the same time. Sitting down gently and keeping his right leg as straight as possible, he discovered, much to his chagrin, that the view of the house was far from perfect but he had no other option, he had to take the weight off his leg. He opened the newspaper and idly leafed through it, trying to look as inconspicuous as possible.

"Come on Molly," he muttered under this breath, "Be predictable, come and get your friend fix." Almost an hour later, he got up and limped slowly to the top of the street and back down again, staying on the other side of the road to Kate and Eddie's house. Glancing up at the bedroom windows he thought he saw a woman's profile. It alarmed him, he couldn't afford to be recognised. Head down, he made his way back to the bench, took the black pen from his pocket and turned to the crossword at the back of the paper. His hand shook, he was cold but he was also excited, he was going to see Molly.

Nearly an hour later, cold, miserable and increasingly stiff, James swallowed two more pain killers and slowly limped up and down the street once more. As he passed Kate and Eddie's house for the second time he made a rash decision. Fed up with waiting around and aching from his fall, he crossed the road and approached the garden gate, checking up and down the street as he did so. The black wooden gate was taller than he'd thought; with his compromised mobility, it was impossible to look over the top. With steady, careful movements, he took hold of the latch and lifted it up slowly, breathing out in relief when it offered no resistance. Pushing the gate forward, he jumped as it scraped noisily against the concrete underneath. He swore silently. He had half expected a squeak from the gate's hinges but the scraping noise threw him. He stopped pushing and looked around again, relieved to see no-one in sight. Trying again, he pushed and lifted at the same time, raising the gate off the ground; it moved backwards silently. A narrow, concrete path led to a half-glazed back door and over to the left, there was a large window. Further along, a set of patio doors overlooked a well-kept garden. Immediately to his right stood an old garden shed which had seen better days. He vaguely recalled this layout, remembered boozy summer barbecues in this garden and children running through water sprinklers.

A dog suddenly started barking inside the house and he jumped. Footsteps were approaching rapidly on the pavement outside. With no time to spare, he jumped behind the old shed, his feet slipping on the frosty paving slabs. A sharp, stabbing pain shot through his knee and he drew in his breath. Someone stepped off the pavement and onto the concrete path. His heart was racing, it had to be her but he couldn't see, couldn't afford to move and the fucking dog was still barking. And then he heard her, heard the sweet bitch's voice. "Only me, I've brought wine," was all he caught before the door shut behind her but it was all he needed. She had played into his hands, she was so predictable, he felt triumphant. Emboldened by the success of his day so far, he cautiously moved out from behind the shed and crept, stealthily, up to the window. Molly and Kate were standing by the kitchen table, Kate seemed to be doing all the talking. Drawn to Molly like a magnet, his heart raced, it was a long time since he'd been this close. He jumped as the dog started barking again. It was a warning, he was taking too many chances. He longed to stay and drink in Molly's image but he needed to go back to the hotel, to get warm and redress his wounds. It looked like a long, boozy lunch was on the cards anyway. He'd return later and complete what he'd set out to do, he was going to find out where the bitch was living. Tracking her down so far had been easy, following her home should be simple; what he'd do then, he'd yet to decide.

***

Molly put the phone down and sighed heavily. The Sunday morning calls with her mother were always difficult but this morning's had been really tough and she felt drained. There had been the usual questions about Seth and James, along with the inevitable recriminations about the mess Molly had made of her life. Today, however, Rita had excelled herself, she had been totally evil. Abusive and aggressive, she had hurled insults at Molly, insults deliberately aimed to cut deep. Today her mother was drunk, had fallen off the wagon, had somehow got her hands on some alcohol. Gin was her preferred tipple but she'd drink anything when the urge took hold. Predictably, the call had finished with a lot of tears, Rita's tears. Molly sighed again, she could tick off another week, duty done for now.

An hour later, with the call to her mother consigned to history, Molly emerged from her front door. Dressed against the cold in her blue duffle coat, she turned the key in the lock and pulled up her fur-lined hood. The coat was old, a relic from the days when she could afford to buy expensive items but it was still the warmest thing she owned and, thanks to its quality, it still looked good. Ethel, the elderly lady who lived alone in the cottage next door, waved at her from an upstairs window. Molly waved back, smiling, she was fond of Ethel. They didn't see each other every day but they had grown close since Molly had moved in. The two women had sat and cried together when Ethel's little dog had died, and Molly did a bit of shopping for her neighbour now and then. She'd even tried introducing

Ethel to the internet but with very limited success. Molly was no expert herself with all things technical and, at times, it had been a case of the blind leading the blind. They had giggled a lot that day. Closing her garden gate, Molly glanced back up at the window but Ethel had gone.

Sunday lunch with Eddie and Kate called for wine and providing a couple of bottles was Molly's customary, small contribution. She headed for the shops instead of taking the usual route through the park. Kate and Eddie weren't wine snobs but they didn't drink the cheap stuff she usually quaffed. Today, thanks to her new job, she felt more inclined to part with her cash, she could afford to. She chose a bottle of Malbec and a more expensive Bordeaux and, as on so many Sundays in the past, she soon found herself walking down Western Drive. She was a little alarmed to find the garden gate wide open. Eddie was usually so vigilant about keeping it closed, he worried about Lottie. She closed the gate, vaguely aware that something seemed odd. Lottie, uncharacteristically, was barking loudly. She knocked briefly on the back door before opening it.

"Only me, I've brought wine." She closed the door behind her. "What's up Lot, why are you barking at me you silly, old thing?" The dog carried on barking, turning in circles as she did so. "Hello, anyone there?" Molly called, her voice competing with the noisy dog.

Lucy, Kate's daughter, came running through from the kitchen. "Molly," she squealed, grabbing Molly and hugging her.

"Lucy!" Molly could hear herself squealing back. "Oh my God, what a nice surprise. I didn't know you were going to be here. Now I get why Lottie's so excited."

"It's all very last minute … a field trip got cancelled. I have some free days, no lectures, nothing. Too good an opportunity... you know ... to come home and see the rents." Molly looked confused. "Rents ... pa-rents. Bloody hell, keep up Molly. You're as bad as Mum."

Molly held Lucy's shoulders and studied her god-daughter. "Wow! You look amazing my lovely. Something to tell me?" The delicate face, pale skin, red hair, Lucy was certainly her mother's daughter, although Molly had always thought Lucy was more like her grandmother. In just the same way that Winnie could light up a room, Lucy had an energy about her, an infectious enthusiasm.

"Good God no!" Lucy replied emphatically. "Having far too much fun." She winked at Molly and Molly, surprisingly, felt herself blushing. Lucy giggled. "Don't look at me like that Molly Pope, nothing you wouldn't do yourself." She turned to lead the way into the kitchen. "I've learnt from the best."

Molly smiled, Lucy didn't know the half of it. She followed the young girl and the excited dog into the warm kitchen, where Kate was preparing vegetables. "Something smells good," she said to Kate, as she gave her a peck on the cheek. "Nice surprise, eh?" She nodded at Lucy.

"Oh gosh yes ... always lovely. If you like noise, mess and a whining dog." Kate laughed, she was clearly happy to have one of her kids home. "Lucy, go fetch Dad from upstairs, tell him we need a glass of wine .... and get Lottie to shut up, will you?" Lucy went out into the hall, followed closely by the doting Lottie. "Molly, before Lucy ambushes our whole day, I just wanted to check how you are? After what happened at the cemetery? I've half a mind to go and see the evil cow."

"I'm fine Kate. I admit it was frightening but she's done worse. She just got lucky."

"I don't know how you can be so calm. What if she actually hurts you next time?"

"There won't be a next time Kate ... I've learnt my lesson. I let my guard down ... it won't happen again."

Kate put the chopping knife down. She was tempted to say more but now wasn't the right time, Lucy would be back soon. "Is everything OK with the job? After I saw Jack yesterday?" She'd been feeling so guilty, she'd said far too much about Seth.

"All seems good." Molly picked up a slice of carrot and bit into it. "I had a text from Sophie last night saying Jack had OK'd it. She wants me to go in tomorrow morning to go through some paperwork but I already have my first rota." She smiled at her friend. "Looks like I owe you one ... again."

Kate smiled back, her guilt slightly assuaged. "Another quick question before Madam comes back. You've heard nothing more from James, have you?"

Molly's smile faded. "No ... weirdly. I don't really know what to make of it." She lowered her voice, she could hear Lucy and Eddie making their way downstairs. "I keep telling myself he's just playing his last, desperate games."

"Having his last hurrah, you mean. Classic James."

Lucy and Eddie burst noisily into the kitchen. Eddie had been giggling, his eyes were moist with tears of laughter. Molly felt a pang of jealousy deep within her. She'd never have that kind of relationship with her own son. She couldn't remember the last time she'd laughed with Seth or seen him look happy; happy wasn't a word you'd associate with Seth. Lunch was always a success when Lucy was home. She had her grandmother's knack for telling a good story and she was a gifted mimic. Her humour was observational and, over a relaxed roast dinner, she repeatedly reduced her parents, and Molly, to tears with stories about life at university. After they'd finished off the last of the treacle pie, a delicacy from the local baker's shop, Eddie suggested a walk but Molly declined.

"I'm going to let you three have some quality time together," she said. "My face aches from laughing so much ... I need a rest." She got up to leave. "Thanks for a lovely lunch Kate. Lucy, will I see you again before you go back?"

"I hope so." Lucy grinned, her cheeks slightly pink from the wine. "I'm going back first thing Tuesday morning. What about a coffee tomorrow while Mum's teaching? I might make you blush again though." She laughed and hiccupped simultaneously.

"Oh, I have no doubt! Time was when we made you blush but the tables definitely seem to be turning," said Molly. "I'm seeing Sophie at the pub at ten thirty. Want to meet me at The Kitchen after that, say about eleven thirty? You can tell me everything you can't tell your parents ... sorry your rents."

"THE rents!" Lucy squealed. "God, you and Mum ... you make me howl!"

Kate walked Molly to the back door. "Good luck tomorrow ... and let me know if you hear from James."

"I will." Molly kissed her friend on the cheek. "Go back and enjoy time with your daughter ... I'll call you."

Out on the pavement, Molly checked to the left and right, the recent incident at the cemetery had made her wary again. With her hood pulled forward, as much for the disguise as for the warmth, she walked quickly down the familiar street, looking through windows of homes where traditional family life was playing out. Children were watching TV, mums were ironing school uniforms and Dads were catching up with the Sunday papers. A car door slammed shut suddenly, startling her. As a precaution, she crossed the road, glancing frequently at the woman who was now opening her boot to retrieve what looked like a small suitcase. She relaxed, this woman wasn't after her. Telling herself, yet again, to stop being so paranoid, she crossed over the road and looked back at Kate and Eddie's house. She felt a tinge of remorse, she hadn't been entirely honest with her old friends. They didn't need their privacy, not from her. She'd been forced to make a lame excuse to get away. Hopefully, Kate hadn't seen through it.

At the entrance to the park she hesitated, it was dark. Common sense told her she should go home the way she'd come but it would be so much quicker to cut through the park and she was keen to get home, she needed to get ready. She looked around her, she'd known every inch of this park since she was a small child. She shouldn't be afraid of it just because it was dark. Her phone startled her, it was a text message.

Be with you in 30 mins
Can't wait to see you!
I'll park on Bridge St and come round the back
I have champagne! H xx

***

James watched as Molly hesitated near the entrance to the park. She appeared to be checking her phone. The solitary streetlight by the gates illuminated her; it made her look lonely and vulnerable. For a moment, he felt something akin to pity but dismissed it quickly, she didn't need to be lonely. He blew warm air into his cupped hands.

"Come on Molly, show me the way," he murmured through chattering teeth. Shivering uncontrollably, he was starting to feel ill, he'd spent too long in the cold. As he watched, Molly suddenly put her phone in her pocket and walked briskly into the park without looking up. James was surprised and a little shocked. Molly wasn't brave, she didn't take risks, she was clearly in a hurry. He limped after her, cursing quietly as fresh, warm blood meandered down his shinbone.

Molly walked quickly down the hill towards the cricket pavilion followed, at an enforced distance, by a distressed James. Not only was he hampered physically but the leather soles of his expensive, designer shoes had no grip and he found himself slipping on the frozen tarmac. He panicked and tried, unsuccessfully, to run. It was useless, after all his hard work, he was going to lose her. A tiny beam of light suddenly appeared ahead and, despite his discomfort, James let a muffled but triumphant laugh escape. Molly had, unintentionally, given him the assistance he needed; the torch on her phone was guiding him to her. He relaxed a little, he still had a chance. Just past the pavilion, Molly, walking more cautiously in the gloom, skirted around the eerie shape of the old bandstand, before appearing to turn left up a steep hill. James, trying hard to keep his knee straight and unsure of the terrain, followed cautiously but despite his very best efforts, the gradient defeated him; it wasn't long before the right leg of his jeans was damp with blood.

Ahead of him, Molly had stopped abruptly. She was just a few feet short of a well-lit pavement. James moved forward quietly. He couldn't afford to alarm her, it would be too easy for her to run away. Seemingly satisfied with her surroundings, Molly stepped out onto the pavement, illuminated once again by a solitary streetlight. She crossed the road and picked up speed. James scuttled after her, as best he could. After a hundred yards or so, Molly turned sharp left into a small side street and opened a low-level wooden gate. James, hiding behind a parked car, held his breath. This had to be it, this had to be where she was living. A door slammed shut and he stood up, quickly scanning the road; he was alone. He approached the wooden gate and gave it a gentle push. It opened silently, swinging back smoothly on its hinges. He limped, warily, towards the white door of a small, stone cottage. Two ugly, stainless steel numbers had been screwed into the door at shoulder height. James was amused, Molly was living at number thirteen. He pressed his ear to the door, soft music was playing, Molly still couldn't bear a quiet house. He tried the door handle but it didn't move, she'd locked the door. Wrestling with his emotions, he leant against the doorframe. He had no choice. He'd have to return to the hotel and recharge his batteries and come back in the morning. The hint of a smile grew, as a cruel idea came to him. Bending down awkwardly, he pulled up the denim of his right trouser leg gagging slightly at the sight of the sticky, fresh blood that clung to the hair on his shin. He placed his left hand tentatively on the gooey substance, wincing at the pain that came with the contact. The palm of his hand and his fingers were soon covered in the tacky residue. Looking around as he stood up, he carefully placed his bloodied hand under the stainless-steel numbers and held it there for several seconds. When he took his hand away a bloodied handprint stared back at him. For James, this was the perfect calling card.

Chapter Seven

Kate placed a mug of steaming, hot tea on Lucy's bedside table and gave her daughter a gentle shake. "Wake up Lucy Loo," she said softly. "I'm off to work but I only have two classes so I should be able to meet you and Molly for coffee around eleven thirty. I want to hear your naughty stories too."

Lucy peered out from under her duvet where she'd been looking at her phone. She smiled up at Kate. "Aren't you lovely to still bring me tea in bed?"

"Yes I am. And don't you forget it." Kate ruffled Lucy's hair fondly, just as she had done when her daughter was a little girl. "Dad's already gone to work but he's suggested we eat out tonight. What do you think? Fancy it?" Kate didn't wait for an answer, eating out was something they all enjoyed. She blew her daughter a kiss and walked out of the room; Lucy soon heard her running down the stairs.

Cradling her tea, Lucy ran her fingers over the rim of the mug. Chipped and stained, it was the mug she'd used since childhood. It represented everything that was good about her childhood, the love, the unity, the consistency. She sipped the sweet tea and looked around her bedroom. It hadn't changed much since she'd left for university nearly three years ago. It was the bedroom of an adolescent girl; childhood memorabilia contrasted with subtle signs of an emerging adult. She'd promised her parents she would sort through all her belongings when her degree was finished, which meant that, for the time being, she could leave it as it was and she was happy with that.

Her phone buzzed beneath her duvet. It was a message from Seth.
Saw on FB that you're home for a few days
How's my Mum?
Lucy's hackles bristled. "Ask her your bloody self," she shouted at the words on the screen. She checked the status she had posted on Facebook.

Spending a few days with the rents, field trip cancelled. Happy days!!

Seth had neither liked her status or commented. She looked again at his text and typed out a quick reply.

Would it hurt to ask her YOURSELF? Or actually go and see her? She's your mum not mine! WEIRDO!

Lucy had known Seth all her life. He and Molly were extended family, closer even than some of her real family. An image of her flustered Aunt Patty and her noisy, young cousins popped into her head. But that doesn't mean I have to bloody well like him, she thought defensively, as she got out of bed and headed for the bathroom. She had liked him once though, had liked him a lot and her brother Bobby still had time for him but Bobby lived in his own bubble of football, gaming, girls and boozing, along with just a little studying. He didn't have time to think about people's feelings. The thought made her feel bad, she was being unkind. For all his failings, Bobby recognised bad behaviour and spoke out if necessary. She wondered if Bobby had ever spoken to Seth about his parents. Their marriage had been a disaster and that had to be difficult. As an only child, Seth may have felt vulnerable and lonely but it happened to loads of people. It had happened to many of her own friends but none of them, not a single one, had behaved like Seth.

Back in her bedroom, after her shower, Lucy checked her phone. There was no response from Seth, which was a good thing. Maybe he'd take the hint and text Molly himself. She got dressed in the standard student uniform of jeans and a hoody and made her way downstairs. "Jeez Lottie, I can hear you snoring from upstairs," she called to the dog. Lottie's response was a repeated thud of her tail on the wooden floor but she didn't move or even open her eyes. "Come on Miss, we're going for a walk." Lottie shot out of her bed and Lucy giggled. Life in the old girl yet she thought, zipping up her coat and slipping on her mum's green wellies.

Kate was already sitting inside The Kitchen when Lucy arrived later that morning. There was no sign of Molly though which didn't surprise her, Molly's lack of punctuality was a standing joke in their family.

"I thought you'd been to work." Lucy pointed to a collection of shopping bags sitting at Kate's feet.

"I have." Kate smiled. "But on my way here, I saw that little boutique on King Street had a sale on … you know I love a bargain."

"You do indeed. Anything for me?" Lucy asked cheekily.

"Might be," Kate teased. "Look, there's Molly. Go and get coffees for all of us … cakes might be good too." She raised her eyebrows questioningly at her daughter and handed over her purse. Lucy rarely turned down cake.

Back at the table, Lucy handed out the coffees along with three generous portions of carrot cake. 'Come on then, what did you get me?" she asked excitedly. Kate handed over a large, bright red, rope-handled bag with the word 'Phoebe' printed delicately down one side. "This is so exciting," Lucy squealed as she peered into the bag and pulled out a pair of tan coloured, leather ankle boots. She squealed again, more loudly this time. "Oh Mum, they're fab, I love them." Scraping back her chair she slipped out of her scruffy trainers and promptly tried on the new boots and then squealed some more. An elderly couple sitting near them laughed, Lucy's good humour was infectious. She performed an exaggerated, catwalk style meander over to the counter, before rushing back and placing a kiss on her mother's cheek. "Thanks Mum."

"You're a lucky girl Lucy Lawson," Molly said smiling. "Nice gear those boots." Kate laughed. "As I said … there's a sale on … but you're welcome my cherub … but there's more. Just a little bit more in the bag." Kate pointed to the bag Lucy had discarded under the table.

"What? Really?" Lucy shot under the table to retrieve the bag and pulled out a delicate ivory coloured, silk scarf decorated with tiny, interlocking, blue hearts.

"Oh … I've got one just like that," said Molly instantly. "I love it. Sophie was saying how lovely it was too." She caught the slightly shocked look on Kate's face. The words had come tumbling out in a rush, she'd never learn to think before she spoke. Looking for a way out, she touched Lucy's scarf. "I don't think mine's silk though … it doesn't feel anything like this. This is quality." She couldn't look at Kate. Kate, more than anyone, knew she couldn't afford to shop in places like Phoebe's, even when there was a sale on. She'd easily conclude the scarf was a gift, especially after the text message from James. "I got mine in the second-hand shop on the Market Place," she lied. "It's not nearly as nice as this." She needed to shut up, she was making things a hundred times worse.

"Speaking of Sophie, how did you get on at the pub?" asked Kate, looking intently at Molly. "Hours all sorted?"

"Yes ... all sorted ...everything's good." Molly was surprised but incredibly relieved that Kate had changed the subject. "They're offering me at least twenty contracted hours a week and Sophie says she can almost guarantee ten more." She felt the need to keep talking, to keep steering the conversation away from the scarf. "Sophie's thinking of putting up a marquee in the garden with an outdoor bar," she carried on, noting sadly both the suspicion and the disappointment in her friend's eyes. Kate was on to her.

***

Molly walked home slowly. Tired physically, she felt overwhelmingly sad too. Harry had stayed late the previous evening and had almost fallen asleep in her bed, something she secretly longed for him to do. They had made love, bathed together and drank good champagne and Harry had talked about the places he'd like to take her. He travelled extensively and was often lonely, he wanted her to travel with him, to keep him company. It had been wonderful to hear him talk about how much he missed her and what fun they could have on their travels. She'd been elated and, with the help of the champagne, she'd fallen under his spell once again, he knew how to make her feel special. But this morning, as on every other morning, she had woken alone. Harry was all talk. He was a married man, he didn't belong to her.

"You've been here before you silly cow," she muttered to herself, as she crossed the road. She should be feeling much happier about life. For the first time in ages she had a proper job, a job she liked. OK, it wasn't a career, and no doubt her mother would have something derogatory to say about it, but it would give her more financial independence than she could remember. Even more importantly, it would put space between her and James. But even that thought didn't lift her mood. She was feeling sorry for herself, sorry that Harry wasn't exclusively hers, sorry that she had so few friends and sorry that Kate had nearly caught her out.

Ethel was at her bedroom window in the cottage next door; she opened it cautiously. "Molly dear, you've just missed your gentleman friend."

"What?" Molly called back. "What friend?" Ethel looked unsteady, hanging on to the open window. "Hold on Ethel, shut the window and I'll use my key to come in through the back. I don't like seeing you hanging out of the window."

"Oh, thank you Molly." Ethel smiled gratefully. "I've never liked heights. I have no problem with the window shut but looking out when it's open, well it gives me the collywobbles."

Molly opened the gate, identical to her own, that led to Ethel's cottage. Using the key the old lady had asked her to keep 'just in case', she opened the back door and let herself into the small but spotless kitchen. An old clock on the wall ticked softly, a slow steady noise in an otherwise quiet home. Ethel was making her way slowly down the stairs; her breathing was just a little laboured. Molly went to meet her.

"That's better," said Ethel. "I'm sorry about that ... can't abide heights. Come into the kitchen where it's warm. Would you like a cup of tea love?"

Molly had not long had coffee but it would do no harm to have a cup of tea with Ethel. She was genuinely fond of the old lady and a bit of company might cheer her up. She sat down at Ethel's kitchen table and watched as the elderly lady slowly heated a teapot and spooned in loose tea, followed by boiling water. She then set cups and saucers on the table along with a matching sugar bowl and milk jug. Molly smiled, Ethel was from a different era, no teabags or milk straight from the bottle for her, Ethel had standards. Today, Ethel was wearing a knee length, dark brown skirt with a cream blouse and a fawn coloured, home knitted cardigan. Her long, white hair was pinned back in a soft but neat bun and little pearl studs shone in her ears. Molly thought she looked lovely and told her so.

"Thank you dear." Ethel pulled at her skirt as if it needed straightening. "I've been to the surgery this morning for an MOT. I can't go there looking like I just got out of bed ... they'll be lining me up for a place in that care home if they think I can't take care of myself. And I'm not having that!" She looked directly at Molly. "I'll be leaving here in a box and that's that."

Molly giggled. "You are naughty Ethel. I hope they told you that you're fighting fit? You would tell me if you didn't feel well, wouldn't you?"

"I passed everything with flying colours," Ethel said proudly. "Nothing wrong with this old girl. I can't say the same for the others I saw in that surgery today though. God's waiting room my son calls it ... he's not wrong either. Anyway, less about me. You've only just missed your gentleman friend." Ethel opened a biscuit tin to reveal homemade chocolate brownies. There was something about the way she called the man a 'gentleman friend' that caught Molly's attention.

"Gentleman friend?" Molly repeated the words. "Did he leave a message?"

"It was only a little earlier ... John had just dropped me back after my trip to the surgery." John was Ethel's son, a man in his fifties who took good care of his elderly mother. Molly thought momentarily of Seth. "It must have been about eleven thirty." Ethel looked up at her old clock. "He'd been to your back door which seemed a little strange to me, although I don't think John noticed." Ethel stopped talking and frowned. "Why are men so unobservant? Do you know John didn't even notice all the early daffodils in the front garden? I had to point them out to him." Ethel made a tutting noise and Molly sighed. Usually, she would have happily spent time bemoaning the inadequacies of the male race but, right now, she wanted to know more about her mystery visitor.

"Did you speak to him ... this man?" Molly asked encouragingly.

"Of course I did dear. I asked him if he was looking for someone." Molly felt like she was being ticked off. "He held the gate for me and said he had just been checking your back door because there was no answer at your front one. But I didn't buy that ... he was lying ... he didn't expect to see me."

"Lying? Really? He didn't give you his name? What did he look like?" Molly was beginning to feel a little anxious and it was reflected in her voice. Could Harry have come back to surprise her? She didn't think so, although she would have loved to see him. And it couldn't be Eddie, Ethel knew Eddie. That didn't leave anyone else. Apart from James. Dear God, she thought, don't let it be James. "Did he leave a message Ethel?" Molly tried to keep her voice calm.

Ethel's hand shook slightly as she poured the tea. "Not really dear. He said he must have got his wires crossed because he thought you'd be at home this morning."

"He thought I'd be at home?" Molly repeated incredulously.

Ethel took a sip from her cup before placing it slowly back on its saucer. She seemed to be weighing up what to say next. "Molly, I wasn't always an old lady you know." She spoke the words slowly and deliberately. "It's easy to imagine otherwise I suppose but, believe it or not, I've led a full and interesting life. There are things I could tell you that would make your hair curl." She smiled to herself as she picked up her cup again, this time with two hands. "Things always worked out well for me in the end but I did things that I'm not proud of ... yet people don't imagine that us oldies were ever anything but old. Somehow, being old turns us into saints ... which most of us definitely aren't ... and weren't."

"Ethel, what are you trying to say?" Molly was curious. Ethel had never spoken to her like this before.

"Molly, I know men like him ... or I did," she said, not taking her eyes off Molly's face. "I can recognise a fake. Suave he may have been but he didn't fool me. Oh, I played along with him ... pretended that I'd fallen for his charms ... I've had a lot of experience in playing the part. You know ... the senile old dear." Ethel hunched her shoulders and shook her hands to intimate a frailer version of herself.

"I still don't understand." Molly was confused but intrigued. "Did he give you his name? Did he tell you what he wanted?"

"Molly, he didn't tell me anything because he didn't want me to know. And why's that do you think?"

"I'm sorry Ethel ... you've lost me," Molly replied quietly. The old lady was rambling.

"You're a beautiful and intelligent young woman Molly," Ethel said very slowly. "But you're very naive too. And I'm only saying this because I care about you." The old lady leant forward over the table. "The thing is ... you need to be more careful." She let the words hang for a second. "I've seen men coming and going at night. Last night for example. I've not said anything ... it's not my business but this is a small town and if you're entertaining during the day now it's only a question of time before tongues start to wag. Not mine you understand but plenty of others would like nothing more, would they? And you've had enough of that already, haven't you?" Ethel had only known Molly a couple of years but, like many before her, she was familiar with the scandal.

"Ethel," Molly gasped. "I'm not ..." Her voice fell away. Her elderly neighbour was accusing her of something close to prostitution. Tears were already forming in her eyes. "How can you think such a thing?"

"Like I said, it's none of my business Molly. You're lonely ... you've had a rough time ... you have very little money ... I understand." Ethel patted Molly's hand. "I'm just saying, be careful. I've seen his type before. They think they're clever ... not clever enough to take his wedding ring off, was he though? Whoever he is dear, one thing's for sure ... it won't end well."

Molly stood up, she had to get away from this embarrassing situation. "I've no idea who it could have been. I wasn't expecting anyone." She wanted to explain about Harry but the words wouldn't come.

Ethel watched as Molly put her coat on. "I didn't mean to upset you Molly," she said. "I just wanted you to know that if I've noticed, then others will have too."

"Ethel, I have no idea who this man was ... please believe me." Molly's voice cracked.

"Well he was a tall man, dark hair, slightly grey in the usual places ... nice shoes too ... not something you see so often on men these days." Ethel got stiffly out of her chair and put the lid back on the tin of brownies. "Oh, and he was limping quite badly. Does that help?"

"No, not really," Molly said as she opened the door. She was desperate to leave. "I've got to go Ethel."

"Here, take the rest of these brownies." Ethel thrust the tin into Molly's hands. "I'd usually save them for Liv, my daughter-in-law. She's started checking up on me, popping in after work sometimes ... that kind of thing. I don't know why ... I'm not an invalid ... I can look after myself." Ethel's voice had become more strident, Liv's visits clearly annoyed her. "I won't be giving her any brownies for a while though ... she's given up chocolate for Lent." She looked around as if checking to see if anyone was listening. "She needs to give up more than just chocolate to shift some of her weight though." She smiled conspiratorially as she placed her hand on Molly's shoulder, any awkwardness about their previous conversation forgotten. "Likes her wine too much that one."

"I'll see you soon Ethel ...thanks for the brownies." Molly opened the door quickly and slipped out. Desperate for the relative safety of her own home, she clambered over the small fence that separated the two back gardens and rushed to her back door. Placing the brownies on a solitary garden chair, she hunched down by the cat flap and stretched her right arm up, to turn the key that sat permanently in the lock. Retrieving the brownies, she opened the door slowly, irrationally afraid of what she might find inside. A champagne bottle sat on the kitchen table, along with the remains of the cheese and biscuits she and Harry had shared. She set the brownies down and moved the dirty plates to the sink, noticing that one of the champagne flutes she'd left there earlier had fallen over and smashed. The glass wasn't expensive, she didn't own anything of value but the breakage saddened her. It was one more crappy addition to yet another dreadful day.

She moved slowly through to the lounge, relieved to see that nothing looked out of place. Whoever her visitor was, he hadn't managed to get in. Close to tears, she sat down wearily on the sofa. Life was so unkind. Even the old lady next door had people who loved her. She started to cry freely, the sobs growing stronger with each breath. In her bubble of self-pity, she failed to spot the second empty champagne bottle, now stuffed full of Ethel's early daffodils, sitting on the small window sill by the front door.

***

Kate and Lucy had lingered over the remains of their coffee. "What do you fancy doing this afternoon?" Kate asked. "No more shopping though, I've overspent already!"

"I'm easy," said Lucy. "Maybe we should take a walk to burn off those cakes?"

Kate arched her eyebrows. "Don't forget, I've taught two classes this morning so the calories were very welcome." She ran her finger slowly round her plate before placing the last remains of the icing in her mouth. "Why don't we walk up to Granny and Grandad's grave ... lay some fresh flowers?"

"Yes, I'd like that. Home first to drop off all this stuff and get Lottie?"

An hour later they had collected Lottie, bought a selection of fresh flowers and were walking slowly up to the cemetery gates. Kate looked down at her feet, she'd been forced to put on her old walking boots, Lucy had commandeered her green wellies. "You and Molly always use my bloody wellies. Perhaps I should buy a second pair as a backup."

"What's yours is mine Mum," Lucy giggled. "Speaking of Molly, I had this text this morning." She found the message from Seth and handed Kate her phone. "I didn't know whether to say anything to her this morning or not ... I decided against it in the end. As much as I think of him as family Mum, he's starting to really piss me off."

"No kidding Lucy. I'm not sure calling him a weirdo was called for though." Kate handed the phone back.

"But he acts like such a prick and he treats her so badly. I hate him for it, it's not fair on Molly. And I resent him for expecting me to do his bloody dirty work for him."

"He has his reasons Lucy." Kate put her arm through her daughter's. "It wasn't always easy for him. He heard and saw a lot of stuff he shouldn't have." That no kid should, she thought to herself. "I personally think they could both work harder at their relationship. And maybe, just in a small way, we should see it as encouraging that he's checking on her through you."

"It's weird though, isn't it? That he thinks it appropriate to ask me how his own mother is? On Facebook he tries to come across as such a decent human being but he doesn't fool me. He needs to grow up."

Kate smiled, seeing things in black and white was a family trait. "Molly and James handled things badly and Seth was unintentionally damaged. It was a tough time. Have you ever spoken to Seth about things?" She looked closely at her daughter. "Did he ever speak to you about his parents?"

"No, not really." Lucy shook her head. "He kind of went into his shell … pushed me away. He was closer to Bobby but boys don't talk, do they? Not about things that matter?"

"That's a bit of a generalisation Lucy. Do you really think Bobby doesn't talk?"

"Bobby's different, he's not a real boy." Lucy laughed loudly. "Sorry," she said quickly. "Forget where I was. Cemeteries don't do laughter, do they?"

"I don't see why not," Kate replied. "You can laugh if you want to … although Bobby might have something to say about your opinion of him."

"I meant Bobby had no choice …he had to talk. Especially having me as a big sister. I've made him listen to all sorts of things in the past. He's surprisingly helpful … sometimes." She lowered her voice to a whisper. "While we're talking about boys … about Seth … can I ask you a question?"

"Sure. What is it?" Kate had squatted down by the side of her parents' grave and Lucy smiled in admiration, her mother was so flexible. "Go on then," said Kate. "Shoot. What's the question?"

"Do you think ... have you ever thought ... that ..." her voice trailed off.

"Bloody hell Lucy! It's not like you to be tongue-tied," Kate said. "Spit it out."

"Have you ever thought Seth might be .... gay?"

Kate straightened up, again Lucy noted the flexibility. "Would it matter if he is?" She spoke the words slowly.

"No ... of course not," Lucy retorted. "I just wondered. He acts like he's hiding something all the time. I wondered if that's what it is. He's never had a girlfriend, has he? There's never anything on Facebook."

"Oh well if it's not on Facebook! Really Lucy, you surprise me. Your generation don't know what you're missing. There's a real life waiting out there for you guys and it's far more interesting than watching what others do with theirs on Facebook."

Lucy grimaced. "Chill your beans woman! I was only asking if it had ever crossed your mind. That he might be gay?"

Kate sighed. "No Lucy, it hasn't. And for what it's worth I don't think he's gay ... but it wouldn't bother me in the least if he were." She chose her next words carefully. "There are things about Seth that only he can share with you. You shouldn't speculate why he's acted the way he has but I'd say being gay isn't one of them."

"What does that mean? There are things about Seth?" Lucy was intrigued.

"Seth went through some horrid things ... things that no kid should," Kate said guardedly. "It's all I'm going to say ... don't push me. But if you feel like he's hiding something, my advice would be to avoid jumping to conclusions ... you're unlikely to get it right." She took up her squatting position once again. "Come on. Help me clean this headstone."

Kate's parents, Winnie and Ted, were buried in the same plot at the far end of the cemetery. Her father had died from a heart attack when she was a teenager and although she had visited his grave with her mother religiously during her adolescence, she hadn't felt an emotional need to do so. That had only come since Winnie's funeral. Looking now at the original inscription on the headstone, the last line reminded her what a nice man her father must have been.

Ted, our father, and our friend

When Winnie had died twenty-five years later, a line from a poem Lucy loved had been added. The simple words seemed even more poignant to Kate since her recent hospital visits.

What will survive of us is love

"Does it make you feel sad Mum?" Lucy's question brought Kate out of her daydream. "Sad they're not here anymore?"

"Sometimes Lucy," Kate replied. "I think we all thought Winnie would go on forever. She seemed indestructible."

"She did, didn't she? I miss her … I think about her a lot. She was hilarious, wasn't she?

Kate smiled fondly at her daughter. It was lovely to hear Lucy reminisce about Winnie, the bond between grandmother and granddaughter lived on.

"You're going to go on forever, aren't you Mum? You're indestructible. I'm always telling my friends what a health freak you are."

Lucy's innocent remark caught Kate off guard; it was too close to the bone. She didn't know what to say, didn't want to give anything away. "Oh Lord Lucy, look at Lottie," she whispered. "Can you go and get her while I finish off here? I'll come and help you in a second."

"Bloody hell," giggled Lucy. "How on earth did she do that?" Lottie, tail wagging furiously, had overturned a waste bin and was on the hunt for food. Pieces of loose paper were floating around in the breeze, some had already landed on nearby graves. On this occasion, Kate was grateful to her greedy Labrador, the dog's constant search for food had got her out of a conversation she wasn't ready to have.

With Lottie back on her lead and suitably chastised, Kate and Lucy started walking home. As they approached the cemetery gates, a tall, blond woman stood back to let them pass.

"Hello Kate," the woman said moving on, clearly not expecting a response.

Kate stopped. "Lucy, stay here with Lottie, will you?" She pushed Lottie's lead into Lucy's hands. "I just need a quick word with that woman."

"Who is she?" Lucy asked frowning but Kate didn't reply, she was already jogging back into the cemetery.

"Fiona ... wait ... Fiona." The woman turned to face her. Tall, lean and broad shouldered, Kate had always found Fiona physically overwhelming. Today, dressed in dark jeans and a three-quarter, cream-coloured, wool coat with her long, strawberry blond hair curling softly around her strong features, was no exception. Kate, wearing her blue anorak, faded jeans and old walking boots, felt dowdy.

"What do you want Kate?" Fiona asked. Her voice was deep and gravelly, almost masculine. "I need to tidy up Will's grave. Cut flowers start to look scruffy quickly in this weather."

"Yes ... it would have been his birthday, wouldn't it?" Kate attempted to find a tone that didn't sound too confrontational but she and Fiona had never really hit it off, even before the scandal with Molly. Privately educated, Fiona had her own social circle, her husband's old school friends had never interested her.

"Oh, I see. The little witch has paid a visit, has she?" Fiona's voice was heavy with sarcasm. "You should tell her not to bother Kate... not to waste her money. Everything goes in the bin. God, I know she's dim but you'd think she'd have realised that by now."

"She hasn't left anything on his grave for years Fiona," Kate said, choosing not to mention Molly's charity donations. This wasn't the time for scoring points. "I suppose you wouldn't have been able to check on the flowers in the dark, would you? Although your aim wasn't bad." Her voice was too high, her nerves were showing. Fiona didn't respond. "You're not denying it then?"

"Kate, what are you talking about?" Unlike Kate's nervous, high pitched shrill, Fiona sounded calm and in control.

"Trying to scare Molly ... throwing stuff at her ... rocks ... it's out of order. It's time to stop. She could have been seriously hurt." Kate's heart was beating rapidly. She glanced back at Lucy, her daughter was, thankfully, glued to the screen on her phone.

"I have no idea what you're talking about Kate," Fiona said slowly. "But if you're saying someone frightened Molly then bravo ... I congratulate them. The evil cow bloody well deserves it. But I can tell you, categorically, that it wasn't me and I don't take too kindly to false accusations."

Kate studied Fiona's attractive face for a few seconds, unable to decide if she was being genuine. "Can I ask you to call your dogs off then? Someone tried to frighten her ... to hurt her. It needs to stop. It should have stopped years ago."

Fiona took a small step closer to Kate and lowered her voice. "I'll ignore that comment about dogs Kate but I'd advise you to choose your words more carefully in future." She held Kate's gaze, letting the veiled threat sink in before she carried on. "She's lucky to have a friend like you ... I mean that. Really, I do. She doesn't deserve such loyalty."

An elderly gentleman walked past them, Kate nodded at him, Fiona moved aside. "Have you heard the latest rumour about Molly?" Fiona continued, once the man was out of earshot. "No? So you don't know that she's at it again?" Kate gasped, James had sent a message implying the same thing. "I see I don't have to spell it out, do I? I don't know who the poor sod is, so I can't give you that little piece of information just yet. Like I said, I don't like false accusations but rest assured, I intend to find out. I'll remember to let you know. Actually, I'll let the whole fucking town know."

***

"I'll have a white wine Dad." Lucy had spotted some of her old school friends in The Crown. "I'm just going to say hello."

"I'm looking forward to the day when you kids buy me a drink," Eddie moaned at her retreating back.

"Don't hold your breath," Kate laughed. She watched as Lucy hugged her friends and eased herself comfortably into her old life.

"Come over here guys." It was Jack. "I've saved you my best table." He made a grand gesture of placing three menus on the table and winking at Eddie.

"Very kind of you, young man," Eddie laughed. "Already got a good crowd in, I see."

"Crazy, isn't it?" said Jack. "I'll send Sophie over to take your food orders in a bit but what can I get you to drink in the meantime?"

"A pint for me please. Kate, do you want to share a bottle with Lucy?" Kate nodded her agreement.

"Hi guys." Sophie had spotted them. "Lovely to see you. I'll come and take your order in a moment ... the menus speak for themselves but any questions just shout. We've also got a specials board by the bar." She pointed to a large blackboard to the right of the bar. "If you like fish, I can recommend the fish pie ... Kim's speciality."

"Thanks Sophie," said Eddie. "No rush, Lucy's still talking to her friends and I've got a pint on the way."

Lucy returned just as Jack brought over their drinks. "Jack, meet Lucy," said Eddie, proudly putting his arm round his daughter. "You've met before ... a long time ago."

"Hi." Lucy smiled appreciatively at Jack, taking in his tall, muscular physique. "Sorry ... I don't remember."

Jack smiled back. "Good ... me neither."

"This place has changed since I was last here ... changed for the better according to my mates over there." Lucy pointed to the table where her old friends were sitting.

"Thanks Lucy, that's good feedback." Jack took a good look at her, she reminded him of a much younger Kate. "It's shocking to think your parents have a daughter your age. Makes me feel old. Grandchildren next, eh?"

"God forbid," said Kate forcefully. "This expensive education needs to be put to good use before she goes down that road. Anyway, she's too busy playing the field from what I hear."

"Times have changed mother. Playing the field … who says that anymore? Haven't you heard of try before you buy?" Lucy laughed and raised her glass. "Cheers Jack, nice to meet you ... or re-acquaint with you."

"You too Lucy. OK … take a look at your menus guys. Sophie has probably recommended the fish pie ... all the pies are good. My personal favourite is the Caribbean chicken ... our chef's family recipe."

"Look, there's Molly." Lucy waved at Molly who had appeared behind the bar. Kate looked up briefly and frowned, she hadn't had time to process what Fiona had told her earlier.

"Thank goodness," said Jack, looking at his watch. "Another pair of hands behind the bar."

An hour or so later Kate scraped the last of her food off her plate. "Well that was delicious," she said, leaning back in her chair. "I take it yours was equally good?"

Eddie's plate was empty. "If we were at home, I'd be licking the plate. This might become a regular thing."

"Fine with me," laughed Kate. "Especially if you're paying."

"How was your food?" Sophie stopped by their table. "I like seeing empty plates."

"It was really good Sophie," said Kate. "You'll be seeing us again ... quite soon if Eddie has his way."

"That's good news. Can I get you anything else? Room for pudding, more to drink?"

Kate patted her stomach. "I think we're done, no room left."

"Oi," interrupted Lucy. "I've got room for pudding ... and I know Dad will have." Eddie raised his eyebrows innocently, as if the thought hadn't even entered his mind. "Sophie, you'll get used to my mother. She has a sensible approach to food ... not like me and Dad. She's the healthy one."

Kate could feel Eddie's eyes on her but she refused to meet his gaze. The irony was almost amusing, the healthy one indeed. Instead she forced a laugh. "Don't let me stop either of you ... it's your waistlines."

"I'll give you a couple of moments to look at the menu," Sophie started to say.

"No need, we know what we're having, don't we Dad?" Lucy handed the menus back to Sophie. "We spotted it earlier. We'll have two portions of Eton Mess please."

"Good choice," said Sophie as she stacked their empty plates.

"Mum, I've just noticed something," Lucy whispered. "You know the scarf you bought for me this morning?"

Kate nodded. "What about it?"

"Molly said she had one a bit like it, didn't she? Well ... take a look. Hang on, wait until she turns around." All three women looked at Molly expectantly, Eddie less so. "There, look ... she's got it on tonight. It's exactly the same!"

"Oh, I noticed that scarf the other day," said Sophie, her eyes still on Molly. "She was looking really nice and I asked her if her jeans were new. She said the only new thing she had was that scarf." Sophie turned back to face Kate and Molly. "She was really coy about it. I asked her where she got it from because it's the sort of thing Kim loves. Anyway, she blushed ... really blushed, and then she said it was a gift." Sophie lowered her voice theatrically. "I think she may be hiding something. If it was a gift, I suspect it was a gift from a gentleman. Ladies, I think Molly has a secret admirer."

"Bloody hell," exclaimed Lucy. "She's a dark horse! She was teasing me about my love life yesterday. She never said anything about her own. Has she said anything to you Mum? Didn't she say she'd found her scarf in the second-hand shop? Cheeky mare!"

"What would I know?" Kate was fighting the impulse to get up from her seat and go over and confront her friend. She was horrified, Fiona had been right.

"Thinking about it, she gave me a dress too ... she said that was a gift that didn't fit," Sophie said thoughtfully. "Definitely a man on the scene I'd say ... and quite a new one if he doesn't know her size yet. Maybe she's waiting to see how it goes before she tells us about him."

"Maybe," said Kate trying hard to keep the bitterness out of her voice. "She's good at secrets though Sophie ... in a class of her own."

Chapter Eight

James had made the difficult return journey to London on Monday evening. Travelling, even in the back of a private cab, had been a challenge and, once inside his own flat, he'd consumed a lot of expensive, single malt whisky in an attempt to ease the pain for a few hours. The downside to this form of self-medication was that, this morning, after a fitful night's sleep, not only did his knee still hurt, he also had a mild hangover.

In his small, elegant kitchen, James filled a glass tumbler with cold, tap water and swallowed two painkillers. He briefly contemplated going back to bed but sleep didn't seem a likely possibility. Instead, he installed himself on one of the leather sofas, taking care to place a couple of cushions under his injured knee. Waiting for the painkillers to kick in, he shut his eyes and replayed the events of the past few days. Despite the injury he'd sustained, he was pleased with himself. Not only had he successfully located where Molly was living but, thanks to her being a creature of habit, he'd even been able to get into her cottage and have a quick look around. With his eyes closed, a familiar, satisfied smile hovered at the corners of his mouth. The 'calling card' he'd left on her front door had been one of his best moves; Molly would have been scared witless. Too scared, it seemed, to even try and remove it; the handprint had still been there on Monday morning. Her fear pleased him; he just wished he'd been in a fit state to witness it himself.

The fact that Molly hadn't been at home when he'd returned the next morning was, considering his impaired mobility, probably a good thing. His longing to see her up close was intense. He yearned to touch her, to smell her but if she'd tried to get away, he'd have been at a disadvantage and, at this stage, there was too much to lose. Gaining entry into her cottage hadn't been his intention initially but Molly had handed him the opportunity on a plate. When they'd lived together at Willow Hill, she had always kept the key to the back door permanently in the lock, it was something her own mother had done. James, obsessive about security, had insisted she stop but she had defied him; it was a habit he couldn't break. When he'd seen the cat flap in the back door of Molly's rented cottage, he knew, without question, that he had a way in. It took just a few seconds to hunch down and reach through the cat flap and turn the key. The satisfaction of hearing the mechanism move outweighed the pain the manoeuvre caused. Once inside, he'd had to resist the temptation to trash the place, to ruin the cosy little environment she had created for herself. Doing so would have been too easy, too obvious. Interestingly, he'd found a print out of a work rota pinned to her fridge. It seemed Molly was holding down a job and, from the shifts on the rota, he concluded that it was a waitressing role. He'd even taken a photograph of the rota with his phone, it might be useful one day.

The only disconcerting discovery had been the empty champagne bottles he'd seen on Molly's tiny kitchen table. She couldn't afford to drink champagne, not even the cheap stuff, he'd made sure of that. Two cheap looking champagne flutes had stood unwashed and upright in the sink. He'd picked one up and held it to the light; a pale lipstick stain hugged the rim. If he had needed physical evidence of her deceit, this was it. Molly had hurried home the previous evening to entertain a late-night visitor and, in his mind, only one kind of late night visitor arrives bearing champagne. She'd made a fool of him yet again. Standing alone in her kitchen, he felt foolish. He'd missed his opportunity, his bloody knee, those fucking dogs, everything had conspired against him. Consumed with anger, his hand had, subconsciously, tightened on the delicate flute until small shards of glass fell noisily into the sink. She was doing it again, she was breaking him.

Now, in the dawn of a new day, James was consumed with the need for instant revenge. Time to call in the troops he thought, time to use Seth. He typed out a quick text message.
Hello son, how's it going?
I have a business meeting in your neck of the woods on Friday.
Are you free for lunch or dinner?
James leant back on the sofa. "You don't know about this, do you Molly?" he muttered. "Your son doesn't want to know you, does he? But me, well I didn't do anything wrong, did I? Seth's my mate."

***

"I think it's a great idea Sophie." Kim was leafing through the paperwork Sophie had placed on the table between them. "But if it's to work, the secret is to keep it simple, really simple ... not just the food but the process." It was eight o'clock, well before opening time, and the two women were sitting at one of the tables at the back of the pub. Kim, dressed in her chef's whites, had come in early to discuss Sophie's plan for a marquee in the garden.

"Well, that's where I need your advice Kim," said Sophie, putting down her pen and leaning back. "Getting the marquee is the easy bit, but I'm worried about the other stuff. The menu, the ordering process, the bar. It's easy for me to think we'll get a good crowd of bikers using the marquee ... especially at weekends ... but I don't want it to detract from what we do in here. And I don't want to bite off more than I can chew."

"You won't know until you try, will you?" said Kim, a large smile spreading across her attractive face. "But you may have just hit the nail on the head. Maybe it should just be a weekend offering? To start with anyway. What do you think? I can have a think about food but it will be staff you'll need. I like the idea of using the cycling theme too. Maybe we could put an old-fashioned bike out there with a trolley behind it. Something classy ... serving quick, hot food."

"I knew I could count on you Kim ... that's a brilliant idea!" said Sophie excitedly. "These guys are hungry when they get here, they want fast food ... but good food. You're right about the staff too. We'll need a lot more help."

"If it's weekends only, we can train up a few students, especially those hoping to follow a catering career. Speak to Doris ... she has loads of grandchildren. She could spread the word for you."

"Spread what word?" asked Jack, as he came through from the kitchen with three large mugs of tea and sat down next to his wife. Sophie gave him a quick breakdown of what they had been discussing.

"What do you think?" she asked her husband, looking over the rim of her mug at him. "Am I being too ambitious?"

"When you first mentioned it, I did think it might be too much." Jack put up his hands as if to defend himself, Sophie was glaring at him. "Don't look at me like that! You asked! But listen … I like the idea of weekends only. I also think we're guilty of having created an awkward situation for some of our clientele ... a situation we need to fix quickly. No offence Sophie, but quite a few of your lycra lovelies can be a bit smelly after a long ride. It's not nice for our other punters who want to come and enjoy a nice meal."

"I know!" Sophie screwed up her nose at the thought of stale sweat. "And I'm often one of them!"

"I quite like the budgie smuggler look myself," Kim said with a giggle, referring to the revealing lycra shorts most of the male cyclists wore. "Although Doris reckons it puts her off her jacket potato."

"Kim," squealed Sophie, tapping Jack on the shoulder as he let out a huge belly laugh. "Did Doris really say that?"

"Yep. Don't laugh ... she was serious. She's clearly been taking a close look."

"OK, all the more reason to get this thing moving," said Sophie, pulling herself together. "I'll speak to Doris ... see if she can recommend any young blood. Kim, you put your thinking cap on." Turning to her husband she said, "you my darling, you will need to think about how we set up a bar in a marquee. That way cyclists won't need to come in here at all ... except to pee."

"One thing," said Kim thoughtfully. "You will need someone to overview a bunch of youngsters. You know, like a Team Leader ... none of us will have time to do it. I'd say it would be ideal for Molly."

Sophie caught the slight shift in Jack's demeanour. He bowed his head and leant back in his chair. "Yes, I agree," she said, watching for her husband's reaction. He didn't look up.

"OK, I need to make a move," said Kim "Thanks for the tea Jack, not a bad effort."

Jack laughed at Kim's retreating back. "Cheeky mare."

"Jack, we are OK about Molly, aren't we?" asked Sophie. "I'm getting a negative vibe from you. We need to be on the same page on this ... we're a team."

Jack sighed. "Yes. I have no complaints about her work Sophie. She's very likeable which is great for a customer facing role."

"I sense a 'but' coming." Sophie picked up the papers she and Kim had been looking through.

"No, not really. I just wish you'd let me fill you in ... or let Kate fill you in on what happened and why some people have a problem. We're not a team if one of us knows more than the other. We're disjointed. And how will you be able to deal with those difficult customers, if you don't know the detail?"

Sophie finished the last of her tea. Jack was a fair man and he had a solid background of handling people in difficult situations. She didn't doubt his integrity and maybe, just maybe, he was right. But she hated gossip and despised rumours. She trusted her own judgement better than any tittle tattle. "OK," she said suddenly. "Let's talk to Kate, just like you did ... if she's OK with it. Will that make you happy?

"It's not about making me happy." Jack looked offended. "I want this business to be a success, just like you do but we are more than just business partners, we are husband and wife and I don't feel comfortable not being able to share stuff with you." He looked away and shook his head. "God, I'm being pathetic. I need to grow a pair."

Sophie covered her husband's hand with her own. "Sorry ... I was being flippant. I didn't mean that ... about making you happy. You're a good man Jack Fox and I'm a lucky girl .... I love you."

"And I love you ... bossy mare that you are. So, you'll do it? You'll have a word with Kate?"

Sophie smiled. "Yes, I will ... but I want you with me. Just in case Kate tells me something you don't know. Same page and all that."

***

Waiting for the kettle to boil, Molly studied the work rota she'd stuck on her fridge door. She had marked her full days off in green, her single shifts in blue and her split shifts in red. Today was a red day, a split shift. She'd be working from eleven o'clock until three and then again from seven thirty until eleven. She yawned and stretched, she'd slept badly; Ethel's words still haunted her. To add to her bad humour, Harry hadn't been in contact, hadn't kept his word. No change there then Molly, she said to herself, as she stirred milk into her tea, men never kept their word.

Her phone in one hand and her cup in the other, Molly walked slowly upstairs to run a bath. The clothes she'd worn the previous evening were lying in a neat pile on the landing floor and she picked them up. Her shirt was, as usual, smeared with food stains. Clearing away dirty plates, in volume, was a skill she had yet to master. Some of her best tops were already ruined and, with a limited range of suitable clothes in her wardrobe, she was struggling to keep on top of the washing. As she moved the bundle of dirty clothes to the small laundry basket, the scarf Harry had given her fell to the floor. She frowned as she picked it up. Delicate and light-weight, it was the kind of item you could easily forget you were wearing. A worrying thought suddenly hit her. Kate and Lucy had been in the pub, they must have seen her scarf, the scarf that had made Kate suspicious. She hadn't spoken to Kate last night, she'd purposely kept her distance but Kate would have noticed the scarf. And, if by some miracle Kate hadn't, then the eagle-eyed Lucy wouldn't have missed it. Her hands trembled as she dropped the scarf into the basket and fresh tears ran slowly down her cheeks.

Emerging from the bathroom nearly half an hour later, she studied her reflection in the bedroom mirror. "You look like shit Molly," she whispered sadly. She checked her phone again to see if Harry had sent a text. Nothing, she'd known there would be nothing. Tossing the phone on her bed in anger, she dressed slowly in an old pair of black jeans and a silver-grey shirt that accentuated her curves. She quickly dried her hair, deciding, for once, to let it hang loose instead of pushing it back into a ponytail. From her bedside table she retrieved her small, silver hoop earrings and her oversized watch, the two accessories she never left home without. She was just applying her make-up, something she took very seriously, when she heard her phone ping with a text message. She ignored it, Harry could bloody well wait, it would do him good. Leaving her phone on the bed, she went downstairs to make breakfast. She might be feeling like shit but her appetite was as good as ever. At ten thirty, feeling considerably better, she went back upstairs to clean her teeth and grab her coat. She retrieved her phone and stuffed it into her bag without checking the messages. This small act of defiance made her feel stronger, more alive. She smiled into her mirror; this morning, for once, she was in control.

On the way downstairs, she spotted the champagne bottle sitting on the small window sill by the front door. Several dead daffodils drooped sadly from its neck. Standing motionless on the bottom step, she gazed at the bottle for several seconds, slowly trying to piece things together. "Fuck off Harry," she muttered at last. "I deserve better than this." She grabbed the bottle and strode purposefully through to the kitchen. Throwing open the back door, she launched the bottle, and the flowers, into the recycling bin. Closing the door behind her, she hunched down to reach through the cat flap and lock the door. When she stood up she was smiling broadly, the earlier tears forgotten.

Chapter Nine

James had finally given in to a nagging doubt and made the short trip to his local A&E. Forty-eight hours since his fall, the swelling on his knee hadn't diminished and he was still finding it painful to walk. After two hours in a scruffy waiting room, he was, however, beginning to regret his decision. Cross, hungry and bored, he was subconsciously making comparisons to the superior treatment he'd always received in France. "Fucking NHS,'" he muttered repeatedly under his breath.

To relieve his growing hunger, he hobbled over to the vending machine and bought crisps and chocolate along with a bottle of water, giving the machine an angry thump when it very nearly failed to dispense his drink. To relieve the boredom, he checked the emails on his phone and responded to some client enquiries. He also checked his calendar for the coming days and weeks. He had intended to drive up to Newcastle to see Seth but catching a train was looking like a better option. Thinking of Seth brought a small smile to his face; his son had become an ally. An intelligent boy, he had drawn his own conclusions about his parents a long time ago. Molly's narcissistic behaviour and her pursuit of a fairy-tale lifestyle had created a distance between mother and son. As a consequence, and unbeknown to his mother, Seth had gravitated slightly towards his father. James wasn't naive about his relationship with his son, he knew that Seth hadn't turned to him out of loyalty or even love. To a confused teenager, James represented the lesser of two evils. But James took what he could, it was a weapon in his armoury should he need it.

With time on his hands, he was tempted to text Molly. He had no reason to text her today and he usually kept to a strict timetable when it came to contacting her but it was time to shake things up a little. The champagne bottles on her kitchen table were never far from his thoughts. He typed out a message, taking care with the wording.

Have business in the UK on Friday so going to meet up with Seth.
Would you like to join us? X

His finger hovered over the send option, as he re-read the short message. The words were innocent, there could be no recriminations, a simple invitation didn't constitute harassment. He pressed send and smiled, confident he'd have a response within the hour.

A young nurse called his name and he hobbled after her to a side room where a doctor, who looked younger than Seth, was waiting to examine him.

"I need a scan." James pushed his chest out, he wasn't going to be messed around.

The young, tired looking doctor wasn't fazed. He indicated for James to lay back on the bed where he carefully examined the injury. "When did you do this?"

"Sunday. I fell whilst running," James replied. "I've tried to patch it up but there's been little improvement."

"And you waited until today to come in?" The doctor didn't wait for an answer, he'd made his point. "Looks like you hit the ground hard." His gloved fingers were carefully feeling around James' knee joint. "With trauma like this we'll need to wait before we do an x-ray, although you'll definitely need a couple of stitches. Once those are done, I'll prescribe you some painkillers and a course of antibiotics. I recommend you get a lot of rest ... ice and elevate the knee. We'll give you a set of crutches which should help for a day or two."

"But don't I need a scan?" James insisted. This wasn't the treatment he'd hoped for.

"We need to settle the pain and the swelling first. We'll know more in a few days." The doctor didn't look up from his notes. "We'll make an outpatient appointment for you ... we'll discuss the need for an X-ray then." James bit his tongue. The doctor may look like a kid but he wasn't wet behind the ears. Handling stroppy patients was part of his day job. "It is very important that you attend your appointment, Mr. Pope." The young doctor had caught the look in James' eye. "If there is acute damage, we will only know once the swelling has subsided."

It took just a few minutes for the doctor to stitch the gash in his knee. James uttered no word of thanks and accepted the crutches ungraciously. Now that his hangover had subsided, he was feeling very hungry. The young nurse printed off an appointment card and directed him to a coffee shop on the ground floor. She reminded him of Molly but every small, blond woman seemed to remind him of Molly.

***

"I can't find my phone charger," Lucy called out to no-one, as she ran out of the kitchen.

Eddie stood by the kitchen table, his car keys in his hand. "We'll post it if need be but we really have to get a move on Lucy. Your train leaves in less than half an hour." His voice got louder as Lucy ran up the stairs. Kate was sitting in the playroom drinking tea, Lottie lying at her feet as usual. He walked over to her and lowered his voice. "I've just got to pop my head in at the office after I've dropped her off. I'll come back for you.... OK? What time is our train?"

"You've got plenty of time," Kate said, stroking Lottie's head. "We can get the eleven thirty train. My appointment isn't until one o'clock."

"Found it." Lucy ran into the room grinning. "I'd already packed it ... just too efficient you see. Right, I'm ready Dad. Aren't you?"

"Bloody cheek." Eddie shook his head but he was grinning. "Come on ... let's get going."

Kate got up and walked to the front door with them. "Text me when you're back," she said, placing a kiss on Lucy's cheek. "Don't forget."

Lucy wrapped her arms round her mother. "It's been lovely to see you both. I'll be back soon for Easter though ... not long, eh?" Crouching down to Lottie, she pulled fondly at the dog's ears. "Bye Lottie, stay out of trouble."

Kate stood at the front door and watched the car until it turned right at the end of the road and disappeared from sight. The house suddenly felt very quiet, as it always did when the children left. She switched the radio on to fill the silence and went upstairs. She had time to do a few chores before

Eddie came back and she wanted to keep busy, to stop herself thinking about what might happen at the hospital. She was stripping Lucy's bed when her mobile rang.

"Hi Kate, is that you? It's Jack."

"Hi Jack, that threw me ... I didn't recognise the number."

"My mobile gets rubbish reception in our flat for some reason ... I'm calling from the pub. Sorry to rush you Kate ... I've got a favour to ask."

"What is it?" Kate cradled the phone on her shoulder, whilst changing pillowcases.

"It's complicated and I'd really like to explain the background face to face. Can Sophie and I pop over to see you? Not today, maybe tomorrow morning? Would that work?"

"Sure, that's fine, tomorrow morning would be good. Just tell me one thing ... is it about Molly?"

Jacked sighed down the phone. "Yes, it is ... but it's a positive thing. She might be part of some development plans we have which would be good for her. But the thing is Kate, I feel quite uncomfortable about how little Sophie knows. I think she needs to hear what you told me."

"Oh, I don't know Jack." She'd told Jack too much already. "I told you just about everything there is to know. Can't you fill her in?"

"I don't like telling other people's stories. In my experience, it's too easy to twist the truth. I don't want Sophie to accuse me of embellishing stuff just for effect. Do you know what I mean? Molly needs me and Sophie to be on the same page."

Kate was silent for a moment. How could she refuse? Jack was being thoroughly fair and professional. "You're a good man Jack," she said softly. "Come early, say about eight. Before Eddie goes to work. I'd like him to be here."

"Thank you, Kate. I really appreciate it." She could hear the relief in his voice. "See you tomorrow."

Putting her phone back in her pocket, Kate wondered if Sophie knew what a lucky woman she was, Jack was a rare breed. She would need to remember to follow his example tomorrow. Negative thoughts about Molly had been running through her mind over the last twenty-four hours but, whatever her suspicions, she mustn't let that distort the truth.

She told Eddie about Jack's call when they were on the train later that morning. "I don't think I know anyone quite so principled," she said, as the train slowed to let passengers on at the last stop before London.

"What did you expect? He's an ex copper ... and he was a copper for a good few years. He likes fair play," Eddie said. "He always did ... even as a kid. I suppose it's just who he is."

"I don't really remember him too much from back then ... you guys are so much older than me." A cheeky smile spread across Kate's face; it took years off her. She was teasing Eddie, waiting for him to bite.

"How rude," Eddie retorted with mock indignation. He was playing along, relieved to see Kate in good humour. Whatever news awaited them at the hospital, she was behaving as she always did, his wife was a glass half full kind of woman. Lying in bed the night before, listening to her quiet, steady breathing, he'd said a private prayer to a God he didn't believe in. But he had said it nevertheless, somewhere deep inside him it had felt like the right thing to do. His wife was a strong woman, stronger than him in so many ways but, if it was cancer, as he feared it would be, he was going to stand by her side every step of the way. Her enemies were his enemies, and that included cancer.

As was usual with Kate, they arrived at the hospital with plenty of time to spare. "Lordy Kate, we're early," Eddie groaned looking at his watch. "It's only twelve fifteen, let's grab a coffee and a sandwich."

"Good idea. I could do with a coffee. I'll get a table and you get the drinks. The usual for me please ... and maybe a toasted cheese sandwich."

The seating area around the coffee shop was busy and Kate had to walk around the perimeter a couple of times before she spotted a man in a dark overcoat step unsteadily out of his seat and, with the help of crutches, vacate his table. A woman on a mission, she squeezed quickly past a trolley full of used crockery and sat down, almost triumphantly, to claim the free table. She smiled to herself, the seat still felt warm. As she leant over to place her bag on the seat next to her, she spotted a discarded appointment card. She looked up, the man on crutches was heading towards the exit. Over at the counter, Eddie was paying for their food. With the appointment card in her hand, she stood back up.

"I'll be two seconds," she called, as Eddie approached. She pointed in the general direction of the exit. "That man has left his appointment card behind." She waved the card in the air and Eddie nodded his understanding. Moving away as he placed their tray of drinks on the table she'd secured, she tried to break into a run but running was out of the question, there were too many people milling around and most of them were moving at a snail's pace. Two old ladies tutted unhappily as she brushed past them and a handbag fell from the smallest woman's shoulder. "Sorry, sorry," Kate mumbled, as she helped replace the bag.

"Look where you're going in future," the taller woman said loudly. "And slow down. This is a hospital not a playground."

Kate mumbled more apologies and stepped away. Through the glass doors, she caught a glimpse of the man in the dark overcoat stepping awkwardly into a taxi. It was no good, she'd missed him. Looking down at the appointment card in her hand, she frowned and glanced up at the taxi again. It was waiting at the traffic lights near the main road. "Shit," she whispered. "What are you doing here?"

***

It had been a long day and Eddie was tired. Glancing over at Kate, as he opened their front door, he could see fatigue etched on her pale face. "Why don't you go and run yourself a bath and I'll quickly walk Lottie up to the park and then get us a fire going."

"Exactly what I hoped you'd say." Kate smiled wearily at him. "What about a bottle of red with that fire?"

"Exactly what I hoped you'd say." It was an old game they played, repeating each other's words. Eddie took his wife's coat from her. "Go on up, I won't be long."

After walking and feeding Lottie, Eddie set a fire in the wood burner. The old dog took up her regular position near the heat, thumping her tail slowly on the floor as she did so. "It's been quite a day Lottie," Eddie said softly, as he walked over to draw the curtains. The evenings were gradually getting lighter and the curtains could have been left open for a while yet but Eddie wanted to shut the world out. He thought about going upstairs to check on Kate but decided against it. One of Kate's ground rules was no fuss, he'd have to be patient and wait until she came downstairs. He heard footsteps on the landing as she made her way out of the bathroom, followed by the high-pitched whine of the hairdryer. They were reassuring noises after the strangeness of their day.

Sitting by the wood burner, stroking the top of Lottie's head, he felt drained, physically and emotionally. The fear that had been bubbling beneath the surface of his consciousness all day was still palpable but he had been offered some hope and this, however small, brought him a huge amount of relief. He'd felt jittery from the moment he'd woken but he'd tried hard not to let it show, he'd wanted so badly to be the strong one. Unsurprisingly, it was his wife, the patient, who had been strong. Whilst tears had rolled slowly down Eddie's unshaven face as they listened to Mr. Patel, Kate's consultant, deliver the bad news, Kate had reached out and gently wiped them away, just as she had done with the kids many hundreds of times. His amazing wife hadn't shed a single tear. Instead, she'd asked a lot of questions, repeating each answer she received, ensuring she understood just what it was she was up against.

"They broke the mould when they made you Kate Lawson," he mumbled, as he opened a bottle of red wine. Kate had been diagnosed with a low grade Non-Hodgkin Lymphoma, a condition she may have been living with for quite a while. Mr. Patel, her consultant, had tried his hardest to explain, in layman's terms, the outcome of the tests he'd conducted during the previous few weeks. He told them slowly and deliberately that Kate had a slow growing form of lymphoma but that didn't mean she wasn't, in general, in good health. Initially her blood levels had been a cause for concern but these had responded to medication and were now acceptable and, critically, none of her major organs were affected at this stage. Mr. Patel said that Kate would need active and regular monitoring but he wasn't recommending any immediate intervention. He had repeatedly used the term 'watch and wait', words that had initially worried Eddie, who, in his ignorance, thought that all forms of cancer needed immediate, invasive treatment. But Mr. Patel had explained that while Kate appeared to be in good health, it would be better to keep an eye on her rather than prescribe anything too radical. She would need regular blood tests and scans but as long as nothing changed, no intrusive treatment would be necessary just yet. The way Mr. Patel put it, the 'wait' in the 'watch and wait' implied that it would be better to delay treatment until it was really needed. This had worried Eddie but Kate had responded more positively and he had tried to follow her lead.

Hearing Kate on the stairs, Eddie picked up the bottle of wine and filled two large glasses. He placed one on the table and took a large swig from the other, relishing the smooth, warm taste. Kate, dressed in blue sweat pants and a white hoody, came and sat next to him and Lottie moved to be closer to her.

"You look like Lucy in that outfit," Eddie said, smiling fondly at her. "How do you feel?"

"Knackered." Kate reached for her wine. "But OK. It's good to hear it said out loud. I've spent too long in limbo." She giggled, albeit a slightly weak giggle. "And I like a plan, as you know. I perform better with a plan."

Eddie placed his arm around his wife's shoulders. "I'm not going to pester you every day with questions Kate. You'd be throwing punches at me if I did that but I want you to make me a promise. If I promise not to fuss, do you promise to keep me informed? I'm a middle-aged bloke ... not a very observant one at that. It might sound selfish but I don't want any nasty surprises."

"Deal ... I promise. But I still want this to be between just us ... I don't want to worry the kids."

"Yes, I respect that," said Eddie sighing. "I think I'd feel the same. But it's not going to be easy ... not with Lucy especially."

Kate placed her head gently on Eddie's shoulder and closed her eyes; husband and wife fell silent. A piece of damp wood hissed in the wood burner and Lottie inched closer to the warmth, glancing back at Kate as she settled into a comfortable position.

"I do have something to tell you though Eddie," Kate said, sitting up and taking another sip from her glass. "Don't worry ... it's not about my health."

"What's that then? Go careful with me though, my head's mashed after today."

"You remember that man I tried to catch up with at the hospital today? The one who'd left his appointment card in the coffee shop?" Kate pulled something from the pocket of her hoody.

"What about him? You said you'd missed him, that he'd got into a taxi before you caught up with him?"

"Yes ... but look at this, look at the name." She handed the card over to Eddie.

"J Pope. Bloody hell Kate, are you saying you saw James?"

"I don't know, I can't be sure ... not entirely. There were a lot of similarities I suppose but I was so intent on catching up with him that I didn't really take in how he looked. The man today was very tall with dark hair and his coat looked expensive. But I didn't immediately think 'God that's James' ... it was only when I saw the name on the card."

"But isn't he supposed to be in France? Isn't that where Molly and Seth think he is? Isn't that part of their deal? What's he doing in central London? In a hospital?"

"I don't know Eddie and yes, Molly thinks he's in France. As for Seth ... well I can't comment. But he's broken most of the terms of their agreement, so why wouldn't he break the one about staying away, staying in France?"

"You said the man you saw was limping. If it's James, maybe he's come back for treatment of some kind."

"What on the NHS?" Kate asked scornfully. "Don't you remember him crowing about how much better the French health system is? I'd be very surprised if that was the case, wouldn't you?"

"I suppose so. Are you going to tell Molly?" Eddie poured more wine into their glasses.

"I don't know, the timing's rubbish." There was a hint of sadness in Kate's voice. "Things aren't great between us."

"Ah ... now she tells me," Eddie laughed. "I wondered why she hadn't looked after Lottie today."

"She's been lying to me Eddie," Kate said quietly.

Eddie looked carefully over his glasses at his wife. "What's she been lying about?"

"What does she always lie about?" Kate took a large gulp of wine. Eddie said nothing, twenty-two years of marriage meant words weren't always necessary. Instead he picked up his wife's small hand. "And last night in the pub, I got some proof." Kate explained about the scarf. "Saying it out loud like this makes it sound a bit pathetic but I know Molly like I know myself. I know she's hiding something. And don't defend her Ed ... not this time."

"You've always been straight with her. Don't resort to playing games, that's more their style ... her and James. Tell her you think you've seen him at least. Be honest. You don't need to talk about her lying to you."

"Oh, but I do ... that's way more important," Kate retorted. She hadn't told Eddie about her encounter with Fiona. He'd be pissed off, he'd already told her not to fight other people's battles.

"You're not going to tell her then?" Eddie was surprised. "Don't you think you should?"

"Bloody hell ... he's not dangerous. I don't think he's here to hurt her. Anyway, we were in London, he's not here, is he? He was only supposed to stay away from her ... not the bloody country."

"That's just it Kate, he is dangerous, we know that. Look at what he's done in the past. If you think Molly is up to something, maybe he does too?" There was an edge to Eddie's voice, he sounded concerned.

Kate sighed. "There's that text message I suppose."

"What text message?" Eddie emptied his glass.

"Last week James called Molly," Kate said. "It would have been their wedding anniversary and he always calls her on their wedding anniversary, you know what he's like." Eddie nodded, he knew all about the bizarre rituals and weird mind games. "Molly picked up the call. He'd rung from a number she didn't recognise. She told him she wasn't going to speak to him. Eddie ... she put the phone down on him. She's never put the phone down on him, not once in over twenty years. Sounds stupid, doesn't it?"

"Sounds childish," Eddie agreed.

"To you and me, and most normal people, it is childish. But this is James we're talking about. He didn't try and call back though which spooked her a bit but then, later that night, he sent her a text message. I thought it was fairly weird, a little stupid, just James being James but now I'm not so sure. Maybe he does know something. Maybe he knows more than me.'

"Kate, you're not making any sense. What did the message say? Why would he know more than you? How could he?" Eddie was confused. "You don't even know anything for sure really, do you?"

"He sent a message saying he thought Molly was up to her old tricks." She didn't add that Fiona had said much the same thing.

"What does that mean? Are you saying he thinks she's having another affair? That's stretching it a bit, isn't it? And even if she is, how would James know?"

"Maybe he's been back for a while? Maybe he's been following her, checking up on her? Maybe it was him in the cemetery." Kate's voice had risen. "We both know what he's like when he loses it, don't we? He's not rational. Eddie ... I'm worried."

"Now who's being overdramatic?" Eddie sighed. "Molly said it was Fiona in the cemetery. It can't possibly have been James, can it? The man you saw today was on crutches ... don't you think Molly might have mentioned that? He just sent her a text message because she put the phone down on him. Classic James. It's so trivial Kate. Remember where we've been today, that's what matters now."

"But there was more to the message," Kate said. "He said something about hoping that Molly didn't kill this one. What does that mean?"

***

"Molly, it's ten past four," Sophie said, pointing at her watch. "You need to go home and put your feet up for a couple of hours."

Molly glanced at the face of her own oversized watch, amazed to see the time. "Well those few hours flew by. OK, if you can manage without me, I'll be off."

"Yes absolutely, off you go and thanks ... I'll see you later. Don't forget, if you come in a little early tonight, Kim will feed you." Sophie offered all her staff the option of one meal a day, a perk they all gratefully took advantage of.

Molly walked through to the kitchen where Doris was diligently cleaning down the work surfaces, the kitchen seemed eerily quiet. "Bye Doris, see you later," Molly called out cheerfully, as she buttoned up her coat.

"I'm not on later," was all Doris said, as she turned her back to Molly and moved over to the double sink.

Molly said no more and walked out. The fact that Doris had been so obviously rude didn't worry her, she was used to it. Plenty of people treated her the same way. But Doris knew her mother, they had gone to school together and she wondered, for a moment, if Doris treated her mother the same way. When Rita was drunk, she would blame Molly for her isolation, saying that it was daughter's fault all her friends had dropped her. Maybe she should try to see Rita more often, try to get there weekly, instead of monthly. But whether her mother was lonely or not, visiting her was no pleasure, it was purely duty.

The cold air hit her as she turned into the Market Place. It was so lovely and warm in the pub, it was easy to forget how cold the weather was outside. She pulled her scarf tight around her face and put her head down, walking quickly, intent on getting home as fast as she could. There were less than four hours before she was due back at work and she needed to rest her aching feet and get some sleep. She still hadn't read the text from Harry but it wouldn't do any harm to make him wait a little longer. She smiled behind her scarf, happy with her new-found strength. FOMO, what bloody FOMO!

Approaching her cottage after the short walk home from the pub, Molly stopped abruptly at the gate, irrationally afraid. Something had happened, there was an odd, sinister shape on her front door. An ugly, dark red stain sat under the house number, it looked like blood. Glancing around her, she crept forward cautiously, at the same time feeling for the housekeys in her coat pocket, they were the nearest thing she had to a weapon, if she needed one. Half way up the path the shape took form; it was a handprint, a bloody handprint. The palm of a hand and four long fingers were clearly defined, the thumb less so. The effect was irregular but dramatic. Oddly, it reminded her of hand paintings Seth had done as a young child, although those had been brightly coloured, cheerful creations. This felt far more ominous. The fake blood looked dry and crusty, as if the handprint had been there for some time but that wasn't possible, she would have noticed. The image of Harry's champagne bottle and Ethel's daffodils swam in front of her, she'd used the back door this morning. She tentatively stretched out her own small hand, the imprint on the door was much bigger, more masculine. "Fucking bitch." Molly spat the words into the air. "Fucking, evil bitch."

Ten minutes later with the help of boiling hot water, a soapy scouring pad and plenty of elbow grease, she had removed most of the offending handprint. Her anger seemed to give her scrubbing added vigour and, despite the cold weather, sweat trickled slowly down the back of her neck. Finally satisfied, she stepped back and examined her work. A tiny, stubborn trace of the fake blood was just visible but it resembled nothing more than a faint blob. The outline of the hand had, thankfully, disappeared. She felt better, Fiona may have renewed her stupid hate campaign but Molly wasn't going to let it get to her. Fiona was a sad, stupid cow, she always had been.

Finally closing the door behind her, she was grateful to feel that the erratic heating system had come on in the cottage. For once, it felt warm and toasty. Hanging her coat and scarf on the small bannister, she took her phone from her bag and walked through to the kitchen. She was going to have a cup of tea and some of Ethel's chocolate brownies before she had a nap, she'd have something more substantial to eat at the pub later.

Settled on the sofa in her sitting room several minutes later with a large mug of Earl Grey and Ethel's tin, Molly opened her phone. She was startled to see several messages waiting for her. The first was from James.

Have business in the UK on Friday so going to meet up with Seth.
Would you like to join us? x

The words hit her like a kick in the stomach and she swore. James was lying. Seth didn't speak to his father, let alone spend time with him. She'd done her very best to ruin that relationship. James had to be lying. She thought briefly about checking with Seth but quickly dismissed the idea, she didn't want to sound desperate. And she didn't want to tempt fate. She felt desolate enough without finding out that her son was on speaking terms with his father.

The next message was from Harry, he'd sent it at two o'clock.
Babe forgive me, my phone died yesterday.
I can't get you out of my mind.
Family possibly away at Easter. I could stay over?
Don't text back, I'll call you. Love you xxx

She had been so pissed off at him, had felt so let down but now her heart soared, even though less favourable thoughts tried to float into her head. He could have borrowed a charger or called from a landline. Banishing these thoughts as quickly as they came, she smiled contentedly, James and his text quickly forgotten. The third message had come through shortly after Harry's. It was from Lucy and she'd attached a photograph.
Lovely to see you at the weekend. Hope the job works out for you.
This pic was in Cosmo. Your admirer has impeccable taste!

Molly enlarged the photograph. It was a picture of a model, a skinny, waif-like creature dressed in black tights and an oversized, baby-blue jumper. She studied the photo closely, irrationally jealous of the woman in the photograph.

Lovely to see you too Lucy! Hope you got back OK.
Explain about the photo - I don't get it. X

Lucy responded immediately.

Look at her hair. Same as ours x

Molly enlarged the image for a second time and studied the beautiful model's hair. Long and dark, it was braided and held back by a delicate scarf, the end of which fell onto her skinny shoulder. The penny dropped, it was the damned scarf, her scarf, Lucy's scarf. The bloody thing was still haunting her. She composed another text.

Admirer indeed, as if!

Within seconds her phone buzzed.

Sophie said you blushed. Blushes mean you have a man. Own up!

Molly gasped and dropped her phone. Lucy had spoken to Sophie about her, about that bloody scarf. "Oh Kate," she whispered into the empty room.

Chapter Ten

"We come bearing gifts ... well breakfast anyway," Sophie said, grinning broadly as Kate opened her front door.

"Oh my, how lovely." Kate peered into the small box of croissants and pastries Jack held forward. "Thank you, come on in. I'll get some coffee."

"I can't take the credit I'm afraid," said Sophie, as she walked into the warm kitchen. "Kim's baking, not mine."

"They smell wonderful. Here Jack, put them on the coffee table and take a seat both of you. Just make sure Lottie doesn't steal one." Kate pointed to the dog who was eyeing the box and sniffing the air. "Eddie's just making a couple of calls ... he won't be long."

Sophie looked around the kitchen. "You've got a nice place here Kate, I love the Aga."

"Thanks Sophie." Kate glanced around the room. She was a little embarrassed, the place was a mess. "We could do with a thorough sort out ... far too much clutter. And if I'm honest, it's too big for just me and Eddie but I'm not ready to move yet. Maybe in a few years."

"Morning guys," said Eddie, coming through from the hallway. Dressed smartly in a navy suit and white shirt, he looked several years younger.

Jack whistled. "Very dapper Ed."

Eddie laughed self-consciously. "Not a look I favour but I have client meetings today. They tend to go better when I dress up." He put his mobile and his glasses on the kitchen table. "I may have to take a call in half an hour or so ... we've had an offer on The Gateway Hotel. I'm just waiting for the owner to come back to me."

Jack was tempted to ask Eddie about The Gateway, he'd half-heartedly thought about taking a look at it himself. Deciding it was a conversation for another day, he turned to Kate instead. "Thank you for agreeing to do this again Kate and I'm sorry to be such a pain in the neck. Shall I start the ball rolling and tell you what we're thinking of offering Molly?" Kate smiled and nodded. She liked and trusted Jack, he had a calming influence, he genuinely seemed to care. "Sophie has, unwittingly, got us into a bit of a pickle with her lycra lovelies." Jack held up his hands defensively, as his wife shot him a steely look. "They are, without doubt, a great boost for business ... there's no denying they have wonderful appetites. But the lycra look, and the accompanying odour can be off-putting for our more discerning diners." He wrinkled his nose for emphasis.

"Yuk," Eddie pulled a face. "That would put me off my pint mate. Let alone my food."

"That too," Jack said laughing. "But seriously ... put yourselves in their shoes. Would you want to sit next to a smelly, mud splattered cyclist when you're trying to do a bit of business over a nice meal or impress a new date?"

"Gosh, I would never have thought you'd have that kind of problem." Kate was genuinely surprised. "I suppose it's a nice problem to have though? Better to have customers than not?"

Sophie nodded and explained her thoughts about a permanent marquee. "It's a bit ambitious for a new business ... a small business at that, but it's the only solution we can come up with that won't cost an arm and a leg. We're hoping we can capitalise on the cyclists' custom, while maintaining a higher-end feel inside the pub."

"Now I think of it, Molly did say something about this the other day," Kate said thoughtfully. "I didn't realise it was so far ahead in the planning."

"It's not ... not really ... but it's not complicated," said Jack. "In a nutshell, we need to take on a lot more staff, mostly at weekends to start with and they will probably be fairly young and inexperienced. Which is where Molly comes in. We thought she might be good in a Team Leader role, someone who could take ownership for the marquee ... and the cyclists. We thought we could even get her involved in the kitchen side of things, possibly offer her some training? It would be good to know what you think. Is she up to it?"

Kate felt slightly uncomfortable, the others were all looking at her, waiting for an answer. "How does Molly get on with the cyclists? Has she come across anyone she knows?"

"Not really, not yet, but she will now she's part of the team." Jack had noticed Kate's hesitance, he had an inkling where it was coming from. He sat forward and looked intently at her. "The thing is, you were really good to me at the weekend. You gave me a candid account of what Molly's been through. I had no idea... as you said, I was away a long time. But you've helped me understand why some people treat her as they do. Please don't think I agree with them but I do get it."

Kate sighed wearily. Molly was her oldest and dearest friend but she was also a liar and a cheat. Despite his claim to the contrary, she wondered if Jack thought this too. "So what else do you need from me?"

"My lovely wife doesn't have a clue about Molly and, admirably, she is reluctant to listen to gossip. But we're a team, we run a business together and that business is our livelihood. If we are to make a success of it ... we feel ... sorry ... I feel ... that there should be no secrets, especially when it comes to staff. And I'm not talking about gossip am I Kate? These things really happened, didn't they? Am I making sense so far?" Again, Kate found herself nodding at Jack. This man could so clearly separate right from wrong. How could you argue with him? He didn't want any nasty surprises when it came to his business any more than Eddie wanted any nasty surprises when it came to her health.

"Can I say something?" Sophie asked, not really expecting an answer. "You guys are old friends and I really respect that ... I do. To stay friends for so long takes some doing. I've no friends from school that I stay in touch with ... I'm a little jealous really." She smiled and looked intently from Kate to Eddie and back to Jack. "But it was important for me, as a newcomer, to make my own friends which, in part, explains the cyclists." She paused for a second. "It was equally important for me to form my own opinions about the people I met, which included the people that Jack had already told me about. People like you guys. I suppose I have a 'live and let live' philosophy. You know ... we all have a past, have some things we aren't very proud of." She glanced at Jack again. "I have so much faith in Jack and we're a team ... a good team. And I'm quickly learning that the business has more potential than I ever thought possible. Anyway, I'm not going to dig my heels in about this any longer. If he really wants me to listen ... then I will." She reached out for her coffee. "Do you know what I call Molly?"

They all looked at her expectantly. "No, what?" Kate asked. "A pain in the neck?"

Sophie laughed gently. "I haven't said this to her face, or indeed to anyone else, but, in my head, she's 'Marmite Molly'. You either love her or you hate her. I hope that doesn't offend you Kate but nobody seems to polarise people ... customers and friends ... even some of the staff, quite like she does." She raised her cup and sipped her coffee thoughtfully. "And the amazing thing is, she either doesn't know it's happening, or she just has an incredibly thick skin which would normally indicate to me that a person has no empathy ... is selfish ... but I'm not convinced Molly's selfish."

Sophie's words resonated deeply with Kate. Molly did split people into two camps but she had never, not once, thought Molly was thick-skinned. Molly cared what other people thought, she was sensitive and had feelings. Just last week there had been tears after the incident at the cemetery. Could it be possible that, in reality, Molly didn't care what anyone thought? Perhaps it was all an act. Shedding tears prompted pity and empathy from others. Were the tears she cried part of a self-centred act? Part of her self-obsession? Did she just want to be looked after, spoilt, idolised? Just as her parents and James had done? Was she searching for love at any cost? To be the centre of someone's world, no matter who got hurt along the way? Kate's mind was racing. James had often said that all Molly wanted was a fairy-tale lifestyle. Had he been right? She shivered and pulled her legs up on to the sofa beside her. She'd promised Eddie she'd talk to Molly soon, she needed to let her know about James. But now there was a much bigger conversation to be had.

Eddie had spotted Kate shiver and got up to replenish everyone's coffees, discreetly increasing the temperature gauge as he walked past the thermostat.

"Is Molly working this morning?" Kate asked.

"Yes, she is," Sophie replied. "She agreed to come in early in exchange for finishing early ... and she has no evening shift, so she has a rare night off. I have to say she's always very flexible with her hours."

"Great, I need to speak to her ... I'll call her later."

Eddie handed fresh coffee to Sophie. "Jack, guess who Kate spotted in London yesterday?"

"Shit Eddie," Kate raised her voice. "Shouldn't we tell Molly first?"

"Sorry Kate ... I didn't think." He looked sheepishly at his wife. An uncomfortable silence descended.

Kate sighed, Eddie and his big mouth once again. "It's no big deal I suppose but please don't tell Molly just yet." She turned to Jack. "I think I saw James in London yesterday."

"Really?" asked Jack. "Isn't he supposed to be in France?"

"Yes, he is. But I'm almost sure it was him." She saw the confused look on Sophie's face. "Do you know, maybe we should come back to this bit of news. I think we run the risk of confusing Sophie?"

Jack looked at his wife and laughed. "Yes, you're right. This news can wait."

"So where do you want me to start?" Kate asked, settling back into the sofa.

"At the beginning Kate please," Jack replied.

***

"I don't get why he stayed away for so long," said Sophie. "If you have definite proof that your wife is having an affair, your immediate reaction would be to confront her, wouldn't it? Why would you stay away? It seems crazy."

Kate nodded in agreement, thinking back to how desperately worried Molly had been when James found out about her affair with Tim. Had it been an act back then too? "We all thought it was odd Sophie, really odd," she said thoughtfully. "Molly was beside herself. Back then she didn't cope well on her own ... she still doesn't. One minute James was saying the marriage was over and that he'd take Seth away. The next, he was promising that things could be different, that they'd work it out."

"And Tim?" asked Sophie. "What happened to him? Did he stick around?"

"No, he dropped Molly and made himself scarce as soon as the affair became public knowledge ... and then ..." Kate's voice trailed off.

"He had a serious car crash shortly afterwards Sophie." Eddie finished off his wife's sentence. "It was fatal unfortunately."

"Oh, dear God," Sophie sat back in her chair. "How very sad."

"He was a good guy Sophie," Jack said sadly. "A real charmer with the ladies but a good guy. A loveable rogue, wasn't he Eddie?"

"Yes ... a good guy." Eddie repeated Jack's words, looking down at the cup in his hands.

"But I don't get the level of resentment towards Molly," said Sophie. "She didn't kill the guy, he had an accident."

"It was a smaller community back then Sophie," Kate tried to explain. "It was a bit of a scandal I suppose. You know ... scarlet woman and all that. But to understand the real resentment towards Molly you need to know about Frosty."

"Frosty?" Sophie asked, frowning.

Jack laughed. "God, I'd forgotten we used to call him that! Kate's talking about Will. He was Tim's step-brother, part of our crowd of friends." He motioned towards Eddie. "A really good friend in fact."

"And he was the man who Molly had another affair with," added Kate. "Just a few months after renewing her marriage vows with James."

Sophie let out a small whistle. "Now I am a little shocked. Bloody hell! You're telling me that she goes through all that ... she rebuilds her marriage, her family and even renews her bloody marriage vows and then she has another affair? It's hard to believe. She's quite a woman our Molly, isn't she?"

Kate nodded silently, momentarily lost in thoughts of the past. Eddie reached out and touched her arm. "Sorry," she said. "I was thinking about Will. He's been gone a long time now but it feels like yesterday."

"Are you saying that Will died too?" Sophie was alarmed.

Kate nodded. "If you think part one was bad Sophie, then part two will shock you. Are you sure you want to continue?" She looked from Sophie to Jack.

"Yes, we do," said Sophie before Jack could respond. "Carry on please Kate." A stillness had settled over the room, Jack could almost feel the expectation emanating from his wife. "So, part two Kate," Sophie prompted. "I'm all ears."

Kate looked at Eddie who nodded encouragingly. She took a deep breath. "We probably need to go back to how things were just after Tim died. In hindsight, things settled quickly for James and Molly ... for all of us really. James was understandably reticent to socialise at first. I thought it was because he felt like she'd made a fool of him but Eddie thought he wanted to keep Molly away from temptation."

"Well, not temptation exactly," interjected Eddie. "I don't think he was worried she was going to go off and shag the first man who paid her a compliment. But, from a male perspective, I think he felt humiliated. You know ... us blokes don't like to think our women can look elsewhere." He smiled timidly. "But I think he was worried about her reputation too. You know ...lots of blokes looking at his wife, thinking she was easy. Sounds foolish perhaps."

"No, I know what you mean," said Sophie. "It's possible Molly felt men were looking at her that way too."

"She never said anything," Kate said, wondering, a little unkindly, if Molly would have minded anyway. Perhaps having men look at her was what she wanted. "Anyway, James kept himself to himself for a while, which meant we didn't see Molly either. To be fair to her, I think she was genuinely trying to put a lot of effort into the marriage ... she certainly seemed to want it to work. Just like he did."

"She was compliant, is how I would describe it," said Eddie. "If James wanted to do something, then she went along with it."

"Is that really how you saw it?" Kate was surprised. "You don't think she was just as excited about all the changes to the house, the extravagant holidays?"

"No, I wouldn't say she came across as excited." A frown appeared on Eddie's face. "She went along with him which is different." He turned to Sophie. "James made her throw out thousands of pounds worth of furniture. He said it was tainted by her and Tim, by the sex they'd had in his house."

Sophie raised her eyebrows. "The bed I suppose?" she asked. "And his house, not their house?"

"Not just the bed," Eddie said. "Which would have been understandable, wouldn't it? No, nearly everything went on the tip. He wouldn't even sell it."

"And it was very much his house in his eyes. Molly was the housewife," added Kate. "Molly didn't have a job, didn't contribute financially."

"Wouldn't it have been easier to move house? Start afresh?" asked Sophie.

"You'd have thought so, wouldn't you?" said Kate. "But James doesn't think like most people. Maybe it was because he was wounded. Either way, it enabled him to have the upper hand. You know ... he could always demonstrate how understanding he'd been, how forgiving. Do you know what I mean?"

"I think so," said Sophie. "He could play the victim. He'd had to make sacrifices due to her infidelity?"

Eddie looked over at Jack. "We really are different breeds, aren't we? Men and women ... the way we think."

Jack smiled. "In some ways. But I've seen men behave like James. They're clever, some are ruthless and the worst ones are potentially dangerous ... very dangerous."

Kate studied Jack thoughtfully, remembering his long and successful police career. He never spoke about his past which she admired, other men might have been tempted to brag. "I do think he's dangerous Jack. Eddie and I were talking about this last night. That's why Molly has to play his games, agree to his demands ... even now. The divorce settlement isn't finalised. Crazy isn't it, after all these years? But he's behaved like a pig. So, until it is, she has to continue to play by his rules."

"And what are those rules," asked Sophie. "Surely if they are legally separated?"

"Gosh, that's a whole other story Sophie," Kate said, pushing her hair back off her face. "I can come back to that but he's been far from kind, bent every rule as regards child support and alimony. He has a clever, if somewhat dishonest, legal team and a corrupt accountant from what I can gather. And God forbid she should start another relationship. He might not have kept his side of the bargain but there's all sorts of clauses in their agreement that Molly shouldn't break."

"Sounds like a nice man this James," Sophie said sarcastically. "So, she needs this job more than ever then."

"But things did get back on an even keel, didn't they?" Jack asked, ignoring Sophie's comment.

"Yes, they did ... by and large. Like I told you last week, they renewed their vows, got new rings and he even let her work part-time."

"Shit! He doesn't sound like my kind of bloke at all ... he let her work part-time?" Sophie was indignant.

Jack laughed. "No, it's fair to say you wouldn't get on, you two. You struck gold with me Mrs Fox."

Kate smiled at them both, they were good together, not like James and Molly.

"If everything was hunky dory, where does Will come in?" Sophie asked.

"That's why I asked about Molly and the cyclists," Kate said slowly. "To see if she'd come across many of them yet." She took a deep breath and looked at Eddie for back up, he nodded reassuringly at her. "Sophie, Molly had a history of taking up hobbies to keep her occupied. She's joined countless gyms, had French lessons … you name it, she's done it. James even paid for her to do a really expensive course in fashion and theatre make-up in London." She sighed heavily. "She had an accident as a kid which left her with some small scars on one arm … nothing too horrendous but Molly fretted … she's a vain creature, you've probably realised that. There was a time, years ago, when she'd only wear long sleeves … but the make-up helped her gain confidence. It's years since she's mentioned the scars."   A small smile played at the corners of Kate's mouth. "She was really good at the theatrical stuff too. The kids were always getting her to fool me. You know the kind of thing, life-like Halloween stuff with bloody, open wounds. Amazing stuff really." She stopped, momentarily lost in thoughts of the past.

"Kate?" Eddie prompted her.

Kate looked up. "Sorry, sorry. What I'm trying to say is that she eventually joined the cycling club … the one you ride with Sophie. And Will was a founder member of that club. That's where she met him. And his wife."

Sophie was visibly shocked. "Shit! I had no idea. I've heard people talk about Will. Bloody hell … what a mess. Jack … I should have listened to you."

"Don't panic Sophie." Jack took her hand. "We can work round this. I just wanted you to hear it from Kate. It's the closest version to Molly's that we're likely to get without asking Molly herself."

"And there's no guarantee that Molly would tell you much anyway," said Kate. "I wouldn't if it was me. I wouldn't want my past used against me like that."

"Kate, we won't use it against her. She still has a job with us," Sophie said gently. "I'm just shocked how this all fits together. Jack … thank you … for making me come here today. I was naive."

121

"You're not naïve." Jack pulled his wife's hand back into his. "I love that you don't judge people but this situation is complicated ... even before we start to think about it from a business perspective."

"Maybe it's not so bad," said Kate hopefully. "If nobody from the club has said anything about Molly yet, then that's a good sign, isn't it? Maybe they've moved on."

"She's not worked a Sunday shift yet so she won't have seen most of that crowd," said Sophie quickly. "Oh Jack," she raised her voice. "I get it now. Get why you said not to put her down for any shifts on Sundays. You didn't want her coming face to face with so many people from the club all at once, did you? Bloody hell, I've been such a fool."

"I had to Sophie," Jack said gently. "Until we were ...."

"I know ... on the same page." Sophie's smile was rueful.

"Sorry Kate," Jack said, turning his attention once again to Kate. "I'm so grateful for your help. Please carry on."

"You know I feel terrible talking about her like this," Kate said, sighing deeply. "Whatever she's done, she's still my friend."

"She did give you permission to talk to me," Jack said gently. "And we won't repeat anything you tell us. I can assure you of our discretion."

Kate studied his good-looking, open face. She hadn't noticed the grey streaks in his hair before. She turned to Eddie, who smiled at her. "I don't cycle myself, so I don't know how it works but I think the two of them, Will and Molly, would often find themselves cycling together. Apparently, it was something Will always did ... you know, take the newcomers under his wing." She looked at Jack and saw the little nod of his head, as if he was agreeing with her. "Molly was far from fit." There was the smallest hint of laughter in her voice. "The most exercise she got, was walking round John Lewis once a week. I think she found it quite tough going. She said she was always at the back, lagging behind and she often had to dismount on hills. It's hilly round here, as you know."

"Yes, it's harder than it looks ... cycling," said Sophie. "Great way to keep fit though."

"I do remember being impressed that she stuck with it though," said Kate. "She hardly ever sticks to anything. Eddie used to tease her ... called her Teflon. Do you remember Ed?" Eddie smiled but said nothing. Kate continued, "I wondered if she stuck to cycling because she was with other people ... you know, being included, part of a group after the Tim thing. Turns out she stuck to it for other reasons."

"She got all the kit, didn't she?" said Eddie, trying to get back to the story. "Definitely looked the part."

"And James was happy with it? Happy with her cycling?" asked Sophie.

"Yes, I think so. Occasionally, when work permitted, he'd join them. We've talked about this too, haven't we Eddie?" She looked over at her husband. "Maybe James thought she couldn't get up to anything surrounded by a crowd of other people ... and on a bike." Again, there was the hint of laughter behind the words.

"It's easy to get separated from the main pack though," said Sophie. "Especially when your fitness levels aren't good. It's easy to take a shortcut. In theory, you could spend several hours with someone on your own. Like you said ... newbie and mentor."

"That's what happened I think, from what I've heard anyway. Good God, I've never judged her on intent though, never judged her at all really." Kate shook her head. "I never thought she intended to have another affair. From what she told me, they both believed it was the real deal. She said they were in love."

"But she said that about Tim too, didn't she love?" Eddie said softly.

"So, what happened?" asked Sophie. "I'm taking it the lovely James found out?"

"It had been going on for some time before anyone found out," said Kate. "But it wasn't just James they had to consider. Unlike Tim, Will had a wife. I think Molly had learnt some lessons from her affair with Tim ... God I can't believe I'm saying these things."

"Will wasn't a ladies' man," Eddie chimed in. "Not like Tim. He was a lovely bloke, wasn't he Jack?"

Jack nodded and smiled. "Yep ... solid, intelligent, caring ... spiritual too."

"Women are attracted to those things too," Sophie smiled gently. "It's not always the obvious that attracts."

"Exactly," said Kate. "Molly described it as a slow burn. She gradually fell in love with him. In many ways, he wasn't her type ... probably too nice." She grabbed a tissue from the box on the table and blew her nose. "She was convinced it was the real deal."

"For both of them?" asked Sophie.

"I never had that conversation with Will," Kate replied. "But he wasn't the cheating type. I can only assume what it meant to him. It can't have been easy for him ... he had a big heart."

"Not big enough to say no, to put his family first, eh?" retorted Sophie. "Sorry guys, you all obviously cared enormously for him but how can you say he wasn't the cheating type? The reality is that he did something as equally as bad as Molly. The people who looked to him for support, his wife, his kids ... well it sounds like they got badly hurt."

Kate looked down at Lottie, a little lost for words and Eddie coughed.

"You're right Sophie," said Jack gently. "He was equally guilty but he paid a higher price."

"What does that mean?" asked Sophie, obviously agitated. "Are you saying he died because of his affair?"

"Yes Sophie," Kate said slowly. "That's exactly why he died."

"This gets weirder," exclaimed Sophie. "Just how can someone die because they had an affair?"

"Sophie, it drove him mad ... the guilt, the shame, the lies." Kate sniffed loudly.

"I still don't get it. He was an adult. An intelligent man by all accounts. He knew what he was doing, didn't he? I'm assuming he had a mind of his own?" Sophie said facetiously. "Sorry, that wasn't necessary ... but you know what I mean, don't you?"

"We do," said Kate. "And I agree. But don't forget we're trying to summarise this for you. To understand what this did to Will, you would have needed to know the man. Jack gave you a clue when he said he was spiritual. He had faith, believed in a God. Call it what you will ... but by cheating on his wife, letting his kids down, possibly giving Molly false promise, he was going against everything he believed in. He couldn't cope with what he was doing to James and Fiona. I don't have a faith Sophie, although religion was a big part of my childhood. I don't understand how someone can do what he did ... from guilt."

"You've lost me Kate. What do you mean, do what he did? I think you'll find a very high percentage of married men, even those who believe in God, have affairs. He wasn't the first, he won't be the last."

"No, I'm not trying to say that," Kate said quietly.

"What then?"

"Sophie, it's complicated but, in the end, Will couldn't cope. He was tormented, he ..." Kate's voice trailed off.

Sophie looked at all three of them in turn. "He bloody what?"

"He took his own life Sophie," Jack said quietly. "He killed himself."

Chapter Eleven

Walking into the pub at nine o'clock, Molly took some small comfort from the benefits of working the early shift. She loved the smell of fresh coffee and warm bread, and the cheery noise of Kim singing along to the radio. The pub was scrubbed clean first thing every morning by a team of cleaners which meant that, at this time of day, there were no stale beer smells and glass surfaces were, for a short while at least, finger-print free.

"Morning Molly," said Kim, coming up behind her with a freshly baked basket of croissants. "These are from an extra batch Sophie asked me to do for her meeting this morning. Why don't you try to sell them at the counter?" She placed the basket on top of the bar.

"How good do they smell!" exclaimed Molly. "I might indulge in one myself. Do you fancy a coffee Kim?"

Kim looked at her watch. "I'd love one," she said, taking a croissant and placing it on a napkin in front of Molly. "Espresso for me please."

"Where have Jack and Sophie gone?" asked Molly, raising her voice above the noise of the coffee grinder.

"I'm not too sure," Kim replied. "But it's rare for them to go out together. This place is taking over their bloody lives."

"Business is good then?" Molly surprised herself, this wasn't the kind of question she usually asked.

"This place is a little goldmine Molly my treasure. It's outstanding how well it's doing and in such a short time too. But with that comes added pressure. You know ... you have to figure out how to hold on to that customer base, keep current. If you don't, they go elsewhere."

"I suspect you're key to that success." Molly placed a small cup in front of Kim. "Not that I know anything about business. You're already talking a foreign language. I'm the most unqualified person I know." Poking fun at herself came naturally to Molly.

"Well life might be about to change for you honey." Kim smiled broadly and picked up her coffee. "You're part of the team now and I have a funny feeling Sophie has plans that include you." She started to walk back towards the kitchen. With her hand on the door, she turned, "Molly ... I've been meaning to say ... don't let Doris get to you. She's harmless."

Molly, a little perplexed, watched the door swing shut. Kim had noticed the animosity between her and Doris. Was that a good thing? If Sophie had plans for her, maybe Doris had been told to put up and shut up. The thought amused her and she sat down on one of the barstools to eat her croissant.

The kitchen door swung open again and Doris approached the bar. She was wiping her hands on the old-fashioned apron that she religiously tied round her waist. Clearly surprised to see Molly sitting on a barstool, leisurely enjoying her croissant, she stopped a few feet short of the bar. "Where's Sophie?" she asked abruptly.

"Good morning Doris," Molly said pointedly but with little apparent effect on the elderly lady. "Sophie's out till later. Can I help?"

"No," said Doris and turned to walk back to the kitchen.

"Doris," Molly called after her, emboldened by Kim's earlier comment. "I know we'll probably never be friends but now I'm working here full-time, can we try to rub along together?" As Doris turned around, Molly's courage started to fade. "Sophie has left me in charge until she gets back. I'd really love to help, if I can." Her heart was beating rapidly, she was irrationally afraid of this old woman.

"Sophie doesn't know you, does she?" Doris almost spat out the words. "She doesn't know what you did? How evil you are? She doesn't realise you have blood on your hands."

Molly gasped. The words shocked and frightened her. "Doris ... that's a lie. You make it sound like it was my fault. I didn't hurt anyone."

Doris walked back to the bar, her footsteps sounded dull on the wooden floor. She stopped just inches from Molly's face, so close that Molly could smell fried food on her clothes. "Didn't hurt anyone?" The old lady's voice was low and waspish, Molly recoiled slightly. "Can you hear yourself? You are a selfish, deluded woman Molly Pope. A good man died, a young woman was widowed, children were left without a father. And you stand there and say you didn't hurt anyone?"

Molly dropped her eyes to the floor. "That's not what I meant," she said softly. "Will ... no-one knew what he was going to do."

"He wouldn't have done it though, would he?" The elderly woman hissed. "He wouldn't have done that dreadful thing if you'd left him alone ... left him to his family. You tried to take something that wasn't yours."

"That's not true." Molly's voice sounded pathetic. "It's not a crime to fall in love."

"People in love tend to be happy people, don't they? They don't make a habit of killing themselves, do they?" Doris stepped even closer, her ice-cold voice was almost a whisper. "If that is indeed what happened. There's plenty of folk who think otherwise."

"What?" Molly gasped. "What are you saying?"

The pub door opened with a loud bang. A young couple and two small children came noisily into the bar. "Are you doing breakfast?" the bearded young man asked, smiling pleasantly at the two women at the bar.

"Yes ... yes." Molly's voice shook slightly. "Please ... take a seat." She led the young family to the tables which had already been set up for food. "Make yourselves comfortable. I'll get the breakfast menus for you." She turned back to the bar, hugely relieved to see that Doris had slipped quietly away.

***

Sophie was as good as her word and at two o'clock she reminded Molly that she could knock off. "Thanks again for coming in early today. I really appreciate it. Doing anything nice with the rest of your day?"

"I thought I might do a little bit of shopping and treat myself to a bottle of wine," Molly replied. "Very rock and roll."

"Sounds good to me," said Sophie. "Have a nice evening and we'll have a catch up tomorrow, shall we?"

"Sure," said Molly. "Is anything wrong?"

"No, not at all," replied Sophie. "See you tomorrow."

Feeling worried about Sophie's request for a catch-up, Molly walked slowly out onto the Market Place. Doris must have said something about their altercation; Sophie was going to tell her off. Just when things seemed to be looking up, a stupid old woman and her evil mouth risked ruining everything. She pulled the sleeve of her coat back to check the time on her watch. She fancied a glass of wine but drinking alone at this time of day was something she tried to avoid. Having a mother with an alcohol problem had made her very aware of good drinking etiquette. At the top of the street she paused by Vinnie's Wine Bar. She'd have a single glass of wine now to take the edge of her bad mood. Then she'd go home and get some sleep.

The interior of Vinnie's hadn't changed much over the years. A dark, low ceiling contributed to the dim, brooding atmosphere. Years ago, before the smoking ban, a constant fog of smoke had pervaded the room, no matter what the time of day. Today, cleaner and sweeter smelling, dim lights hung from the same dark ceiling but they did little to brighten the room. Several old-fashioned booths lined the external walls, the red leather seating bore testament to years of service. Large, circular tables, set with red and white checked tablecloths, occupied the remaining floorspace. Molly ordered a large glass of Sauvignon Blanc at the bar and settled into a booth near the back. A large, noisy group of women were sitting around a table to her left. She quickly scanned their faces, making sure neither Fiona, or any of her cronies, were among them. Empty wine bottles littered the table, explaining, in part, the level of loud, excited laughter. Reassured that none of the women represented a threat, she relaxed into her seat, sipped her wine and examined each woman closely, greedily taking in the designer clothes, the carefully highlighted hair and the expensive, ostentatious jewellery. She experienced a small pang of jealousy. If things had worked out differently she could have been a lady who lunched, she could have been one of these women. Instead, she was working as a barmaid. Life, and James, had been cruel to her.

Several hours later she was still in the bar and, surprisingly, she was having a really good time. The group of women having a long lunch had insisted she join them, and had repeatedly filled her glass for her. They were all drunk, some more so than others, and they were curious about her. Why was she sitting drinking on her own? Didn't she have a man to go home to? Molly found herself enjoying the attention and, as the wine flowed, she laughed along with them, happy to be part of their crowd. She felt, however temporarily, as though she had a group of friends. In need of the loo, she weaved her way slowly up the rickety old stairs to the Ladies toilets on the first floor. She giggled to herself, she'd done this a few times in the past with Kate. It felt good to be drunk with a bunch of other women again, it almost felt like old times.

"Busted." Molly jumped as a large, blond woman, dressed in a tight but ill-fitting, red dress blocked the entrance to the Ladies. Over the woman's shoulder two other women were hanging out of a large window, dragging greedily on cigarettes. "Oh no, don't panic, it's OK ... she's one of us." Coming closer to Molly, the blond woman put her chubby finger to her wine stained lips. "Sshhh," she said dramatically. "Don't tell Jenny ... the old dragon downstairs." She pointed her finger down to the bar below them. "She'd have a fit."

Molly grinned, childishly pleased to be entrusted. "Your secret's safe with me."

"And yours is safe with me." The woman winked dramatically. Molly was startled but she said nothing. The big blond was drunk, she was just having a laugh. "It's OK love," the blond continued, slurring a little and reaching out to put her arm around Molly's shoulders. "Don't look so worried ... the others don't know. I'm sorry, I'm a bit pissed, I shouldn't have said anything. I'm only putting two and two together ... but you've not been very discreet, have you darling?"

"I don't follow," Molly said slowly, recoiling slightly at the smell of cigarettes. "I don't know you, do I? What are you talking about?"

"That's true enough but you do know my mother-in-law, Ethel, don't you?" The woman covered her mouth as a loud hiccup emerged. "Ooh, excuse me."

"Ah yes, Ethel. I live next door to her," Molly smiled warmly. "You must be Liv? You've given up chocolate for Lent, right?" Liv looked confused. "Sorry, Ethel told me. I still don't understand though. What secret's safe with you?"

The other two women had finished their cigarettes and were trying, unsuccessfully, to shut the window. They were giggling like young girls. Liv lowered her voice conspiratorially. "I pop in and see Ethel when I'm on nights ... I'm a Nurse. I've seen your gentleman friend coming and going." She looked back at her friends and put her mouth directly to Molly's ear. Her breath was warm against Molly's skin. "I know his wife."

"What?!" Molly pulled back, startled. Gentleman friend, Ethel had used the same expression.

"I can't blame you, can I though? He's absolutely gorgeous. But don't worry darling." Liv put her hand onto a nearby sink to steady herself. "My lips are sealed. She can be a bit of a cow anyway ... his wife ... with her flash airs and graces. But a word of advice from someone who's older and wiser. Don't think you're the only one giving out favours. Or the youngest, or the prettiest for that matter. Sorry ... no offence. Not saying you're not pretty. You're lovely." Liv giggled to herself. "Let's just say he likes to play the field. Even my friend the Merry Widow's taken a shine to him and she's got a heart of ice." Liv opened the door for her friends. "But when you look like him, it's easy to win over an ice queen, isn't it? I think you'd do well to steer clear love. For your own sake. Come on, we've another bottle ordered ... the night's young yet."

"I'll be down in a minute," Molly heard herself say.

The three women filed out of the door, unsteady now on their high heels, leaving Molly alone. Liv's words repeated on a loop in her head. She hadn't mentioned Harry by name but it was clear who she was referring to. She must have seen him arriving at her cottage, just like Ethel had. The two women had probably laughed about it. She walked over to the mirror above the basins and looked at her sad reflection. The familiar tears were already coming and she watched as they fell slowly down her cheeks. Did Liv, just like Ethel, think she was prostituting herself? Had she said as much to the women downstairs? Was that why they had asked her to join them? Were they laughing at her, behind her back? Rumours spread like wildfire in this town. Pinning something like prostitution on her already blemished reputation, would be the final nail in her coffin.

A few minutes later, she'd composed herself enough to make her way carefully down the stairs, holding on to the rail on the wall as she did so. She crept over to where she'd been sitting and picked up her bag and her coat. Waving to the noisy women she mumbled her goodbyes, shaking her head when they implored her to stay. She concentrated on heading for the door, on escaping. Out on the street she was disorientated, it was dark, she'd been inside for hours. The air was bitterly cold and she tried, clumsily, to fasten her coat as she weaved her way, unsteadily, through the throng of people. She stumbled as her shoulder connected with someone else's and she mumbled an apology. Her bag fell from her shoulder and she tried, ineffectually, to pull it back. She stumbled again. This time, with her balance already compromised by the alcohol, the ground rose to meet her and she let out a single, shocked scream as her head hit the pavement with a sickening thump. As she lay there, staring up at the blurred faces that quickly gathered around her, the bile rose in her throat and she turned her head to throw up. The smell of undigested wine rose quickly in the cold, winter air.

***

"Just call me a taxi ... please," Molly pleaded with the couple who had picked her up and taken her back into the dimly lit but warm entrance of the bar. "I'm OK. Fairly embarrassed but OK." Someone directed her to a chair and pushed a tissue towards her. She used it to wipe her mouth, praying there were no traces of vomit on her chin or, God forbid, in her hair. Somebody else, a member of staff, offered her a small glass of water which she sipped slowly.

"You need to get looked at. Your head's bleeding slightly," said the woman. "I think you may have concussion. It's possible you need an ambulance." Molly assumed she worked in a bank, the nylon, striped blouse and blue blazer reminded her of a bank uniform.

"I think she might be right." The voice of the man. "Better safe than sorry, eh?" She noticed the expensive looking scarf wrapped loosely around his neck and what looked like a suit underneath his formal overcoat.

"OK, I'll get a taxi to A&E. Please just call me a taxi." She stole a look to the back of the room grateful that her new-found friends hadn't noticed the commotion. A member of staff walked past with a bucket full of hot, soapy water, the steam floated behind him. Mortified, Molly realised he was clearing up her vomit.

"Is there anyone we can call for you?" asked the man softly. Molly noticed his polished shoes and it made her think of James. She looked up at his face. He had kind eyes, James didn't have kind eyes.

"No, I'll be fine," Molly replied. She didn't want to share her embarrassment with anyone else, not that there would be a long line of people queuing up to come to her aid.

"Are you sure? Well maybe I should come with you." The man wasn't giving up. "You can't go on your own."

Molly sighed wearily. This was no good, she couldn't have a stranger, however charming, shadowing her. Her head was hurting, she just wanted to go home. "Look, I'll call my friend," she said, reaching for her phone in her bag and wincing at the sharp pain in her shoulder.

"See," said the woman, a little too triumphantly. "You're in pain, it's obvious. You need to get checked out."

"Here, give me the phone." The man gently took the phone from Molly's hand. "Who shall I call?"

"Kate. Please call Kate, my friend Kate." Molly dropped her head as the tears came again. She could hear the man talking on her phone.

"Kate will be here in a few minutes." The man sat down next to her and patted her knee reassuringly. "She tells me your name is Molly. I'm Simon. You'll be OK Molly."

Molly smiled at him through the tears and nodded. She noticed the gold wedding ring on his left hand, the good ones were always taken.

Chapter Twelve

Kate woke up early, she'd been dreaming but the dream was fading. There'd been a hospital and a grave. Her subconscious was playing tricks on her. Eddie was still sleeping soundly, his regular breathing a reassuring sound in the dark. She slipped out of bed quietly and shivered as she put on her dressing gown. The digital clock on Eddie's bedside table read five thirty, the heating wouldn't kick in for another hour and the house was cold. She pulled the bedroom door open quietly, checking to see if Eddie moved at all but his rhythmic breathing continued.

They had put Molly in Lucy's room when they returned from the hospital the night before. Kate opened the bedroom door gently. She wasn't surprised to find the bedside light on and Molly checking her phone. "Morning, how do you feel?" she asked, struggling to look Molly in the eye. "No, don't answer that. I'll go and make some tea. Come downstairs, it will be warmer."

Molly smiled weakly. "OK. Can I have a quick shower first though? I'm a mess."

"I couldn't get you to shower last night. I couldn't get you to do anything." Kate walked over to Lucy's wardrobe. "There's some of Lucy's old sweat pants and tops in here. Help yourself. I'll put your stuff in the wash."

"You don't have to do that. It's my mess." But Kate had already picked up Molly's clothes and was walking through the door. Molly stared after her. She didn't want to go downstairs. Kate wanted answers, answers she couldn't give.

Molly took her time showering, trying in vain to put off the inevitable. The hot water stung the graze on her shoulder and washing her hair was painful. When she eventually ventured downstairs more than twenty minutes later, she found Kate sitting in the playroom. The room felt warm, the Aga had taken the chill off. Lottie padded over and nuzzled her while Kate got up to refill the kettle.

"You don't look too bad for a pisshead. How's your head?" Kate's voice was harsh.

"Sore. I'm not sure if it's due to the alcohol or the bang it received." Molly smiled tentatively and massaged the tender spot on the back of her head. "My shoulder hurts too." Kate wasn't looking at her, she was concentrating on making tea. "Sorry Kate, I didn't want to bother you last night but that bloke wouldn't hear of me going anywhere on my own. I'm sorry I hijacked your night... and Eddie's."

"Simon? He's a nice guy. I know his wife. She comes to Pilates sometimes." Molly looked away, afraid Kate might see the look on her face. She'd clocked how nice Simon was. "Anyway, it's not the first time we've had to come to the rescue, is it?" Kate handed Molly a cup. "Where do we start Molly? I've got stuff to tell you but you've clearly got stuff to tell me too."

"Shit Kate." Tears were already coming to Molly's eyes. "How do you put up with me?"

"Stop it!" Kate shouted so loudly that Lottie jumped. "Don't you dare go looking for fucking sympathy." She stopped shouting abruptly, simultaneously letting the words sink in and trying to compose herself. She continued in a quieter voice, "Not that you'd ever think to ask but I've got my own shit going on ... important shit."

"Sorry Kate. I'm not looking for sympathy," Molly started to say but Kate cut her off.

"You're always looking for bloody sympathy. Just tell me what you're up to. I know about the scarf. It was a gift, wasn't it? A gift from a man. You certainly can't afford to shop in Phoebe's." Molly bit her lip and nodded. "And Sophie tells me you gave her a dress that didn't fit," Kate continued. "A dress that was a gift too apparently. Just like the scarf." Molly gasped. "Don't worry, she wasn't telling tales. It came up in conversation. You, of all people, should know nothing stays a secret forever. Who's buying you nice clothes Molly? Who are you seeing?"

Molly sighed and looked down at her hands, the tears were plentiful now. "I knew you were on to me Kate. The other day with Lucy, I could tell."

"Shit Molly, words fail me. Are you actually fucking mad?" Kate banged her cup down on the coffee table. "And I take it he's married? You wouldn't be so bloody secretive otherwise. Do I know him?"

"You don't know what it's like. I'm lonely." Molly sounded like a child. "You're so lucky. You have Eddie and kids who actually want to spend time with you. I've got no-one ... I don't even have a dog." She smiled ruefully, she could usually bring Kate round with a funny line.

"You're lonely?" Kate was furious, her usually pale face bright red. "And as for me being lucky, you have no bloody idea. You're so wrapped up in yourself, you never ask what's going on in my life." She drew her breath in.

"I can explain," Molly said timidly.

"I can't believe you. You think the way to remedy your so-called loneliness is to start seeing another married man? Jesus Molly, you swore you'd never be that fucking foolish again." Kate was speaking through clenched teeth. She didn't want to shout, didn't want to wake Eddie. "Have you learned nothing? Did Will's death mean nothing to you?"

Molly looked up, stung by Kate's words. "That's not fair Kate. I loved Will. You know I did. I didn't know what he was planning."

"Jesus Christ. If you loved him, really loved him, you would have known how tormented he was. Tormented by what you, both of you, were doing."

"But it was bigger than us," Molly interjected.

"Shut up with the claptrap Molly." Kate's voice conveyed every ounce of her anger. "You're not a bloody teenager. You knew there would be consequences. You saw what it did to Fiona and her kids, to your own child for God's sake. You have damaged Seth beyond belief." Kate stopped speaking for a moment, she didn't want to bring Seth into it but she couldn't help herself. "I can't believe you are selfish enough to do it again, to even think about doing it again. You disgust me. Seriously disgust me."

"It wasn't like that Kate." Molly tried to wipe away her tears with the back of her hand. "He came on to me. He did all the chasing. You don't know what it's like to be lonely."

"You should hear yourself. You're one sick individual Molly, always putting your own needs first." Molly pulled her knees to her chest and put her head down, she was sobbing but Kate took no notice, poignantly she felt no empathy for her friend. She tried to compose herself before she spoke again. "To do it all over again Molly, how can you be so fucking evil? Don't you care how other people feel? What they think?"

"Of course I do," Molly's head was hurting. "Have you got any paracetamol? My head's banging."

Kate got up and opened a kitchen drawer. She threw a box of tablets harshly at Molly. "So, who is he?" she asked, sitting back down across from Molly. "And don't give me any bullshit Molly. I'm so pissed off right now. I'm not going to take any more of your shit. I deserve better."

Molly bent down to stroke Lottie's head. The old dog looked up at her with trusting eyes. "I can't tell you who he is ... but I am going to finish it. I promise."

"You make me want to scream," Kate hissed. She reached for a box of tissues on the coffee table and threw it at Molly.

"Listen Kate ...please," Molly pleaded, taking a handful of tissues. "I found something out last night. Something I'm ashamed of."

"Oh ... at last? You're ashamed! What is it? In addition to shagging yet another married man?" Kate's comment hit Molly like a well-aimed punch.

"Kate, last night someone I don't even know told me she knew I was seeing him. This woman said she knew my secret." Molly shook her head and sighed. "I couldn't believe it. We'd been so careful."

"Fucking unbelievable," hissed Kate. "It's all about you, isn't it? You're such a bitch."

"Kate listen, this woman told me something awful about him. She said ...." her voice trailed off.

"What? What did she tell you about him? What did she say about your married man?" Kate asked sarcastically.

Molly started to cry again and her shoulders shook. "She said that I'm not the only one. He's got several lovers. I'm just one of them. There might be younger, prettier lovers. Jesus ... she even said he's been targeting widowed women. They must be older than me."

Kate moved forward until her face was just inches from Molly's. Her voice was low and she spoke slowly. "Seems Karma may have caught up with you at last, eh Molly? About bloody time. You have no shame, do you? You're only prepared to finish with him because you are one of his many whores? But you'd happily carry on shagging him, if it was just his wife and kids you had to deal with? I take it he has got kids?" She could see from the look on Molly's face that the comment had hit home. "Fucking hell Molly, how low can you go?"

***

"It's nothing too serious Jack." Eddie cradled his mobile on his shoulder, as he opened his office door. "She banged her head when she fell. The Doctor at A&E said there didn't seem to be any sign of concussion but the recommendation is that she take it easy for a day or two."

"Bloody hell, how did it happen?" Jack asked.

"Not too sure really, sounds like she wasn't looking where she was going. I think she just tripped up." Eddie hated lying to Jack but he didn't want to let Molly down. Saying she'd been pissed up and drinking alone wouldn't help her at this stage. "She said she'd be back tomorrow. If that's OK with you?"

"Yeah, sure. Tell her not to come back until she's confident she's OK," Jack replied. "We'll miss her ... but we'll manage."

Eddie sat down at his desk. "I'll tell her. Jack, can I ask you something?"

"Of course," said Jack. "What is it?"

"I've been doing a lot of thinking," Eddie said timidly.

"Dangerous," Jack joked.

"Indeed!" Eddie laughed. "Has any of this talk about Molly got you thinking? Raking over the past has started me wondering."

"Go on. Wondering what?" Jack was instantly curious.

"You're going to say I'm crazy but I think James might have had something to do with Tim's crash ... with his death."

Jack let out a long, slow whistle. "Bloody hell. What makes you think that?"

"Nothing specific," Eddie said. "I've just been thinking about how James stayed away, and how nobody else was involved in the crash. Do you think James could have caused it? Maybe he wasn't in France? That might have been his cover."

"The police would have investigated the accident Ed," Jack said.

"But I don't think anyone thought for a minute that James was involved. Not at the time. Kate and I didn't. Why would we?" Eddie's voice trailed off. "It's just a hunch."

"Hunches are good Eddie." Jack could hear the disappointment in his friend's voice. "But evidence is better. Even coincidence is better."

"Is the coincidence of Will dying better?" Eddie asked slowly, willing Jack to be enthusiastic. "Maybe James had something to do with that too? Do you think Will killed himself?" Jack was quiet on the other end of the line. "Sorry Jack. I've clearly been doing too much thinking. I can't get the thought out of my head. Could James be implicated in both events?"

"Eddie, I've got to go," Jack said softly, as if he didn't want to be overheard. "Come over tomorrow night. We'll have a beer and a chat. I'm not saying you're on to something though. Let's just say you've pricked an ex-copper's curiosity."

Eddie placed his phone on his desk. It buzzed almost immediately with a text from Kate.

I was right

He sat back in his chair and sighed heavily. Kate had been right about Molly lying, about her having another affair, that's what the message meant. He didn't text back, there was nothing to say. Molly had been in a real mess the previous evening. Clearly disorientated, either from the bang to her head or the amount of wine she'd consumed, she'd worried him, even alarmed him. Physically she'd looked dishevelled, the normal smart facade ruined by the smell of stale wine and traces of vomit. But it was the emotion pouring out of her and not her appearance, that had shocked him the most. She'd cried heavily from the moment he and Kate had arrived at Vinnie's and she hadn't stopped during the long hours at the hospital. The doctor who treated her had hinted at shock, coupled with alcohol. When, several hours later, they'd got her home, she was too exhausted to eat or even clean herself up and Kate had put her to bed with a pint of water and a hot water bottle.

"Were you planning on speaking to her about James tomorrow?" he'd asked when they had finally got to bed. "I don't think I've ever seen her so emotional. Do you think she's up to it?"

"I'm going to talk to her about a lot of things," Kate had replied. "As for all the emotion, just remember what Sophie said about Molly's thick skin. Don't be taken in by the tears Ed. She's only crying for herself."

This morning, when he'd gone downstairs, he'd found Kate and Molly in the playroom. Molly had seemed relieved to see him, as though he offered her some refuge from Kate. That had struck him as odd. Kate had always protected Molly and now Molly looked frightened of her. He'd made some breakfast for everyone, scrambled eggs on toast and mugs of strong coffee and had been pleased to see both women devour everything he put in front of them. He'd thought about staying a little longer to see how the land lay but Kate had given him the look, the look that said, 'leave us alone.'

He opened his laptop. Was he being ridiculous? Tim's accident and Will's suicide were just that, weren't they? An accident and a suicide? He opened his search engine and typed in Tim's name. There were a few football references and match reports but little else apart from an article covering the accident. As he scrolled down, he saw a photograph of Tim taken at around the time of his death. He reached out and touched the screen, surprised at the sudden ache in his chest.

Typing in Will's name, he whistled softly. The suicide had been heavily reported, there was a lot to go through. Eddie looked at his watch and called the switchboard to ask them to field his calls for a couple of hours. Then he fetched a cup of coffee from the small staff canteen and walked back to his office, closing the door behind him. Back in front of his laptop, he clicked open the first link. He was going to read every piece of information, every last word about Will's death. He didn't know what he was looking for, but he had a hunch he'd find something. He had to have something to show Jack.

***

Kate opened the back door and let Lottie out into the garden. She felt slightly guilty that she hadn't walked the old girl this morning but she needed to finish what she'd started with Molly. Lottie would have to wait for once. "Hurry up Miss," she called to the dog. "It's bloody freezing out here." Back in the warmth of the playroom, Molly was playing with her phone. "Why won't you tell me who he is Molly," Kate asked softly.

"I can't," Molly muttered. Kate's softer tone relieved her.

"You're not thinking of seeing him again, are you? Bloody hell, don't tell me you want to end it face to face. Moll, you know that won't work. You'll fall for any old excuse he comes up with. You're so fucking weak."

"Calm down …please." Molly didn't want Kate to get agitated again. "I don't want to see him. But I do want to speak to him, not just send a text."

"Why? What will it change?" Kate's voice was rising again, her frustration was creeping through.

"Don't you understand? I feel cheap enough as it is." Molly pulled the dark red, sofa blanket over her bare feet. "I need to start getting some self-respect back. I can do that better by speaking to him."

"Molly, you have no idea how angry I am. Angry and incredibly disappointed." Kate's voice conveyed every ounce of her disappointment. Molly started to say something but Kate held up her hand. "But there is something I need to tell you." She got up and walked over to the same kitchen drawer where she'd found the headache tablets earlier. She pulled out a small printed card and handed it to Molly.

"What's this?" Molly asked, scanning the card and turning it over. "What's going on Kate? This says J Pope. Does this have something to do with James?"

"It's possible. I found it in a coffee shop. A man left it on the seat. I tried to run after him, to return it but he got into a taxi."

"Was it James? What coffee shop? Was James here?"

"I don't know. I can't be sure, not really. I think so." Kate stumbled over her words. She couldn't tell Molly exactly where she'd found the card, not yet.

"Was it him Kate? What are you saying?" Molly turned the card over repeatedly.

"I only saw the back of him as he got into the taxi, so I can't be sure. It wasn't until I looked at the name on the card, after he'd gone, that I began to wonder." Kate avoided looking directly at Molly, staring instead at the card in her friend's hands.

"He's supposed to be in France," Molly mumbled. "He lives in bloody France."

"Look, I haven't seen him for a few years, so it might not have been him. Maybe it was just a guy who looked like him," said Kate. "But I had to tell you. It seems too much of a coincidence, doesn't it? This man was tall and he was wearing a long, expensive looking overcoat. That sounds like James, doesn't it?"

Molly was staring at her. "But he lives in France Kate. He promised."

"Oh no you don't Molly. Don't start playing the victim. You don't get away with things that easily." This news about James had played into Molly's hands, she was, once again, looking for sympathy.

"I'm not," Molly whispered defensively. "But this isn't exactly good news, is it?"

"Molly, your separation agreement is a bag of shit. Always has been. James got away with murder. And you let him." Kate had never voiced this opinion before. She'd always protected Molly but something between them was changing, it was time for tough love. "The guy I saw was limping quite badly, so there's a chance it wasn't James. But if it was, maybe there's a perfectly plausible reason. What is it, what's wrong?" Molly's hands had flown to her mouth.

"A man with a limp was at my cottage on Monday. He spoke to Ethel. He told her he was an old friend."

"Jesus Christ Molly! Are you sure? Ethel's an old lady. She might be wrong." Kate was grabbing at straws, Ethel was a sharp, old girl.

"I told you he sounded weird on the phone." Molly got up and started pacing the room. "He's been snooping on me Kate. Why else would he come to the cottage? And why's he sent this?" She found James' latest message and handed her phone to Kate. "The bastard even put a kiss at the end."

Kate read the message. "He's meeting Seth? But I thought they weren't in contact?"

"Me too," groaned Molly. "Got that spectacularly wrong, didn't I?"

"Sit down Molly," Kate coaxed. "Did you respond to this? Did you check with Seth? James might be making this up."

Molly sat back down and pulled the throw over her legs. "God Kate. I'm so stupid. I was playing games. I thought it was a text from him. You know, the married man. I was making him wait. I was cross with him. He'd kept me hanging on and I was trying to get my own back ... playing stupid, teenage games. I knew I'd had a message but I ignored it. I didn't read it until hours later. I figured the damage was done by then."

"And he's not contacted you since?" Kate asked. She wanted to add that playing games with married men was a waste of time but she stopped herself. "You've not checked it out with Seth?"

Molly shook her head. "No, there's no point."

There was so much Kate wanted to say but she was too tired. She needed some time to herself, to process her thoughts. She got up and walked over to a large bookcase on the far wall, each shelf was full to overflowing. Several old photo albums were piled one on top of the other on the bottom shelf. "Look at this," she said, walking back to the sofa with an old album open in her arms. "This is a photo taken when you renewed your vows." She laid the album on the coffee table in front of Molly. "Look." She pointed to a picture of James and Seth standing in front of the church. They were both looking directly into the camera. The smile on James' face seemed genuine, Seth looked bored. "I don't think I've got anything more recent and I'm guessing you haven't kept any photos, have you?"

"Are you kidding? James wouldn't let me keep any of the old albums. They're part of the settlement. He's supposed to hand them over when we complete." Kate nodded, she hadn't heard this story before but it didn't surprise her. James had fought Molly over everything. "Why are you showing me this Kate? It wasn't the best day of my life." Molly studied the photograph, her eyes drawn to the unsmiling face of her son.

"No, I know." Kate pulled the photograph from the album and handed it to Molly. "Take it, go on, take it. Next time you see Ethel, check with her. Check if that man she saw was James. And please … contact Seth."

Chapter Thirteen

James stepped carefully off the train with the help of his crutches. Five days on from the fall his knee was feeling surprisingly good, the enforced rest had certainly helped his recovery. He'd thought about discarding the crutches but he wanted to make an impression on Seth, and seeing the look of concern on his son's face as he walked towards him, he was glad of his decision.

"Man alive! What have you done to yourself?" Seth asked, staring at his father's raised, right leg. Theirs wasn't a relationship where hugs were offered, or hands shaken, but James could see Seth was visibly concerned and this pleased him, Seth cared about him.

"It's nothing, just tripped whilst jogging and landed badly. The crutches make it look worse than it really is."

"Do you need me to get a wheelchair?" Seth looked around the platform.

"Hell no," said James. "I'm not totally incapable. I am starving though. Where are we going for lunch?"

"Let's get you into a taxi Dad. No way am I putting you on the Metro like that. We'll go to the Quayside. You're not on any medication, are you? You can have a drink?"

"Since when did you turn into such an old woman?" James chastised his son. "You're nineteen, you don't need to worry about me like that."

"I'm twenty actually Dad and I'm studying medicine. Let's just say I know a thing or two about the abuse of medication." Seth opened a taxi door. "Anyway, some things are just common sense."

"And now you sound like a parent," James said, laughing. "You need a drink. It's the weekend."

Ten minutes later they were sitting inside a trendy bar near the river. A friendly waitress had escorted them to a table where James could comfortably extend his leg. Seth watched, with amusement, as his father turned on the charm with the pretty, young blond. She giggled girlishly at his jokes and blushed at his overt innuendos. His father must be approaching fifty but he looked good, kept fit and still attracted female attention. He was always impeccably dressed and prided himself on his appearance. No high street clothes for James, he was a designer label man. He had a few grey hairs now, even more than Seth remembered seeing at Christmas but his father still had 'it' whatever 'it' was. Seth certainly didn't think he'd inherited this thing called 'it'. He had his father's height and lean frame but, in contrast to his father's olive complexion, Seth had inherited his mother's milky white skin and pale, blond hair.

"Have you seen your mother recently?" James asked Seth when their drinks arrived. It was always wise to get the conversation about Molly out of the way as soon as possible.

"No, but I've been thinking I should go home soon." Seth laughed at the look of surprise on his father's face. "Yeah I know. It sounds a bit weird, doesn't it? But I feel a bit guilty about not seeing her over Christmas."

"I'm sure she was fine," James replied, taking a large swig of his beer and smacking his lips in appreciation.

"She was, she was at Kate's. There were photos on Facebook. It looked like they had a really good time." Seth was looking at the menu as he spoke. "She looks well."

This rankled James but he tried not to let it show. "Does she?" he asked, motioning to the waitress to get them two more beers. "That's good. I've not seen her for a long, long time."

"Kate and Eddie look just the same though. Especially Eddie, he never seems to change." Seth smiled. "I like Eddie."

"Everyone likes Eddie," James said with a heavy touch of sarcasm. "Great guy, Eddie."

"What's that all about? What's Eddie ever done to you?" Seth didn't like his father's tone.

"Nothing," James replied. It felt strange to be chastised by his own son. He needed to change the subject. "I don't do the whole Facebook thing, probably too old."

"Rubbish!" Seth picked up his phone. "Plenty of people your age love Facebook. Look … it's simple. It's just an app ... see." He flashed his phone in front of his father. "You should give it a go. Maybe you could hook up with some old friends."

James laughed. "No thanks son. Quite happy as I am."

"I don't believe you Dad," Seth retorted. The beer had hit the spot, it was making him unusually bold. "You've not had a serious relationship since Mum and it's not right. You don't need to be lonely."

James nearly spat out his beer. "Lonely, me? Whatever gives you that idea? I have plenty of female company but I have it when I want it. I literally just have to click my fingers." He shook his head slowly. "I prefer not to get into anything deep. Women are hard work Seth." And they lie, he wanted to add.

"Do you want to see?" Seth put his phone down on the table in front of James. "Go on. Take a look, while I go for a pee. See what social media could do for you."

James hadn't lied to his son, he really wasn't interested in Facebook, he valued his privacy. The longing to see photos of Molly however was too great. Seth had left the app open on Molly's page and James scrolled quickly up and down, greedily scanning the photos of his wife. Seth was right, she did look well but more than that, the bitch looked genuinely happy. "Fuck you Molly and fuck your friends too," he said quietly to the screen. A picture of Molly and Kate caught his attention. They were smiling for the camera, wine glasses in hand, paper hats placed precariously on their heads. He'd always wondered if Kate had been complicit in Molly's affairs. Good friends covered for each other, didn't they? Had Kate and, even Eddie, known about the other men? Had they entertained them in their home? Kate had sworn that she knew absolutely nothing but, looking at the picture of the two women together, he began to think Kate had known more than she'd ever admitted. Theirs was a unique friendship, she must have known. Women were liars and Kate was no different.

Several hours later Seth helped James up the steps and back onto a train. They'd both drank a fair amount of beer but his dad, surprisingly, hadn't handled it too well. James could usually drink anyone under the table and Seth suspected his father hadn't been too truthful about his painkillers but he felt little sympathy. If James was mixing his medication with ale, then he'd have the mother of all hangovers in the morning and it would serve him right.

"You'll be back in London in about three hours." Seth placed a bottle of water on the table in front of his father. "Wise decision, booking first class. You might get some decent shut eye."

"Thanks son." James stretched his right leg out in front of him. "It's been a good day, hasn't it? We've had fun."

"Yes Dad, it's been fun," Seth agreed grudgingly. It had been fun for James, less so for him. After a few beers, his father had got talking to a bunch of students sitting at the next table. They were third year students nearing the end of their Politics degree. James, fuelled by beer and sheer arrogance, had goaded them about their own political beliefs. He'd been confrontational and borderline rude. Seth hadn't joined in, he'd seen his father do this too many times, there were too many embarrassing memories.

As he stood on the platform and watched the train pull away, Seth let out a sigh of relief. He didn't really do family and, as much as James was, in many ways, an easier option than his mother, one day in his company, especially when it involved alcohol, was more than enough. He did, however, feel an unfamiliar stab of guilt. He should go home and see his mother. His feelings towards her had begun to mellow, maybe it was time to try again. Easter was coming up and he could spare a few days away from his books. He'd need to check with Bobby first though. A few days back home would only be bearable if he could escape to the normality of Bobby's house. Bobby's parents weren't weird like his parents, they genuinely cared about each other and their kids. Eddie didn't show off in front of Bobby's friends and Kate didn't flirt with them. And then there was Lucy. She'd been like a sister to him growing up, they'd shared many childhood adventures and got into a lot of scrapes together. Over time, he'd started to feel something stronger for her but the torrid unravelling of his parents' relationship had affected him deeply. His inability to discuss it had put a distance between him and Lucy and he wasn't sure there was a way back. He pulled his phone from his pocket and typed in a message to Bobby.

Thinking of going home for a few days over Easter
Am counting on you to be there too bro!

About to close his phone, he noticed a Facebook notification on the screen and opened the app. He groaned inwardly, his father clearly wasn't as pissed as he'd thought. The notification was a Facebook friend request from 'JP' Pope. He accepted the request knowing, as he did so, that a few eyebrows would be raised back home.

***

"Let me." Eddie grabbed the door and smiled at the young woman in front of him who was struggling to control an excited little boy. A man in a dark suit followed closely behind, with a younger but equally excited child in his arms. "Friday night treat?" Eddie asked, still holding the door.

"Thank you," replied the man. "Friday night treats aren't what they used to be." He nodded at the wriggling, little bundle in his arms whose face was heavily smeared with traces of tomato ketchup.

"No, I can believe that," Eddie sympathised. He was about to say that things would get easier but stopped himself, it was a condescending comment. Instead he patted the man on the shoulder, the gesture of one man simultaneously consoling and reassuring another.

Sophie was behind the bar and smiled a warm welcome. "On your own Eddie?"

"Yes, for now," Eddie replied. "I've just sent Kate a text. She's got a class until half past seven but I've tried to entice her down here by offering to buy her some supper. I think it will work."

"It'll be nice to see her," said Sophie genuinely. "How's Molly?"

"She's much better. I think she's planning on coming back to work tomorrow."

"Wonderful," Sophie said. "Jack's in the cellar ... he'll be through in a minute. Pint?"

"Yes please." Eddie watched as Sophie picked up a pint glass and moved over to a pump at the end of the bar. Thoughts about James and what he might have done had occupied his mind all day. Naively, he'd thought he might come across something online that would incriminate James. Instead, he'd opened old wounds and now he was feeling more than a little sad. He also had serious doubts about what he should say to Jack. Maybe he should just leave things as they were, let the proverbial sleeping dogs lie.

"Eddie, fancy giving me a hand mate?" Jack popped his head around the corner of the bar. "I've had an increased delivery and I need to shift the boxes before someone trips over them."

"Sure." Eddie stood up. "Where do you want me? Can I bring my pint?"

Jack led the way to the store room at the back of the building. The corridor leading to it was full of boxes and crates, an assortment containing bottles, cans and snacks. "Health and Safety hazard," Jack grinned. "But a perfect opportunity to speak to you without people listening in."

"What? You left this here on purpose until I came in?" Eddie was laughing. "Devious!"

"Call it planning Eddie," Jack replied, picking up a box. "Come on, I'll show you the system."

The store room was meticulously tidy which surprised Eddie. He'd worked in a lot of pubs as a student and, from his experience, most store rooms resembled an Aladdin's cave, always full to the brim with everything apart from the one item you were looking for. Jack's store room couldn't be more different. Bright lights shone from the ceiling onto boxes and crates regimentally arranged on heavy duty shelving. A large screen was bolted to the wall at the far end and a laptop sat on a small desk underneath it.

"Everything's been checked in," said Jack. "Just make sure you work to date order."

"This is very impressive." Eddie looked around. "Not what I was expecting. I don't remember you being organised."

Jack smiled and handed Eddie a pair of gloves. "Come on then, run me through your theory." Eddie glanced back to the corridor. "Don't worry, Sophie won't leave the bar. Not at this time on a Friday night. And if she really needs me, we have this." He pointed to what looked like an intercom.

"I don't know where to start Jack. I'm not sure what's going on in my head." Eddie put on the gloves. "We've all been raking over the past, haven't we? All the talking seems to have cleared the fog for me, or at least I think it has."

"What fog?"

"I was caught up in the emotion. I think I can be more objective now," Eddie replied.

"Slow down mate. You're not making any sense. What emotion?"

"Sorry, I told you I didn't know what was going on in my head. Look … when Tim died, it felt like a totally separate event to what was happening between Molly and James. Sure, there was a connection because Molly and Tim had been having an affair. But I didn't make a connection about Tim's death. About how he died. But now I'm not sure."

"You think James had something to do with Tim's accident?" Jack asked in a matter of fact way.

"Yes, I do but I have nothing to back it up with," Eddie said sadly. "Like I said though … it's just a hunch. You probably think I'm stupid … some kind of pathetic, amateur sleuth."

"What can you tell me about Tim's death?" asked Jack. "Details?"

"I don't remember that much unfortunately and I only found one article online which didn't give much away," Eddie replied. "But I do know it was recorded as accidental due to driver error. That seems strange to me."

"Why?" asked Jack. "We're all human, aren't we? All make mistakes? It only takes a moment's lack of concentration behind the wheel and you can be in serious trouble."

"For you and me maybe but did you know what Tim did in the Army?" Jack shook his head. "No, I don't think so. Not the specifics."

Eddie stepped back, looking for more space on the shelves. "I don't know why I never thought of it before but Tim was part of the Army's School of Transport. He rarely talked about it but we narrowly missed a pile up on the motorway once. It got us talking." He turned to look at Jack. "He trained combat drivers, trained them to cope with the harshest driving conditions in the world."

"Really?" Jack was genuinely surprised. "The Army run blue light training courses for emergency vehicles. I did one of those courses ... it changed the way I drive. I'm ashamed to say I thought Tim was ... well... a squaddie."

"And that's what he wanted everyone to think," said Eddie smiling. "No hidden agenda with that man remember."

"Are you saying you believe the chances of Tim having an accident are minimised due to his expertise behind the wheel of a vehicle?" Jack had stopped what he was doing to ask the question.

"You think it's a long shot, don't you?" Eddie replied.

Jack nodded. "Four out of five road accidents in this country are due to driver error Eddie. Ordinary things like failing to look, speeding, ... everyday distractions. It's hard to argue with statistics like that, isn't it?" It was Eddie's turn to nod his head. "The accident would have been investigated." The two men fell into silence as they continued to stack boxes. "Will's death intrigues me though," Jack said after a while.

"It does?" asked Eddie, feeling strangely pleased. "You don't think he did it himself? I don't, I know a lot of people think it was because of his faith but I don't get that. If anything, his faith would have stopped him, wouldn't it?"

Jack walked over to the door and closed it. "How much do you know about drowning Ed?"

Eddie sat down on one of the crates. "Honestly? Very little. It's a form of suffocation, isn't it? I'm guilty of not really wanting to know I suppose."

"It's a slow, agonising death mate. It's certainly not an obvious choice for those contemplating suicide. Even those who want to do it that way, well they often fail. Once the lack of oxygen makes itself felt, the survival instinct kicks in. The instinct to get air into your lungs takes over." Jack shook his head. "Drowning yourself isn't an easy option."

"You've come across people who've tried and failed?" Eddie was curious.

"Unfortunately, yes and most who try it are either high on drugs, or pissed up. Most still fail."

"I've read loads on the internet today about Will's death," Eddie said. "I didn't see anything about him being drunk."

"Eddie drunk or not, it makes no difference. Most drownings are recorded as accidental. Without evidence of any inflicted injuries that's just what they look like ... accidents. Alcohol in their system changes nothing." Jack took off his gloves, Eddie thought it was a sign the conversation was over. "I'm interested why a suicide verdict was given though."

"Can we find out?" Eddie asked hopefully.

"Possibly ... but have you thought about it logically, Ed?" Jack sounded a little frustrated. "It's relatively easy to hold someone under water and kill them but there would be a scuffle, a confrontation. Will was a fit bloke, more than a match for James. If they'd fought, there would be evidence on Will's body ... bruising, scratches ... that kind of thing."

"I don't remember anything like that." Eddie was crestfallen.

"The circumstances around the drowning are crucial. What do you know? Were there any witnesses? Where did it happen? There's a shed load to consider. What about his mental history? Would his infidelity and his faith have collided? Would the shame have driven him to do it? Did he leave a suicide note? What did it say? To be recorded as a suicide there has to be evidence of that nature and that intrigues me."

"You're confusing me Jack. Are you saying you think it's possible he could have been killed? That it wasn't suicide?" He couldn't answer Jack's questions. He'd promised Kate he would say no more about Seth.

The intercom squeaked into life and Eddie jumped. Sophie's voice rang out from the small speaker on the wall. "Jack, can you let Eddie know Kate's arrived? Aren't you two done yet?"

"To be continued," said Jack, switching off the laptop. "Let's go and have a beer."

Chapter Fourteen

"I'm coming, I'm coming," Molly grabbed both her phone and her dressing gown, and ran down the stairs. Someone was banging repeatedly on her front door.

"Good morning." A small, wiry man with a receding hairline was standing on her doorstep. Molly looked from his smiling face to the enormous bouquet of flowers he was pushing towards her.

"I think you may have the wrong house," she said, pulling the belt of her dressing gown tightly around her waist. "These aren't for me."

The man checked the small envelope peeking out from the centre of the bouquet. "Molly it says here. Is that you?" Molly nodded. The man pushed the flowers towards her again. "Well Molly, they're for you then, aren't they," he said. "Nice surprise, eh?" Molly smiled politely back at him and reluctantly took the flowers. The man turned to walk away. "Have a nice day Molly," he called cheekily over his shoulder. Molly was vaguely aware of him whistling, of the gate swinging shut.

In the kitchen, she placed the bouquet of flowers on the table and removed the envelope with her name on it. Inside, on a plain white card, six words had been hand written in smudged, red ink.

Before you hurt, feel
Before you hate, love

"Fuck off Harry," she whispered. "Just fuck off." Expensive flowers and fancy words weren't going to change her mind, she wasn't going to be his booty call anymore. Opening the back door, she launched the flowers headfirst into her recycling bin. The white card with the red writing escaped and fluttered onto the concrete below. She bent to pick it up and tossed it on top of the flowers where it landed face down. Unnoticed by Molly, in the same red ink, a rough outline of a small hand had been drawn on the reverse of the card.

Back in the kitchen, Molly filled the kettle and sat at the table, waiting for it to boil. Her phone buzzed in her dressing gown pocket and her heart leapt. It was Seth's name on the screen.

Are you home for Easter?
Could get a train on Wednesday?
A smile crept across her face, as she tapped out an answer.

Always welcome

She added a heart and a smiley face. Seth would cringe when he saw the emojis but she'd seen Kate using them when texting Lucy and Bobby, she badly wanted to be able to speak to Seth like Kate spoke to her kids. Better to embarrass him with silly text messages than to subject him to the mess of her love life. Seth was coming home at a good time, he'd fill the void left by Harry. Walking upstairs with a fresh cup of tea, she stopped to look out of the tiny, side window, a feature all the cottages in her street shared. Ethel and her son were walking down the path towards his waiting car. John was holding Ethel's elbow and gently guiding her, his hair was as grey as his mother's. The simple scene gave Molly hope. There was still a chance for her and Seth. He'd volunteered to come home and she was going to try her best to be a proper mum, to be more like Kate. Watching Ethel, as John settled his frail mother into his car, Molly suddenly remembered the photograph of Seth and James. She needed to ask Ethel if James might be her mystery visitor but with the good news about Seth still uppermost in her mind, there was less urgency. She had something James didn't, she had a relationship with her son.

***

Molly was still feeling good when she arrived at the pub a little later.

"How are you feeling?" Kim asked, as soon as she walked into the kitchen. "You've been in the wars, haven't you?"

Molly smiled sheepishly. "No lasting damage fortunately. I just need to watch what I'm doing in future."

Kim came closer. "You do look pale though Molly. Are you sure you should be here?"

"God yes," Molly replied. "I'm going mad watching crap TV at home. How have things been?"

"Busy ... as usual," Kim said, emphasising the last two words. "We've got some new faces coming in today. Several youngsters are having a trial."

"Really?" Molly was surprised. "How come?"

"Oh, I'll let Sophie fill you in ... like I said before, she has plans." Kim winked at her. "There's some fresh brioche on the counter in the bar. Get some before it disappears."

Molly made her way into the bar. It felt a little odd, as if she'd been away for a long time instead of just a few days. The place gleamed, the cleaners had already waved their magic wands.

Sophie came in behind her. "Molly! How are you?" She took Molly's arm. "Not too sore?"

"No, I'm fine. A little embarrassed still." Molly blushed, unsure how much Sophie knew about the events of Wednesday night.

"Don't be daft, nothing to be embarrassed about." Sophie waved her hand. "It's good to have you back though. Do you know if the schools have broken up for Easter yet?"

"Er yes ... I expect so." Molly was thrown off-guard by the question. "Easter's next weekend, isn't it? They usually have a two-week break. Why do you ask?"

"Kim and I weren't sure. We've never had kids, we don't know the kind of stuff you know," Sophie explained. "We can expect more of the nasty, little ankle grazers than usual then ... great."

"Not a fan of kids, I take it?" Molly laughed.

"No. The small ones in particular." Seeing the grin on Molly's face, Sophie giggled. "And don't try and convert me Molly. It won't work! Many have tried and failed. Fancy a quick coffee?"

Molly nodded. "Yes please. Don't worry, you won't hear me banging that drum. It's difficult being a parent." She surprised herself, she rarely spoke about family. "Kim said something about some new people trying out today?"

"Oh yes," Sophie said, warming milk in a jug with one hand and setting out cups with the other. "I need to talk you through some ideas I have for the pub which means taking on new help. Today's lot are all fairly young ... students I think. Kim and Doris are taking two in the kitchen and we're going to have two in here. I'd like your feedback on them, when they're done."

"Sure," said Molly. "I suppose it's going to be busy over Easter. It will be good to have extra help. Actually, my son's coming home for a few days." Molly offered the news timidly.

"That's great news," said Sophie with genuine warmth. "I look forward to meeting him."

"It is good news," Molly agreed enthusiastically. "I can't wait to see him. He doesn't get home often."

The four students arrived promptly at eleven o'clock and, after a short induction from Sophie, Molly found herself working with an intelligent looking boy called Daniel and a nervous, skinny girl called Lily. They shadowed her as she worked the tables, delivering food and clearing plates. Both were quick learners and it wasn't long before they were using the tills and operating the huge coffee machine. Daniel was friendly and polite but there was something reserved about Lily. Molly's antennae told her the young girl knew her story.

"Daniel's great," she told Sophie, as she got ready to go home a few hours later. "Very switched on .... I think he'll work out fine. I'm not sure about Lily though. She seems capable enough but either she doesn't like me or she's just shy."

"Really? OK. I'll have a word with her," Sophie said thoughtfully. She hadn't considered that any of the youngsters might hold a grudge against Molly. She'd assumed Molly's past would be old news, that only the older generation would have an opinion. If Lily had a problem she'd just have to deal with it, either that or find another job. She smiled reassuringly at Molly. "I hope you're going home to put your feet up?"

"Yes ... I feel a bit pooped actually." Molly gently touched the back of her head. "But I'll be fine after a nap." She reached out to put her handbag on the workbench in front of her but misjudged the distance, the bag fell loudly to the floor scattering its contents at Sophie's feet.

"Ooops, let me help." Sophie bent down to retrieve a lipstick, some loose change and a tube of hand cream. A notebook had fallen on its spine scattering some receipts and a couple of photographs on the kitchen floor. "Wow, is that you and Kate?' Sophie picked up the first photograph. It showed two young women sitting on a sandy beach. They were smiling happily into the camera.

"Oh my God, how embarrassing. A lifetime ago." Molly took the photo from Sophie. "What on earth were we wearing? Horrendous."

"It's lovely Molly and it's even lovelier that you carry it around with you. And this?" Sophie picked up another photograph of a man and an adolescent boy.

The smile disappeared from Molly's face. "Ah that's Seth, my son," she said, looking at the photograph Kate had found in her old photo album. "Again, a fairly old photo now."

"Who's that with him?" Sophie concentrated on keeping her voice neutral.

Molly dropped the photo back into her bag. "That's James, Seth's Dad. My ex."

***

It was after midnight when Sophie locked the main doors and switched off the lights in the bar. They'd had a good crowd in again but it had been difficult to persuade people to go home, they had been having far too much fun. She was yawning as Jack came through from the kitchen.

"Oh dear," he said gently. "Someone won't need rocking tonight."

"I'd forgotten how tiring it is to mentor someone let alone four of them." Sophie leant into her husband for a cuddle. "Trying to explain what I'm doing bit by bit ... whilst remaining pleasant ... well, it's really tiring. But it was worth it. I think we've got a few good ones there."

"Kim even had one of them making pastry tonight." Jack stifled a yawn. "She certainly doesn't waste any time." He followed Sophie up the stairs to their small flat. "These kids. Are they coming back for more tomorrow?"

"They are, all of them, although I'm not sure about Lily. Do you know which one she is?"

Jack nodded. "Doris' granddaughter?"

"I might need to keep an eye on her. Not sure she's the right fit. Apart from that, I'm pleased. Just as well really, as I still haven't rostered Molly to work on Sundays. I need to have that conversation but I just don't know what I'm going to say."

"Just be honest love." Jack led the way to their tiny kitchen. "She's going to have to work on Sundays ... we all do. It's your cycling friends I'm more worried about. We can't predict what their reaction will be."

"Oh my God, I forgot to tell you." Sophie pulled the elastic from her hair and let it fall over her shoulders. "I know who that bloke is, the one from last week. The one who acted weirdly."

"You're going to have to be more specific than that." Jack opened the fridge. "A lot of our customers act weirdly, especially with alcohol inside them."

Sophie accepted the bottle of water Jack offered her. "What was his name? JP? Yes, JP. The man who helped me with my helmet on the train."

"Ah yes, the guy who couldn't escape fast enough, once you showed your face," Jack teased.

"Well today, when she was leaving, Molly dropped her handbag on the floor and loads of stuff fell out." She lifted the bottle of water to her lips and took a small sip. "There were a couple of photos ... one of Molly and Kate when they were teenagers."

"What's this got to do with that bloke?" Jack put his hands on her shoulders and pushed her gently towards the bedroom. "What was his name again?"

"JP. There was another photograph. One of a man with a teenage boy." She turned and looked up into Jack's face. "You'll never believe it, the man in the photo was JP."

"What are you saying?" Jack asked. "That JP is a friend of Molly's?"

"No, not a friend exactly. The boy in the photograph was Seth, Molly's son."

"So?" Jack was yawning again.

"And the man with him was his Dad," Sophie said slowly. "Jack, our friend JP is James."

Chapter Fifteen

Despite his negative comments to Seth, James was getting to grips with Facebook. He'd initially been impressed and more than a little surprised, to learn that his son had several hundred friends but, as his understanding of the site grew, he realised that many of these friends were just acquaintances, often merely friends of friends. Nevertheless, what he'd discovered about Seth surprised him and he'd been forced to reconsider his opinion of his son. The troubled teenager of yesteryear had disappeared. The new Seth was confident, amusing and likeable. He was clearly having fun in Newcastle and was making the most of his student lifestyle. This surprised James. He'd assumed Seth would hate university, that he wouldn't know how to fit in. There were hundreds of photographs. Most were of Seth with his friends, male and female, in bars or in clubs. Some showed him taking part in various organised road races; he seemed to belong to a running club. More interestingly, a few showed him smiling triumphantly with a finisher's medal hanging from his neck. James had experienced intense sadness looking at these photographs, he hadn't known his son was a runner.

Sitting in his flat, drinking his second cup of coffee early on Sunday morning, James was in a reflective mood. He and Seth were strangers; they didn't have a regular father and son relationship. In fact, they didn't really have a relationship at all. Studying a new post on Seth's page, James longed to make amends, to correct the errors of the past; he wanted Seth to be his friend. He'd noticed familiar names among Seth's Facebook friends. Eddie was listed but he didn't seem to be very active, although his kids included him in a lot of their posts, mostly pictures of their bloody dog. He instinctively reached down to rub his knee. Kate didn't seem to do a great deal either, apart from promoting her yoga classes. He clicked open Lucy's page and immediately spotted a photo of Lucy and Molly, taken just a week ago in Kate's kitchen. The caption read, 'Love this Lady #trendygodmother'. He studied the photo and laughed out loud. Little did

Lucy know that he'd been in their garden that day, that he'd even taken a furtive peek through the kitchen window. He scrolled down to the next entry, another photograph of Molly. This time the caption read, 'Never too old. Admirers and expensive gifts #sassygodmother'. He was immediately pissed off, Lucy was suggesting Molly had an admirer. Lucy's next entry was a collage, a couple of photos of Lucy and a cut out from a glossy magazine. Lucy had written, 'As seen is Cosmo #stylequeens'. Molly wasn't in the collage but for some reason Lucy had tagged her. Why would she do that? It made no sense. No matter how many times he flicked back to the post, the meaning eluded him. He sighed, women spoke in riddles.

He moved to Molly's page and studied her list of friends. There were a few names he recognised including Kate's sister, Patty. He grimaced, he hadn't liked Patty. He remembered her as an opinionated career woman, nothing like Kate. Looking at her profile picture, he was surprised by the change in her. Pictured with two young kids, she looked bloated and old. Her husband was listed too but James didn't recognise him. Out of interest, he clicked on the husband's page and whistled when he saw his posts. This guy was seriously into his wine. There were spectacular photographs of rolling, green vineyards taken in exotic locations, along with close-up shots of the guy tasting wines in atmospheric cellars. His profile picture was a solitary, wooden table standing on a pale, sandy beach with nothing but the blue ocean in the background. The table was groaning with uncorked bottles of champagne glinting in the sunlight. James was curious and slightly jealous.

***

Molly had spoken to her mother, as she always did on a Sunday morning and had been pleased to hear Rita in much better form this week. There had been no tears, or raised voices and no slurred recriminations, her mother was sober. The pleasure in Rita's voice, when Molly mentioned Seth might be coming home had been palpable and Molly had, for a split second, felt a little guilty. Her mother was lonely, it must run in the family.

Shortly after speaking to her mother, Molly walked over to Ethel's cottage with the photograph of Seth and James in her hand. She knocked on the back door and waited while Ethel found the key and unlocked the door.

"Hello Molly," said Ethel. "Come in dear, cup of tea?"

"Only if you're having some Ethel," Molly replied, taking a seat at Ethel's small kitchen table. But Ethel was already picking up the kettle and walking to the old, white sink to fill it up.

"How's your new job going?" Ethel asked. "Are you enjoying it dear?"

"Yes, thanks Ethel. It's busy but I like it. Jack and Sophie, the new owners, are really lovely."

"Did your visitor come back?" Ethel opened a tin of home-made shortbread biscuits and placed them in front of Molly. Molly couldn't help but smile, Ethel was as skinny as a rake but she was always baking, there was always something sweet to have with a cup of tea.

"No, at least not while I've been at home." Molly picked up the smallest piece of shortbread she could see. "I was going to ask you the same thing. You haven't seen anyone while I've been at work?"

"No sorry Molly ... I don't think I've seen anyone." Ethel shook her head.

"Has Liv?" Molly asked, watching Ethel carefully.

"Liv? My Liv? What do you mean?" Ethel stopped pouring the tea.

"I bumped into her the other day. She said she drops in when she's on nights."

"Molly, I'm not a gossip," Ethel said sharply. "You're implying I told Liv about you. What I said will go no further. I would have thought you'd know that."

"Sorry Ethel, sorry." Molly felt guilty. She shouldn't have thought so badly of her elderly neighbour. She was judging Ethel by her own poor standards. "Ethel, it's just possible that I know who he was, this mystery visitor. Kate and I were talking about it the other day." She pushed Kate's photograph across the table. "We think it might have been the man in this photograph."

Ethel picked up her reading glasses from the chain around her neck and peered down at the photograph. "Is that Seth?" she asked, pointing at the young boy standing slightly apart from the man next to him. "He doesn't look too happy."

Molly smiled slightly. "Camera shy teenager."

"Let me see." Ethel held the photograph closer. "Yes, Molly that's him. Yes, that's your friend. He looks slightly older now of course. What's his name?"

"It's JP," Molly said trying hard to keep the smile on her face. She didn't want to alarm Ethel. "If you see him again please try not to speak to him Ethel. I don't want to see him again."

Ethel took off her glasses and studied Molly for several moments before speaking. "Of course, dear," she said slowly. "If you're sure."

Molly reached out and patted Ethel's hand. "Thank you, Ethel, I appreciate it."

Back in her own cottage Molly called Kate. "Kate, it was James. I showed Ethel the photograph. He's been looking for me."

"Shit. I thought it would be. He's not been in touch?"

"No, not since the text about Seth." Molly was fighting to keep her voice steady. She wanted to tell Kate how frightened she was but the memory of what had been said the other day stopped her. Kate had accused her of always looking for pity, now wasn't the time for tears.

"Molly, about Seth. How much do you look at Facebook?" Kate asked.

"Are you kidding? Me? Facebook? I'm the one with no friends remember. Why?"

"Lucy sent me a text yesterday," Kate explained. "You're not going to like this but it looks like James did go to Newcastle on Friday."

Molly's heart dropped. "He's been to see Seth?"

"Yes. Well it looks that way," said Kate. "Lucy saw a notification on Facebook saying that Seth is now friends with JP Pope."

"Does that prove he went to Newcastle?" Molly asked.

"No, but Lucy did some snooping. James checked in at Newcastle Central Station on Friday night ... and he tagged Seth. I'd say he was trying to prove a point."

Molly felt the familiar stomach churning emotion that always hit her when James managed to get the better of her. "What's he doing Kate? I'm scared."

Kate ignored the comment, she'd promised herself she wasn't going to fall for Molly's tricks anymore. Instead she said, "What about calling his bluff?"

"What do you mean?"

"Fight fire with fire. Show the bastard he can't get the better of you. You should have done it years ago. I bet he doesn't know Seth's coming home. Upload something and tag Seth. It's harmless but it speaks volumes."

Chapter Sixteen

Kate was enjoying a leisurely coffee and a croissant at The Kitchen. In the past, she would have headed straight home after two teaching sessions but, since her diagnosis, she was making changes. Treating herself to a coffee, instead of rushing home to Lottie and the inevitable chores, was a baby step but it was a start, she was putting herself first. On a Monday morning, The Kitchen was usually quiet but the school holidays changed all that. Most seats were occupied and the queue at the counter snaked almost to the door. It didn't bother Kate at all, the busy atmosphere was uplifting.

"How are you stranger?" She looked up to see her sister standing over her.

"Patty!" Kate jumped up to kiss her sister on the cheek. "What a surprise. What brings you here? Don't you do your shopping in London?" Patty lived twenty miles out of town, in a pretty village where properties demanded incredibly high prices, prices that were way out of Kate and Eddie's league.

Patty sat down heavily on one of the seats opposite Kate, placing various shopping bags on the floor beside her. "I do Kate, I do. But my friend, Sally" she pointed to a woman queuing up for their drinks. "Sally said there was a nice little boutique here now .... Phoebe's? Designer stuff? She wasn't wrong as you can see." Patty gestured to the bags at her feet.

"Phoebe's? Gosh yes, it's a lovely place, I've bought a few things there myself. In the sale usually though." Kate looked down at the bags. "Looks like you've had a successful trip but you should have given me a call. We could have had lunch?"

"Sorry Kate. It did cross my mind but I've got to pick the bloody kids up from holiday club. I've had to let the nanny go. Like many before her, she liked my husband more than she liked my kids."

Kate was familiar with the stories of Patty's nannies and the challenges of motherhood. The nannies never lasted long, either too intimidated by

Patty or too smitten with her good-looking husband. "You won't need a nanny soon, surely?" Patty's kids weren't babies any more.

"That's what everyone bloody well says but where would that leave me? Doing all the chores for two thankless brats? No, thank you. I'm thinking of trying an au-pair instead." She smiled as a small, chubby woman with short, dark hair approached their table. "Sally, this is Kate, my sister. Kate, this is Sally, the friend who, along with the shopping, holds my sanity together."

"Nice to meet you Sally," said Kate, smiling at the heavily made up woman. Sally looked like she'd put on every piece of designer clothing she owned. The result was that nothing matched; Kate thought she resembled an overstuffed teddy bear. The gold bracelets she wore on both wrists clinked loudly as she put the drinks down on the table.

"You too Kate," said Sally in a strong, northern accent. Kate was surprised, she'd expected cut-glass, boarding school tones. "This is quaint, isn't it?" Sally gestured at the shabby chic interior of The Kitchen. Kate wasn't sure if Sally was being genuine. It sounded derogatory but she let it go and asked Patty about the children instead.

"Oh, don't Kate," Patty said, stirring sugar into her coffee. "They're more badly behaved than when you saw them at Christmas. If I can't get a decent au-pair, I'm seriously thinking of weekly boarding. It's not like we can't afford it."

Kate took a closer look at her sister, there was no doubt they came from the same gene pool. To look at, Patty was a chubbier, bustier version of herself. But they were, inherently, very different people and, as a consequence, they had avoided each other as young adults, silently and mutually acknowledging their differences. But Kate knew that, deep down, Patty was a good person and she was proud of her sister's charity work. Patty had a knack of making her rich friends put their hands in their pockets and had raised thousands of pounds over the years. But there was no denying that her wealth made her look at the world from a different perspective. Unfortunately, Patty, like many of Kate's more wealthy clients, believed money was the solution to all her problems. It wasn't a sentiment Kate shared.

Most people, Kate included, had thought Patty wasn't interested in children, that her career would always come first. But then, just when her biological clock had started to slow down, her sister had married and produced two children in quick succession. She'd found motherhood hard and had turned to Winnie, their mother, for support. But Winnie hadn't been well herself and when Patty's eldest child was just a year old, Winnie had suffered her first stroke. Patty, pregnant with her second child, had employed a nanny almost immediately. She'd had one ever since.

"Lucy and Bobby are coming home for Easter," Kate said to her sister. "You should come over one day for lunch?" The invitation sounded vague, she knew Patty's diary would already be full. You had to organise things well in advance with her sister.

"Thanks Kate. It would have been lovely to see Lucy and Bob but we're going away. Well, when I say we, me and the children and, hopefully, an au-pair." Patty put her hands together as if praying. "Sally's got a lovely place in Cheshire. We're spending most of the Easter break there."

"What about Harry?" Kate asked. For all his failings, Kate didn't want to think of her brother-in-law being alone over Easter.

"He's going on another buying trip." Patty's dissatisfaction was evident in her voice. "South Africa again, I think."

"Oh well, his loss darling," said Sally. "We'll have the most fun."

They parted about half an hour later, Patty promising to get in touch soon and Sally making a point of rattling her Range Rover keys in front of Kate. You can choose your friends but not your family, Kate thought as she watched the two women walk down the hill. She had chosen Molly though and look what had happened there. Patty might be ostentatious with her cash but she was genuine. Her sister would never be so cavalier with people's feelings.

***

Molly walked out to the garden with a tray full of tea mugs, followed by Sophie holding a basket of freshly baked muffins.

"It's smaller than I thought it was going to be," Molly said, looking at the recently erected marquee to the left of the garden. "But it looks good, doesn't it?" The team of men who had spent all morning putting the marquee together, spotted the tray of tea mugs and started to make their way over.

"You wouldn't believe how many options there are to choose from," said Sophie. "But I'm pleased with it, as a temporary measure for the summer anyway. It will give us some breathing space at least."

Molly placed the tray of mugs on a table and the men tucked into the muffins. "Nearly done Mrs. Fox," said one of the men picking up his tea. "Just a few bits to finish off with the flooring, then it's all yours."

Molly noticed the men were all wearing branded polo shirts. "Sophie," she said, as they walked back inside. "Have you ever thought of having branded shirts like those men? You know, maybe with The Crown written on the front and a logo?"

Sophie looked back at the men who were now sitting at the garden tables making the most of their ten-minute break. "No, I haven't," she said thoughtfully. "But I like the idea Molly, really like it in fact. It's probably a bit late to get anything done before Easter though, which is a shame."

"There's a place in town that does that kind of thing. I think they can do stuff at quite short notice. It might be a solution until you can sort something more permanent?"

Sophie turned and smiled at Molly. "Give me the shop details and I'll give them a call."

"I can do it if you want," Molly offered, a little timidly. "I know how busy you are."

"Wonderful." Sophie reached out and hugged her. "That will be a great help. It's a wonderful idea ... free advertising."

"It will stop me ruining my clothes too," Molly laughed looking down at her top. Somehow, she had managed to spill tea over her white shirt. "I've a lot to learn when it comes to waitressing."

"Did I tell you my friend Annie is coming to stay over Easter?" Sophie said. "You know? The Minesweeper?"

Molly smiled. "Oh yes, the Minesweeper. It seems like everyone's going to be in town for Easter. Kate said that Lucy and Bobby are coming home and I'm expecting Seth at some stage."

"Maybe we should have a bit of a get together here at the pub? What do you think? I could ask Kim to join us. It would be nice to have some downtime together."

"That sounds really nice Sophie." It would be wonderful for Seth to meet Jack and Sophie, to see how far she'd come, how normal her life was.

"OK, leave it with me. By the way, do you think you could swap a few shifts? Maybe do the lunchtime shift on Easter Saturday and Sunday?" Sophie watched Molly's face closely, there was no indication that working on Sundays would be an issue. She carried on, "I think we'll need a lot of staff. I may even have to put Annie to work when she gets here. I could swap some other shifts for you to compensate."

"Yes, no problem," Molly replied, still thinking how nice it would be to have everyone together again. "If you're stretched for staff, I'm sure Lucy, Kate's daughter, would help out. She does some bar work at uni."

"Why didn't I know that before?" Sophie threw her hands up in comic despair, as she headed towards the kitchen. "Right, I'll have a word with Kate."

Jack was restocking the fridges when Molly walked back into the bar. "The marquee looks good," she said.

"Yes, it does, doesn't it?" Jack stood up and stretched his back. "I've got other kit being delivered this afternoon, so hopefully we'll be up and running by Friday. I know Sophie's keen to try it out over the holiday weekend. No bloody patience that woman." He turned to look at the door as a group of walkers came noisily into the bar. "But just when we think we've dealt with one problem, we get another. Not as smelly as Sophie's lovelies but just look at their bloody boots." Molly looked on, a little horrified, as large clumps of mud fell from the walkers' boots. "I'll serve this crowd. Can you deal with those two?" Jack pointed towards the entrance, as two men came through the door. Molly turned to look. Jack, already pulling pints next to her, spotted a subtle change in her demeanour. She was blushing.

"Hello Molly. Fancy seeing you here." The man who'd spoken was smiling, looking directly into Molly's eyes, clearly thrilled to see her. Jack recognised this behaviour. Molly and this guy had shared something intimate, there was a tangible electricity between them.

"Hi Harry," Molly said. "I could say the same to you. What can I get you?"

***

There was no denying it, James was hooked. Consumed by an irrational need to know what Molly and Seth were doing each day, he had quickly fallen into a new routine of checking Facebook the very instant he woke up. If there was little activity, he'd check on Kate, Eddie and their kids, often frustrated by the security settings he'd only recently come to understand. Once he'd showered and dressed and checked on urgent emails, he'd do it all over again. There was a significant downside to his snooping though. Each new post on Seth's page provoked overwhelming feelings of sadness, resentment and even jealousy. A nagging voice in his head kept telling him to stop it, to give it a break, that it wasn't good for his mental health. But he had no willpower, Facebook was becoming a dangerous distraction.

This morning he'd had a lot of work to do and had spent several hours on the phone closing various deals. He was far more comfortable in this corporate world where, unlike the world of social media, everyone spoke in business terms. He was highly respected within his industry and, despite his disastrous private life, his reputation remained unblemished.

After ending a call with a new client, James played back the voicemails that were waiting on his phone. The first was from Colin Adams, his well-spoken, privately educated solicitor who, despite his privileged background and prestigious client base, wasn't averse to bending the rules. He'd been a great, if expensive, ally to James over the years.

"*James, it's Colin. Why don't you ever pick up your bloody phone man? Call me, we've run out of time. It's time to sign and pay up ....*"

Standing by the full-length window that looked out over the Thames, James deleted Colin's message before it finished. The view was sensational but James wasn't taking it in. He had no intention of returning Colin's call, he wasn't ready, he'd never be ready. He looked up as a helicopter flew overhead and turned to the east, heading for the nearest Heliport. If he signed the papers Molly would have won, she'd be free of him, free to marry again, free to take another man's name. His hands tightened around his coffee cup and his breathing quickened. He played the second message.

"*Hi Dad. I just wanted to let you know I'm going home to see Mum for Easter. Hope you're OK.*"

He opened Facebook, Seth had been tagged in a photograph by Molly. A much younger and distinctly uncomfortable looking Seth, wearing a suit and tie, stared out of the screen. Despite the bad humour that had descended on him after hearing Colin's message, James was tempted to laugh. He studied Molly's words.

Looking forward to seeing this young man soon x

James studied the photograph for a long time. It wasn't one he recognised or even remembered. Seth in a suit had been a rare event, especially at that age. He enlarged the photo and examined the detail. At the very bottom, in the right-hand corner of the picture, there was what looked like the tip of someone else's shoe. It was a man's black dress shoe. Seth had been standing with someone when this photograph was taken. James swore loudly and thumped the window with his fist. The shoe was his, the bitch had cut him out of the photograph, just like she'd cut him out of her life.

***

Molly could feel Harry's eyes following her around the bar. Each time he managed to catch her eye, he threw her one of his dazzling smiles. She tried not to succumb, not to smile back, he could save his energy for his other women. But her willpower was weak, she was too gullible, too easily flattered. Aware that he was watching her every move, she found herself exaggerating her movements, using her femininity. She was showing him what he'd lost.

"Do you think they're settling in for a session?" Jack asked, as he walked past. "Friends of yours?"

"No, not really." Molly dropped her eyes to the floor. "Friends of friends, that's all."

Jack raised his eyebrows. He didn't believe her but it was none of his business. "Can you manage on your own for half an hour?" he asked, heading towards the kitchen. "My delivery for the marquee has arrived." Molly nodded and moved behind the bar.

"Molly, can I settle up?" It was Harry, she hadn't heard him approach. "I'd like a quick word too, if that's OK."

She looked around to see if anyone else was listening. Harry's friend was talking on his phone and a couple sitting nearby were just finishing their coffees. The walkers that Jack had served were tucking into their food and a group of women at the back of the pub had only just bought another bottle of wine, they'd be here for a while yet. She printed off Harry's lunch bill, took the card he offered her and fed the total into the card machine. "I don't want to hear anything you've got to say Harry. It won't change anything. I said everything I had to say last night."

"You don't mean that. I miss you Babe."

"Don't call me that." Her voice rose a little. "I'm not your babes."

Harry looked behind him, checking to see if anyone was listening, just as Molly had done a few seconds earlier. "Don't shout Babe, I need to see you." He handed the machine back to her and tried to touch her hand. His fingers connected with the wide leather strap of her watch.

"I ... said ... don't ... call ... me ... Babe." This time the couple sitting nearby turned to look at her. She took note and lowered her voice. "What are you doing here Harry?" Despite the whisper, her voice was harsh. "I told you to leave me alone. Don't cause trouble for me."

"I miss you B ..." he stopped in mid flow. "Sorry. But it's true, I do miss you. I've been a fool although, to be honest, I think I've had some bad press. I'm not seeing anyone else. Why would I when I've got you?"

"Really?" she whispered incredulously. "Bad press! Is that what you call it? I can think of other names for what you do but none are repeatable in here." She tore Harry's receipt from the machine and threw it on the bar. "And if you think I can be bought off with flowers from Ethel's garden or fancy florists then you really don't know me at all."

Harry frowned. "Ethel's garden? Flowers? I don't know what you're talking about. Look, let me explain. Over a coffee?" He leant closer over the bar and whispered. "What time do you finish? Do you want me to come round?"

Molly turned her back on him. "I hope you enjoyed your lunch."

"Later then?" he asked. "This evening? We can talk about the weekend. I'll be home alone, remember?"

Molly couldn't help herself, she turned back to face him. "Harry, you lied to me, and you nearly got me into trouble with Kate."

"What?! Kate knows?" Harry's smooth demeanour instantly changed.

"Oh, don't panic Harry, you're safe," Molly said sarcastically. "She doesn't know about you. But she guessed I was seeing someone. Kate's not stupid."

Harry patted his chest dramatically, as if he were having palpitations. "Shit! I thought you'd told her it was me." He turned briefly to look at his friend who'd finished his call and was putting on his coat. Turning back to Molly he said, "Wow, you had me worried."

"Worried about what?" It was Sophie.

"Sophie." Molly was startled. "I didn't hear you. You gave me a fright."

"Sorry," Sophie patted Molly's arm and smiled at her reassuringly. She turned to Harry. "Is everything OK here? What were you worried about Sir?" Molly spotted the appreciative look Harry gave Sophie. His eyes lingered just a little too long on Sophie's slim waist and generous bust.

"Nothing wrong at all. Just having a laugh about my card," Harry joked. "The wife's been on a spending spree recently. For a minute, I thought it was going to be declined." Sophie smiled but said nothing. She'd worked in hospitality a long time, she knew when she was being fobbed off. "I'd best be off. Please give my compliments to the chef." Harry stepped away from the bar. "My food was superb. I appreciate you going the extra mile to explain the ingredients in so much detail on your menus. So helpful for someone like me."

"Someone like you?" Sophie was confused.

"I have a severe peanut allergy. Not many people understand the consequences. For the sake of a few quid some restaurants are prepared to play fast and loose with our lives. People can die." He stopped and ran his hand through his thick, blond hair. "Sorry, lecture over. I just wanted to say it's nice to see how much you care." The look he gave Sophie would have made most women melt but Sophie remained impassive and it was Harry's turn to look confused. "Anyway, it was good to see you Molly. See you again soon, I hope."

As the door banged shut behind Harry and his friend, Sophie turned to Molly and raised her eyebrows. "My sixth sense is going into orbit here Molly. Fill me in."

Molly could feel herself blushing. "Oh, that's just Harry, he's a local flirt. Ignore him."

"Really? Well he's a good-looking flirt. Do you two have history?"

"No, absolutely not." Molly turned away quickly to clear a table. "Every woman in this town knows to steer well clear of Harry."

Chapter Seventeen

It was the end of the working day and Eddie was sitting in a long queue of cars outside the entrance to the station. A train had recently arrived from London and he watched as a flow of commuters emerged onto the steps. Most ran towards the waiting cars and taxis, or rushed over to the bus station. Each time he watched this hectic scenario, he thanked his lucky stars he didn't have to commute to another town, or city, to work. These unsmiling, tired looking people always reminded him of unhappy worker ants, scurrying repeatedly from one task to another. No matter what the financial reward might be, he would never want to join their ranks, life was too short.

The queue moved on and the cars slowly inched their way forward. Taxi drivers beeped their horns and people wandered aimlessly along the pavement searching for their lifts, their mobile phones glued to their ears, displeasure and fatigue etched on their faces in equal measure. Suddenly, the front passenger door flew open and Bobby climbed in, grinning broadly with the wires of his trademark earphones hanging loosely on each side of his face. And he wasn't alone. Eddie turned as Seth opened the rear passenger door and threw his rucksack in.

"Hi Dad." Bobby sank into the seat next to Eddie. "Look who I found on the train."

Eddie squeezed his son's shoulder. A gesture that said, 'Welcome home, I've missed you.' He simultaneously turned around and smiled at Seth. "I heard a rumour you might be showing your face over the holidays. It's really good to see you Seth."

Seth pulled on his seatbelt and returned the smile. "Thanks Eddie. I'm a day early. I'm going to surprise Mum."

"She'll be really pleased to see you. Where do you want me to drop you? At the cottage or at the pub?" Seth looked confused. "She's got a job at The Crown. Didn't you know?"

"No," said Seth slowly, a little crestfallen. "That's bad of me, isn't it?"

"Don't worry about it. She's only been working there a few weeks." Eddie pulled the car out from the queue of traffic. "Why don't we drive up to the pub? A good excuse for a quick pint, eh boys? If she's not there, I'll drop you at the cottage."

"Gets my vote," Bobby said eagerly. "I could murder a beer. As long as Mum's not waiting for us?" He looked innocently at his father.

Eddie laughed. "Drop the act Bobby. Your priority is beer. Even your Mum knows that! "

Jack was behind the bar when Bobby and Seth walked noisily into the pub. For a moment, he didn't spot Eddie behind the tall, lithe youngsters.

"Hi Jack, meet Bobby and Seth." Eddie gestured to the boys. "One's mine and one's Molly's."

"Nice to meet you lads." Jack shook hands with both boys. "Home for Easter I take it?"

"Yup," said Bobby. "Three whole weeks." Jack was struck by the family resemblance, although Bobby was considerably taller than his father. They both had the same easy going and approachable manner, Bobby might just be a chip off the old block.

"Is my mum working tonight?" asked Seth, looking around the pub. "I've come home early. I wanted to surprise her." He seemed impressed by his surroundings. "This place has changed, hasn't it Bob?" Bobby was already drinking greedily from a pint Jack had handed him, he nodded as he licked his lips.

"Molly's not working tonight Seth," said Jack. "Sorry, she didn't mention her plans. I don't know what she's doing."

"OK Bobby," said Eddie who had been texting Kate. "I have orders to get you back in an hour. Seth, you can always stay at ours, if we can't track Molly down."

"Great," said Bobby and Seth in unison. Jack laughed, he and Eddie had been like this, always ready for a few beers. The smile that had come with the laugh faded quickly though, Will had been part of that carefree world too.

Just under an hour later Eddie stopped his car outside Molly's cottage and Seth got out. "Looks like she's home," he said, hitching his rucksack over one shoulder. "I can see a light on."

Eddie looked over at the single light shining weakly from the small window next to the front door. "I'll hang on, just in case."

Seth pushed open the low-level gate and walked quickly up to the front door. He didn't have a key; this cottage had never been his home. He knocked three times with his knuckles, noticing for the first time the numbers on the door. One and three, thirteen, not the best number on the street. He put his ear to the door, music was faintly playing. A childhood memory came momentarily to mind; his mother doing the housework at Willow Hill. She'd always played loud music when she was cleaning. From his bedroom, the noise had seemed to resonate off the walls. It was only recently that he had matched this memory with his liking for rock music. He looked back at Eddie and shrugged his shoulders. "Going to take a look round the back," he called.

The path that led to the back of the cottage was narrow and Seth stumbled on a loose paving slab. He cursed quietly, as he steadied himself, and looked through the kitchen window. Two sets of keys had been left on the table. He knocked loudly on the door and waited, still no response. He turned the door handle but it wouldn't budge; the door was locked. About to give up and return to the car, he spotted the cat flap. It made him think of his father. Lowering himself to the ground, he put his shoulder to the door and reached through the opening until his hand found the key. "Yes!" He let out a small, triumphant laugh. God bless his mother and her habits. He turned the key anti-clockwise, rejoicing inwardly as the mechanism moved. Standing back, he wiped his hands on his jeans and tried the handle once more; the door swung open. The music was louder now. It wasn't the rock music he had known as a child but something more melodic. His mother's tastes in music must have mellowed.

Shutting the door gently behind him, Seth walked quietly through to the sitting room. The light from the small lamp in the window by the door, threw shadows into the neat and tidy room. Following the sound of the music, he walked towards the staircase in the opposite corner of the room. A pair of men's expensive looking, tan coloured, leather lace-up shoes were resting on the bottom step. He stepped quickly back into the shadows as a man laughed upstairs. A woman's giggle followed, his mother's giggle.

A young boy was standing in front of a white door, his freckled nose level with the chrome handle. He was wearing red and white striped pyjamas and his feet were bare, his little toes sank into the carpet. He was sleepy and disorientated, strange moaning noises were coming from the other side of the door. "Mummy."

More muffled noises from upstairs and a deep voice calling his mother's name, startled him. He crept back to the kitchen intending to leave as quickly, and as quietly, as he could but the keys on the table caught his eye. It was easy to spot his mother's set. A small keyring held a photo of himself as a much younger child, a happy little boy on a tricycle. A lifetime ago. The second set of keys were larger, seemingly more masculine. A couple of Yale keys and a small memory stick had been attached to a chunky BMW smart key. Nothing personal, no pictures of small children. On impulse, he pulled the memory stick from the keyring and put it in his pocket. Back outside, he dropped to the floor and, once again, put his arm through the cat flap.

He shook his head as he approached Eddie's car. "No answer I'm afraid. Is it OK if I stay with you guys tonight?"

Chapter Eighteen

Molly was alone in the Ladies toilets, trying on one of the shirts she had ordered for the pub. The short sleeved, black polo shirt had a small crown motif in the top left-hand corner. She was pleased, it looked simple but effective. She grabbed her bag and walked briskly into the kitchen where Kim was putting bacon under the grill. Doris was unpacking a vegetable delivery at the back of the room. "What do you think?" she asked, pirouetting in front of Kim. "Work in progress but not bad for a first effort, don't you think?"

Kim stood back with her hands on her hips. "That looks the business, Molly. Good job."

"Really?" Molly was thrilled with the praise. "I took a bit of a risk not getting Sophie, or Jack, to approve them but I was short of time." She looked down at her shirt. "I love them."

"So do I." Kim giggled, as Molly continued to pirouette around the kitchen. "You've got a spring in your step this morning lady. It's nice to see."

Molly beamed at Kim. "My son's coming home from university today, I'm so excited."

"Ah, is that it?" said Kim, buttering several large slices of fresh bread. "For a moment, I thought you'd been struck by Cupid's love arrow."

Molly stopped dancing immediately. She was truly excited that Seth was coming home but Kim had touched a nerve. She'd been weak, had given in to Harry. It wasn't going to happen again. "Good God no … I avoid all that. Been there, got the bad memories. It's just that I haven't seen Seth for months. I'm quite giddy."

"Are you bringing Seth to this little soirée Sophie is organising at the weekend?" Kim asked.

"I am indeed," Molly replied, relieved that Kim had changed the subject. "I'm really looking forward to it."

"So am I," said Kim. "It will be nice to get out of these for a change." She pointed to her chef's whites. "Here, can you take this order through please? Table four."

Molly was surprised to see how busy the bar was, the holiday weekend had started early. After delivering the two plates of food to a couple sitting at the far end of the room, she slid round behind the bar, tapping Jack on the shoulder as she did so and mouthing a greeting. They worked comfortably alongside each other, dealing with the breakfast rush for another twenty minutes before Jack noticed the polo shirt.

"How good does that look!" He smiled broadly at Molly. "Where's mine?"

"There's a bag in the kitchen with several different sizes. I only ordered twenty to start with. I wanted to be sure you and Sophie were happy with them." Molly looked worried.

"They're great." Jack twirled Molly round to get a proper look. "Hope you ordered an extra-large for me."

"Yes, I did." Molly was relieved with Jack's positive response. She could feel herself blushing slightly. "I'm so pleased you like them."

Jack started stacking glasses in the dishwasher. "I bet you were chuffed to see Seth last night. He's a nice lad Molly, you must be proud."

Molly's stomach flipped and she stared at Jack's back, as he continued to load the dishwasher. When she spoke, her voice was tight. "Seth?"

Jack turned to look at her. "Shit! Me and my big mouth. He didn't find you, did he? Sorry Molly, I just assumed you'd be at home."

"I don't know what you're talking about Jack."

"Eddie brought Seth and Bobby in here last night. Seth was looking for you. He wanted to surprise you by coming home early. He must have missed you. I'm so sorry Molly. Did you go out last night?"

"I had an early night ... I didn't know."

"Don't panic. You weren't meant to know. He wanted to surprise you." Jack placed a reassuring hand on Molly's arm. Her skin felt slightly sticky to the touch. "Eddie was with him. He probably stayed at Kate's."

"But he didn't call me." She looked away, she didn't want to cry in front of Jack.

"Maybe he didn't want to disturb you? He'll probably call you once he surfaces this morning."

Molly smiled weakly and walked slowly away to collect some plates from a nearby table. Her son, the child who had distanced himself from her, had come home early, had wanted to surprise her. This was such good news, such a step forward, she should have been elated. She imagined Seth knocking at her door, smiling, eager to see her. She'd done it again, she'd let her son down. A saving grace was that Seth didn't have a key to the cottage, what could have happened didn't bear thinking about.

"Nice shirt Molly," Sophie said, surprising her. "Did you get enough for everyone?"

Molly blinked rapidly. "Yes ... although I didn't want to get too many, just in case you didn't like them."

"I love them. Would you be able to order some more?" Sophie caught the look on Molly's face. "Molly, you look like you've seen a ghost. Are you OK?"

Molly nodded. "Sorry, I was miles away." She looked at her watch, it was only a little after ten. She'd text Seth when she finished work and meet up with him. She'd make it up to him, she'd tell him the truth. It was time to put Seth first.

***

Dressed in just their shorts and T-shirts, Bobby and Seth were sitting on the sofa in the playroom, eating huge bacon sandwiches. Lottie, as usual, had placed herself at Bobby's feet, carefully watching for crumbs. Fine lines of drool hung precariously from both sides of her soft mouth. As Bobby reached the end of his sandwich, he pulled off a crust and gave it to the waiting dog, stroking the top of her head as she rapidly consumed the treat.

Kate carried over two large mugs of tea and placed them on the coffee table. "Right, I'm off to work. What are you two doing today?" The two boys looked at each other and shrugged their shoulders.

"I'm hoping to locate Mum," Seth joked. "At least she's expecting to see me today."

"Have you called her yet?" Kate studied the blond-haired Seth. She had been pleasantly surprised to see the transformation in him when he'd arrived with Bobby the night before. Chatty and amusing, he was so different to the troubled teenager she remembered. University had clearly been good for him.

"No." Seth shook his head. "Do you think she'll be working today? I might pop into the pub and still try to surprise her."

"Now I like that idea," said Bobby, slapping his friend's thigh. "Shall we go for a lunchtime pint?"

Kate sighed. "Bobby! Anyone would think you couldn't go a day without a drink."

"I'm a student Mother! That's what we do."

Seth smiled at Kate. "Don't worry, I'll keep an eye on him."

Bobby picked up the nearest cushion and lobbed it at Seth. "Yeah right, lightweight. I'm not the one who needs looking after."

Seth sprang forward in playful retaliation and stuffed the cushion into Bobby's chest, pinning him back on the sofa. Kate smiled as she watched. This was a familiar scene, a scene that had played out in this room since these two were small boys. They were good friends and she hoped they always would be. She and Molly had that special friendship but as this thought popped into her head, she frowned. She wasn't sure their friendship was so healthy right now.

"Enough, enough," Bobby groaned coming up for air. "Shit! Have you been working out? You're stronger than you look."

"No, you've just gone soft." Seth released his hold on Bobby's arms. "I'm going for a run. Wanna come?"

"You on crack?" Bobby replied scornfully. "I'd rather have my toenails pulled out. I'll wait for you though. We can go for that beer."

Ten minutes later Seth was on his way. Cutting through the park, he joined the wide track that hugged the side of the river until he came to a small, brick bridge. The track narrowed here and he had to slow down as he passed a young couple with a small child in a pushchair. Several people were out walking their dogs. Each one obligingly pulled their pets to one side, as he ran past. Boats of all shapes and sizes were moored on this part of the river, the people working on them looked up and acknowledged him with a friendly nod or a smile. After nearly four miles, he turned to cross the river, using an old wooden footbridge which rattled disconcertingly. On the other side, he ran across the grass towards Willow Hill. The gradient meant that fewer people used this side of the river and he pushed himself hard to get to the top. Re-joining the road back into town, he stopped to catch his breath and looked back at the valley behind him. This pretty, little town was home but he had no affection for it, too many bad things had happened. Taking in the view, he realised he wasn't far from the house he'd lived in as a child, the house he'd shared with both his parents. Curiosity got the better of him and, pulling his headphones from his ears, he jogged down the road until he came to the entrance to the old vicarage. A long, gravel drive, lined by mature oak trees led to a tall, carefully manicured hedge and a set of wrought iron gates, behind which stood the imposing red brick house. The years fell away, everything looked and felt incredibly familiar. He started to walk, tentatively, down the drive, glancing behind every few steps. At the iron gates, he stopped and looked up at the house. His eyes were drawn immediately to an upstairs window, his old bedroom window. The image of what he'd seen and heard in his mother's cottage the night before floated into his mind. Things like that had happened in this house too.

 He pulled the gates open slightly, surprised to feel them move so easily. For some reason, he'd assumed they would offer more resistance. Squeezing through the gap, he approached the house; the gravel crunched noisily under his trainers. All the curtains on the ground floor were pulled shut and the house gave the impression of having been mothballed. Following a wide, hedge-lined path he skirted the side of the house, stopping only when the path merged with a wide terrace. Looking around, he was confused by the vast panorama of the back garden. It wasn't a layout he remembered. Something had changed, something was missing.

A young, skinny, blond haired boy was running in the garden, laughing and squealing with excitement. A dog, a bouncy, young, black dog was chasing him, barking excitedly and jumping up at the boy's hand as he ran. The boy had a yellow ball in his hand, a tennis ball. It was the dog's ball.

Seth looked down at his own hand. His fingers were cupped, as if he was cradling a ball. He flexed his fingers and shook his hand, he was imagining things. At one end of the terrace, garden furniture had been carefully wrapped up for the winter in protective green covers. Seth peered through the windows at the back of the house but, once again, all the curtains had been pulled tightly shut. He walked to the far edge of the terrace where a narrow stone path followed the slope of the grass. It came to an abrupt end after about thirty metres, as if it hadn't been finished, it didn't lead anywhere. Seth walked slowly along the path, trying to remember where it had led but the memory wouldn't come. Like so many memories, it was firmly locked away. He vaguely recalled a big wooden trellis, covered in a thick layer of ivy, an oblong wall of green.

The boy was running again but this time he was running away from something. He ran across a stretch of green grass, as fast as his long, skinny legs would take him. The boy was bare chested. He looked frightened, his mouth was open, the boy was screaming.

Seth shivered, his body had cooled down and he was getting cold. He shouldn't be here, it was time to leave.

Back at Bobby's house he headed for the shower. He'd known his way around this house since he was a little boy and, as he walked across the landing towards the bathroom, he collected a towel from the cupboard that housed the hot water tank. In many ways, this house felt like home, he had nothing but good memories. Something he certainly couldn't say about the other house he'd just seen. Stepping under the hot water, he let his thoughts wander, cautiously, back to his childhood. On a day to day basis, this wasn't something he allowed himself to do. It was a taboo subject but going to Willow Hill had opened a door. He wasn't sure it was a wise move but, standing under the hot water, he gave his mind permission to skirt around the memories he'd fought so hard to bury.

He'd had a lot of therapy. His tutor at uni had suggested it, had almost insisted on it. And, despite his reluctance and occasional bad humour, the therapy had helped, he'd learnt how to deal with the past. Most of the bad memories were firmly packed away, compartmentalised into the 'before' and 'after.' The images that he'd conjured up earlier at Willow Hill seemed to have little significance, he couldn't tap into their relevance.

Going to university and working with a tutor who recognised his urgent need for help was, without doubt, the best thing that could have happened to Seth. It had literally saved him from himself and taught him that, fundamentally, he wasn't alone, most people had demons. Seth had gone to Newcastle a quiet, angry and deeply disturbed teenager. He liked to think that person belonged in the past. He'd moved on. Ultimately, he'd grown up. He'd be lying though, if he said his visit to Willow Hill hadn't troubled him. The lid had come off the memory box surprisingly quickly and he was, disturbingly, completely unprepared.

Pulling on his jeans ten minutes later, his hand brushed against the memory stick he'd taken from his mother's cottage the night before. He placed it on the palm of one hand and slowly turned it over with the other. He was unsure now, in the cold light of day, why he'd taken it. It was something the old Seth would have done, the devious Seth, the pre-therapy Seth. He slowly put the memory stick back in his pocket, he'd find a way to return it to its rightful owner. Whatever had happened in the past, his mother was entitled to a life.

***

Eddie was looking out of the window at the far end of his office, watching cars come and go from the car park. Today was his last day at work before the Easter break and he was feeling 'demob' happy. Bobby was already home and Lucy would be back in a few hours and, thankfully, Kate seemed well. He was looking forward to some time off with his family. The phone on his desk buzzed and the receptionist informed him he had a visitor, a Mr. Fox.

"What brings you here?" he asked, as he opened his office door. Jack's wide, tall frame almost filled the corridor outside.

"I haven't got a lot of time but I wanted to pick your brain mate," Jack said, shaking Eddie's hand.

"Can't guarantee you'll find anything." Eddie closed the door behind him. "Coffee?"

Jack nodded and sat down on the leather chair Eddie pulled out. He waited patiently while his friend called the receptionist to ask for two coffees. "Eddie, can you tell me why it's such bad news that James might be back?" he asked, as soon as Eddie put the phone down.

Eddie was surprised. "What makes you ask that?"

Jack sighed. "He came into the bloody pub."

"Shit! When?" Eddie sat forward in his seat. "Are you sure it was him? Did you speak to him?"

Jack held up his hands to stop the onslaught of questions. "It was him. Randomly Sophie met him on the train. It's a long story and a total fluke. But then she saw a photograph of him in Molly's bag. He introduced himself as JP."

"Molly carries a photo of him?" Eddie was shocked.

"Seth was in the photo too," Jack explained. "Tell me Ed. Why is he such bad news?"

Eddie sat back in his chair. "He's dangerous Jack."

"So everyone keeps saying." There was evident frustration in Jack's voice. "But how dangerous? I know you think he had something to do with Will, and even Tim. But where's the evidence?"

Eddie shook his head. "I know, I told you it was just a hunch. I've read everything I can find online and there's no hint of any foul play." He paused for breath. "Maybe I just want to pin their deaths on him. I'm not sure why. He unsettles me."

"He bloody well unsettles me too. Thanks to you!" Jack exclaimed.

Eddie sighed. "It's complicated Jack. James is complicated." The receptionist tapped at the door and placed their coffees on the table. Eddie smiled and thanked her, waiting until she had shut the door behind her before continuing. "I think what he did to Molly would come under the 'abuse' banner. More emotional than physical, although there was a fair amount of physical."

"But you said he only attacked her once." Jack was a man for detail.

"There was only one sustained attack but he was still violent," Eddie said slowly.

"Fuck it, Eddie." Jack banged the palm of his hand on the table, spilling his coffee. "Why are you being so economical with the truth?"

Eddie put his coffee down. "OK, OK. James was clever. Twisted maybe but clever. When he found out about Molly's affair with Tim, he played mind games with her. There was the one serious incident of physical violence. We told you about that, didn't we?" Jack nodded. "It's not my place to say any of this Jack but I think he took to thumping her occasionally too, to keep her in check. Kate will kill me for saying this to you."

"What the hell? Why would Kate not say that before?"

"Calm down mate. She was only providing you with a reference for a job, wasn't she?" Eddie defended his wife. "She wasn't giving you a fucking witness statement."

"Sorry Eddie, I didn't mean to offend ... and I am grateful to Kate." Jack held up his hands, a conciliatory gesture. "I'm just shocked. If you knew it was going on, why didn't you do something about it?"

"Like what? Molly wouldn't report him and there was rarely any proof. I think she learnt how to avoid making him cross and, gradually, it got better. Until the affair with Will."

"Shit Eddie, what are you hiding? If he's that dangerous I need to know. Sophie tried to befriend him. He came into the pub looking for her. But then he got edgy, like he'd been caught. I may be way off the mark, I certainly hope so, but I don't want my wife put in any danger."

"He wouldn't hurt Sophie," Eddie said quietly. "He's only ever wanted one woman."

"Have you ever thought he might hurt someone to get to Molly?" Jack asked.

"He's a bully Jack, a violent bully. And like most bullies he picks on the most vulnerable. He wouldn't hurt Sophie."

"Did he ever hurt Seth?" Jack's tone was softer. He was reverting to type, he was trying to coax information out of Eddie.

"Not directly, not physically." Eddie sipped his coffee, fighting for time. He needed to steer the conversation away from Seth. He'd promised Kate.

"Not directly? What does that mean?"

Eddie sighed and took off his glasses. "Look. I'll give you an example. You know Lottie? Our dog, Lottie?"

Jack nodded. "Where are you going with this Eddie?"

"We've always had dogs, me and Kate. We wouldn't have it any other way. Some people don't get it but that's just the way we are. Our family wouldn't be complete without a dog." He looked over at the photo of Lottie on his desk. "When we got Lottie, Seth came with us. He was always with us to be fair. He was there the day we went to see the litter of puppies; dead cute they were." Jack smiled but said nothing. "Seth was a bit of a spoilt brat back then. He kicked up a big fuss about wanting a dog himself. Just like his mother, Seth got everything he wanted. He wanted a puppy and he got one, named him Scooby."

"I'm still not sure where this is going," said Jack quietly.

Eddie held up his hand to stop Jack talking. "Lottie's over twelve now, so Seth would have been about seven or eight I think. He was old enough to learn how to care for a dog. James was surprisingly keen on the idea. Remember, this was before he and Molly had any problems, before Tim. He was traveling a lot, he liked the idea of a dog being in the house when he wasn't around." Eddie looked at the photos of the kids and Lottie again. "Scooby was a huge success. I think he filled a gap with Seth being an only child. They were inseparable. He put our Lottie to shame. He was the clever one of the litter but he wasn't keen on James. We used to think it was a possessive thing, with James being away so much. He wasn't aggressive towards him or anything like that. He just gave him a wide berth. Like I said, he was clever." Eddie got up and walked over to the window that looked down on the car park. He was quiet for a few seconds.

"Eddie?" said Jack. "What is it?"

"Molly told James about the affair with Will herself. She didn't want him to find out any other way. Not like he had with Tim."

"You're losing me Ed." Jack tried to pull Eddie back to the story.

"We didn't know about the affair Jack. Maybe if she'd told us, or told Kate, things might have worked out differently." Eddie turned back from the window, his face downcast. "We only found out when James turned up at our house with Scooby, a dead Scooby."

"Dead?" Jack's voice rose. "What has a dead dog got to do with this?"

"I think it was a Sunday morning. Kate had taken the kids swimming. I was in the kitchen. I saw him come through our garden gate. He had the dog in his arms and he laid him on the grass. The poor thing was a mess, there was blood everywhere. I remember checking Lottie was with me. For a dreadful moment I thought it was her." Eddie's voice caught in his throat and he gulped. "James said Scooby had been knocked down by a van and that Molly was on her way. Then he just left, he walked away. He left me alone with his dead dog."

"I'm still not following you Eddie," Jack said gently, as Eddie brushed away a tear.

"Molly arrived shortly afterwards. She had the start of a black eye, a gift from James." Eddie grimaced. "She'd told James about Will. They'd been walking with Scooby. She'd planned it that way. She'd wanted to be out of the house. She thought she'd be safer in broad daylight."

"Let me get this straight. Are you saying James punched Molly and killed the dog?" asked Jack.

Eddie nodded slowly. "It didn't go well, he didn't take the news well. I think he flipped. Forgot where he was."

"And the dog?" Jack had to prompt Eddie to continue.

"Scooby was collateral damage, wrong place, wrong time." Eddie stuttered over the words. "They were walking up by the flyover. James got violent hence the black eye." Jack had a feeling he knew how this story was going to end but he remained silent. "He's a loose cannon Jack. It could easily have been Molly. He told her it was a warning. What he could do to the dog, he could do to her."

"What did he do? The dog didn't get hit by a van, did he?"

Eddie's eyes were watering again and he sniffed loudly. "James threw that poor, defenceless creature off the flyover. Scooby never stood a chance."

Jack walked to the window and put his hand on his friend's shoulder. "Bastard." The two men stood together for a while, both staring out of the window. "He is dangerous then," Jack said at last. "Disturbed at the very least."

"When I said he walked away, I mean he literally walked out of our lives." Eddie wiped the tears from his eyes again. "He walked away and never came back. I assumed he went to France."

"But the news was out I take it? Molly and Will were official?" Jack was trying to form a timeline in his mind.

"Well no, not really. Will told Fiona at around the same time." Eddie took a tissue from his desk and blew his nose. "Molly and Will had agreed to do that. But Will died just a couple of days later."

Jack turned sharply to face his friend. "And it never entered your head that James might have had a hand in his death?"

"Bloody hell no! I've told you, I only started to think that could be possible recently. I'm a chartered surveyor Jack, I have a habit of believing what people tell me."

"Sorry Ed. Old habits." Jack paced the room. "Eddie, I'm sorry to have to ask but is there anything else you haven't told me?"

Eddie kept his eyes on the car park. There was plenty left to tell. "Probably," he said. "It was a period of time I don't like to think about."

"OK," sighed Jack. "I understand that. Look, I don't want to alarm you but I think we should keep an eye on James for a while. I'm not going along with your theory about Tim. I doubt whether there's anything to disprove. His accident was probably just that, a tragic accident but I have some suspicions about Will."

Eddie turned, hope illuminated his face. "Really?"

"Don't get excited mate. There's very little we can do to prove James was involved, even if he was. But I'd like to have him on the radar. The appointment card Kate found? When was James supposed to go back to the hospital?"

Chapter Nineteen

Annie had been trying to pack her bag for over an hour but with little success. She had absolutely no idea what you needed for a few days in a country pub and Sophie had offered little advice.

"Just normal stuff, everyday stuff," Sophie had replied when Annie had posed the question. For Annie that meant skinny jeans and trainers, unless she was working, then it was standard issue uniform and steel capped boots. To cover all bases, she put her weekend bag back in the cupboard and selected a larger suitcase and threw clothes for all occasions in it. She was just pulling the zip shut when her phone rang.

"Annie, what time are you due in?" Jack asked.

"Sixteen hundred hours, Sir," Annie said automatically and then laughed. She couldn't drop the habit. "Sorry, four o'clock Jack."

"Great, that means you can do something for me before you catch your train. I'll put the details in a text. You might need to call in a few favours."

Annie put the phone down and checked her watch. It was only ten o'clock, she should have enough time to do whatever it was Jack wanted. She had planned to pop out and buy something nice for Sophie and Jack, a little gift for their new home but that might need to be put on hold for now. The text from Jack came through in less than a minute.

Can you go to Orthopaedic Outpatients @ Royal London?
James Pope. Mid 40's, 6'2", dark hair, lean build
11.15 appt. May have a limp
Let me know if he turns up and get home address?
Bottle of Malbec waiting for you

Jack had sent a photograph with the text which revealed a white, averagely good-looking man with dark hair. Annie saw hundreds of men every week, there was nothing different about this one. Jack was right, she was going to have to call in a favour. She pressed a speed dial number on her phone and waited for one of her colleagues to answer. When he did, no introductions were necessary. "Tom, I need an ID check." She cradled her phone between her shoulder and her ear and reopened her suitcase. She'd changed her mind, she was going to travel light after all. Grabbing a rucksack from her spare room, she went back to the suitcase she'd just finished packing. She reopened it and transferred the essentials to the rucksack. Tom came back on the line.

"Got a pen?" he asked.

"Can you text me?" She was being cheeky but her hands were full.

"Beers on you," Tom said and the line went dead. Annie smiled. Tom hadn't asked what was going on, and he certainly wouldn't have waited for a thank you. They were old colleagues, they just got on with the job. Grabbing her leather jacket, she swung her rucksack onto one shoulder and picked up her house keys. As she walked out to the street, she typed a quick message to Jack.

On my way. Will keep you posted.

Tom's message appeared on her screen.

James Pope, date of birth, 18.09.70. Flat 22, Stenton House, St. Archibald's Road, Canary Wharf. No convictions. Next of kin Molly Pope.

Annie was intrigued and excited. Jack was behaving like a policeman, maybe her visit to the country would be interesting after all.

***

It was ten forty-five when Annie walked through the main entrance of the busy hospital. This was familiar territory. This hospital had been on her patch when she was a rookie, she knew her way around. She headed straight to the coffee shop and purchased a large mocha before starting the long trek to Orthopaedic Outpatients. Walking slowly, she discreetly observed the people around her. She'd done this kind of thing a million times before but she still got a buzz from it and today, on a day off and out of uniform, it felt different somehow. In the tired-looking waiting area, she picked up an even more tired looking magazine. In a bid to stop anyone trying to make idle conversation with her, she plugged in her earphones but she didn't play any music, she just wanted to appear unapproachable. Slowly sipping the coffee, she scanned the room. Several small children, bored with being forced to sit still, had taken to running around the back to back, plastic seating. Their high-pitched, excitable screaming was clearly grating on the patience of those around them. Annie took no notice, focusing instead on the men in the room. Most were elderly apart from a young, self-conscious adolescent wearing a brace on his foot. Confident her man hadn't arrived, she pulled her phone from her pocket and studied the photo Jack had sent. She scanned the elderly gentlemen in the room again, double-checking their faces before typing out a message to Jack.

In situ. Nothing yet. Home address is Canary Wharf.
What's he done?

Jack responded instantly.

Not sure. Possible harassment, domestic violence, maybe more.

Annie looked up as a middle-aged woman in a wheelchair tried, unsuccessfully, to negotiate her way around the noisy children and their toys. Exasperated by the lack of help on offer from the useless parents, Annie got up, the magazine still in her hand, and helped the lady clear a path through to the nurses' station. She was forced to shout at the children to get their attention. Some of the parents glanced up but said nothing. Raised voices was clearly something they were used to. A tall man came through the double doors as Annie sat back down. The dark, expensive looking overcoat and what looked like a cashmere scarf set him apart from the other people in the room. Dropping her eyes to the floor, just for a second, she clocked the highly polished, dark-brown loafers. This man certainly wasn't trying to be discreet.

"I'm here for a follow up appointment," she heard him say, in a voice that demanded attention. "I think it's at eleven fifteen but I've lost the card I was given." He had an average accent, nothing too posh but classier than her own east London twang. The nurse consulted her computer and said something that Annie couldn't quite hear, the man turned to take a seat. A small sneer appeared on his face when he spotted two small boys climbing over some empty seats and he purposely gave them a wide berth. Annie looked up innocently, seemingly engrossed in her music. She took a good look at his face. It was him, she had her man. She typed a message to Jack.

He's here

***

James had learnt, from bitter experience, that hospital follow up appointments were an opportunity to ask questions most GP's couldn't answer. He didn't want to be here but, as a runner, the last thing he needed was a serious knee injury. Sitting down on an uncomfortable plastic seat, he picked up a magazine from the table next to him but put it down when he saw the date of publication, it wasn't yesterday's news, it was last year's. Shaking his head in disbelief, he fished his phone from his pocket and opened Facebook. There wasn't much else he could do whilst he waited and the good old NHS would, no doubt, keep him waiting a while yet.

As usual, he went straight to Seth's page, surprised to see his son had just been tagged in a new post by Molly. The woman who did so little on Facebook was suddenly becoming a regular contributor. The post showed a photograph of a smiling Seth with another young man. They were sitting on a large, leather sofa, behind a low, wooden table and they were holding pints of beer. Molly stood behind them with a tray of empty glasses in her hands. She was smiling broadly into the camera. He studied her closely; one day, she'd smile at him that way again. He traced her image on the screen with his finger. He still knew every inch of her so well, the blond hair, the blue eyes, the pale skin around her neck, the carefully applied make-up. Sophie, the attractive woman he'd met on the train, was standing at the edge of the photograph. Both she and Molly were wearing black polo shirts, they looked like uniform issue. He enlarged the photo and studied the shirts; Molly was working for Sophie, she was a barmaid. The rota he'd seen in her kitchen was from the pub. He frowned, he didn't like this. Being a waitress was one thing but working behind the bar in a small-town pub was quite another. An incorrigible flirt, Molly would have relished the male attention. He half-heartedly wondered if she was sleeping with the boss himself, with Jack Fox but then he looked again at Sophie. Jack didn't need to look elsewhere, he had all he could ever want at home.

James looked up as a screaming child fought with its mother. Unwilling to be strapped back into its buggy, the child, a little boy, had thrown himself on the floor in defiance and refused to move. The mother, embarrassed and close to tears, made an unorthodox decision, pushing the empty buggy, she headed for the exit. Sensing danger, the child panicked and ran after her, screaming even louder. James glanced at a woman sitting to his left but she was wearing headphones and her head bobbed to a rhythm no-one else could hear, she was clearly untroubled by the noisy youngster. Wincing as the child started to scream again, he turned back to his phone wishing he too had some earphones. Refreshing the Facebook page, he noticed plenty of people had liked Molly's photograph and a couple had already posted comments. It still surprised him how many people were tuned in to social media, no matter what the hour of day. He scrolled down the list of names who had liked the photograph. Lucy, Kate's daughter, was the only name he recognised. With time to kill, he clicked on each individual's page quickly discovering most were students, friends of both Seth and the young man with him who appeared to be Bobby, Kate's son. The last name he clicked on sounded vaguely familiar. Opening the page, he remembered that Harry Smith was Kate's brother in law, the poor guy who'd married the overbearing Patty. That wasn't so odd he supposed, Bobby was in the photograph and Bobby was his nephew by marriage. The guy's page and the fabulous photographs of sunny, green vineyards were as intoxicating as the last time he'd looked. His eyes were drawn again to the photograph of multiple champagne bottles nestling on a wooden table. He enlarged the photograph and studied the green and gold labels. A creeping sense of realisation engulfed him, he'd seen these labels before, he'd seen them in Molly's kitchen. He cursed loudly. An old man in the seat behind tutted disapprovingly. The young woman in the headphones caught his eye but she gave him a bored, disinterested look and turned back to her phone, to the message she was typing. He looked back at the photograph; his mind was racing, he was furious.

"James Pope." He was vaguely aware of a nurse calling his name. "James Pope," the nurse called again, more loudly. James stood up and marched briskly towards her.

Bad guys came in all shapes and sizes, Annie knew that more than most people but this man didn't look dangerous and he certainly didn't conform to any criminal stereotype. As the curtain closed behind James, she typed out a message to Jack.

With Medic. No limp. Seems pissed off?

Jack responded immediately.

Great. Be careful x

Annie smiled. Those two words had always been Jack's hand off. No matter the nature of the job, he'd always asked his team to be careful. Watching the striped curtain James Pope had disappeared behind, she was reminded how much she missed having Jack around. She didn't dislike his replacement but he had big shoes to fill, the team hadn't really been the same since Jack had quit.

James emerged from the cubicle after fifteen minutes and headed for the exit. Annie waited until he was nearly at the double doors, before she stood up to follow him. As a precaution, she pulled a woolly hat from the side pocket of her rucksack. Even though she'd done her best to look as though she was engrossed in both her music and her phone, she was pretty sure she'd been noticed. Out in the corridor, with no visible sign of any leg injury, James was already some distance ahead and Annie had to walk briskly to keep him in sight. Assuming that he was heading back to the main hospital entrance, she broke into a jog and pushed gently past several people. Skirting wide of James, she headed towards the revolving doors. The taxi rank was to the left of the exit, just near the patient drop-off area. She took a gamble and jogged over to the queue of waiting people, hoping that James would follow. Standing behind an old couple, Annie took her rucksack off and pretended to look for something inside. Glancing back to the hospital, she saw two young girls approaching, they were deep in conversation. Behind them, James was striding towards her. She looked away and waited. Several taxis drew up and the elderly couple inched their way cautiously to the curb. For a moment, Annie thought James was going to force his way past them but he stopped and waited his turn. Taking her time to open the door of her own taxi, Annie heard James bark an address at his driver.

"Jack, he's in a taxi ... he's going to Canary Wharf which tallies with his address," she said breathlessly when Jack picked up her call. "I'm in a taxi. I have time to follow him, if you want."

"Thanks Annie, great job," said Jack. "No need to follow him. You've tied up a loose end for me. I'll tell you more when I pick you up later."

***

Molly had been overjoyed to see Seth walk into the pub. Throwing her emotional caution to the wind, she had rushed from behind the bar, taken him in her arms and hugged him fiercely, slightly overwhelmed but delighted to feel him hug her back. Now, nearly twenty-four hours later, they were having a late breakfast in The Kitchen. Molly sensed a distinct change in her son. Physically, he looked the same but the sullen, distracted teenager seemed to have disappeared and a pleasant, well-mannered, young man had taken his place. She owed a debt of gratitude to Newcastle University.

"What are you grinning at?" Seth asked, as a waitress placed a generous portion of grilled bacon and scrambled eggs on the table in front of him.

"Nothing," Molly replied smiling. "It's just so good to see you. You look so well." Seth, mouth already full, grinned back at her. "I'm so sorry I missed you on Tuesday. I'm so cross with myself. Here, take this." She placed a silver Yale key on the table. "Get a copy made while I'm at work. That way you won't get locked out again."

"Stop apologising, it's no big deal." Seth was secretly thinking how embarrassing it could have been for both of them, if he'd had a key the other night. "It gave me a chance to catch up with the Bobster ... and Kate and Eddie."

"And the opportunity for a session yesterday too." Molly pulled a face. "You like a drink, you boys, don't you?"

Seth took a sip of his coffee and wiped his mouth with a paper serviette. "To quote Bobby 'we're students, that's what we do'. Although I agree, Bobby was on a mission. It was good fun though. And Lucy turning up was a real bonus. I expect she's got a monumental headache this morning though."

Molly smiled fondly at him. It had been so good to see the three kids together yesterday, even if she had been slightly shocked at how much booze they'd consumed. Several old school friends, who were also home for the Easter holidays, had joined them and it had turned into a noisy evening. Jack and Sophie had been very tolerant. Eventually, long after her shift had finished, she'd taken a slightly wobbly Seth home and put him to bed. She'd stood in the doorway for a while, listening to his breathing, cherishing the feeling of having him home. Whatever magic the people around him in Newcastle had performed, she was thankful, the change in Seth was miraculous.

"How long have you been working in the pub?" Seth asked, pushing his empty plate to one side. "The place has really changed and Jack and Sophie seem like good people."

"Not long, a few weeks," Molly replied. "Yes, they are ... good." She was surprised by his choice of words but it seemed an apt description. "Sophie has big plans for the place, and Kim, the chef, is bloody amazing. We'll eat there one night."

"Isn't there something happening this weekend?" Seth asked. "Kate mentioned it."

"Yes, there is," said Molly excitedly. "Sophie is putting on a little something for staff and friends. It will be nice to have some downtime together. I'm looking forward to it."

Seth studied his mother's eager face. Like his father, she looked good for her age, although she didn't have his advantage of a designer wardrobe. But she had something money couldn't buy, something James didn't have. Molly was altogether more approachable than James and she was quick to smile, even after all her heartache. She also seemed to have the ability to bounce back. He was glad to think that she might have met someone else and, just as he had tried to encourage his father to get on with his life, he decided to broach the same subject with his mother. "Do you have a date for this get together at the pub?" he asked, winking playfully.

Molly was startled. "A date?"

"Yes, you know ... a fella?" Seth persisted.

Molly started fiddling with her coffee cup, turning it slowly round and round on the table. "What makes you say that?" she asked quietly.

"Sorry, I was only joking Mum." Seth felt bad, his mother was embarrassed. "I wasn't prying, honestly. But it would be nice to meet someone, wouldn't it?"

"Has someone said something to you?" she asked timidly. Gossips were everywhere in this town.

"No. Is there something to tell?" he asked encouragingly. It really was none of his business but he wanted her to be happy. He couldn't mention what he'd seen and heard the other night, that wouldn't be fair, wouldn't do either of them any good but she was still a young woman, she had a life to lead. A few years ago, he would have confronted her about the near miss, or he might have saved it as ammunition to use cruelly, as and when an opportunity arose. Thankfully, he wasn't like that anymore. Many hours of discussion with his therapist should ensure that intentionally cruel acts towards his mother were no longer part of his behaviour pattern but her defensiveness surprised him. Maybe she just wasn't ready to go public, maybe the relationship was very new. Looking at her worried face, he decided not to push any more. If she needed more time, then that's what he'd give her. "I'll have to be your date then, won't I?" He was pleased to see her body relax and a smile return to her face. "Come on, you'll be late for work. I'll walk you up there and find somewhere to do this key."

***

The train was full to bursting and many passengers were forced to stand but there was some good-humoured banter being shared. The prospect of a long weekend was lightening the mood. Annie, sitting in a window seat, watched as the urban sprawl she knew so well, gave way to a less familiar, more rural vista. Born and bred from generations of city people, Annie rarely ventured out of the metropolis. The uniformity of the fields and the quintessentially English farmhouses, reminded her of pictures in the storybooks she and her sister had shared as small children. It all looked very pretty but it wasn't her cup of tea, she preferred the chaos of the concrete jungle.

The train slowed down and Annie watched, in fascination, as people started pulling their belongings together, simultaneously bumping into and apologising to one another. It amused her, it was so very British. Several long seconds ticked by until the doors opened, disembarking passengers waited patiently without complaining. Then, weighed down with laptop bags and briefcases, they poured quickly off the train, some stopping to replace the coats and jackets they had, briefly, taken off in the stuffy carriages. It made her think how very different most people's lives were to her own but she wouldn't trade places. She loved her job passionately. She wasn't convinced the people around her would say the same thing, if asked. Still watching the departing crowd as the train doors closed, someone on the platform caught her eye. He was near the back of the queue, waiting to go through the ticket barrier. The dawdlers behind him were obscuring her view but there was something familiar about his tall frame. She kept watching as the train pulled away but he didn't turn around and she lost interest. He could be anyone, she certainly came across a lot of people in her line of work.

Twenty minutes later she got off the train and headed towards the ticket barrier. Jack was waiting for her on the other side.

"Good to see you little lady." Jack swept her up in a huge bear hug. She squealed as her legs dangled in the air.

"Good to see you too but put me down. I can't breathe." She laughed as he released her.

"Thanks for earlier." Jack smiled down at her. "Like I said, you tied up some loose ends for me. Come on, this way."

"So, what's the story?' Annie trotted after Jack. "He didn't look very dodgy. Grumpy, definitely but not dodgy."

"It's complicated. He's complicated." Jack said. "I'm going to take you for a drink before we go back to the pub. I'll run you through it. But you'll need to keep it to yourself. A lot of people are involved. People you'll meet over the weekend. I have a funny feeling something is about to happen. I don't know what but the man you saw this morning is up to something and he concerns me. He's disturbed."

"Disturbed?" Annie asked, raising her eyebrows. "That's a new one. He's not a known offender. I checked."

They got into the van and Jack headed for a pub that would be quiet at this time of day and where no-one would know him. "From what I know James is affluent, well educated, and successful. Most of the time he functions normally, just as you and I do. In fact, probably better than you and me. Like I said, he's a success."

"And at other times?" Annie asked.

"A trigger, and it seems it's always the same trigger, interrupts the normal pattern of his life," Jack answered. "The status quo is disrupted with tragic consequences."

"And what's the trigger?"

"His ex-wife, a lady called Molly ... a member of staff."

"Ah ... OK ... interesting. And the consequences?"

Jack parked the car outside a dowdy looking pub on the outskirts of town. "Well, in addition to the harassment and violence that Molly has endured, there seems a possibility, and I stress that it's only a possibility ... but he may have something to do with the death of a man."

"Who?" Annie asked, as they walked inside the pub. Jack put a finger to his lips while they ordered their drinks. "So, who?" she asked again, as soon as they were seated.

"It won't sound plausible until I give you the background." Jack looked around the bar, it was almost empty. A couple of conservatively dressed, middle-aged men were sitting near a window and a group of younger men were playing on a fruit machine. Another man was sitting in the far corner with two children who were squabbling over a tablet. "Molly has had two affairs and both men have died," he said quietly, as he turned back to Annie. "And both men were friends of mine. I'm almost sure Tim, the first guy, died in an accident. Tragic but not suspicious. However, something's niggling at me about Will, the second guy."

Annie whistled softly, as she picked up her beer. "Now I'm interested. But before you tell me more, I've just realised there's something else I should tell you about this James."

Jack sipped his beer and grimaced at the taste. "You'll get a better pint later. What else?"

"It's weird but I think he was on my train," she said. "He got off two stops before me. I couldn't work out why I recognised this bloke although I only saw him from behind, which didn't help. I didn't give it much thought but now I'm sure. It was the bloke in the hospital this morning. It was your man, James."

"Shit! Are you sure?" Jack reached for his phone. "I need to tell Eddie."

Annie grabbed his arm. "No, you don't, not yet. First, you're going to tell me everything."

***

Seth spotted Lucy and Lottie walking slowly ahead of him. He picked up speed. "How's your head this morning, Lucy Loo?"

"Shit! You made me jump. Don't call me that ... you know I hate it." It was a childhood nickname, one she only tolerated from her parents. "I feel like death if you want the truth. You guys are animals." She looked up at

Seth, squinting slightly against the bright sun as she did so. "What about you? How do you feel?"

"Fine and dandy," he said, making a fuss of Lottie. "Ran it off this morning. Would a coffee help?"

"Difficult." Lucy held up Lottie's lead. "Dogs not welcome."

"What about a take-out and a bench?" He pointed to a group of wooden benches outside the entrance to the grounds of St. Mary's, the old Catholic church. "The sun's out."

Lucy nodded and followed Seth across the road towards the coffee shop. "It was a good night, wasn't it? What I remember any way."

Seth laughed. "Yes, it was. Maybe we should do it more often?"

Lucy groaned. "My liver and my finances won't like that. No student loan until after the holiday."

"Bank of Mum and Dad?" Seth asked.

"Oh yes, that's a good one," Lucy laughed. "Have you met my parents? You get nothing for nothing. You should know that." Lucy waited outside the coffee shop with Lottie while Seth went in to collect their drinks. "Seth, I think I owe you an apology," she said, when he reappeared.

Seth looked surprised. "Really? Why?"

"That text you sent me a few weeks back about your mum. I bit your head off. I'm sorry."

"Don't worry about it." Seth carried their coffees over to the benches by the church. "My past behaviour preceded me."

"That sounds deep. What do you mean?" Lucy sat down next to him and tied Lottie's lead to the bench.

"It's taken me a long time to realise it, but not everything revolves around what's going on in my family," Seth said, choosing his words carefully. "I wasn't particularly friendly towards you when you offered to help in the past. I was mean to you. There's a lot I can't remember but I did things I'm a little ashamed of. Maybe it's me who owes you an apology." Lucy started to say something but he put his hand up. "Let me finish. My parents were odd. They probably still are but what's happened between them is just that ... between them. But I didn't get that until I went to Newcastle. Lucy, a lot of people I now consider to be good friends, have gone through family break-ups and lost people they love. They haven't let it define them."

Lucy smiled. "That's almost, word for word, what I said to Mum after you sent that text through. But now I know there was nothing wrong with your text. I was basing it on the old Seth, the pre-university Seth. The new Seth gets it, doesn't he?"

It was Seth's turn to smile. Lucy made it sound so easy, as simple as turning a page. She clearly remembered very little, maybe she didn't even know. "Yes," he said. "The new Seth just wants them to be happy. I want them to meet other people. Sounds corny, doesn't it?"

"No, not at all. And I think your mum may have already met someone anyway."

"Really?" Seth raised an eyebrow. "How do you know? Are you sure?"

"Someone's been buying her presents, fairly expensive presents." Lucy emphasised the penultimate word. "We caught her out, me and Mum. It was a total fluke but she got very flustered."

Seth thought about the man he'd heard in his mother's cottage. "You might be right." He hadn't realised he'd spoken out loud.

"Really?" Lucy was excited. "Has she said something? Who is it?"

"No, she hasn't. I shouldn't have said anything. Just call it a feeling."

"That's not good enough Seth. That's what the old Seth used to do, keep secrets, tell lies. You're not telling me everything."

"Why do you say that?" Seth asked. "Did I tell a lot of lies?" He knew the answer to this question already, it was a recurring theme during his therapy sessions.

"Yes," Lucy said honestly. "Sorry, it was a long time ago. You were going through stuff."

Seth took a sip of his coffee and nodded his head. Going through stuff was a catch-all term, it implied so much yet barely scratched the surface.

A bare-chested boy was struggling. He was fighting someone, kicking out and biting. The taste of blood was metallic in his mouth.

"Seth, Seth ... are you OK?" He looked down, Lucy's pale hand was on his arm.

"Sorry, miles away." He turned to face her. "I'm sorry for those lies Lucy. I hope I didn't hurt you. I've changed."

Lucy held his gaze. "Yes, I can tell," she said softly. "You weren't a very nice kid but, like I said, you had stuff going on."

"Indeed," Seth agreed. "But lots of people have stuff going on ... "

Lucy laughed suddenly. "Oh, you're clever. You nearly had me there. I'm hungover but not stupid. You're doing this on purpose, aren't you? Steering the conversation away from Molly? Come on! Tell me about her new man."

Seth was relieved. He wasn't ready for a deep conversation with Lucy, one day maybe, but not yet. "OK, if I tell you, I need you to keep quiet about it. Mum will tell us when she's ready. I've already tried to broach the subject and she shot me down in flames."

"Seth just tell me, I won't say anything," Lucy pleaded, inching closer.

Seth took a deep breath. "OK. When I went home the other night, you know, the night I had to stay at your place?"

"Mum said Molly had locked you out," Lucy smiled. "Oh my God, are you saying she had a date?"

"Yes. Well no, well kind of, I suppose." He was already having misgivings about confiding in Lucy. "Please don't say anything to her. Promise?"

"Just bloody well spill, will you?!" Lucy almost screamed.

Seth took a long, slow sip of his coffee before speaking. "Lucy, I did get into the cottage. Do you remember the old cat flap trick?"

Lucy giggled. "Oh my God. Is that how you got in?"

Seth nodded. "But I didn't get very far. I heard voices. Well a man's voice ... from upstairs."

Lucy squealed, startling Lottie. "Oooh, the naughty mare. I said she was a dark horse. And you have no idea who it was?"

"Jesus! As soon as I heard voices, I got out of there, I can assure you." He wrinkled his nose in disdain. "I had no desire to see what was going on, thanks very much. Shit Lucy! This is my mum we're talking about."

Lucy was laughing. "Don't be a prude Seth. Sex is the most natural thing in the world. Did you recognise the man's voice?

"What?! Can you hear yourself? No, I didn't recognise his bloody voice."

"And there was nothing lying around that gave any hints?" she asked. 'No clothes on the floor? No coat at least?"

"As if I was going to start rifling through his coat pockets. Although there was something." He put his hand in his pocket and pulled out the memory stick.

"What's that?" Lucy asked. "I don't get it."

"It's his. It belongs to Mum's mystery man. I don't know why I did it but I took it from his keys. God knows why, I shouldn't have." It was the old Seth, he said to himself, the troublemaker.

Lucy squealed in delight. "Bloody hell, Seth Pope, you little tea leaf. I knew you could be devious but that's genius. And you laughed at my suggestion of going through his coat pockets. I love it. Have you looked at it?"

Seth turned the memory stick over in his hand. "No, I'm not sure I should."

"Aww Seth ... don't spoil my fun. Aren't you curious? What harm can it do?"

"I don't know but it makes me feel uncomfortable. It's like I'd be snooping." Seth put the stick back in his pocket.

"Well, let me know if you change your mind," Lucy sighed. "If you want to return it, you need to look at it, don't you? But don't look at it without me. Promise?" He didn't respond. "Seth," she said more forcefully. "Promise?"

Seth looked at Lucy's earnest face and laughed. "God, you don't change, do you? OK, I promise."

Chapter Twenty

If someone had broached the subject of religion with Kate, she would always profess to be a Catholic, albeit a seriously lapsed member of that flock. Catholicism was in her blood, plain and simple. As a child, she'd had no choice. Winnie, her mother, had been in charge and had insisted her daughters attend Mass, in their best clothes, every Sunday morning. As the girls entered their teenage years, being forced to go to church became a serious bone of contention and Kate remembered, with regret, many heated arguments. She couldn't pinpoint when, or how, it had happened, but there had come a day when Winnie had simply stopped insisting the girls accompany her. Recently, this thought made Kate feel sad and guilty. Her mother's faith had been important to her and her daughters had been rude and dismissive about it.

As her illness took hold, Kate found herself drawn to the sombre interior of the church where her mother had spent so much time. She didn't come to worship, or pray, as her mother had done. It was the solitude the church offered that drew her in. The tests she'd undergone, while waiting for her diagnosis, had made her question her future, analyse her present and look back at her past. The peacefulness of the church allowed her the privacy to process these thoughts. She hadn't told Eddie about her visits yet, not because she was fearful that he would mock her, Eddie wasn't that kind of man. The truth was that, above all, Kate wanted to be alone. Within these cold, stone walls she felt stripped of responsibility. She was Kate, not Kate the wife, or Kate the mother, or even Kate the friend, or the yoga teacher. She was just Kate.

Today, on Good Friday morning, with the kids sleeping late and Eddie taking advantage of the unexpected good weather, to potter in the garden, Kate had taken Lottie for a walk up to the church. Leaving the old dog tied tightly to a bench by the enormous, wooden doors, she walked quietly inside and sat in a pew near the back. She didn't feel it was appropriate to bless herself or to kneel as she saw others doing. She was, after all, a lapsed

Catholic. Instead, she sat with her hands clasped together on her lap and looked slowly around her, trying to remember what had brought her mother here every Good Friday.

"Are you here for the Stations of the Cross?" a soft voice asked from behind her. Kate turned around, surprised to see a dark-haired, young man wearing a priest's dog collar. Dark-rimmed glasses enhanced his bright blue eyes. He smiled encouragingly at her, prompting her for a response.

"Err, no," Kate mumbled. "Sorry. I'm just here to ...." She couldn't put it into words.

"No problem," the young man responded. A perceptible nod of his head indicated he understood her reticence. "Please feel free to join in, if you wish."

The young man walked away, stopping briefly to speak with two elderly women who were arranging flowers near the alter. Mesmerised, Kate watched as people started to drift in through the doors, one or maybe two at a time, until there were roughly twenty people standing with the priest. She felt like an intruder, she had no idea what was happening. The priest led the small group, mostly women Kate noticed, to stand by a small image on the church wall. He started to softly recite a prayer. The group responded with a soft 'amen' and then, collectively, they moved to the next image on the wall. The Stations of the Cross, the priest had said the words as if she would know what he was talking about but the words meant nothing to her. She watched, transfixed, as the group made their way from image to image. There was something deeply respectful about their behaviour, these people were, unashamedly, devout. Sensing they were nearing the end of proceedings, Kate got up and tiptoed quietly outside, relieved to see Lottie still sitting, waiting patiently for her. She sat down on the bench and stroked the dog's soft head. What she'd seen had evoked memories of a time gone by. A time when life had been simpler, when the demands of modern life were less oppressive. She leant back, turned her face to the sun and shut her eyes. She wanted to park herself in the moment, to feel unencumbered by her thoughts.

"Kate? Kate! Are you OK?" Someone touched her shoulder softly. She opened her eyes and squinted into the sun. It was Molly.

"What are you doing here?" Kate asked.

"Don't you mean what are you doing here?" Molly put her bag down and sat on the bench. Lottie strained on her lead, she wanted some fuss. "I'm on my way to work. You know I come this way. What are you doing here?" She pointed to the church. "Something to tell me?"

Kate frowned. "No, why?" she asked defensively. "I was walking Lottie. Just thought we'd sit for a few minutes in the sun."

"Is Lottie OK?" Molly reached over and stroked the dog.

"God! What's with all the bloody questions?" exclaimed Kate. "I'm not doing anything wrong, you know."

"You just looked strange ... a bit lost. You worried me. Are you sure everything's OK? You would tell me, wouldn't you? I don't like not knowing."

"I'm fine, absolutely fine," said Kate, standing up and thinking, a little ungraciously, that Molly was fairly late to the party when it came to asking about her wellbeing. "Come on, I'll walk with you to work. Do you get paid double for working on a Bank Holiday?"

"I don't know." Molly was easily distracted. "It would be nice if we did, wouldn't it? I'm only working a few hours though. Seth and I are going to take my mum out for afternoon tea."

"Ah, that will be nice." Kate linked her arm through Molly's.

"For her maybe," laughed Molly. "Less so for me. Not sure about Seth."

"Seth seems more settled." Kate chose her words carefully. "University seems to have been good for him."

"I know, hasn't it?" Molly's smile lit up her face. "We've had a lovely couple of days. He's been so ... oh I don't know ... nice."

"Nice?" laughed Kate. "Strange way to describe your own child."

"It was his idea to go and see his grandmother. In the past, he would have run a mile."

"Like I said, university, this year especially, seems to suit him," said Kate. "I noticed it myself the other night when he stayed over."

"Oh God! I'm so sorry about that Kate. I don't know why I didn't hear him. I had an early night. It won't happen again ... he's got a key now."

"No need to apologise." Kate glanced at her friend. "It wasn't a big deal Moll. It was lovely to see Bobby and Seth together again, as friends ... and young men."

"I'm just cross with myself." Molly kept looking ahead, she didn't want to look Kate in the eye. "I feel such a bloody fool."

"A fool? Why? Anyone would think that you'd done something to be ashamed of. Stop beating yourself up. You only had an early night. You didn't know he was coming home early. Bloody hell, it was just one night."

"Yes, it was just one night," sighed Molly.

***

James sat in the hotel restaurant, slowly stirring sugar into his coffee. The remains of his scrambled eggs were slowly congealing on the plate before him. He was, unaccustomedly, unsure what to do next. Yesterday, when he'd made the devastating connection between Molly and the champagne bottles, he'd acted irrationally. In a moment of madness, he'd bolted from the hospital, hurriedly packed his overnight bag and boarded a train, driven by the need to get to Molly. But doubt had steadily crept in, as he sat on the crowded train; he wasn't a man given to knee jerk reactions. On the contrary, he always considered his options and planned accordingly. Frustrated with himself and the situation, he'd got off the train a couple of stops later and found a hotel. But he'd slept fitfully, images of Molly in a black polo shirt and the champagne bottles constantly disturbing his sleep.

Sitting in the nondescript hotel restaurant and sipping on the bitter, lukewarm coffee, James was agitated. Despite his snooping on Facebook, he still hadn't come up with a plan. He put his cup down, the crockery clattered noisily in the quiet room. Deep down he knew he should get on a train, go back to London, sign the papers, pack his bags and distance himself, maybe catch a flight to Paris. That would be the sensible thing to do. And maybe, just maybe, he would have done that, had it not been for the champagne. He picked up his phone, turning it over and over in his hands. He typed out a message to Seth.

Glad you're fixing things with your mother
Have a good time. Big plans for Easter?

There was so much more he wanted to ask but Seth wasn't stupid. He needed to keep his cool and maintain his facade. His phone buzzed, it was Seth.

All good so far. Off to see Granny later. What about you?

"Tell me more Seth," James muttered. He typed out another message.

Back in sunny France. Say hello to Rita for me. Hide the Gin!

He smiled ruefully, he was blatantly lying but it was for the best.

Taking her for afternoon tea. No alcohol on the premises. Enjoy your trip.

End of discussion, there was nothing else to say. He opened Facebook, something he now did numerous times each day. There were no new posts on Seth's page. He scanned the list of his son's friends, there were hundreds of them. He looked again at Molly's page, she had very few friends. It was clearly a generational thing, he'd been right, Facebook was a toy for the young. He opened Kate's page, a thought was forming in his mind. He was a fool, he should have thought of it earlier. Kate, Molly, their extraordinary friendship and his nugget of information, it couldn't be easier. Molly's affair with Harry wouldn't be common knowledge; Kate certainly wouldn't know. What would Molly do to keep him from sharing that particular piece of grubby news with her oldest friend? She'd do anything he bloody well wanted her to. He got up quickly, knocking the table with his injured knee but the slight, shooting pain didn't register, he had the beginnings of a plan. He'd outwitted her yet again and, this time, there would only be one winner.

On his way back to his room, he stopped to ask the friendly, young woman at reception to organise a hire-car for him. He waited impatiently as she rang a local firm and negotiated a deal on his behalf. She was pretty, blond and curvaceous, not unlike Molly when they had first met, before she'd changed, before she'd ruined his life. He listened, as the young woman poured on the charm with the poor guy on the other end of the phone. She was running circles around him, using her femininity to get the best deal for her client. That's what they all did. They flirted with you and treated you like a God but only until they had what they wanted. Once they'd stripped you of your masculinity, you found yourself surplus to requirements. They moved on to their next target without a care for the mess they left behind.

"Your car will be delivered at eleven o'clock Sir." The young blond was pleased with herself and was looking for praise. He ignored her efforts to be friendly. She was a nobody, he had more important things to do.

***

Jack watched nervously as several cyclists queued up at the small bar in the marquee. A few had already purchased their drinks and were sitting in groups at the round, wooden tables. The hotdog stand, attached to a vintage, white bike, was being manned by one of Sophie's newbies and the queue there was even longer. He shook his head in wonder and headed inside, standing aside quickly as a group of small children ran excitedly towards the small play area, at the very end of the garden.

"Bloody hell, Sophie," he said, walking up to her as she cleared some plates from an empty table. "It's busier out there, than it is in here."

Sophie laughed. "I might have told some people the marquee would be open for business today." She skillfully piled plates into a small mountain. "I think they're checking us out."

"But the garden's packed with kids too," Jack said worriedly. "It's like a playground."

"That's not my fault. That's due to the good weather and the holidays. And I, for one, would rather have the little buggers out there, than in here any day."

"Are we going to be able to manage? Will Kim be OK? Do we have enough staff on?"

"Stop worrying." Sophie handed him the stack of plates. "Make yourself useful and take those into the kitchen. I've looked after everything. You just need to get your arse behind that bar and do what you do best."

"And what might that be?" asked Annie. Neither of them had seen her come into the bar. "On second thoughts, don't tell me. I've not had enough coffee yet."

"Headache?" Jack asked, smiling.

"Just a little one," Annie replied, using her thumb and forefinger to demonstrate how small her bad head was. "How do I look?" She pulled at the shirt Sophie had given her. "Like part of the team?"

"Indeed you do," said Jack. "Remember though, no minesweeping."

"Cheeky sod," exclaimed Annie. She glanced at the plates Jack was carrying. "Seems busy, what can I do to help?"

"Nothing," said Sophie. "At least not yet. Let's grab a coffee and go outside. I want you to meet Molly."

The two women walked outside with their coffees, Annie whistled when she saw the marquee. "Very swanky," she said. "Must have cost a bit."

"It's not really all that grand," said Sophie but she was chuffed with Annie's reaction. "We're just trialling it over the summer." She lowered her voice. "It will keep the smelly cyclists away from our more discerning customers." She spotted Molly collecting glasses and waved her over. "Molly, this is Annie. Annie meet Molly."

"Nice to meet you Annie." The two women shook hands. "I've heard a lot about you."

"Nice to meet you too Molly." Annie decided it wouldn't be wise to say she had heard a lot about her too, it wasn't fair. "All good I hope?" she asked instead.

Molly glanced at Sophie and smiled coyly. "Yes, all good."

"Shit Sophie! You've warned her, haven't you?" Annie's voice sounded offended but her eyes danced. "Do you know what Molly? Maybe you and I can have a glass of wine later? I'll tell you a thing or two about Princess Sophie. She's not as perfect as you'd think."

"No you don't Annie," laughed Sophie. "What goes on tour, stays on tour. Remember?"

"This sounds interesting," Molly giggled. "Tell me more."

"There's absolutely loads to tell." Annie jumped out of the way, as Sophie tried to place her hand over her mouth. "Tonight? Or are you working?"

"No, I'm not working tonight." Molly found herself warming to this little, blond woman. "I was going to come in actually, bring my son in for something to eat."

"Fabulous." Annie laughed out loud as Sophie put her head in her hands. "You may well cringe Sophie. I have so much ammunition."

"Enough already!" Sophie pulled Annie away. "Come on, Molly's busy. Let's go back inside. You could probably do with some food. Feed that hangover?"

"See you later Molly," Annie called over her shoulder, as Sophie pushed her away. The two women were still laughing as they headed back to the bar.

"You're incorrigible," Sophie giggled. "I'm her boss. Go easy with what you say."

"From what I hear, she gets up to far juicier things than you and me. Maybe I'll turn the tables on her."

"Do you know what Annie?" Sophie opened the door into the bar. "Maybe that's not a bad idea. Everything we know about Molly and all her problems is hearsay, anecdotal."

"What? You don't believe some of it?"

"I believe all of it. The affairs, the men dying, the horrible ex. It's undeniable. But I've never heard any of it from the horse's mouth, as it were. Up until recently I really didn't want to. I've always maintained it's all in the past. Always thought it should be left there."

"But this JP ... James ... whatever his name is, he worries you?"

"To be honest I don't know what to think," Sophie replied. "It's frustrating. Part of me thinks that we're all making huge assumptions. So, the guy's a nasty piece of work but there's plenty of them out there. You know that more than anyone. You see it every day."

Annie nodded. "I sure do. See much worse, if I'm honest."

"But he's not a criminal like most of the guys you deal with," said Sophie thoughtfully. "Or is he? Has he come back specifically to do something bad and what might that be? Jack's worried but I don't know why. Like I said, I don't know what to think." They were still standing in the doorway as a tall, blond man came through from the bar and tried to push past. Sophie was shocked to see him, intentionally, place his hands tightly around Annie's lower hips and squeeze her bottom.

"Sorry Babe, can I have a moment?" Annie's face changed and her body tensed.

"Are you mistaking my friend for someone else?" Sophie put her hand gently on Annie's arm to restrain her. Her friend might be small in stature but Sophie had seen her in action; you didn't mess with Annie.

The man looked from Sophie to Annie. "Oh my God! I thought you were Molly. I'm so sorry. Bloody hell, please believe me. I'm sorry." The guy was stuttering over his words, genuinely embarrassed. "The hair, the shirt. I am so sorry."

"No harm done," said Annie through slightly clenched teeth. Sophie smiled, the words were harmless but the tone said, "Fuck off you twat." The mortified man walked back to the bar with his head down. "Who the fuck is that?" Annie dusted imaginary dirt off her thighs. "Molly's boyfriend?"

"She hasn't got one." Sophie frowned, the man looked familiar. "Not officially."

"He didn't leave much to the imagination, if you get what I mean … he got mighty close."

"I'm sure I've seen him here before. I've seen him speaking to Molly." Sophie turned back to Annie and looked her up and down. "Funny thing is you do look like Molly and you're wearing one of our shirts. I hadn't thought about it before."

"And that excuses him? Not where I come from Sophie," Annie said. "No man, or woman, has the right to touch without invitation. I don't mind the compliment though, if that's what you're getting at. Pretty woman that Molly."

***

Eddie heard the familiar noise of the gate banging, as Kate and Lottie came back into the garden.

"Just in time," he said, coming out of the shed. "Lucy's making coffee."

"Wonderful." Kate let Lottie off her lead. "Sorry I was so long. I bumped into Molly."

"Everything OK? Did you tell her what Jack told me? About James being just up the road?"

Kate sat down on the old wooden bench next to the shed and turned her face to the sun. Eddie thought she looked tired. "No," she said. "She's in such a good place at the moment with Seth being home. They're seeing Rita later today and I didn't want to burst her bubble."

Eddie sat down next to her. "I've been thinking about it this morning. I don't think we should say anything."

"But you were adamant that she needed to know." Kate turned her face from the sun to look at Eddie.

"I know. I think I over-reacted," he said, a little sheepishly. "What good would it do to tell her? And what exactly would we tell her? We don't want to spoil these few days she's having with Seth, do we?" Kate turned back to the sun and closed her eyes. "Kate, are you still cross with her? About the married man thing?" Eddie asked quietly, stealing a look at the back door in case Lucy was nearby. "You've not said much since she got pissed and hurt herself. But you're OK you two, aren't you?" Kate didn't move. "Kate?" he persisted.

Kate sighed. "Yes, we're OK Eddie," she said slowly. "Let's just say that some of the lines that define our friendship are more blurred than they used to be. That's all."

Eddie frowned. "What the heck does that mean?"

"Nothing bad but things change, don't they? People change. I think our friendship has fundamentally changed. Maybe I took Molly for granted. I didn't understand what she needed."

"You wouldn't take anyone for granted," Eddie said indignantly. "She takes you for granted, more like."

"But I think I did Eddie, which makes me as bad as James. I never knew she was so lonely, so desperate for company."

"But she has you. She's always had you ... and us." He gestured towards the house. "You've always been there for her. Jesus, she's still got her own mother alive. Neither you or I have that privilege. I know Rita has her own issues but she's her mother for God's sake. She's probably far more lonely than Molly."

Kate held her finger up to her lips mouthing a silent 'shhhh' as the back door opened.

"I saw you come back." Lucy smiled at Kate. "I assumed you'd want coffee too." She placed a tray with two cups on the patio table, pushing Lottie's face away as the old dog lifted her nose, ever hopeful of something edible coming her way.

"Thanks love." Kate took a cup and passed it to Eddie. "Aren't you having one?"

"No, I'm on my way over to see Seth for a couple of hours," Lucy replied. "Bobby's still in bed. Let him know where I am if he surfaces."

"Nice to see her and Seth getting on so well again," Eddie said, as Lucy walked back into the house. Kate nodded and sipped her coffee. "Kate, I'm very fond of Molly you know that. If she's lonely or desperate for company, male company, it's not your problem. She needs to make better decisions. Learn from her mistakes."

"I know," sighed Kate. "But she must have been in a pretty bad place to consider taking the risk. And I didn't spot it. That doesn't make me a very good friend."

"Stop it Kate, you're making me cross." Eddie leant forward on the bench. "She's a bloody grown up. Shit happens to everyone. I take it you still haven't told her about your own issues, have you?" Kate shook her head. "It's a bloody two-way street, isn't it? You've propped her up for years. Don't get me wrong, I'm not resentful. But maybe some of that support needs to come the other way." They fell silent, the noise of a nearby lawnmower filled the void. "Did she tell you who it is? This man she was seeing?" Eddie asked eventually.

"No. She wouldn't. She promised me she was going to finish it."

"And you believe her?" Eddie asked. "Do you think we know him?"

Kate shrugged her shoulders. "She discovered recently that she isn't his only extra-marital interest. He's a player. That's why she's going to finish it."

Eddie shook his head in disbelief. "Oh my God. Poor Molly."

"So now it's poor Molly, is it?" Kate asked, a little incredulously. She picked up their empty cups and started walking towards the house. Glancing back at Eddie, she stopped. "Sorry for snapping. It's hard to work out which side of the fence to come down on, isn't it? Do we feel sorry for her because she's lonely and an easy target for a womaniser? Or do we judge her as a home-wrecker, who can't learn from her mistakes? Either way, we can't abandon her, can we? And now we have an added complication .... James."

***

"What on earth are you doing?" Lucy held her hand up to shield her eyes from the sun. Seth was standing at the top of a ladder.

Seth looked down at her upturned face. "What does it look like?"

"Well, I can see what you're doing. But why are you doing it? Shouldn't you leave that to an expert?"

Seth threw a wet sponge in her direction, narrowly missing her head. "Mum can't afford window cleaning experts, can she? Anyway, how do you know I'm not an expert? I'm a man of many talents."

Lucy laughed and pointed to a downstairs window. "You missed a bit. Need to keep working on your expertise, I'd say."

"Make yourself useful, you cheeky cow." Seth pointed to a biscuit tin on the floor. "Go and make some coffee and take that tin with you."

"What's in it?" Lucy asked, picking up the tin.

"Brownies, good brownies. A thank you from Ethel." Seth nodded towards Ethel's cottage. "Mum's house-sitting for her. She's gone away for Easter."

Lucy walked into Molly's small kitchen and placed the tin on the table. The room was strange to her, she didn't know the layout. Molly always came to their house, never the other way around. She found some cups in a cupboard on the wall and was spooning in coffee, when Seth appeared at the back door.

"Where's Bobby?" he asked, washing his hands in the small, enamel sink.

"In bed ... as usual." Lucy handed him a cup and took a brownie from the tin. "Mmmm, really good brownies. Where's your laptop?"

"In the sitting room. Why?" Seth asked cautiously.

Lucy raised her eyebrows and smiled innocently. "Thought we might take a look at that memory stick."

"I had a mental bet with myself that you wouldn't let that lie." Seth followed her into the sitting room. "You always were a nosy cow."

"Curious," she corrected him. "Just curious. Don't try and tell me you're not."

Seth couldn't help but smile at her. Lucy had always been able to do this, been able to get people to do what she wanted. He pulled his laptop out from under the sofa and retrieved the memory stick from his pocket.

"I think you're going to be disappointed." He placed the stick in a USB port. "It's probably going to be extremely dull stuff, boring spreadsheets, that kind of thing. That's what most people use memory sticks for."

"We won't know, if we don't take a look," she responded, edging closer to him on the sofa. "Aren't you just a tiny bit excited to see what's on it? What if it's kinky? You know ... sexy pictures of your mum?"

"Bloody hell Lucy, don't say that! Now I really don't want to look." The thought hadn't entered his head. "Shit! I shouldn't have taken it, it's theft." They both watched as the screen populated with folders. "There's loads on here," Seth said in amazement. "Now I feel even worse. This might be important stuff for him."

"If we find out who he is, we might be able to return it." Lucy was excited. "There seem to be a lot of folders starting with the letters PV. Maybe that's his initials."

As Seth had predicted, there were a lot of spreadsheets and, frustratingly, some were password protected. The ones he could open were heavy with data. "This is going nowhere, it might as well be in a foreign language."

"There are loads of abbreviations. They seem to be on all the documents." Lucy pointed to several columns marked Ch., Rg., Bl. and Rs. "They're the only common denominator that I can see."

"No idea," Seth murmured. "These tabs," he held the cursor over the tabs at the bottom of one sheet. "Could they be company names?" He moved the cursor again. "These figures could be prices?"

"How boring. I had my hopes up for something much more interesting," Lucy groaned.

"I told you you'd be disappointed."

"Pipe down, boy." Lucy retorted. "You're no fun."

Seth leant back on the sofa. "A lot of work has gone into these documents Lucy. Whoever owns them probably needs them back. I shouldn't have taken it ... I'm such a retard."

"You give up way too easy." Lucy grabbed the laptop from Seth. "Come on, keep looking. There must be a clue somewhere. If PV isn't his initials, maybe it's an abbreviation for a product?"

"Or a brand or a business?" Seth looked at his watch. "Shit! I had better get ready. I'm meeting Mum in forty minutes. We're going to see Gran."

"Really? Doesn't sound much fun." Lucy said sarcastically. "Go on then. I'll carry on here. You go get ready."

Lucy shut the spreadsheet folders and searched for text files. There was nothing she could open. Whoever this guy was, he was security conscious. She heard Seth come out of the shower and walk across to his room. There was one folder left, it was marked PV-HS. Her heart beat faster, there were photographs in this folder. Despite her earlier comment to Seth, she really didn't want to find any kinky photographs of Molly, Seth would be distraught. Holding her breath, she clicked nervously on the first image, surprised, relieved and then a little disappointed, when a photograph of a wine bottle and a single glass emerged. She clicked on the next photograph, again it was a wine bottle, this time it had been opened and the glass next to it appeared half full. She worked her way, methodically, through all the photographs, her disappointment growing as each one revealed more of the same.

"Find anything?" Seth was at her shoulder. She had been so engrossed, she hadn't heard him come downstairs.

"Not really." Lucy was faintly aware of Seth's aftershave. "There are a lot of photos of wine. Posh wine by the looks of it."

"Really? Show me."

"Nice photos ... professional, I'd say." Lucy clicked through the photographs. Without saying anything, Seth lowered himself onto the sofa and took the laptop from her. He reopened one of the spreadsheets.

"I think I've worked out the acronyms." He held the cursor over the top line. "Look ... Ch might stand for Champagne, Rg for Rouge, Bl for Blanc and Rs for Rosé. What do you think?"

"You absolute genius." Lucy's voice rose and she clapped her hands excitedly. "And the countries make sense too then, don't they? Wine producing countries? Or clients in those countries?"

"Lucy, I think we should stop." Seth snapped the laptop shut and removed the memory stick. "We should have left it alone."

"What are you talking about, you idiot?" Lucy was indignant. "This is great. We must be on the right track. Those spreadsheets? It's clearly business data. The pictures? They support the acronyms. Whoever this guy is he ..." Her voice fell away and she turned to look directly into Seth's eyes. His face had turned grey. "Fuck! You'd already worked it out, hadn't you? It's Harry, isn't it? My Uncle Harry. Fuck. What do we do now?"

Seth placed his hand on hers. "I don't think we do anything Lucy. This doesn't prove anything. It's not necessarily Harry."

Lucy pulled her phone from her jeans and found Harry's Facebook page. "Planet Vino! His business is called Planet Vino. P fucking V. Now tell me it's not him. What the fuck is she doing? He's married to my bloody aunt for God's sake." Lucy was shouting. "Talk about shitting on your own doorstep. How could she?"

"Hang on Lucy." Seth got up and pushed his laptop back under the sofa. "I'm not defending her but it takes two, doesn't it? I don't think he was here because she forced him."

Lucy looked up at Seth's troubled face, her indignation subsided a little. "She's your Mum Seth ... I get it. And you're right. It does take two. But this is low. Shit! She shouldn't even think about going there. What about my mum? I don't think she'll forgive her ... not this time."

Seth turned his back to Lucy, he didn't want her to see the disappointment on his face. He'd instinctively defended his mother but that didn't mean he wasn't embarrassed, ashamed even.

The little boy, dressed in blue and white striped pyjamas was standing on the landing with his head pinned up against the wooden bannister, the pale carpet was soft under his feet. His mother was in the hall below him, she was looking at her reflection in a large, ornate mirror. His father was behind her, he had his head bent, he was gently kissing her exposed shoulder. The little boy watched as his father raised his hand to move his mother's blond hair aside, revealing the pale white skin of her slender neck. She was smiling at her reflection. His father raised his head to return the smile. The little boy gasped and recoiled from the bannister, the man downstairs wasn't his father.

"Seth .... Seth," Lucy pulled on her coat. "Are you OK? What's the matter?"

Seth, the grown man, had gasped just as the little boy had. "Sorry, sorry," he said, shaking his head "I was thinking about something."

"What do we do?" Lucy asked.

"I don't know Lucy, not yet anyway." Seth's voice was tight in his throat. "But you have to promise me you'll keep quiet for now ... until I've figured this out."

"But ..." Lucy was about to object.

"No buts Lucy." Seth cut her off and walked to the front door, gesturing for her to follow him. "Promise me."

"Promise," Lucy said quietly. They left the house in silence, each one struggling with their own thoughts. Peeling off to walk home through the park, Lucy suddenly placed a kiss on Seth's cheek. "Call me later ... and don't worry." A trite comment but she didn't know what else to say, Seth's silence worried her.

Seth carried on towards town, walking slowly. A year ago, this latest discovery would have found him packing his bags and heading back to Newcastle without stopping to say goodbye but part of his recovery, if that's what it could be called, was the deal he'd made with himself to stop running from his parents. He'd worked hard to convince himself that his parents were just ordinary people, with ordinary flaws. Define ordinary though, he said to himself as he approached the pub. The evidence against his mother was conclusive. She was, yet again, having an affair with a married man. However you looked at it, she was as guilty as hell. He pulled the memory stick from his pocket and forced the security catch out of place, until it looked like it could have easily fallen off a key ring. He had no qualms about doing it, it was something the old Seth would have done.

Chapter Twenty-One

Molly would think afterwards that she could have handled things differently but Fiona was the last person she expected to see on the other side of the bar. "Yes please, ladies," she said to the two blond women. "What can I get you?"

Fiona turned from her friend, a twenty pound note visible in her hand. Molly was immediately struck, as always, by Fiona's appearance. Tall, athletic and strikingly good-looking, Fiona epitomised a woman clearly comfortable in her own skin. She exuded understated class. Long, strawberry blond hair fell in gentle waves past her shoulders, perfectly manicured nails were painted scarlet red and Molly noticed, with a pang of what felt like guilt, that Fiona was still wearing her rings. A distinctive, sapphire engagement ring sat proudly above a diamond encrusted wedding band. Molly dropped her eyes. She'd had a ring just like that in a previous life, she'd had expensive manicures too. Fiona may have lost Will but she hadn't lost her comfortable lifestyle; unlike Molly.

"What the hell are you doing here?" Fiona spoke slowly. Her throaty voice was icily cold. Her companion reached out and placed her hand gently on Fiona's arm. Molly's stomach lurched, the young woman was Will's daughter, Nicola. Tall and pretty, Nicola's face carried many of her father's features. The restraining gesture from Nicola seemed to have the desired effect on Fiona and she took a step back. "Two glasses of white wine." She placed the twenty-pound note firmly on the bar.

Molly was aware of several heads turning to look in her direction. Those with good memories were clearly curious, they were waiting, expectantly, to see how this situation would unfurl. Those not so well informed were merely nosey, the undisguised animosity was palpable. Molly wanted the ground to swallow her up, to rescue her from Fiona and the garden full of curious onlookers. She'd been on the receiving end of Fiona's anger before and it never, ever went well for her. Red faced and with shaking hands, she poured out two glasses of white wine, putting them on the bar and placing Fiona's change, carefully, next to them.

"I hadn't finished." Fiona spat the words. "I need a pint of lager too." Molly picked up a pint glass and poured lager from the nearest tap. Without looking at Fiona, she picked out the necessary coins from the change still sitting on the bar. The crowd were still watching. "It wasn't me, you know," Fiona said quietly. Molly didn't look up or reply. "In the cemetery," Fiona continued, her voice still low. "Kate told me about your latest adventure. It wasn't me."

Molly willed herself to ignore the comment. Tempting though it was to prove to Fiona that she knew the hate campaign had recommenced, a comment about the bloody handprint wouldn't help. She needed to remain calm and keep quiet. "Yes please," she said to the next customer, a small, dark haired woman, dressed in colourful lycra. "What can I get you?"

"Careful Steph," Fiona called out. "Keep your eye on Pete. This one has a thing for married men." Molly looked at the woman called Steph, willing her to place her order but Steph giggled nervously, clearly embarrassed and uncomfortable. Some people behind her, a group of women, laughed openly. Molly could feel the flush of embarrassment spreading across her face. "I'd ask for someone else to serve me, if I were you Steph," Fiona said, even more loudly. "This one's dangerous, she's got blood on her hands." The image of the bloodied handprint swam into Molly's head. She willed herself to ignore it. Fiona was playing games with her, she was deliberately baiting her.

"What can I get you?" Molly prompted Steph again, as another thought hit her. Blood on her hands, Doris had used that expression. Her enemies were everywhere, watching her, waiting for an opportunity to attack her. Steph looked warily from Molly to Fiona, clearly unsure what to do next. "Here, let me make it easier for you Steph, I'm almost finished for the day anyway." Molly pulled Daniel, one of the new recruits, to her side. "Daniel here will take your order." Summoning up as much courage as she could, she turned back to face Fiona. "You need to show a little more decorum.

Will would be really proud of you and your childish games, wouldn't he?" Fiona's eyes registered her shock and, for a split second, Molly experienced the joy of having delivered a verbal body blow but the joy was short-lived.

"Proud? Decorum?" Fiona's eyes darkened with rage. "You're a fine one to talk Molly Pope." She inched closer to the bar and lowered her voice to a menacing growl. "Liv's told me about your dirty little secret, you filthy, fucking whore. Don't talk to me about decorum"

Molly was shaking now and she wiped away a tear as it escaped from the corner of her eye. This was insane, her heart was thumping loudly in her chest, she shouldn't have goaded Fiona. She tried to move but Daniel was pulling pints and blocking her way. "Daniel," she said shakily. "Can I get past?" Daniel didn't move, he hadn't heard her, her voice was a whimper.

"Who is it Molly? Whose husband are you shagging now? From what Liv's let slip, you're not the only one lucky enough to be sharing that bed, are you? Ha! Didn't know that did you, you stupid cow? Plenty of others get to go to that gig too." Fiona's eyes danced with delight. "Now then. What was it you were saying about pride and what was it? Decorum. Yes, fucking decorum." Each syllable was heavy with hatred. "People in glass houses Molly. People in fucking glass houses."

Stunned, Molly turned her back to the bar, sobs threatened to erupt from her throat. She fought to compose herself. With her back turned she had no way of knowing that Fiona hadn't finished. Emboldened by rage and possibly alcohol, Fiona picked up the pint of lager Molly had placed on the bar and launched its contents at Molly's back. A collective gasp went around the bar as the liquid landed on Molly's shoulder blades, instantly soaking her pony tail and her shirt. People sitting at nearby tables, turned to see what had happened.

"Shit ... Mum!" It was Nicola remonstrating with her mother but Molly didn't stay to hear any more. She pushed past Daniel and ran towards the relative safety of the pub, she didn't look back.

Kim looked up as Molly slammed the kitchen door behind her. "Hey what's the matter? What on earth's happened?"

"Nothing," Molly mumbled, wincing inwardly as she caught Doris staring at her. "Nothing," she repeated, turning away.

"Bollocks. Don't give me that." Kim placed a hand on Molly's arm. "You're wet ... your shirt." She picked up a tea towel and patted it firmly against Molly's back. "I'm guessing this wasn't an accident?" Molly shook her head but said nothing, she was trying hard to keep back the tears. "If you don't want to tell me, that's fine but sit down for a few minutes. Get your breath back." She pushed Molly on to one of the two chairs near the kitchen door. "I'll get you a coffee ... and another shirt."

"I'll be OK in a minute," Molly said, wiping the beer from her arm and the back of her neck. Doris was staring at her, she couldn't bear it. Accepting the spare shirt Kim handed her, she headed for the toilets to change.

"Molly. Thank God. I've been looking for you." Harry was hovering in the corridor.

"Harry, what the hell are you doing here?" She looked around nervously. "Why would you be waiting for me? Go ... please, before someone sees you. Shit Harry! Just fuck off ... get out of here! I'm in enough trouble."

If Harry sensed the desperation in Molly's voice, he didn't acknowledge it. "Did you find a USB at your house the other night?" he asked. "I can't find it. It was on my car keys. It's got important stuff on it ... confidential stuff." The words came out quickly but quietly.

"What? A USB?" Molly wasn't really paying attention, she had her eyes on the marquee.

"Yes, a USB. A memory stick." Harry moved towards her.

""A stick?" Molly pushed him away, he was blocking her view of the garden.

"A bloody memory stick ... a USB. Fuck it! I don't have time to play games Molly," he hissed. "I know I had it that day. I used it. And I've looked everywhere else. I need to find it ... urgently."

"Is this what you're looking for?" Harry and Molly spun round to see Seth standing behind them, a memory stick in his outstretched hand.

"Seth ... Hi." Molly wondered how much her son had heard. "Where did you find that?"

"Hi ... Harry, isn't it?" Seth stretched out his other hand, intentionally ignoring Molly's question. "We've met before. I spent a lot of time at Kate's house growing up. I know your wife." He hadn't meant to mention Patty, the words had just come out but the poignancy of his comment was lost on Harry. From the look on his mother's face, it was lost on her too.

"Pleased to meet you Seth." Harry's innate charm kicked in. "You've not been eating peanuts, have you?" he asked. Seth, nonplussed, shook his head as Harry grabbed his hand. "Sorry. Your mum will explain ... got to dash. Thanks for this, you're a lifesaver." He stepped over and kissed Molly on the top of her head before she had time to pull away.

"Looks like the catch is broken," Seth called out, as Harry walked away. He turned back to his red-faced mother. "Get a move on then. Granny will be waiting for us."

***

Molly might have been consoled by the fact that Fiona had been asked to leave the pub after the lager throwing incident. Kim, quietly and discreetly, had gone out to the marquee and questioned Daniel.

"Excuse me, are you Fiona?" she said to the striking blond woman Daniel pointed out. "Could I have a private word, please?" Kim walked Fiona over to the quietest corner of the garden before giving her an ultimatum. "Fiona? Are you OK with me calling you Fiona?" Kim's tone was friendly.

Fiona nodded. "What do you want?"

"I'll be discreet Fiona," Kim said slowly but firmly. "I want you to leave the premises ... for today. You're welcome to come back another day, if you promise not to behave like a lager lout again. There are things we, the management, won't tolerate and being rude, or physically abusive, to our staff, is one of them. So, for today we, the staff and our customers, have had enough of your company. Take it as a verbal warning." Kim smiled graciously and took a step to indicate the conversation was over. Anyone watching would never have guessed at the message being delivered, Kim had clearly done this kind of thing before. "I'd be grateful if you'd leave quietly ... now."

"Who the hell do you think you are?" Fiona hissed. "How dare you talk to me like that? You don't know who you're dealing with."

"You'd do well to keep your voice down Fiona, if you don't want your friends to know you're being thrown out," Kim continued in the same, even tone.

"Maybe you should be more careful who you employ." Fiona put her hand out to take Kim's arm.

"Don't." Kim pulled her arm away sharply. She waited several seconds before she spoke again. "Who we employ here, has nothing to do with you."

"Molly Pope is a witch. People will stop coming here. I'll make sure of it." Fiona clearly believed she had that kind of power. "No-one wants to see that devious bitch's face, not after what she did."

Kim was unfazed. "I'll be back in five minutes Fiona. If you're still here, I'll have you escorted from the pub and possibly barred. Your decision ... your credibility."

***

"Seth, your Mum's hammered." Bobby nodded in Molly's direction. "Have you two been here all day?"

"Leave her alone, she's having fun." Lucy picked up her phone and took a photograph of Annie and Molly. Both women smiled happily for the camera, raising their wine glasses in a toast. Lucy's gaze lingered on Molly, despite what she and Seth had discovered she couldn't bring herself to hate the woman. She was cross, disgusted even but she didn't hate her. And she wasn't going to behave differently towards her until she'd had the chance to ask her, face-to-face, what was going on.

"Don't get me wrong, I think it's great," Bobby laughed. "She and that Annie are really going for it."

Seth looked over at his mother who was laughing loudly now at something Annie had said. Despite the turmoil going on in his head he smiled, it was good to see her like this. They'd had a rare but successful afternoon with his grandmother. Rita had been delighted to see him and had wanted to hear all about Newcastle. He'd been very aware of his mother switching off in the background, only contributing to the conversation when directly asked to do so, but Rita hadn't seemed to notice or maybe she was just used to Molly's indifference. After visiting Rita they'd had dinner in the pub and Annie, Sophie's friend, had joined them. The two women had steadily worked their way through several bottles of wine. Seth, desperate for company of his own, had sent a text message to Lucy and was relieved to see her, and Bobby, turn up twenty minutes later.

"We haven't been here all day Bob but she has certainly hit it off with Annie and I think she always needs a drink, or several drinks, after an afternoon with my grandmother." Seth was laughing. "I might need your help walking her home at this rate."

"Always happy to oblige," said Bobby, finishing his pint. "I wouldn't mind walking that Annie home either."

"Euwww Bobby!" Lucy slapped her brother's arm. "She's old enough to be your mother."

"And your point is?" Bobby ruffled his sister's hair playfully. "You girls are always getting your hands on older men. What's wrong with it being the other way round? Ha! Got no answer, have you? Call yourself a feminist!"

"Shut up, you idiot." Lucy laughed. He was right, she didn't have an answer.

"Same again?" Bobby picked up Lucy's empty glass.

Lucy watched Bobby walk to the bar. "I haven't said anything to him," she said quietly. "About Harry."

"Good," Seth replied. "Don't."

"Did you say anything to your mum about the stick?" Lucy was still watching Molly and Annie.

"No, I didn't have to." Seth quickly described the scene that had been waiting for him earlier.

"Oh shit," Lucy groaned. "What are you going to do?"

"Nothing," Seth said. "It's none of my business."

"Seth, you have to do something." Lucy checked the bar to see where Bobby was. "They're having an affair."

"No shit Sherlock!" Seth said sarcastically. "They're both consenting adults. They both know what they're doing."

"But Patty ... the kids?" Lucy was shocked at Seth's attitude.

"Lucy, isn't it a bit too late? They're having extra marital sex ... well he is. Doesn't that mean the harm has already been done? That the trust has been broken? What's the good of me wading in now? Just when I'm starting to build a relationship with her again?"

"Don't be such a twat. Are you saying you're happy to sit by and let things run their course whatever the consequences?" Lucy had clenched her teeth, she was so cross. "It's my family we're talking about. You're only thinking of yourself. You've never been interested in having a relationship with her before."

Seth flinched. "If we hadn't looked at that memory stick, if I hadn't come home early ... well we would be none the wiser, would we?" he whispered. "And maybe we should just bide our time. Not let things run their course but bide our time. See how the land lies. Who knows? It may fizzle out. From what I saw today, they certainly didn't look like lovers. They certainly weren't talking like lovers either."

"You're full of fucking clichés," Lucy hissed, watching Bobby make his way back with their drinks. She sat back in her chair, frustrated. "If you learn anything Seth ... and I mean anything, however small, then you tell me. Give me your word." She glared at him.

"I give you my word," he said, smiling at Bobby as he dropped back into the chair next to him.

Lucy glanced up as Molly got up from her seat and wobbled towards the Ladies. Molly waved and Lucy found herself smiling and waving back. For many years Molly had been like a much older sister, an integral part of her extended family. During her early teenage years, she had confided in Molly when she hadn't been too sure how her own mother would react. She'd always loved the slightly scatty, fun-loving naughtiness of Molly. Looking at her now, as she weaved unsteadily past other drinkers, Lucy thought, sadly, of her aunt and her cousins. They didn't deserve this. Despite what Seth had said, she felt the need to say something.

"No, you don't," Seth said, as she started to stand up. He had her arm and was pulling her back down into her seat. "She's drunk, no point and we had a deal." He wasn't cross but she felt chastised. And, deep down, she knew he was right. Alcohol would probably make Molly talk but it could exacerbate the situation too. What she wanted to say, should probably be said and heard sober.

Lucy looked around the packed bar, smiling at familiar faces, young and old. She saw Sophie, empty glasses in her hands, stop and speak to Annie, who, despite Bobby's earlier comment, did not seem to be nearly as drunk as Molly. They looked like close friends, a bit like her mum and Molly. She imagined her mum sitting at home watching TV with her dad and Lottie. What was Kate going to say when she found out about Molly and Harry? Can friendships survive such deceit? She didn't have the answer. Seth was right, she needed to leave things alone, for now anyway.

Seth's phone buzzed on the table and he reached out to read the text message. He laughed as he handed the phone to Lucy.

Getting taxi home. Can't drink anymore. See you in the morning. Sorry x

"She's ghosted?" Lucy asked, turning to check where Molly had been sitting earlier. Annie was now talking to another couple. "Will she be OK?"

"She'll be fine and so will I." Seth pulled his keys from his pocket and dangled them in the air. "At least I won't have to get in through the cat flap this time."

***

Molly made it to the Ladies and sat in a cubicle, listening to the footsteps of other women come and go. It was no good, she was pissed, she needed to go home. She flushed the toilet and washed her hands, splashing some water onto her face. Her reflection confirmed the need to get home. Her make-up was a mess and her cheeks were as pink as the wine she'd been drinking. Concentrating on walking without wobbling, she slipped out into the corridor and opened the door into the dimly lit garden. Swaying a little, she put her hand on one of the garden tables and lowered herself onto the bench beside it. She pulled her phone from her jeans pocket and typed a message to Seth, putting the word sorry and a kiss at the end. She was a bloody useless mother and a rubbish role model but, at this exact moment, she'd just have to hope and pray that he'd understand. She got up and shuffled forwards slowly, her left hand feeling for the brick wall of the pub. Sophie had been right about Annie, that woman certainly liked a drink, she'd been a stupid cow to think she could keep up. Out on the pavement she paused as a young man came out of the pub. She didn't want anyone to see just how drunk she was.

"Are you OK, Mrs. Pope?" The young man leaned in towards her.

Molly squinted up at him, she didn't know who he was. "Fine, fine, fine," she said, trying hard not to slur. "Just waiting … my lift."

He smiled at her and turned away, and she watched as he raised his hand, he was hailing a taxi. She looked over at the taxi rank but she couldn't see any waiting cars, the young man was out of luck. A car horn sounded and she jumped, a car had pulled up from the other direction. The young man got into the back seat. This was good news, there were taxis around after all. She opened her bag and clumsily checked the contents of her purse. Her fingers located a note and she giggled. A taxi was an extravagance but, sod it, she needed to get home. She held her arm up just like the young man had and giggled again, as a car glided to a stop in front of her. She was in luck.

A familiar smell hit her nostrils as she climbed into the back of the car but she couldn't place it. "Victoria Road please," she said. "Number thirteen." She leant back against the soft leather, yawned and closed her eyes. It had been a long and eventful day, she was utterly knackered. All she wanted to do now was to climb into her own bed. The car pulled smoothly away from the pavement and the driver turned up the volume on the radio. Slow, relaxing music embraced her and, as she dropped off to sleep, she made herself a promise. She would speak to Seth in the morning, she'd explain about Harry. It would be best to come clean. Seth was old enough and seemingly well enough, to know the truth.

***

The gravel crunched under the car's tyres, as James pulled the rented BMW to a halt on the drive. Gazing up at the house in the fading light, he was totally unprepared for the rush of emotion that swept over him. He'd been happy here, he'd mistakenly thought they had all been happy here.

The key moved easily in the lock and the front door swung open silently. James switched on the hall light and quickly stepped over to the alarm. He punched in four digits, Molly's date of birth. His footsteps echoed loudly on the tiled floor, as he walked across the hallway to the large kitchen at the back of the house. Flicking on more lights, he looked around the empty room, surprised at how familiar it felt, even after all this time. Memories, some good, some bad, filled his head. Wandering into the dining room and then the lounge, he was a little surprised to see so much furniture. Molly had taken some smaller pieces but most of it was too big for her needs. He'd taken nothing, preferring to leave the house as intact as possible. Doing so was his way of keeping the dream alive, the dream that Molly would return, that they'd start again. He gently ran his fingers over bookcases and ornaments, everything was spotlessly clean. The agency he'd engaged to look after both the house and the garden, were obviously keeping their side of the bargain.

James returned to the car to fetch his overnight bag and several purchases he'd made en-route. As he passed the central heating thermostat in the hall, he increased the setting, after the warmth of the car, the house felt cold. He stopped at the bottom of the stairs and gazed upwards, momentarily indecisive. There would be nothing to see but he was, unexplainably, apprehensive. He took a breath and walked slowly up the carpeted stairs, all the doors on the landing were closed. Years ago, he'd secretly dreamed of filling these empty bedrooms with brothers and sisters for Seth. Molly hadn't been so keen, arguing that pregnancy didn't suit her, that it was hard work, that Seth was happy on his own. Looking at each of the bedroom doors he wondered, not for the first time, whether things would have been different if they'd had more children, if he'd had his own way.

The master bedroom felt cold. Full-length windows spanned much of one wall. In the morning, with the shutters open, they would reveal a breath-taking view of the gardens and the river. The en-suite was almost as big as the bedroom with stylish his and hers sinks, a walk-in double shower and an enormous roll top bath. James let his fingers linger on the edge of the bath, he and Molly had bathed together in the early days. He drew his hand back, suddenly stung by the alarming thought of other men lying in this bath with Molly. He'd never considered this possibility before. Even after all this time, thoughts of her infidelity could still shock him.

He returned to the bedroom and sat on the edge of the bed, the bed he'd been forced to buy after Molly's first affair. A photograph, in an ornate frame, caught his attention and he picked it up off the bedside table. He'd seen this photograph many times but holding it now, alone in this house, he felt like he was seeing it for the first time. It was a wedding photograph, a professional picture taken of him and Molly, on the occasion of their first wedding. Everything about it was old-fashioned. His dark grey suit, cutting-edge fashion at the time, looked dreadful, too big and square for his lean frame. Molly, petite next to him, was drowning in voluminous white lace and netting. The two newlyweds were smiling openly at each other, a truly happy moment caught in time. Using his thumb, he gently stroked Molly's face. He needed to see her smile at him like that again, to see the same adoration in her eyes.

He lay back on the bed, he felt drained. A shower and an early night would do him good. He could decide how to execute his plan, with a clear head, in the morning. He'd acted irrationally too often recently, he needed to think things through. Looking up at the ceiling and despite his fatigue he smiled, getting Molly back was going to be so easy. He pulled his phone from his pocket and opened Facebook, a little surprised to see that Seth had posted a photograph of himself with Rita and Molly; all three were beaming happily at the camera. Seth had his arm round his grandmother's frail shoulders and James was, momentarily, shocked to see how much Rita had aged. He'd always got on with his mother-in-law, she had been an ally. Now, however, looking at the cosy picture of three generations, he felt a familiar anger, he was always on the outside.

"Traitor,' he said aloud to the smiling Rita. "Fucking traitor." The photograph had been loaded at four o'clock. The three of them had been having afternoon tea, just as Seth had said. There were a few comments under the photograph.

Bobby had written, 'What you up to later?'

Seth had responded, 'Dinner in pub with Mum.'

James sat up and checked his watch. Stalking Molly this evening wasn't a good idea, he needed to get the house ready, to work on his plan but he was riled. He jumped up off the bed and ran down the stairs, grabbing the car keys from the hall table on his way. A look, he would just take a look, nothing more. A sense of urgency descended over him and he drove at speed, he was going to see Molly. Entering the Market Place from the east, he parked in a space facing the pub, slightly in front of the empty taxi rank and next to a mud splattered jeep. Two middle-aged couples were chatting on the pavement. James studied them, he didn't recognise them. Adrenalin coursed through his veins and he drummed the steering wheel with his thumbs, vaguely aware that he was, yet again, acting irrationally.

He opened Facebook. Lucy had just posted a photograph and tagged Seth. She had entitled it 'Your Mum … such a heartbreaker'. The words struck him as odd. In the photograph, Molly and another blond woman were raising their wine glasses to the camera. Molly's face was clearly visible, her smile radiant but her eye make-up a little smeared. He shook his head; the stupid cow was pissed already. The other woman held her wine glass in front of her face, making it impossible to tell if she too were in the same state. He could only assume she was. His eyes were drawn to Molly, to the pink flush that spread from her neck to her cheeks when alcohol got the better of her. She had always been a party animal, always up for one more drink, one more dance but tonight, by the look of her, Molly wouldn't see the night out. A noisy group of young people startled him as they crossed the road and he lowered the interior visor of the BMW as a precaution.

He refreshed Facebook. Lucy had just posted another photograph and tagged Seth and Bobby. The caption read, 'And then there were 3.' What did she mean? Where was Molly? He swore out loud and punched the steering wheel with his fist. A young man, emerging from the pub, caught his attention. He seemed to be talking to someone in the shadows. A dim memory of a beer garden surfaced in James' mind. There was another entrance, he'd forgotten. A car approaching from the other direction beeped its horn, starling him slightly. He watched as the car stopped and the young man climbed inside. Slowly and unsteadily, the other person emerged from the shadows and James started the engine. It was her, it was Molly.

The BMW glided forward silently. James knew he should speed up, to anyone passing by he looked dodgy, like a middle-aged kerb-crawler. He swore, he had no idea what he was doing. And then he saw her raise her arm, she was waving a bank note in the air. The stupid, pissed-up cow was hailing a cab. He looked nervously in his rear-view mirror, a taxi's headlights were a hundred yards or so behind him. Putting his foot on the accelerator, he drove the car quickly, stopping just a few feet in front of Molly. He held his breath, the taxi was right behind him. Molly stumbled over to the BMW and opened the rear passenger door. His fingers tightened around the steering wheel as she climbed, awkwardly, into the back seat, bringing with her a rush of cold air, the smell of alcohol and a familiar waft of the scent he remembered so fondly. Despite the tension, he grinned. Molly didn't hate him, this was proof. The expensive perfume he sent, care of Rita on each and every birthday, was still being put to good use.

***

After Kim's ultimatum in the pub garden, Fiona and Nicola walked home in silence, one mortified by what she'd witnessed, the other consumed with indignant rage. Once inside their own four walls Nicola, feigning a slight headache, escaped to the privacy of her own room. As she closed the door, she heard the distinctive, familiar noises of ice cubes landing in an empty glass and a wine bottle being pulled from the fridge. Her mother was going to drink herself into a stupor and wallow in her own misery. Nicola sighed wearily, it was all so predictable.

Two hours later, gripped by an almost maternal need to check on her mother's welfare, Nicola went downstairs. She found Fiona sitting in the dimly lit snug, just off the kitchen. This was her mother's favourite room, one that hadn't changed at all since her father's death. His favourite chair, now rarely used, still sat near the patio window. Fiona had already finished off one bottle of white wine and was half way through a second. Nicola, still in maternal mode, filled a pint glass with cold tap water and handed it to Fiona.

"Drink it Mum," Nicola said gently. Fiona shook her head. Nicola pushed the glass forward. "Drink it, you'll regret it."

"She's a fucking bitch." Fiona slurred the words. The alcohol had worked its magic, foul language would be the norm for the remainder of the evening.

"Leave it Mum ... please." The anger was nothing new, Fiona was always cross with someone or something but Nicola didn't want to hear yet another character assassination of Molly Pope. She sat down. "Let's do something tomorrow ... the weather's going to be good. Maybe we could call David? Meet him for lunch?" David, her elder brother, had escaped to London several years ago and rarely came home. She couldn't blame him, it was no fun baby-sitting Fiona.

"I'm not going to take this lying down, you know." Fiona ignored the comment about her son. "That bloody witch shouldn't still be here, not after what she fucking did."

"And you shouldn't be throwing pints of lager over people, should you?" Nicola surprised herself, she rarely stood up to her mother. But she needn't have worried, Fiona clearly wasn't listening.

"You know she's been skulking around with another married man, don't you?" Fiona's voice was heavy with contempt. "Dirty ... fucking ... cow."

"I'm not interested Mum. I'll make us some supper. Why don't you go into the lounge? I'll bring it through. We could watch a film maybe?"

"Liv wouldn't tell me who the nasty cow's shagging. Can you believe it?" Fiona made no attempt to move. "Said she'd made a bloody promise to keep a secret. When has that fat cow ever kept a secret, for fuck's sake?!"

Nicola tried to hide a smile. Liv, a large, gregarious woman, was one of her mother's recently acquired friends. Nicola liked her, she was a breath of fresh air. Liv wasn't afraid of Fiona, like so many other women were. She stood up to her, argued with her and even took the piss out of her. She'd recently taken to calling Fiona the Merry Widow, which secretly amused Nicola. And it was a moniker that looked like sticking, the more Fiona raged against it, the more Liv employed it. Fiona was right about Liv though. The woman was a dreadful gossip but, to her credit, she knew how to manage Fiona, some pieces of juicy gossip were better not shared. Liv, whatever her reasons, was doing the right thing in guarding Molly's secret, if indeed she had one. Her mother would have sung that piece of news, true or false, from the rooftops.

"I'm going to bloody well find out though. Liv owes me ... I'll make her tell me!" Fiona's voice was strident.

"Leave it Mum. She's on holiday, don't go disturbing her. Did you hear what I said about seeing David tomorrow? Shall I call him?" Fiona's phone pinged with a text message and Nicola watched as, for the first time that day, a genuinely happy smile appeared on her mother's face. "Well?" she insisted. "What do you say? David?"

"What? David? No ... no need." Fiona got up with sudden, renewed energy. "I'm going to bed. Goodnight darling."

"Un...be ... liev...able ..." Nicola muttered under her breath, as her mother walked unsteadily across the kitchen. Fiona had clearly received a better offer, the possibility of a day with her kids had been outbid. Another ping from the hallway indicated a text conversation was in full flow. Nicola picked up her mother's wine glass and took a sip. "Happy Easter," she said into the empty room.

Chapter Twenty-Two

It was Saturday morning and Eddie had his regular chores to do. He'd often grumble, to anyone who would listen, about Kate's endless shopping lists but he only did so in jest, the reality was that he cherished his Saturday mornings. He loved the routine of walking Lottie around the local shops, frequently stopping to speak to people he'd known since childhood. Many of the independent shops, on both the High Street and the Market Place, had disappeared in recent years but the shopkeepers who'd remained knew him by name. This morning, his first stop was at Jenkins the Bakers, a shop that, thankfully, hadn't moved with the times. The original stone floor and low, beamed ceiling emphasised the wonderful smell of freshly baked bread. Old Mr. Jenkins had officially retired many years ago but, on a Saturday morning, he still liked to sit on a high-backed chair behind the counter, with a freshly laundered apron tied tightly around his skinny frame. Approaching ninety, his watery, beady eyes missed nothing and staff were often berated publicly for any silly mistakes. His son, known as young Mr. Jenkins, was in charge now but wasn't too far off retirement himself. Eddie wondered, as he waited to be served, what would happen to the shop in years to come. Young Mr. Jenkins did have sons to hand the business over to but the eldest two had moved away long ago and he doubted if Joe, the youngest, would be interested. Joe was here this morning, helping out over the busy Bank Holiday weekend, but he was a musician, a guitarist in a local band and a small bakery business wasn't where his future lay.

"Hello Mr. Lawson." It was Joe. "What can I get you?"

"Two large brown loaves Joe. Can you slice them too, please?" Eddie asked, stepping up to the counter.

"Of course." Joe took the loaves over to the slicing machine. "I saw your Bobby in the pub last night," he called above the noise. "Lucy and Seth too."

"Yes, they seem to be spending a lot of their time in there at the moment." Eddie smiled. "Boosting profits."

"It's a nice place these days." Joe packed the sliced loaves into neat bags. "I was speaking to the owners about my band doing some small gigs there during the summer. They seemed quite keen on the idea."

"Knowing Sophie and Jack, they would love that kind of thing." Eddie handed over a ten-pound note. "Sorry Joe, I'm out of change."

"No problem." Joe took the note. "By the way, did Seth's mum get home OK last night? She seemed pretty wasted."

"Molly?" asked Eddie, in a surprised voice, as he held out his hand out for the change. "Wasted?"

"Sorry ... a bit drunk ... tipsy," Joe elaborated.

Eddie laughed. "Man alive Joe! I know what wasted means. I'm not in my dotage just yet. I'm just surprised you're talking about Molly."

Joe smiled sheepishly. "I was waiting for my mates to pick me up and saw her outside the pub. I don't think she recognised me. Sorry, she seemed pretty far gone. She said she was waiting for a lift?"

"Well, I haven't heard anything, so I can only assume that she got home OK. She probably has a stinker of a headache this morning if she was that drunk. Sorry ... wasted." Eddie winked at Joe who laughed.

"I think Bobby might have one too," Joe said. "There were a few wasted people in there last night."

Eddie's next stop was at the Butchers to buy bacon and a joint of beef for Sunday lunch. The shop was busy, as usual, and while Eddie waited to be served, he thought about what Joe had said. It was true, Molly liked a drink as much as the next person but he found it hard to believe she would be in the kind of state Joe had described. She'd been with Seth, she would have kept herself in check, especially after her recent experience at the Wine Bar. Back outside on the pavement, he stopped to check Kate's list.

"Hello Mr Lawson." A young, attractive blond woman bent down to stroke Lottie.

"Hello," Eddie replied. It wasn't uncommon for people to stop and speak to him, or Lottie, but he didn't recognise this young woman.

Sensing his confusion, she helped him out. "Nicola," she said. "Nicola Frost."

"Ah yes ... sorry Nicola," Eddie apologised. "How are you?"

"Fine thanks." Nicola was still fussing over Lottie.

"Good." Eddie was cross with himself for feeling awkward. This young girl hadn't done anything wrong.

Nicola stopped fussing the dog and straightened up, Eddie was shocked by her resemblance to Will. "Can you do me a favour please, Mr. Lawson?" she asked, timidly.

"Eddie ... please call me Eddie."

Nicola smiled, it was Will's smile. "Could you apologise to Molly for me please?"

"Apologise?" Eddie was surprised.

"For my mother. For what she did in the pub." Nicola nodded across the road, towards The Crown.

"I'm sorry Nicola. I don't know what you're talking about," Eddie said, frowning slightly.

"My mum let herself down again ... threw a pint over Molly." Nicola cast her eyes down as she said the last few words. "I wanted Molly to know how sorry I am."

Eddie studied the young girl's profile for a few seconds. "I'll tell her Nicola. Molly's not mentioned it but you shouldn't be feeling guilty. It wasn't your fault, was it? Surely your mum can apologise herself?"

"I should have stopped her," Nicola said. "I'm sorry."

"There's history there Nicola." Eddie put his hand on the young girl's shoulder. "It seems some things can't be forgotten, or forgiven, but you shouldn't be taking responsibility for your mother. She has to do that herself."

Nicola smiled gently. "I know. Easier said than done though."

"How is she?" Eddie felt a little guilty, he hadn't stayed in touch with Fiona. A subconscious decision taken years ago, due to his closeness to

Molly. He shouldn't have done that, he should have made more of an effort, Will had been a close friend.

"Driving me mad," Nicola said, laughing gently. "No change there. She's busy packing again … going away later."

"Really? Where's she going? Aren't you going with her?"

"No. It's something she does quite often … treats herself. Sometimes it's a Spa, sometimes a shopping trip. She always comes back in a better mood than when she left, so I don't worry about her." Nicola bent down to fuss Lottie again. "Anyway, if you could let Molly know."

"What are you doing tomorrow?" Eddie asked, surprising himself. The thought had only just formed in his mind and he hadn't cleared it with Kate but it felt like the right thing to do. "If your mum's not going to be around, why don't you come to ours for lunch? The kids are home. We'll be having a big Sunday roast."

***

Several people were sitting at the wooden tables in the garden when Eddie tethered Lottie to a hook on the pub wall. After his encounter with Nicola, he fancied a quick pint and he was pleased to see Jack behind the bar.

"Morning Eddie, nice to see you." Jack turned to the coffee machine. "What's your poison?"

Eddie glanced at his watch to check the time. "Make it a pint this morning. It's a holiday weekend after all, isn't it?" He looked around the bar astounded, as always, at how many people were eating a leisurely breakfast. Most of the tables were already occupied and a steady trickle of young waiting staff were coming backwards and forwards from the kitchen. He looked back at Jack and shook his head in wonder. "I know it must be hard work Jack," he said. "But this place is always busy. You're definitely onto a winner here."

Jack nodded in agreement. "You're bang on about the hard work. Very different to my previous life, as I'm sure you can imagine."

Eddie took a sip from his pint. "I'm often told by my clients that there's something to be said for being your own boss," he said. "Do you have enough staff?"

"We have plenty of youngsters. I'm always being asked if there is any weekend work going but, to be honest, we need more experienced people. Not necessarily experienced in this trade but experienced in life. More like Molly, I suppose."

Eddie couldn't help but chuckle. "Funny to think we were all a bit worried about Molly working here and now you want to clone her." He wondered whether Jack knew that Fiona had thrown a pint of beer over Molly. He decided not to mention it, it was Molly's business.

"Maturity teaches you things, doesn't it?" Jack smiled, recognising the irony. "You know, how to deal with difficult customers, how to win over people. She's quite a flirt though but, in this business, that can have its advantages."

"A flirt?" Eddie was surprised. "Really? With customers?"

"God, yes," said Jack. "Don't tell me you've never noticed? I've even seen some chemistry going on."

"Bloody hell. I thought she'd stopped all that." Kate would have wanted him to find out more but he couldn't bring himself to ask, he almost didn't want to know. In a quieter voice and almost to himself, he said, "she's a conundrum, isn't she?"

"Aren't all women conundrums?" laughed Jack. "Speaking of which, here's one of the best." He nodded at Sophie as she approached them, her arms full of paper serviettes.

"Morning Eddie," Sophie said cheerfully. "Are you two talking about me?"

"Not you," Eddie replied, a little defensively. "Women in general."

"Experts in that subject are you, the two of you?" Sophie stacked the serviettes behind the bar.

"Anything but, my darling, anything but." Jack was still laughing as he turned to serve a customer.

"Eddie, I hope you and Kate are still coming in tonight?" Sophie asked. "Kim's doing a few bits of food for us, on the house."

"We're looking forward to it and you know how much I love Kim's food." Eddie put both hands on his stomach and winked at Sophie. "I think the kids are using this place as a second home now though," he added. "Let me know if it becomes an issue."

Sophie wave her hand dismissively. "Don't worry. They're good kids, they know how to behave. They were in again last night ... Molly too. She really hit it off with our friend Annie." She looked at her watch with a slight frown. "Actually, Molly should be here by now. I hope she remembered she's working today."

"Ah, she's not renowned for her time-keeping is our Moll. Sorry. We didn't tell you that, did we?" Eddie said, almost shamefully. "An important piece of information to include on a reference in hindsight."

Sophie smiled. "She stays late often enough so it works both ways but you can see how busy it is already. I'm sure she'll be here soon."

Eddie was tempted to say that Molly's lateness was probably due to a hangover but he thought better of it. If Molly had been drunk last night so be it, she didn't need him telling tales. He finished off his beer and waved goodbye to both Jack and Sophie. Outside, he found Lottie had attracted an audience, several young children had gathered round her, some were tentatively stroking her soft black head. "Come on Lottie," he said, untying her lead and pulling her, reluctantly, away from the children. "Let's go and see if everyone's surfaced. It's time for some bacon sandwiches."

Back at the house, he found Kate alone in the kitchen. "Don't tell me they aren't up yet?"

"I've heard very little." Kate took the shopping from him. "The smell of bacon should get them moving." There was a knock at the back door and Seth let himself in.

Eddie laughed loudly. "Bloody hell. The lure of bacon ... amazing."

"Idiot," Kate laughed. "I take it you'll join us Seth? Bacon sarnie?"

"Yes please," Seth smiled. "Aren't they up yet?" He looked up at the ceiling.

"No." Eddie turned as the kitchen door opened. A pale faced Lucy appeared, followed by her sleepy looking brother. "I take it back, they're up but they don't look too lively."

"Shut up Dad." Lucy groaned. "I feel like poo."

"You don't look too great Lucy Loo," Seth said. "I didn't think you were that bad last night."

Lucy ignored the nickname, her head hurt too much to chastise him. "I wasn't, until that Annie started with the drinking games," she moaned. "Everything's a bit of a blur after that. The woman's an animal."

"She's great, isn't she?" Bobby filled a large glass with tap water. "She's my new hero. I've never known a woman sink a pint so quickly. Not even the girls on the Ladies Rugby Team at uni."

"Praise indeed." Kate raised her eyebrows as she placed a plate of sandwiches on the table.

"Bobby's got a crush on an older woman," Seth teased. "Punching a bit too high, aren't you Bobs?" Bobby threw a wet sponge in his direction. Lottie, thinking it was food, chased it across the floor.

"Shut up candle," Bobby sat down and swiped playfully at Seth's head. "You don't have the greatest of track records yourself, do you?"

"Candle?" Kate asked tentatively. "Did you say candle?"

"Mum, come on!" Lucy groaned. "Really?!"

Kate looked confused but she was laughing, she wasn't exactly sure why. "I'm lost."

Bobby came to her rescue. "Candle, Mum. That's what Seth is, he's always being blown out."

Seth shook his head. "Ignore him Kate. He has no idea … and no hope."

"Want a bet?" Bobby challenged. "Me and Annie? Want a bet?"

"I don't fancy the odds if I'm honest Bob," Eddie laughed. "Although I admire your ambition. Speaking of older women Seth, I bumped into Joe this morning. You know Joe Jenkins, don't you?" Seth, his mouth full of bacon sandwich, nodded his head. "He said he saw your mum last night. He said she was a bit .... let's say he thought she was a bit tipsy." He refrained from using Joe's more graphic description. "He wanted to know if she got home OK. Not sure why he thought I'd know but did she? Get home OK?"

Seth swallowed and reached for the orange juice Kate had put on the table. "Yes, I think so. Well she must have. I haven't seen her this morning, to be honest. She'd left for work before I got up but Joe was right ... she was a bit the worse for wear."

"She ghosted on us Dad," said Lucy sarcastically. "Did a runner. Couldn't keep up with Annie I think. She was going to get a taxi home, wasn't she Seth?" Seth, finishing off another sandwich, nodded again.

"Always the sensible thing to do, get a taxi." Eddie was relieved. Seth had confirmed Molly was on her way to work, she wasn't going to let Sophie down.

"What are you guys doing with what's left of the day?" Kate asked, as she collected empty plates.

Seth glanced at Bobby. "We do have a plan, all three of us." Lucy looked at him blankly.

"We do?" asked Bobby innocently.

"No good playing dumb guys." Seth reached for his rucksack and pulled out one of his trainers. "Those games of Annie's? The forfeits?"

"Oh shit!" Bobby dropped his head to the table. His voice was muffled when he spoke. "It's all coming back to me."

"What?" Kate and Eddie asked simultaneously.

Lucy groaned. "You're not serious, are you Seth? You're not really going to make us do it? Not after all that alcohol?"

"Do what?" Eddie couldn't help but laugh. "It can't be that bad, can it?"

"Seth ... I can't," Lucy pleaded.

"If I'd lost, you'd make me do my forfeit, wouldn't you?" Seth looked from Bobby to Lucy.

"Do what?" Eddie asked again.

"Shit, I can't do it Seth," Lucy groaned. "I'll throw up."

Bobby rose slowly from the table. "OK, I'll go get ready. Come on Lucy, no backing down. A forfeit's a forfeit. It might even help with the hangover."

"Will one of you bloody well tell me what's going on?" Kate threw her arms in the air. "I can't stand the suspense."

"Bloody Annie and her frigging games. Losers' forfeit ... that's what's going on," Lucy rose slowly from her seat. "Bloody woman."

There was a glint in Seth's eye. "Beer goggle bravado disappeared, has it?"

"What's the forfeit?" Eddie asked.

"A training run. We're going to put them to the test."

"We?" asked Eddie. "Who's we?"

"Me and Annie," said Seth, smiling gleefully. "We're meeting her in half an hour. Why else would Bobby be so keen?"

Chapter Twenty-Three

A hand landed softly on her shoulder, the shake was gentle. Molly, eyes closed and half asleep, turned her face away.

"Let's get you inside." It was a command, gently delivered. Molly acquiesced, opening her eyes and blinking rapidly as she took in her surroundings. In the gloom, she was alarmed to find herself still in the taxi. Disorientated, she searched for her bag; a dull headache manifested itself as she did so. The wine, she thought, Annie and all that bloody wine.

"Come on, let's get you inside." The same command. The taxi driver was being kind but she was embarrassed.

"Thank you, thank you" she mumbled. "I'm sorry, I must have fallen asleep. It's been a long day." She was mortified. "I don't normally do this." She tried to laugh, her default behaviour kicking in. "How much do I owe you?"

The man said nothing but pushed her gently forward, gravel crunched, noisily, under her feet.

"Where am I?" Her mouth was dry. "This isn't my house."

"Yes, it is. This is your home Molly."

Her mind was playing games on her. He'd used her name, he knew who she was. In the darkness, she heard a door close and a key turn in a lock. "Who are you?" Her voice shook. "Please don't hurt me." The man took her elbow and pushed her forward again. His gentleness confused her, she felt compelled to cooperate. A familiar smell hit her nostrils and she stopped abruptly. "Who are you?" she asked again. Soft light suddenly illuminated the room and she gasped. She was in her kitchen, her old kitchen, she was at Willow Hill.

"Well Molly, how's your head?" James came towards her with a glass of water. "Here, drink this." Another command. She took the glass from him cautiously. "It's just water Molly ... no need to look so afraid." He took her arm again and led her to the dark green sofa, the sofa she'd bought in John Lewis all those years ago. "Go on. Drink it. You'll be dehydrated after all that booze." Despite her fear, Molly took several small sips, grateful for the clean, fresh taste. James sat down next to her. She pulled back, sensing, incorrectly, that he was going to touch her.

"Better?" he asked eventually. "You had a lot to drink last night." She turned her wrist to look at her watch, shocked to see it was nearly five o'clock. James caught the confused look on her face. "You fell asleep so quickly once you got into my car," he explained. "I didn't want to wake you. I drove around for a few hours, I thought you'd benefit from some sleep. I even stopped and grabbed a couple of hours myself but the cold woke me up. I have to say it's been a long time since I slept in a car."

"What are you doing James?" Molly asked cautiously. "Why did you pretend to be a taxi? Why have you brought me here?"

James laughed loudly and she flinched. "I didn't pretend to be a taxi Molly. Imagine ... me ... a taxi driver." He was offended. "I was driving past and saw you staggering about drunkenly. You waved me down and got into my car. Got in willingly, no-one forced you."

Molly sipped more water, he was right. She had a vague recollection of hailing a taxi, of a car stopping, of climbing into the warm interior. "What are you doing here?" she asked nervously. "You signed an agreement."

"We both signed that agreement Molly." He let the words hang for a second, he didn't want to use his trump card just yet. "You got into my car uninvited ... and drunk."

"Why have you brought me here?" Molly looked around the familiar kitchen. A dreadful thought occurred to her. "Don't tell me you still own this? Shit! It doesn't make sense."

"It's our home, Molly," James said, looking intently at her. "Why would I sell it? Where else would we go?"

***

"Where the fuck is she?" Jack hissed, as Sophie walked into the kitchen. "It's manic out there. Those kids are doing their best but they can't cope on their own."

"Don't swear at me Jack, I don't know where she is." Sophie picked up a loaded tray and walked over to the door. "I've left a voicemail and sent a text message but she's not responded. What else do you expect me to do? Anyway, you don't need to get your knickers in a twist. If you'd bothered to ask, I could have told you Annie's just gone upstairs to get changed. She's going out there to lend a hand."

"I'm sorry but it's not good enough Sophie." Jack held the kitchen door open for her. "It's a Bank Holiday weekend and the good weather is driving everyone outside. She knows we'll be busy."

"I know, I know. I'm just worried she may have forgotten I changed a few shifts." Sophie paused in the doorway. "Should I call Kate?"

"I'll do it," Jack said. "Thank God Annie's here."

"Thank God indeed," said Annie, running down the stairs. "OK, where do you want me? In the marquee?"

"Yes please." Jack walked outside with her. "Thanks for this Annie. It's not much of a break for you really. You're supposed to be on leave."

"Don't be daft, happy to help but could you do something for me?" she asked. "Text those kids ... Seth and the others? I was supposed to go training with them this morning."

"You can tell them yourself." Jack pointed to where Seth, Lucy and Bobby were sitting on a bench. "Looks like they're waiting for you."

Annie trotted over to them. "Morning guys. I'm really sorry but we have a bit of an emergency here and I'm needed behind the bar. You'll have to run without me." Lucy made no attempt to hide her relief. Bobby, on the other hand, looked crestfallen.

"That's a shame," said Seth. "No problem though. I can put these two through their paces. What's the emergency?"

Annie looked up at Jack who had joined them. "Seth, do you know where your mum is?" he asked in a matter of fact tone. "She's not turned up for work yet. It's not like her."

"Really?" Seth looked surprised. "I've not seen her today. She'd already left when I woke up this morning. How late is she?"

Jack looked at his watch. Molly was nearly two hours late but, despite his anger, he didn't want to alarm Seth. He'd wait until he'd spoken to Eddie. "Don't worry," he said, in a reassuring voice, deliberately not answering Seth's question. "It's possible that Sophie and your mum got their wires crossed. A last minute change was made to the rota. She didn't say anything to you though, did she? About not working today?"

Seth shook his head. "Sorry Jack. I don't think so, I don't really remember. When I didn't see her this morning, I just assumed she'd be here. Have you tried calling her? Sorry, stupid question."

"Sophie has. No need to panic. We've got Annie with us so we're covered." Jack grinned at Lucy and Bobby. "Seems you two get a reprieve … for now at least. Believe me she's a tough cookie." He patted Annie on the head. "She might be small but she's as fit as a flea. I wouldn't have fancied your chances."

"OK Jack, no need to frighten them." Annie laughed and turned towards the marquee. "Right, I'll see you guys later, enjoy your run. Let me know how they get on Seth."

Watching the kids walk out of the garden, Jack rang Eddie. "Ed, do you or Kate know what Molly is up to today?" He spoke quietly.

"No idea mate. Isn't she working?"

"I don't want to panic you but she's not turned up and we've had no word from her. I've just spoken to Seth. He reckons she'd already left for work when he got up this morning. Eddie … she's over two hours late."

"Shit! Are you thinking what I'm thinking?"

"Do I think it's got something to do with James? Yes, Eddie I do. I think there's a strong possibility."

"Oh God, fuck," was all Eddie could say.

"Can you and Kate come over here? In an hour or so? The lunch rush should be over by then. I'd like to retrace her steps and put some pieces of the jigsaw together."

"What have you said to Seth?" Eddie asked. "He'll be back here in a while. I don't want to scare him with our news about James."

"Scare him? Why would Seth be scared of his dad? Are you still keeping things from me Eddie?"

***

She was a bloody prisoner, not a prisoner in her own home but a prisoner in her old home. The irony was almost amusing. Slowly releasing her left hand from the grasp it had on her bag, she placed her fingers on the soft green fabric of the sofa. She wanted the touch to reassure her but the familiar feel only served to prove that she wasn't dreaming, that this wasn't just a horrendous nightmare. James walked across the kitchen towards her, his trademark expensive shoes echoing on the tiled floor. Even after sleeping in a car, he looked immaculate. In contrast, she felt shabby, her cheap, high-street jeans and work shirt, poor comparisons to his well-made, designer clothes.

"You're probably hungry." He handed her a cup of tea. The tall, white china cup was familiar, it had been part of a wedding gift. She tried to remember who the gift was from but couldn't, there had been so many gifts, so many people to thank. He sat down next to her, she shifted; he was too close. "I expect you'd like a shower first, wouldn't you? Or do you need more sleep?" She took a mouthful of tea. It tasted good, hot and slightly sweet. "Or maybe you'd prefer a bath?" James was still talking. "It can't have been too comfortable in the back of the car. A nice hot bath might help relax you."

"I'm not staying James." She was relieved to hear some strength in her voice.

"Of course you are." James adopted the persuasive tone of a parent encouraging a reticent child. "You're home now, where else would you go?"

"This isn't my home." She saw his shoulders droop. Knowing her refusal to cooperate was hurting him, gave her some strength. "And Seth will be worried about me."

"You think?" James asked, raising his dark eyebrows. There was a familiar, cruel edge to his voice. "He wasn't worried about you at Christmas, was he darling?"

"What do you mean?" The endearment made her cringe but she was too frightened to remonstrate with him. "He's home from uni. Of course he'll be worried."

"Oh, I doubt that. Seth doesn't waste time worrying about you."

"I'm supposed to be at work." He wouldn't know about her job. "My boss will be worried too."

"Now don't lie to me Molly." She could have been a child, he was admonishing her. "Let's promise. No more lies."

"What makes you think I'm lying? It's the truth. I'm due at work."

He sighed in mock disappointment. "Molly, please stop being so tiresome. You're not due at work today. I've seen your rota." As shock registered on Molly's face, he smiled triumphantly. "People underestimate me you know, you included apparently. It's a quaint little place, isn't it? Your cottage? The rota's on your fridge. You used to put Seth's drawings on the fridge in here. Do you remember?" He gestured over to the huge fridge in the corner of the kitchen.

"You've been in my cottage?" she asked breathlessly. "Why? How?"

James sighed. "I needed to check on you Molly, check what you were up to. You gave me reason to check. Like I said, you signed an agreement too."

"You needed to check on me? Christ James, you're supposed to stay away from me. You have no right going into my cottage. How the hell did you get in?"

"Oldest trick in the book darling. The cat flap trick." He roared with laughter, the noise hit her like a gust of wind. "You really should be more careful."

She couldn't look at him, he was so pompous, he made her feel sick. "James, I don't care if you got into my cottage," she said, desperately. "I've nothing to hide from you or anyone else." She shifted forward, thinking how easily the two of them had fallen back into a war of words. "I already knew you were looking for me." For a moment, she had the upper hand. "It was only a question of time until you did something stupid."

"The silly old maid next door snitched on me, did she?" he asked scornfully. "Interfering old cow." Molly put her hand in her bag. "Looking for this?" He held up her phone.

She closed her eyes in defeat. "I am due at work today, it's the truth. The rota changed. People will be looking for me." She said a silent prayer, she hoped to God people would be looking for her.

"Who? Seth? I doubt it." There was something close to contempt in James' voice. "Like I said, he wasn't worried about you at Christmas, was he? And do you really think the lovely Sophie will be worried? She'll just be cross you haven't turned up. She seems like an organised lady, she'll have a back-up plan."

Molly gasped. "How do you know Sophie?"

James threw himself back on the sofa. "Oh Molly, you are so blond. How the hell have you managed without me?" He was enjoying himself. "You don't know about me and Sophie, do you my love? Don't look so shocked. Unlike your friendships with members of the opposite sex, it's nothing sordid. Sophie and Jack bought me a drink a couple of weeks back. In return for a favour, of course."

"I don't know what you're playing at but I'm not staying here." She was shouting now, she couldn't help it. "Don't you see how inappropriate this is? We're getting divorced."

"Inappropriate?" James scoffed. "I love it. Inappropriate? Me? You really need to examine your own conscience Molly."

"Stop it." She got up unsteadily. "Stop playing your stupid fucking games. I'm leaving."

"Sit down." His tone changed. "You're not going anywhere until we discuss something. I have a deal to propose to you."

She sat down obediently, deflated and close to tears. "A deal?"

"Good girl. That's better." The master of mood swings, he smiled at her encouragingly. "It's a wonderful deal. I'm just a little disappointed with myself for not thinking of it sooner."

"What are you up to? Why do you want to do a deal with me?" He'd spent years playing games over the divorce, she couldn't tolerate more excuses. She deserved better.

"Tell me, how much do you value your friendship with Kate? Could you ever imagine life without her? Odd question I know, but could you? You two are joined at the hip, aren't you?"

"Oh God James, stop talking in riddles." She dropped her chin to her chest, her head hurt. "What deal are you talking about? We already have a deal."

"Do we? I'm not so sure anymore. But this new deal is failsafe."

"James, stop it. I want to go home."

"And Kate is integral to this deal," he added slowly. "Look at me when I'm speaking to you Molly." She raised her head and met his gaze. "That's better." He smiled softly. "I know how much you rely on her, on Kate. How many times has she picked up the pieces? Sorted you out? Kept you sane?" She shook her head, there was nothing she could say. It was true, Kate had always been there for her. "And it doesn't stop with Kate, does it?" James continued. "Good old Eddie's part of the package, isn't he? Dependable, old Ed. God, what a dreadful bore that man is." The smile disappeared. "But he's always there when you need him, isn't he Molly? An arm you can lean on? Visit the dead with?

"You evil bastard!" Molly screamed. "It was you! You were in the cemetery! You're a fucking madman. Bloody hell James, you could have hurt me." Her hand moved to rub her shoulder, under her shirt there was still a slight bruise, the result of her collision with a headstone.

James sighed. He was sitting so close, she could feel his breath on her face. "Oh Molly, if only you knew. Hours of fun... watching and waiting for you."

She looked at him closely now, at the face she had once known as well as her own. His thick, dark brown hair looked healthy, with just a little grey showing at the temples and his skin was smooth, even with the onset of early morning stubble. The chocolate brown eyes, framed by long, poker straight eyelashes and the slightly prominent bridge of the nose, were all familiar to her. She was struck, suddenly, by ugly facial characteristics she'd never observed in isolation before. She noticed, for the first time, how small his mouth was, how mean and bitter it looked. And his chin, James had a small, weak chin. It made her skin crawl to think of the intimacy they'd once shared. She shuddered.

James misunderstood the shudder. "Kate wouldn't be very impressed if she knew what you'd been up to, would she? It might be the last straw, don't you think?"

"What the hell are you talking about? I have nothing to hide from Kate." Frustration was making her brave.

James feigned surprise. "Really? I wouldn't be quite so sure darling."

"James, I want to go home." She was close to tears. "If you don't tell me what game it is you're playing, I'm walking out that door in two minutes."

"Not so fast ... play along darling. I want you to consider, for a moment, what life would be like without Kate and without her wonderful family." Each word was heavy with sarcasm. "Without her friends too? Let's face it, they only tolerate you because of her. Personally, I don't think you'd cope. You'd turn into your mother Molly. You'd turn into a lonely, sad, old woman."

"I don't know what you're talking about." She desperately wanted to remain calm, he wasn't going to see her cry.

"Really?" He paused, the fridge hummed softly in the background. "I'll spell it out for you, shall I?" He uncrossed his legs and readjusted his sitting position. "Kate's been good to you, hasn't she? She epitomises friendship. She's stuck by you repeatedly. God knows why. You haven't deserved it. You've done some truly, wicked things, haven't you? Things even Kate doesn't know about. Things that could get you in a lot of trouble." He let the words hang in the air. "But let's be honest," he pulled her face round to look at him. "Your latest piece of news is too close for comfort, isn't it? Not in the same league as some of your old tricks maybe but definitely a friendship destroyer I'd say."

"Shut up James. You're talking shit. You always did. You're a fantasist. I've done nothing wrong."

"Shagging Patty's husband, her sister's husband, is a step too far Molly ... even for Saint Kate, don't you think?" The silence that fell between them was deafening, again the fridge hummed. Pleased with what he saw in her eyes, he slowly let go of her chin. "Not rushing to deny it then? I knew what you were up to. I just needed a little time to work out who it was."

"You don't know what you're talking about."

He put up his hand. "Don't go there Molly. You're as guilty as hell. I got into your cottage remember. There was evidence. You should clear away your empty bottles, his champagne bottles to be exact but then you always were lazy. Do you want to hear the deal?" He sounded childishly excited. "You've probably worked it out for yourself by now anyway, haven't you? It's very simple, a little like you." He forced a cruel laugh. "Sorry, I couldn't resist that one. Cheap joke." He drew his breath in. "So, my deal with you Molly is that I keep quiet. It's as simple as that. I won't tell Kate about your sordid little affair with Harry, the guy who's married to her sister, the father of her niece and nephew." He studied her face without pity. The tears she'd tried to hold back were in free-fall. "Have you guessed what I want in return?"

Molly dropped her head. "The settlement. You want me to walk away from the settlement." He'd won, after all this time, he'd won. She was never going to have any money, she was destined to a life of just getting by.

"You never fail to disappoint, do you? You're so very stupid but equally endearing." James was, once again, consumed with laughter. "I don't care about the bloody settlement. I never have. Good God Molly, you were getting very little of my money. So little I wouldn't even have noticed, a mere drop in the ocean." He paused to compose himself. "Go on, have another guess. What do I want in return?"

Molly wiped away the tears and looked up at him, dread slowly descending on her. He couldn't be serious, he wasn't in his right mind. "James ... no."

"What?" He sat forward until his face was just inches from hers. She could see the cracks in his dry lips and smell the staleness of his breath.

"You can't be serious. You can't expect me to do that." Her voice was just a whisper.

"What Molly? What can't I expect?"

"No. No way. Please ... no."

"Molly, you're not being any fun," he chastised her. "What happened to the fun-loving Molly? Where did she go?"

"Fun loving?" Molly asked, her voice momentarily stronger. "Fun costs. I have nothing."

"We can change that though, can't we? We can get the old Molly back. The deal works in your favour too."

"James, you can't mean it?" she sniffed. "Not after all this time?"

"Stop with the tears woman. There's nothing to cry about. From what I've seen of your life lately, you should be grateful I'd even consider it. Take it or leave it. Carry on with the divorce and I will happily tell Kate everything ... and, this time, I mean everything." He walked over to the curtains and pulled them back to reveal a bright, sunny morning.

The sunlight startled Molly, time had moved on. "I don't want to be married to you James." There was nothing else she could say, it was true. But James had the upper hand, he'd always had the upper hand.

***

Seth led Bobby and Lucy through the Market Place at a gentle pace, jumping on and off pavements to avoid pedestrians. He was heading for the river and the dirt track where, for the most part, it would be easy for them to run three abreast. Lucy had put on her sunglasses and plugged in her earphones. Grumpy and hungover, she was being deliberately noncommunicative. Bobby, on the other hand, had ditched his customary earphones and was happy to chat.

"Shame about Annie, eh?" Bobby said, breathing hard. "I was looking forward to seeing her in lycra ... to running behind her."

Seth laughed. "Out of your league mate but I agree, it's a shame she couldn't come. You guys might have tried harder for her."

"Oh believe me, I'm trying," gasped Bobby, as they narrowly avoided being chased down by a playful Jack Russell. "I'll be having words with your mum later. She's ruined my morning, making Annie work."

Seth laughed again but he said nothing. He wasn't sure whether he should be overly worried about Molly's no-show at the pub. From what Jack had said it was probably just a mix up in rotas, which was easy to believe, she was, after all, a dizzy blond. He pointed to a path that skirted the newly built housing estate; Bobby and Lucy followed him in single file. Their laboured breathing, coupled with the sound of their trainers hitting the dry track, competed with the noise of various activities going on behind the garden fences. Lawnmowers were making a comeback after winter hibernation and children were playing.

Coming back on to the wider track, Seth slowed down and touched Lucy's elbow to get her attention. "You OK?" he mouthed. She put her thumbs up in response. "She's fitter than I remember," he said to Bobby, as they crossed the wooden footbridge.

"She plays for the uni hockey team. She's always moaning about the training but it looks like it's paying off. Shit! Do you expect me to run up that fucking hill?" Willow Hill wasn't particularly steep but the incline was lengthy, for non-accustomed runners it could look, and feel, never-ending.

"I do mate, I do." Seth hit the gradient. "Come on, dig deep."

"I'm done." Bobby stopped abruptly. He was breathing hard. "Wait for me at the top."

"Wimp!" Seth shouted as he sprinted after Lucy who was coping well with the gradient. Catching up with her, he tapped her on the elbow, gesturing for her to take her earphones out.

"What?" Her tone was impatient.

"You can carry on, or you can wait for Bobby." He pointed behind him to where Bobby was making hard work of the incline. "I'm happy to wait for him."

Lucy looked down at her brother and groaned. "He wouldn't be walking if Annie was here." She put her hands on her hips to further demonstrate her displeasure.

"Still in a bad mood then?" Seth asked.

"Shut up Seth."

"I'll take that as a yes. See that?" He pointed to a house further up the road. "Does that look familiar to you?"

"No, what? What am I supposed to be looking at?"

"See that turning on the left, the long drive, and the oak trees?" he asked.

"Yes, what is it?"

"That's my old house. Our old house. The Vicarage."

"Really?" Lucy asked. "Are you sure?"

"Of course, I'm sure, you idiot. I used to live there. Why wouldn't I be sure?"

Lucy shrugged her shoulders. "I don't know. It was a long time ago. Come on, we should take a closer look."

"What about Bobby?" Seth looked behind him. Bobby was, at last, getting closer.

"Come on!" Lucy was already jogging towards the drive. "What are you scared of?"

"Hold on," he shouted. "Wait for Bobby."

"I spend my life waiting for Bobby. I'm going to take a peak. I'll meet you at home," Lucy shouted. She'd already put a good distance between them. Seth watched her for a few moments, there was so much he admired about Lucy. She was impulsive and brave, she was everything he wasn't.

"Where's she going?" gasped Bobby, as he climbed the last of the hill and stepped onto the pavement next to Seth.

"See that house over there, behind the oak trees?" Seth pointed ahead. "That's my old house."

"The one with the enormous pool!" Bobby exclaimed. "I remember that house. You had a trampoline too, years before anyone else. But you had everything, didn't you?"

Seth was surprised by this comment, Bobby had a good memory. "Come on, jog" he said.

"No mate I can't, I'm done. I've got blisters on top of blisters and I've got stitch." Bobby sat down on the grass verge and took off one of his trainers. "You carry on. I'll walk back."

"I'll wait. Get your breath back." He looked up the road, there was no sign of Lucy. He had no longing to follow her anyway, he'd seen enough of his old home yesterday. Lowering himself onto the grass next to Bobby, he tried to sound casual. "What did you mean when you said I had everything?"

"What? Oh … just that you had every toy going mate. Rooms full of them and your dad built you that train track in the garage. Don't you remember? It was amazing. We used to spend hours in there."

The garage, the trains, the intricate details of the small engines and the noises they made as they navigated the winding tracks. He'd blocked out so many memories, some of the good ones had been blocked along with the bad. "I'd forgotten about the trains," Seth said thoughtfully. "And the pool." The pool, the trellis, neither were there anymore. They'd been dug up, filled in, obliterated. Just like some of his memories.

"Sorry Seth," Bobby said. "I didn't think. I guess there's a lot you'd rather not remember."

"Don't apologise … I'd just forgotten." Seth got up, he wasn't sure how much Bobby knew. "Although some things are probably best forgotten."

Bobby pulled off his sock to examine the damage to his foot. "Pretty hard to forget though? Some things can't be unseen, can they? You've come out the other end now, haven't you? Everything's cool, isn't it?"

Seth managed to smile. Bobby, in his own way, was asking him if he was OK. "Yeah, everything's cool," he said. "Thanks to my therapist."

"Shit! Really? You have a therapist? You never said." Bobby was shocked.

"Yes, I have a therapist Bobby. His name is Charles. He's old-school ... white-haired, well educated, quite posh. Get the picture?" Bobby nodded. "He's helped me deal with things ... made me a better person I think." Seth had only ever discussed Charles with his tutor, this was new territory.

"Bloody hell," was all Bobby could manage to say.

Seth considered whether he should say more. "You seem surprised?"

"Yes, no, maybe. I just thought that after so long ..." Bobby's voice tailed off.

"What? That life goes on?" Seth shook his head. "Life went on for everyone else but I needed help. I didn't know it, my tutor spotted it. Thanks to him, and Charles, I've managed to park a lot of that shit. I wasn't very nice back then, was I?"

Bobby shrugged his shoulders. "You were OK."

"No I wasn't. I was a nasty, little shit. I did some horrid things." Seth felt guilty, this was too much for Bobby. "I've learnt to deal with it though." He tried to sound upbeat. "I rarely think about everything that happened and, when I do, there's a lot I can't recall. I think it's better that way ... for everyone."

"Sorry Seth. I'm no good at this stuff. I never know what to say but I'm here if you need to talk. Maybe I should have said that before."

"We were kids. Crazy things happened. Don't apologise, there's nothing to apologise for." Seth was touched by Bobby's sincerity. He put his hand on his friend's shoulder. "I'm over it ... really I am." It was time to change the subject, he couldn't afford to dwell on things too long, he only did that with Charles. Dwelling on things opened the memory box where wounds, fear and irrational behaviour lived. And most worryingly of all, dwelling on things reminded him that there was still a crucial piece of the jigsaw missing. "Come on," he said, in a voice that sounded much more positive than he felt. "Jog, you'll get cold otherwise."

***

Lucy stopped at the gates. She was surprised, this house was familiar after all. The enormous front door, the wide, sash windows, the tall chimneys; it had all seemed overwhelming and a little bit frightening to a small girl. Today, in the bright sunshine, the house looked austere and aloof but not threatening. Curious, she took a step closer and slipped through the gates. Up close, the house was huge. It made her wonder, briefly, if Molly had wanted more children. A house this size was screaming out for lots of kids but the thought of Seth with siblings was disturbing; Seth was unique.

Creeping furtively closer to the house, she peered through the downstairs windows. The rooms, although beautifully furnished, didn't look lived in. They were too perfect, like something she'd seen in expensive magazines. A path led to the back of the house where a huge expanse of perfectly manicured lawns sloped down to the edge of the river and the woods. She had no recollection of this, the garden she remembered had been less formal. There had been swings, a slide and even a climbing frame.

"Can I help you?" Lucy jumped. A tall, dark-haired man had stepped out onto the terrace. She was struck by his appearance; a crisp, white, cotton shirt, blue jeans, a discreet belt, leather shoes. Just like the furnishings she'd seen in the front rooms, this man's clothes looked expensive.

"I'm sorry," she said, a little self-consciously. Dressed in her running gear, she felt exposed. "I didn't realise anyone was here."

"Manifestly." His tone was impatient. Lucy half expected him to advance towards her but he didn't move, his left hand remained firmly attached to the door handle.

"Sorry," she said again. "I used to know the people who lived here. I was passing." She indicated her running gear. "I was being nosy … I've not been here in a long time." She opted to tell the truth, he didn't look like the kind of guy you could mess with.

The man looked behind him briefly, through the open door. "Who did you know?" he asked. His tone was far from casual.

"I had a friend ... I have a friend. His name's Seth. Seth used to live here." She was struggling to string a sentence together; this man was intimidating. "I remember playing here ... in this garden. It looked different back then."

A voice shouted something from inside the house and the man turned his head. "Sit back down, don't move." There was an unpleasant shift in his demeanour. Lucy took a step back, irrationally afraid. "I think you should go." The man shut the door and took a step towards her.

She didn't need telling twice. "I'm going ... sorry." She turned and raced along the path. From behind her she heard a cry, it sounded like a child. The gates were still open and she flew through them, catching her elbow sharply on the bolt as she did so but she didn't stop and she didn't look back. Panting heavily as she re-joined the pavement, she crossed the road and jogged more slowly down the hill. She'd been such a fool, Seth would be furious. Not content with taking a look from the gates, like most people, she had pushed her luck and wandered through private property. It was little wonder the bloke had been cross, she had been trespassing and he was probably worried about his kids. She made a decision there and then. She wouldn't tell Seth about the man, she wouldn't tell anyone.

Chapter Twenty-Four

Kate hadn't been able to wait. Sitting at home, doing nothing, wasn't an option; she needed to find Molly. She'd called her friend's mobile number multiple times, her frustration growing each time the calls went to voicemail. Making up a poor excuse, she had even tried calling Rita. It was a long shot and Rita, somewhat confused by the call, had confirmed what Kate already knew, Molly wasn't with her mother. Finally, when she couldn't wait any longer, when the pacing of her kitchen was driving her mad, she'd raced up to the pub with Eddie following in her wake. Frustratingly though, the waiting continued, they were just waiting in a different location.

The lounge in the flat above the pub was very small but perfectly adequate for Sophie and Jack, on a day-to-day basis. Two brown, leather sofas sat at right angles to each other and were covered in brightly coloured, scatter cushions. A long and low, wooden coffee table sat in front of the settees and a discreet, flat-screen TV hung from one wall. Two pretty Tiffany style, floor lamps were the only other pieces of furniture. It was a stark reminder of how cluttered her own home was.

"God, this was a bad idea," Kate said, sighing. "We should have stayed at home, we should have waited to speak to Seth."

"I don't think Jack wants us to speak to Seth until we have the facts." Eddie was trying to be reassuring but his mind was racing. There was so much he hadn't told Kate.

"Facts?" hissed Kate. "What bloody facts? Molly's gone AWOL and James is probably behind it. We should go to the police."

"And tell them what," asked Jack. Kate jumped, she hadn't heard him come into the room. "Sorry Kate, I know you're worried. Believe me, I'm quite worried too but the police won't be able to do anything, at least not with any speed, until we pull what we know together."

He was right, but her body ached to be proactive. Sitting and waiting was eating away at her. "OK," she said quietly, as Jack sat down next to her.

"But it's hard Jack, the not knowing. She's not a child, she can come and go as she wants but she'd tell us, she'd tell me. This feels wrong and I'm scared." She looked down at her hands afraid to keep looking at Jack, afraid to let him see her tears. She hadn't cried when she'd been told about the cancer, she wasn't going to cry now.

"One step at a time." Jack put his hand reassuringly on her arm. "OK, what have we got? From what I know he, James, has been back here a couple of times recently. When Sophie met him on the train, he said it was his first visit back in years. We don't know if that's true but he certainly returned a few days later. He came in here, into the pub. That was before we knew he was James though. Sophie and I knew him as JP. We had no reason to suspect him of anything. In fact, he'd helped Sophie out of a potentially embarrassing predicament on the train. She had reason to be grateful to him." Kate sighed but said nothing. It gave her no pleasure to think of James as some kind of knight in shining armour.

"What next?" Jack asked Kate directly. "You saw him in London, didn't you?"

"Yes. Well I think I did," Kate said. "But if you're looking at this chronologically, then it was Ethel who saw him next. She saw him before I did."

"Ethel?" Jack asked. "Who's Ethel?"

"Molly's neighbour," said Eddie. "The old lady from the cottage next door."

"She told Molly that a man had been looking for her," said Kate. "From her description, it sounded like James."

"Is she a reliable witness?" asked Jack.

"Bloody hell, is that what she is?" asked Eddie. "Is it that serious?"

"You tell me Ed. You guys are the ones who think James is dangerous, aren't you?" Neither Kate or Eddie responded. Jack continue, "can Ethel verify the man she saw was James?"

Kate nodded. "Molly showed her a photograph."

272

"Hang on, Sophie told me something about this. So that's three sightings in the last few weeks?"

Kate nodded again. "And then there's the texts."

"Let's come back to those later," said Jack. "You can explain those when we talk about reasons and motives. At the moment, we're trying to establish a timeline of sorts ... establish who's seen him and when."

"Reasons? Motives?" Jack's terminology shocked Kate. "There's nothing else. Nobody else has seen him."

"That's not exactly true." Jack glanced at Eddie. "You haven't said anything?"

"No." Eddie looked at Kate sheepishly. "I didn't want to worry you, not with everything else going on."

Kate shot him a warning glare. "What haven't you told me?"

"Annie. Have you met her yet?" Jack asked, sensing the tension between his two friends.

Kate shook her head. "No, I've heard about her ... my son has a crush."

Jack laughed. "Really? That surprises me. I thought his generation were more tuned into these things." Kate frowned. "Annie's gay," he explained. He was about to say more but stopped himself, this wasn't the time or the place. "Annie's an old colleague, she's still with the police. I asked her to do me a little favour the other day."

"What's this got to do with Molly?"

"You know the appointment card you found?" Kate nodded. "I asked her to go to Outpatients ... to see if James turned up?"

"You did? Is she allowed to do that? Did he?" The questions were tumbling rapidly out of her mouth.

"She was off-duty Kate and she was just doing me a favour." Jack tried to sound reassuring. "He did turn up. She was able to positively ID him."

Kate picked up one of the cushions and wrapped her arms around it; Jack and Eddie waited for her to speak. "I don't know why I'm surprised," she said at last. "He had an appointment, didn't he? Chances were he'd turn up. I should have thought of it myself."

"Kate," said Jack, softly. "In addition to going to the hospital, Annie did a bit of digging. James has a London address."

"He has? So the bastard's been lying all this time? Could he have taken her there?"

Jack put his hand on her arm again. "Slow down Kate. He may have two homes, possibly one here and one in France. There's certainly no law against it. He owns a property in Canary Wharf, in London and he appears to use it."

"Why can't he leave her alone?" Kate said sadly, more to herself than to the two men in the room.

Jack glanced at Eddie again. "Kate, we know a little bit more too."

"There's more?" Kate was alarmed. "What?"

"Well, by chance, just sheer bloody chance, Annie saw him on the train the other night," he said. "The night she arrived here. Thursday night. He may be here Kate."

"Oh, dear God," Kate muttered. "Then it's definitely him. He's taken her, hasn't he? Jack, do something … please."

***

Increasingly concerned about his mother's welfare, Seth let himself into the cottage; it was, as he'd known it would be, empty. He checked upstairs, wishing, as he opened her bedroom door, that he'd taken the time to check the night before. Unsure what to do next, he returned downstairs and sat on the small sofa under the stairs. He wasn't expecting her to offer an explanation when she showed up, he didn't really want one. She let people down, broke hearts, messed up families, that's what she was good at but she was still his mother and one thing he'd come to appreciate over the last few days, was that she was lonely and more than a little vulnerable. He knew how that felt, he'd been there himself. The thing with Harry would, like her other relationships, end badly but this time, unlike the others, she'd need him, Kate wouldn't be available.

He unlocked his phone and looked at Facebook. Some of his friends were trying out their barbecue skills, beguiled by the unexpected and prolonged spell of sunny weather. Others were moaning about revision, something he'd forgotten about, exams beckoned when he returned to uni. He looked at his mum's page knowing, as he did so, that it wouldn't help. The photograph of him, as a young boy, stared sadly back. He couldn't remember where it had been taken or who had taken it. That memory, along with many more, was packed away. Out of curiosity, he looked at Harry's page, scrolling repeatedly up and down, carefully examining each entry. Most posts were work related, pictures of sunny vineyards and expensive looking wine. Two young kids, a girl and a boy appeared in a few, recent photographs. They looked like normal kids, happy and healthy and blissfully unaware of the trauma his own mother was about to unleash on their childhoods.

A loud knock at the door startled him. Through the small, side window he caught a glimpse of shoulder length, blond hair. "Thank God," he said, flinging the door open but it wasn't Molly. "I thought you were her."

"Sorry Seth." Annie smiled. "No sign of her, I take it?"

Seth held the door open and beckoned for Annie to come in. "No, nothing."

"I hope you don't mind me popping over. Sophie gave me your address. I wanted to check you were OK." She was lying but it sounded plausible. "I wondered if you wanted me to help track down your mum."

"Track her down?" Seth was confused. "She's not missing."

Annie looked around the small, tidy room. "Have you lived here long?" she asked. She'd have to be more careful, Seth was a bright kid.

"A while, yes," Seth frowned. "We've lived in a few places since my parents split up. I haven't spent much time here though. I went to uni about the time she moved in. It was more economical for her to move to a smaller place and you can't get much smaller than this, can you?" He gestured to the tiny proportions of the room.

"I'm in that club too." There was just the tiniest hint of sadness in Annie's voice. "The divorced parents club. Does your dad still live locally?"

Seth shook his head. "No, he left ages ago."

"Where does he live? Do you get to see him often?" Go gently Annie, she reminded herself, it's not an interview.

"France ... just outside Paris." Seth had no reason to suspect that Annie was digging for information. "He does a lot of work here though still. Well I think he does. He only tells me what he wants me to know. To be honest, I'm guilty of not showing a great deal of interest. I did see him a couple of weeks ago though. He came up to Newcastle ... a rare visit."

"Nice when they make the effort, isn't it?" Annie had a hunch there might be more to Seth. There was something hidden behind his eyes, something deep, something sad. "What are you studying?" she asked.

"Medicine," Seth replied. "Dad went to Newcastle too but he got disillusioned with medicine after a while. From the little I know he got greedy, got lured away by pharmaceutical sales. And the money and lifestyle that came with it of course."

The hint of sarcasm wasn't lost on Annie. This boy intrigued her. He presented himself as a decent, hardworking, polite, young man but there was an edge to him. "My dad was in the police," she offered. "Some things run in families, don't they?"

"You're a police officer?" Seth was surprised. "Why didn't I know that?"

"Because you've only just met me." Annie giggled. "I don't wear the uniform all the time."

"Sorry, you just don't look like a copper. Sorry ... that's not the right thing to say, is it?" He giggled too.

"I think my dad was disappointed he never had a son." Annie surprised herself, she rarely shared this kind of personal information. "His dad had been in the force too, so perhaps it was my destiny, despite my gender." Annie wondered if Seth knew about Jack's previous life. She doubted it, Jack didn't advertise his past. "My parents don't really talk since they divorced," she added after a moment, hoping to get Seth to open up a little. "My sister's wedding was a challenge."

"Mine don't either. I'm not even sure if they're officially divorced yet, even after all this bloody time," laughed Seth. "There's no love lost, on my mum's part anyway. Although I don't think Dad's ever got over it."

"Really?" She tried to sound only politely curious.

"He claims not to care, to be well rid," Seth said quietly. "But mum hurt him badly. I spent a few days with him over Christmas ... it was an eye-opener."

"Oh dear. Alcohol induced revelations?" Annie smiled gently, encouragingly.

"Kind of." Seth was thinking back. "I don't know really. He got hurt badly but he didn't want a divorce. When he's had a drink, he jokes about them getting back together. But sober, he's evil about her."

"Sorry Seth, I don't want to pry." Annie felt guilty, she knew so much already.

"It's OK, you're not. Anyway, it's common knowledge around here." Seth sounded slightly emotional. "Mum's never told me the full story but the kids at school did a pretty good job."

Annie studied him. He wasn't looking for pity but a feeling of sorrow washed over her anyway, some parents had a lot to answer for. Her parents' marriage had broken down because of her dad's job and the long, unsociable hours. There hadn't been any cheating or deceit but the unravelling of the marriage had left its mark on all of them. There was no such thing as an amicable divorce, someone always got hurt. Annie just thought the degree of residual pain differed from person to person. Seth's pain felt raw, it seemed to simmer just below the surface. They both jumped a little when Seth's phone pinged in his pocket.

"Not her?" asked Annie, seeing the disappointment on his face.

"No. It's Bobby," Seth replied. "He wants to know what time I'm going tonight."

"Do you think she'll be back before then?"

"I don't know ... I'll wait here until she gets back. I have to speak to her."

Annie looked at her watch. "I had better go," she said. "See if Sophie needs me. I'm sorry I haven't been much help."

Seth got up. "Can I ask you a question Annie?" Annie nodded. "What do I do if she doesn't come back? She's done stupid things before."

"Are you asking me as a friend ... a new friend? Or as a police officer?"

"As a friend, I think." He smiled bashfully. "Although the police thing might help."

"As a police officer, I have some questions. You just said she's done stupid things before. Do you think that's what this is? Is it another stupid thing? You seem confident that she'll come back. Do you know more than you're letting on?"

"No, why?" Seth lied. His loyalty was to his mother.

"I don't know if it will help you ... or worry you," Annie offered. "But I've taken a quick look at the pub's CCTV."

"And?"

"It shows your Mum speaking to a young man."

"Joe Jenkins," he replied. "Joe told Eddie she was drunk."

"Yes, Joe Jenkins." Annie chose her next words carefully. "Then is shows her staggering a little and waving down a car. Unfortunately, the camera didn't catch the plates. But Seth, it was a private car ... not a taxi. It looks like she was waiting for a lift from someone she knew."

Seth didn't seem too surprised by Annie's revelation. "What kind of car was it?"

Annie frowned. "Does it matter?"

Seth nodded. "It might."

Annie laughed. "I'm supposed to be the detective." Seth smiled but said nothing. "A BMW ... like I said, the footage isn't brilliant. Does that tell you something?"

"It does." Seth sighed and sat back on the sofa. "We don't need to look any further Annie. I know who owns that car."

"You do? Who?" Annie asked. Seth had lied to her, he clearly knew more than he'd let on.

"I can't tell you Annie," Seth replied. "That's for my mum to do. Will you tell everyone not to worry anymore? That she's absolutely fine? Who knows? She might even turn up tonight."

"I'm sorry Seth, that's not good enough." Annie was stunned by the boy's attitude. "Whose car did she get into?"

"I told you … I can't say. Not until I've spoken to her."

Annie got up. "Seth, I don't want to alarm you but there's stuff you don't know. People are worried about your mum. You need to come to the pub and speak to Jack. There's a lot more at stake than you appreciate."

"Annie, I know how much is at stake, believe me." Seth moved to open the door. "My mum has everything to lose this time … everything."

Annie followed him to the door. His comment perplexed her. "So why are you so relaxed?"

"Relaxed?" Seth asked. "I'm not relaxed Annie. Maybe I'm just desensitised to the drama. Some things never change."

***

Molly scrambled off the bed and ran to open the shutters. The soft beam of sunlight confirmed her fears, she was in her old bedroom at Willow Hill. Through the window, the garden was still bathed in sunshine but the shadows cast by the house seemed longer. A quick glance at her watch confirmed it was early evening, she'd been asleep for a long time. More than a little confused, she stared out of the window for several seconds. The lawn, where Seth's climbing frames had once stood, now sloped away, uninterrupted, down to the river and the woods, beautifully manicured but empty. The vegetable patch she and a much younger Seth, had spent many hours toiling over, quite unsuccessfully she remembered fondly, had gone too, as had the big, ivy trellis. The little area of decking at the far end of the garden, the one James had built to catch the last rays of sun on a late, summer's evening, had also vanished. Slowly, with the trellis gone, she made the connection, the pool was missing. All that remained was the path that now led nowhere. James had wiped it all away. For once, he'd done the right thing.

In the familiar en-suite bathroom, the shelves were groaning with luxurious toiletries and fresh, soft towels; her longing for a shower was overwhelming. Ensuring the door was securely locked, she undressed quickly. Unlike the shower in her cottage, the water was intensely hot, almost painful. Head bent and gasping as the powerful jet of scalding hot water stung her, she forced herself forward. The pain was welcome; it was a release valve. As she started to sob, she lowered herself to the shower floor, cradling her knees close to her chest. "Will." Just a whimper, one word, one name. This house held so many memories, James may have tried to destroy the physical reminders but the emotional scars could never be eradicated.

With one towel wrapped around her wet hair and a second around her body, Molly eventually ventured back into the bedroom. In search of something clean to wear, she opened her old wardrobe. It was empty; perhaps James wasn't so prepared after all. Turning to retrieve her dirty clothes, a glossy, blue carrier bag sitting on the floor at the end of the bed, caught her attention. She shouldn't have underestimated him, James was always prepared. The delicate white underwear he'd chosen slid over her pale skin, a perfect fit. The soft, pink, silk blouse nipped in at her waist and cleverly tailored, dark blue jeans enhanced her curves. A silk scarf, charcoal grey in colour, reminded her briefly of Harry's present. She left it the bag and pushed Harry from her memory; Harry was history.

Convinced that James would be waiting outside the bedroom door, she took her time pulling on soft, new socks and black, leather ankle boots. James, for all his failings, had taste and he still knew her style. Sneaking one last satisfied look in the mirror, she slowly opened the bedroom door. There was no sign of James; the landing was, thankfully, empty. Pulling the door shut behind her, as quietly as she could, she tip-toed over to Seth's old bedroom. Her heart lurched as she opened the door, it was the room of a young boy.

"A bit young for him now, don't you think?" James made her jump. "But that's easily remedied. You used to love organising all that stuff, didn't you? The painters, the furniture. It could be your first project." He was standing right behind her, looking over her head into the bedroom.

"I'm not staying James, you can't make me." She tensed, thinking he was going to reach out and touch her. She had tolerated so much but she couldn't have him touch her.

"That's true ... I can't, as much as I'd love to." He studied her new clothes. "Stunning," he said simply. "Come on, I've cooked."

"What on earth does that mean?" She rushed after him as he descended the stairs. "You'll let me go?"

"You can go anytime you like Molly." He ushered her to the kitchen table and pulled out a chair. "You're not a prisoner ... but this will always be your home. Let's remember, you were drunk and you got into my car. You could say I helped a damsel in distress." He seemed to find the thought amusing. "I can't say I'm not disappointed. I thought that a few hours' sleep might help you make the right decision."

"Did you drug me James?" she asked, as she sat down.

"Drug you? Why would I drug you?"

"I don't remember going upstairs ... going to bed," she said quietly.

"So now I'm a rapist, on top of everything else, am I?" James sat down opposite her. "Be careful Molly. Claims like that can get you in trouble."

"I didn't say that," Molly said quickly. "I just don't remember."

James studied her face for a moment, he seemed to be considering what to say. "I want you back Molly but not under duress. That's why you're free to go. If you want to leave, then leave. I've made clear what the consequences will be ... it's your choice."

"You don't think a lot of Kate, do you?" Molly was looking hungrily at the food in front of her. "She's got a big heart ... a good heart. She'll understand."

James didn't answer. Something had caught his eye in the garden and he got up to close the curtains. "Stay where you are," he whispered, as he unlocked one of the glass doors that led onto the terrace. There was someone outside, Molly got up to take a closer look. "Sit back down,"

James shouted viciously at her. She did as she was told. "Don't move." He turned away again. This time he pushed the door shut but not before she heard another voice, a woman's voice. She inched her way out of her chair and crept to the window.

"I told you not to move." James was rattled.

"Who was that?" Her voice trembled. "They're looking for me, aren't they? I told you they would. It was Lucy, wasn't it?" She started to scream. "Luuuucy .... Luuuucy"

Clamping one hand over her mouth, James pushed her harshly against the wall. She fought back and tried to bite but he was too strong, she couldn't move. "Shut up!" he whispered harshly. "Shut the fuck up." She obeyed, she had no choice, he was frightening her. Seemingly satisfied that Lucy wouldn't be coming back, he released his hand and led her to the table, pushing her, a little roughly, back into her seat. He picked up his glass and took several large gulps of wine. "OK … where were we?"

"You were going to let me go," Molly whispered. "Kate will understand that it wasn't my fault." There was fear and desperation in her voice; she'd pushed him too far. "I was at a low ebb … I got taken in. Harry's a well known womaniser. There have been others before me." She thought briefly of Liv and Fiona; both women had, in their own ways, warned her.

"Jesus Molly. Are you kidding me? That makes it OK, does it?" The wine seemed to be helping James regain his composure. He spooned a large portion of a rich looking, beef stew onto a plate for her.

"I'm not saying that." Kate had said something very similar. "But she knows most of it anyway. She knows I was seeing someone and she knows that I was about to finish it."

"But that was a lie too, wasn't it? You didn't finish it, did you?"

"Have you been fucking stalking me?" Molly was indignant. "You need to get a fucking life."

James ignored her. "Eat up. You must be starving."

She fell greedily upon her food and for several minutes the only noise in the room was the sound of cutlery moving over crockery. "So, I can go?" Full, Molly sat back in her chair, both hands clasped around her wine glass.

"I've said as much, haven't I?" James refilled his own glass. "This is your home. It's not a prison."

"And the deal?" she asked hesitantly.

"The deal still stands. Don't underestimate me though," he said calmly, without emotion. "If you walk out of here, I drop round to see Kate and Eddie. I might even pay a visit to Harry ... warn him what he's let himself in for. Give him time to think what he's going to say to that awful woman he married."

"Shit James! Why?" Molly pleaded. "What have I ever done to you?"

James reached for a paper napkin and folded it slowly, his hand shook slightly. "Do you really expect me to answer that?" he growled. "What the fuck goes on in that head of yours? Do you know what you are?"

"What? Selfish? OK, guilty as charged," she screamed. "But you're no fucking saint either, are you? It's all your fault, all this. This shitty life I endure is all because of you. You ruined everything."

"Oh, I see, we're playing the blame game now, are we? I've done some bad things Molly. I put my hand up to that but, in my defence, I did them because of you." He waited a few seconds before he spoke again. "And I never once looked at another woman. It was only ever you Molly ... it still is."

"So why have you made my life such hell?" she screamed. "Sane people don't treat the ones they claim to love, the way you've treated me."

"I'm not going to get into a shouting match ... there's been too many of those already." His left eye twitched and he rubbed it with the back of his hand. "I've been difficult, I've made things hard for you, I'm not denying it ... but you did much worse, didn't you? All you ever had to do was come back. You knew that. I always forgave you Molly."

"You make me want to scream." She slammed her glass down hard on the table. James watched as the red wine dripped down the stem. "A decent human being wouldn't have done what you did." Molly's face had turned red. "You used me as a punch bag. You killed Scooby.... and Will would still be here, if it wasn't for you."

The fridge hummed as before; neither of them spoke. She'd overstepped the mark, said too much. She'd done this before, pushed his buttons, taken him to breaking point. She got up slowly, waiting for him to react but he didn't move. She counted the seventeen steps it took to get to the door. Still James didn't move.

"I did hit you Molly." His voice was quiet and controlled. "But I swore I would never do it again and I didn't." He turned his hands over and studied them, as if looking for signs of the beating he had given Molly, all those years ago. "I'm not proud of what I did, men shouldn't hit women." She had the door open now, she was nearly in the hall with just one more door to negotiate. "Scooby died instantly," his voice was stronger, he was making sure she could hear him. "He didn't stand a chance. He ran in front of the van Molly. You were there ... you saw it happen. And I never laid a finger on Will. I wanted to ... Jesus I'm guilty of that much. But it wasn't me who killed him Molly ... why would say that when you know the truth?"

Molly ran across the hall, her new boots echoing noisily on the tiled floor. She stole a look behind her as she released the latch on the front door. James was standing by the kitchen door holding out her phone.

"I take it there's no deal then?" he asked, walking towards her.

Stumbling across the gravel, she heard him roar in anger but she didn't look back.

***

"It's a bit of a squeeze in here, isn't it?" Jack looked around the room apologetically. "Sorry for that but I wanted to get everyone's input." Seth, Bobby and Lucy had joined them in the small living room above the flat.

"Is this all to do with my Mum?" asked Seth. "I told Annie ... I think she's fine."

Jack looked at him, there was no time to beat around the bush but he didn't want anyone to be unduly alarmed. "Seth, some of us are a little concerned that your mum didn't show up for work today and that she isn't answering her phone." Seth nodded but said nothing. "And I want to emphasise that Seth. That it's just a concern at this stage. And usually, in situations like this, if we discuss what we know together, as a group, we might find the answer. One of us may have a vital piece of information we might have overlooked, some information that will give us a sensible explanation. Does that make sense?"

Again, Seth nodded. He glanced at Annie briefly. She was clearly waiting for him to speak, to share what he knew. "Where do we start?" he asked nervously.

"OK." Jack could feel Sophie watching him closely. He'd promised her that he'd keep this simple, that he wouldn't overwhelm or frighten everyone unnecessarily, most of all that he wouldn't sound like a copper. "Molly was here last night, as were most of us, apart from Eddie and Kate." He nodded at Eddie and Kate sitting together on one of the sofas. "Does anyone remember her saying anything about what she might be doing today? Anything about not working?"

"I was with her just before she left last night," Annie said, looking directly at Seth. "She mentioned tonight's drinks party, she was really looking forward to it."

Kate, sitting with her feet tucked her, sighed. "I feel like I'm clutching at straws but maybe she's gone shopping. She's been pretty short of cash for a while but with the regular hours here at the pub, maybe she's more flush? I suppose she could have gone into London. Maybe her phone's died. Maybe that's it." Her voice grew in confidence as she spoke, the idea felt plausible.

"OK." Jack smiled reassuringly at Kate. "That seems like a possibility. If there was a mix up with the rotas, maybe she decided to go shopping. Her phone's dead but we've all done that, haven't we? Not charged our phones?" Nearly everyone nodded their heads in agreement. Seth glanced at Annie who raised her eyebrows questioningly. "Eddie," Jack turned to his friend. "The Jenkins boy said she was waiting for a taxi last night, didn't he?"

"No, not exactly," Eddie replied. "He said he saw Molly outside the pub." He glanced at Seth, feeling stupidly uncomfortable about what he was going to say next. "Joe said she seemed pretty wasted ... his words. She told him she was waiting for a lift, not a taxi exactly."

"It's true! She was drunk, wasn't she?" interrupted Lucy, turning to Seth. "But she sent you a message saying she was going to call a taxi, didn't she? It's easy to say lift and mean taxi when you're drunk, isn't it?"

"What did the message say Seth?" Annie asked. Jack glanced at her, there was something about her tone, she seemed irritated.

Seth reached inside his jacket for his phone and read out the message. *"Getting taxi home. Can't drink any more. See you in the morning. Sorry."*

"So," said Jack. "The taxi. Annie, you've looked at the CCTV?"

"Yes," she said, her eyes still on Seth. "It shows her getting into an unmarked private car. Not a taxi." She glanced over at Jack. "A BMW."

"Plates?" Jack asked. Annie shook her head. "Can anyone think who drives a BMW? Who might have given her a lift? Late at night?" He looked around the room, at the concerned faces.

"No," said Kate. "There's no-one. Molly hasn't socialised much in recent years."

"Seth?" Lucy said slowly. "Time to share?" Seth frowned and shook his head.

"Seth." Annie's voice was harsh. "If there's any chance you know something, this really is the best time to share it. None of us want to go to the police and then find out we've wasted their time, do we?"

Seth shook his head. "I don't think we'll need to go to the police. Mum's been seeing someone ... it's his BMW." He glanced apologetically at Kate. "I only found out recently. I'm not sure how serious it is."

"It's not serious at all." Kate surprised him. "She's finished it. She told me ... she's finished it."

"You know?" Lucy was incredulous. "And you're OK with it? No way!"

Kate shook her head. "I only found out recently too," she said. "Although I've had my doubts for a while." She glanced at Sophie. "Someone was buying her gifts, stuff that she couldn't buy herself ... stuff she couldn't afford."

"The scarf," Lucy and Sophie said in unison.

Kate nodded. "I confronted her. She didn't want to admit it ... we had an argument."

"I'm not bloody surprised," said Lucy. "I'm amazed you didn't batter her. Anyone else would have."

Kate frowned at her daughter. "What does that mean?"

Seth put his hand out to stop Lucy speaking. "Kate, did she tell you who she was seeing?"

Kate shook her head again. "No. Sorry Seth. She refused to tell me ... I have no idea. But it doesn't matter who he is, does it? She can't be with him. It's over."

"Jesus," said Lucy. "This gets worse. Mum, how many times has she lied to you before? You never, ever, think badly of her. She walks all over you."

"Lucy," Seth hissed. "I'm warning you ... back off."

"But it wouldn't have been him giving her a lift," Kate insisted. "She promised me it was over. She'd been humiliated by him ... big time."

"Did she finish it before I got home from uni?" Seth asked.

"I think we might we getting off track Seth," Jack said, surprised when Seth held up his hand to stop him talking.

"Kate, did she finish it before I got back from uni?" Seth asked again.

"Yes, just a day or two earlier." Kate was confused. "Why?"

"Do you remember the night I came home? The night I couldn't get in because she'd locked up and gone to bed?"

Kate nodded. "Of course."

Seth couldn't hold Kate's gaze any longer, he looked back at Lucy instead. "I did get in but I found that she wasn't on her own. She had company ... male company."

The room was quiet, the hum of activity from the pub below, audible in the silence. Jack was the first to speak. "Seth, I have to ask. Do you know the man?"

Seth nodded his head slowly. "I didn't. I've found out since. Although she doesn't know that I know. Maybe I should have said something ... but she has a life of her own. What she does isn't my responsibility."

Jack was surprised at his words. "Can you tell us? Who is he?" he asked encouragingly.

Seth nodded his head. "I'll tell you Jack ... in private." He glanced at Kate.

"Oh, for fuck's sake Seth! Grow up!" Lucy stood up, she'd lost her patience. "What's the point in keeping it secret anymore? It won't change anything." She glared at Seth, waiting for him to speak. When he didn't she turned to Jack. "It doesn't give me any pleasure to tell you this Jack but Molly was with Harry that night". She knelt down next to Kate and picked up her hand. "Mum ... Molly's having an affair with Harry."

"I'm sorry Kate," Seth said quietly. "I'm so sorry. The BMW ... it's Harry's. I saw his keys at the cottage ... he's drives a BMW."

***

Kneeling, just as she had done all those years ago, with her hands clasped tightly together and her elbows digging into the hard wood of the pew in front of her, Kate was back in church. Years ago, she had knelt next to Patty and Winnie like this, three red heads bent in individual prayer. So clear was the image in her mind, she could see the detail of her mother's green winter coat and the emerald brooch she always wore. Winnie had been old school, her generation dressed for church.

To her right, a door opened and footsteps echoed on the worn, stone slabs. A pew, on the other side of the aisle, creaked as another woman blessed herself and knelt forward to pray. Like her, she was seeking comfort. The thought had come from nowhere and it shocked her. Was she really seeking comfort? Wasn't she just hiding? Initially from her cancer diagnosis and now from the news about Molly. Her knees were beginning to ache and she looked down, the padding on the kneeling rail had seen better days. She pulled back to sit on the pew and, as she did so, a hand touched her gently on the shoulder. It was the same young priest she'd seen before.

"Hello," he said, amiably. "It's nice to see you again." His accent was Australian, she hadn't noticed that before. "Are you here for confession?"

"Hello." No matter how sad her mood, Kate felt compelled to return the smile. "No ... confession ... no ... I'm not. Sorry." She cast her eyes over to the confessional box. She hadn't made a confession in years, it was too late now.

"No problem ... don't apologise." She noticed the strong dimple in the priest's chin, it reminded her foolishly of her late father. "If you change your mind, I'll be in the vestry."

"Thank you." Perhaps she looked like she needed to make a confession but she wouldn't know where to start.

The priest smiled warmly at her and laid his hand, gently, on her shoulder again. "I'm Father Patrick. Peace be with you."

He walked up to the alter and turned left, out of sight. Peace be with you. They were religious words that had meant little to her as a child but they touched a nerve now and she felt guilty. Consumed by self-pity, she was seeking comfort in the establishment she had abandoned as a teenager. Winnie would have disapproved. She was using and abusing the one thing her mother had held most dear. Worried that the priest would come back and ask her more questions, Kate made her way out of the church. It was time to dust herself down and get on with things. That's what she was good at.

Back at the house she found Eddie waiting for her. "You disappeared," he said. "Are you OK?"

"I'm sorry Eddie." She still couldn't tell him where she'd been. "I just needed some air, to get my thoughts together."

"That's what I figured." Eddie reached out and hugged her. She remained within his embrace for several seconds, it was a good place to be. "We are not going to change our plans because of this," he said quietly into her hair. "We're going back to the pub and we're going to enjoy our evening. Do you hear me? We can deal with this other stuff tomorrow."

Kate nodded. Eddie was right, they could deal with Molly another day.

Chapter Twenty-Five

"Earth calling Sophie." Jack nudged his wife. "You were miles away."

"Was I? Sorry. I was just thinking about Kate. It's going to be hard for her this evening." She hadn't seen Eddie standing next to Jack, she blushed. "Sorry Eddie ... no offence."

"Don't apologise Sophie. You're right. Things may be tough for a while but Kate's strong, she'll cope." Eddie glanced over at his wife, who was talking to Annie. Behind the smiles, he knew she was anxious. "Can you promise me something guys? No more talk about Molly tonight please? I'm kind of bored of it."

"Sure," Sophie smiled.

"Of course." Jack patted Eddie on the shoulder.

"Thanks. Come on then, let's get this party started." Eddie picked up the tray of drinks Jack had prepared and took them over to where Kate was sitting with Annie and the kids. Kim, out of chef's whites for once, had just joined them. In a soft, cream-coloured jumpsuit which accentuated her lean frame and dark skin, she looked like a supermodel.

"What do you think he means by that?" Sophie asked Jack, her eyes on Kim. "Bored of Molly?"

"Sophie, a lot of us have spent the last ten days worrying about Molly and what her ex-husband may or may not do. Let alone, what he may or may not have done in the past." Jack had also spotted how good Kim looked, it was a few seconds before he spoke again. "Eddie has been particularly worried. And now he's probably thinking she doesn't deserve his concern."

"I suppose you're right," Sophie agreed. "A little too close to home."

"Master of the understatement you, eh Soph?" Jack laughed. "OK, the kitchen's closed and the signs are up." He pointed to two handwritten signs he'd placed at each end of the bar.

'No Food Service After 6pm
Normal Service Resumes Tomorrow'

"Doris," he continued, nodding towards Doris as she walked past with two bowls of chips in her hands, "is happy to serve plates of chips to the needy but everything else is off ... for one night only. And Kim has made some wonderful "freebies" which we'll put out later to keep the locals happy."

Sophie reached out and spread her arms around his waist. "Feels ever so slightly naughty, doesn't it? Like bunking off school."

"As if you ever bunked off school," Jack scoffed. "Right, go and join the others Miss Goody Two Shoes. Tansy's here, as are the two new boys and I'll join you shortly. Go on ... join your friends. No excuses ... it's time to chill."

Jack's words made her smile, it hadn't taken long to forge new friendships. "You look amazing," she said, as she squeezed in beside Kim. "I can't take my eyes off you. God knows how the boys are managing." She nodded towards Bobby who was clearly intoxicated by Kim's appearance. "And damn you," Sophie groaned, as she munched on one of the small pastries Kim had brought out from the kitchen with her. "You cook as good as you look. Is there anything you can't do?"

"Where's Molly?" Kim asked quietly. "I might be wrong but I sense a vibe."

"Ah, I should have told you what's been going on." Sophie lowered her voice, simultaneously wiping some pastry away from her mouth. "Let's just say she's nobody's favourite person right now. I'll fill you in when we get a moment but my advice is not to mention her tonight."

"Intriguing." Kim raised her eyebrows. "Not an affair of the heart, is it? I noticed she had a certain spring in her step the other day ... she denied it though."

"Am I the only one who never knows what's going on?" Sophie laughed to hide her exasperation. "You're not too far off though ... but it's a little delicate."

"Delicate or not Sophie," Kim said, reaching for Sophie's arm and pulling her round until they were both facing the main entrance to the pub. "Look who's here."

"Shit! We don't need this now ... not here," Sophie muttered. She shot a look at Kate. It was too late, Kate had already spotted Molly.

"Mum!" Seth jumped up and grabbed Molly by both arms, deliberately creating a human shield between her and everyone else. "Where have you been?" He glanced quickly behind him at Kate. "I ... I've been worried. Didn't you get any of my messages?"

"Sorry Seth," Molly said breathlessly. "I got here as soon as I could. I seem to have lost my phone." She reached out to hug her son tightly.

A man laughed loudly in the background, a chorus of high pitched giggles followed.

"Mum." Seth pulled himself away from Molly's embrace. "We were worried."

"It looks like you've been shopping." Sophie was keen to diffuse a potentially difficult situation. "New jeans?"

"What? Oh yes," Molly replied, looking distractedly down at her jeans, as if seeing them for the first time.

"And boots?" Sophie carried on. "We were right folks. We thought you might have gone shopping."

"What?" Molly looked confused. "Shopping? Why would you think that?"

"We must have got our wires crossed Molly." Sophie was desperate, she didn't want a scene. "No harm done. Annie was here to help."

"I don't understand." Molly looked from Sophie to Annie.

"I thought I'd asked you to work today," Sophie said. "But don't worry. Like I said ... no harm done."

"That's why we were worried about you Mum," said Seth. "And then when you didn't answer your phone, we got even more worried."

"Oh ... I see," Molly looked down at her new boots. The gravel from the drive at Willow Hill had left dusty white marks on the leather.

"Is that it?" It was Eddie, a very angry Eddie. "Is that all you have to bloody say? No apology? To Sophie at least?"

Sophie put her hands up. "No apology needed Eddie ... really." She moved closer to Molly. "Come on, come with me, I'll get you a drink." If she could just get two minutes alone with Molly, she had a chance of managing and even rescuing this situation. Molly would be sent home, Kate could deal with her another time.

"Hold on Sophie," Eddie barked. His voice was uncharacteristically sharp. "If you weren't shopping Molly, where were you? Like Seth said ... people have been worried."

Eddie's anger seemed to galvanise Molly. "I'm sorry Sophie ... Eddie's right. I should apologise. But something really weird happened ... and I lost my phone. I couldn't contact you. I can explain ... it wasn't my fault."

"Mum, let's go home," pleaded Seth. "I need to talk to you." He put his arm through Molly's and tried to pull her away. He had an overwhelming urge to protect her, she was his mother.

Molly meekly took a step to go with him. It was Kate's voice that stopped her. "It's over this time Molly. I'm done ... once and for all."

Molly stared at her old friend. "What? What are you talking about?"

Sophie tried to step in and push Molly gently towards the exit. "Molly ... come on ... go with Seth."

Molly stood her ground. "What's going on? Why are you all behaving so weirdly? Have you got any idea what I've been through?" She looked wildly around the group of familiar faces, few would make eye contact.

"What you've been through? Jesus! It's always about you ... even now." Kate pulled herself free from Eddie and thrust her finger in front of Molly's face; her hand was shaking. "You wreck lives Molly. It's what you're good at. I knew that ... I've always known that ... but I continued to defend you, you were my friend. Jesus Molly! I fought for you, time after fucking time and you repay me by doing this? Our friendship ends here ... now. There's no way back. There are no words." Tears were running down Kate's cheeks. Eddie tried to pull her back but she shook him off. "Did you ever give Patty or her kids a single thought? Of course, you didn't. No-one else matters, do they Molly? You're one selfish cow!" Molly gasped as Kate's open hand slapped her cheek. "Get out of here Molly before I do something much worse," Kate screamed. "Get out!"

Sophie, painfully aware of the hush that had descended over the entire pub, spoke first. "Seth. Take your mother home. Now!"

"He's been here, hasn't he? He got to you before me?" Molly screamed. People in the pub were straining to witness the action. Seth grabbed Molly's arm but she pulled herself free. "The bastard, he said he'd give me a head-start."

"Go with Seth Molly," Eddie grinded out the words. "Now isn't the time or the place. Don't make a scene here. Sophie and Jack have been good to you. You owe them."

"I can explain. Please, let me explain." Molly insisted. Seth pulled her away forcefully. "It was James … it's not my fault."

"Shit Molly! Change the bloody record," Eddie said sharply. "You're in enough trouble, you've done enough harm. Stop the lies. Why, in God's name, can't you stop?"

**

"That wasn't quite the evening I'd planned," Sophie said, handing cups of coffee to Jack and Annie. Eddie and Kate had long since made their excuses and gone home and Lucy and Bobby had gravitated towards a group of their old friends who were devouring the free food Kim had organised. Surprisingly, Kim had accepted the offer of a drink from a customer and was now deep in conversation with him, in one of the alcoves at the other end of the bar. Watching them, Sophie thought they looked good together. Kim, elegant with a subtle sensuality was leaning forward, listening intently to what her tall, chiselled date was saying. An unwelcome thought crossed her mind briefly; Kim was out of place in this setting, she belonged in London. Somewhere within her, she knew that Kim would, sadly, be moving on.

"Who said living in the country was boring?" Annie laughed, deliberately trying to lighten the mood.

"You did." Jack laughed too.

"Well I take it back." Annie pulled a face. "It's a hotbed of …. I don't know the word but it's definitely a hotbed."

"Intrigue?" asked Jack.

"Infidelity?" added Sophie, looking over at Kim. Hopefully, the man who was plying her with champagne wasn't married but Kim was smarter than that, smarter than Molly.

"I'm no good with words but there's a lot going on behind the sleepy facade of this place, that's for sure." Annie pushed the coffee aside and picked up a glass of red wine. "It's like one of those books I usually read on a beach."

"I saw that Annie," Jack laughed loudly. "Minesweeping again. You don't even know you're doing it!"

"Sod off! It's my glass … that's not minesweeping." There was indignation in Annie's voice but her eyes danced. She loved being teased by Jack, loved the playfight that usually followed.

"I'll let you off," Jack chuckled. "What do you think Molly meant when she said that stuff about him getting here first, the head start?"

"I've been thinking about that," Annie replied. "She mentioned James, didn't she?" Jack nodded. "But that seems to be her default setting, doesn't it? Everything is his fault?" Jack nodded again. "Do you think she was talking about Harry? Maybe they had an argument? Maybe he had a crisis of conscience? Had threatened to come clean?" She stopped talking abruptly, Sophie was giggling. "What's so bloody funny?"

"Crisis of conscience! Where the hell did that come from? You said you were no good with words." There were tears of laughter in Sophie's eyes. "Sorry. I think I'm a little hysterical. It's been a weird day."

"Hidden depths. Clearly!" Annie feigned indignation. "Shit! Sophie look … at the bar. It's that man again." Jack and Sophie looked up to see a tall, blond man speaking to Tansy.

"Isn't that the guy who mistook you for Molly?" Sophie whispered.

Annie nodded. "He's coming over. Surely he doesn't think I'm her again." They watched as the tall, slim man walked quickly towards them.

"Hi," he nodded at Jack. "Sorry to interrupt but the girl at the bar said you're the owner of this place?"

"That's right," Jack replied. "Jack Fox, my wife Sophie." He gestured towards Sophie who smiled. "And Annie ... our friend."

"Harry ... Harry Smith." The man sat down.

"You're Harry?" Sophie was unable to disguise her shock. "Sorry." She could feel herself blushing. "We've met before, haven't we?" She pointed at Annie. "Mistaken identity last week?"

Harry looked over at Annie, his confused expression quickly turned to one of embarrassment. "Ah ... yes," he said. "I'm so sorry about that."

"Don't worry about it." Annie waved the apology away. "No harm done." Harry's face creased into a warm smile and Annie suddenly understood. The smile welcomed you in and put its huge arms around you. It didn't work for her but she knew it would work for many of the fairer sex.

"I was looking for Molly ... again," Harry said nervously. "I've been trying to get hold of her all day."

"She's not been at work today," Sophie said, cautiously. "And I think she's misplaced her phone."

Jack had sat forward in his seat. "Harry, are you saying you haven't seen Molly at all today?" There was a hint of urgency in his voice.

"No," Harry replied. "I couldn't get hold of her."

"So, you didn't pick her up last night?" Jack felt Annie lean forward next to him. Her thought pattern was matching his. "From here? After work?"

"Last night? No. I haven't seen her for a couple of days. Why?"

"Must have got my wires crossed," Jack said, trying to disguise his concern. "I thought she said she was getting a lift home last night. I'm afraid I assumed it was you. I saw the way you were with Molly the other day when you ate here. I assumed you two were an item."

"Really? Damn ... we'd been so careful." Harry smiled ruefully.

Sophie smiled back, she couldn't help herself. She wanted to be so cross with this gorgeous man but it was impossible, he was such an open book.

Annie wasn't so easily won over. "Unbelievable," she muttered.

Harry either didn't hear or didn't want a confrontation. He looked directly at Sophie and asked, "Is she working tomorrow?"

Sophie didn't want to get involved but she wanted Harry to leave Molly and Seth alone, they needed time. "She's got plans with her son," she lied. "She's not working."

***

Despite his show of good humour in the pub, Harry was seriously pissed off. He'd worked hard to ensure his wife and kids were away for the long weekend and now Molly was playing hard to get, just because her feelings were hurt. On top of that, she'd already made other plans, she'd wasted his time.

Standing outside the pub, he pulled his phone from his jacket. "You've had your chance, Molly, my love" he muttered, as he typed. "I've got a weekend pass and I'm going to use it." He pressed send.

"Sorry to keep you waiting Foxy Lady – I got caught up in something. The coast is clear. Come on over."

A satisfied grin appeared on his face when a response came back immediately, this blond was so much more accommodating than Molly. She wasn't nearly as much fun but at least she was willing. He composed a quick message to Molly.

Shame you couldn't spare me any time this weekend Molly. Still love you Babe. There's only you! Another time maybe? x

A car sounded its horn as he stepped off the pavement and he jumped back, startled. Engrossed in composing the text message, he hadn't heard the car approaching. He was shaken, he'd had a lucky escape. Looking more cautiously up and down the road, he quickly pressed send and pocketed his phone. Harry, the man who lived a double life, had, for once, not followed his own rules. Taking the time to check his texts had kept him out of trouble for years, sending the text intended for Molly to another of his lady friends was a schoolboy error. One that would cost him dearly.

Chapter Twenty-Six

Seth took a deep breath and knocked at the familiar door which, in the space of just a few hours, had become a line he couldn't cross. Lottie barked a warning as the door opened to reveal a tired looking Kate.

"Seth." Kate smiled, despite her fatigue. "Is there something wrong with the door?"

"No," Seth said quietly. "I just wasn't sure."

Kate looked at him through weary eyes. "You weren't sure?" she asked. Faint frown lines creased her forehead.

"Last night." He didn't know what else to say.

"Oh Seth, please don't." Kate stepped forward and wrapped her arms around him, squeezing tightly. "We're OK, aren't we?" she whispered into his chest.

"I hope so Kate," he replied, slightly overcome by her display of affection. "I really hope so." He returned the hug.

Kate pulled him gently through the door. "Go through," she said. "I'll make you a cuppa." Lottie was waiting for them behind the kitchen door, Seth bent down to rub her ears.

"Morning Seth," Eddie called from the playroom. "No sign of life from upstairs yet, I'm afraid."

"It was you two I wanted to talk to actually." Seth took a seat next to Eddie.

Kate handed him a cup of tea. "How's your mum?" She sounded normal, Seth was reassured.

"She's not great," he said, sipping the hot tea. "She's upset ... she hasn't slept."

Kate had to bite her tongue. Spiteful, dark thoughts threatened to find a voice. "No ... sleep's been a stranger in this house too."

"She had a bit of a meltdown when we got home," Seth confessed. "I'm worried. She's rambling, not making any sense."

"What do you mean?" Eddie found it easier to show more concern than Kate. He'd been livid with Molly the night before but, in the light of a new day, he felt more compassionate. Whatever Molly was guilty of, she hadn't done it on her own. It took two to have an affair. And Molly was vulnerable, she was an accident waiting to happen.

"You're going to think it's as weird as I do." Seth was struggling to find the right words. "She's .... she's convinced Dad set her up."

"Set her up? Your dad? Why on earth would she say that?" Eddie took his glasses off and rubbed his eyes. "Your dad's got nothing to do with this. We haven't seen or spoken to him in years." Kate made a small tutting noise and frowned at Eddie. He was telling the truth, they hadn't spoken to James for many years. But he had been seen. She shook her head, hoping Eddie would understand but say nothing. Sharing this bit of news with Seth, at this precise moment, wouldn't help.

Seth, sitting next to Eddie, was oblivious to Kate's efforts at tacit conversation. "I know. I've explained that to her. But she's not listening to me. She's hysterical. Sorry, I don't mean to sound dramatic but she's worrying me."

"Has she expressed any remorse?" Kate wanted to hear Seth say Molly was ashamed.

Seth shook his head. "No ... not really. Sorry Kate. She's obsessed with Dad. It's crazy. She said she was with him yesterday. She's saying he drugged her ... kidnapped her."

"What?" asked Eddie, incredulously. "He what?"

"I know!" Seth almost laughed. "Dad's in France. I spoke to him just the other day. But she's convinced he took her to the old house, the one on Willow Hill."

"Bloody ridiculous," Kate muttered. Molly had always been able to talk herself out of situations in the past but this was sheer fantasy.

"She's adamant. Do you think I should get her to see a doctor? She's saying crazy things. I don't know what to do."

"Where is she now? asked Eddie. "Do you want me to talk to her?"

It was the offer of help Seth had been hoping for. "I'd appreciate that Eddie. She's at home, trying to get some sleep." He looked up at Kate. "I don't think she's intentionally lying to me but I'm her son. She's sparing me the gory details."

Kate turned away, she couldn't hold Seth's gaze. Molly had all but abandoned her son all those years ago on a self-indulgent whim. Whatever story she was feeding him now, it was nothing but make-believe. Molly didn't suddenly care about Seth, she didn't care about anyone.

"Are you OK with that love? If I go and see Molly?" Eddie asked. He knew his wife better than anyone. Kate was struggling to contain her rage.

"Sure." Kate's tone was business like. "I'll walk Lottie ... and get the lunch sorted. It's Easter Sunday. We've got Nicola coming."

"Nicola?" Seth was surprised. "Nicola Frost?"

"Yes Seth, Nicola Frost," Kate said slowly. This was dangerous territory. She shouldn't have mentioned Nicola. Seth might not be ready. "Eddie's invited her for lunch."

"I bumped into her yesterday, she mentioned her mum was going away. It felt like the right thing to do." Eddie shrugged his shoulders, lost for further explanation.

"I've not seen her for a long time," Seth said thoughtfully but without any apparent concern. "It's weird how things work out, isn't it?"

"Yes Seth ... it's weird," Kate replied. She wanted to add that the common denominator, the troublemaker, was his mother but she didn't. None of this was Seth's fault, or Eddie's for that matter.

***

The drive from Kate's house to Willow Hill would normally take twenty minutes, due largely to the dreadful one-way system. By cutting through the park, the journey could be done, on foot, in much the same time. Kate, with Lottie in tow, set out to investigate, she was going to call Molly's bluff. Enjoying the feel of unexpected, warm sunshine on her back, she meandered slowly down the hill towards the old wooden footbridge. Lottie, unhappy at the prospect of crossing to the other side, needed gentle encouragement. It made Kate smile, Lottie, brave, fearless animal that she was, had always hated this rickety old bridge. The steep steps that led up to the road presented Lottie with another challenge and Kate was forced to stop frequently. It was a painful reminder of Lottie's declining fitness.

Standing at the entrance to the old vicarage, five minutes later, Kate was caught off-guard. Time seemed to have stood still, everything was so familiar. The immaculate drive and the neatly trimmed hedges hinted at a much loved and well-maintained home. The large, red brick house standing at the bottom of the drive was, as it always had been, a spectacular sight. Grand and imposing, it had always felt cold to Kate, both inside and out, but just like the drive, it appeared well cared for. The lawns to the front were neatly mowed and the flower beds regimentally tidy. Molly and James had both been obsessed with tidiness. For James, it had bordered on OCD. Kate smiled to herself, James would have been pleased to know the new owners were looking after the place. With both hands on the cold iron gates, she studied the house looking for signs of life. The old vicarage stared impassively back at her, undeniably stately but inherently sad. Lacking the confidence to go any further and concerned that Lottie's impatient barking might draw attention to them, Kate turned around and headed back down the drive. Molly had been lying, she hadn't been here, she'd been with Harry. With her back against the wall, she'd done what she always did, she told lies.

Kate and Lottie were just a few paces from the main road when a large, grey car pulled into the drive at speed. Stones and pebbles flew into the air, as the surprised driver hastily applied the brakes. The car slid to a noisy, juddering halt. Lottie, sensing danger, squealed and jumped back. Kate, surprised by both the car and Lottie's sudden agility, lost her balance. The two of them fell awkwardly into the hedge.

"Shit! I didn't see you. Are you OK?" The driver scrambled out of the car to help. Dust hung in the air.

"We're OK ... I think." Kate was checking on Lottie, running her hands softly down the old dog's legs. "Sorry, we shouldn't have been ...."

"Kate? Bloody hell ... of all people." James was shocked.

"James?" Kate was incredulous. "My God! What are you doing here? You could have killed me ... and Lottie."

James studied her for several quiet moments, simultaneously taking in her appearance and considering how he should reply. "Kate, this is my house. I have every right to be here," he said at last. "What are you doing here?"

Kate was stunned. "This is your house? Still? She's telling the truth?"

James reached down to stroke Lottie but Kate pulled her away, James had history when it came to dogs. "Are you talking about Molly?" He kept his tone light. "She was here yesterday. We had a talk."

"She was here? She's not lying?" Kate was struggling to understand. 'You did it then. I didn't believe her."

"Did what Kate?" James leant forward to stroke Lottie again, Kate didn't pull her away a second time.

"She's saying you kidnapped her ... Seth told me."

"Kidnapped?" James laughed, just a little too hard. "She really said that? Why doesn't that surprise me? Kate, that woman lies through her teeth, even when the truth makes a better story."

"I don't know what's going on James but I'm very confused. I had no idea you still owned this place."

"Sorry Kate." James sounded genuinely apologetic. "You've had a fright. Perhaps you'd like a cup of coffee? Give me a chance to explain." She stepped back, irrationally afraid. "Ring Eddie. Ask him to come over too." James could sense her fear. "There's no need to look so scared Kate ... I don't bite. It's time you both heard my side of the story."

***

"She's what?" Jack shouted down the phone. "Is she fucking mad?"

"I'm on my way there now Jack. It's OK ... she's OK. He's got stuff he wants to tell us." Eddie was running over the same bridge Kate had crossed half an hour earlier.

"I don't understand." Jack was striding up and down the garden, holding his mobile phone close to his ear. "Why didn't you tell me he had a home here? And why the bloody hell is Kate with him?"

"Molly said that's where she was yesterday. We didn't believe her," Eddie explained. "Kate, typical bloody Kate, went up there to take a look. It's a long story Jack. We didn't know he still owned the house." Eddie's breath was coming in gasps, as he scaled the stone steps that led up the hill and out of the park. "I was on my way to see Molly when Kate called me. I decided Molly can wait. I need to be with Kate."

"Fuck! This just gets weirder and weirder," Jack said. "That's why I called you Ed. To tell you she wasn't with Harry yesterday. He came here late last night, looking for her."

"You're kidding? Where was she?" Even as he posed the question, he realised he knew the answer.

"Is Seth with you?" Jack walked into the pub. "What about Molly? I don't like how this is unravelling Ed."

"Seth's gone home ... I haven't told him anything. He thinks I took an urgent call from a client." Eddie was standing on the pavement, waiting for a gap in the traffic. "The lad's worried about his mum. He's going to stay with her. Look, I've got to go. I'll call you later."

On the other side of the road, Eddie trotted towards the old vicarage, making a silent pledge to himself, as he did so, to do something about his weight. The regular walking of an elderly dog clearly wasn't enough exercise, the sweat was pouring off him. In the driveway, he stopped briefly to get his breath back. The red brick house loomed ahead. It wasn't to his taste, it had always made him feel inadequate but he held a grudging admiration for it nevertheless. He approached the open gates and stepped onto the gravel. A few steps short of the front door, he stopped again to brush himself down. He wiped the sweat from his forehead and ran his fingers through his thinning hair. In the same way as the house made him feel like a poor relation, James was a master at one upmanship. Eddie had never been able to compete. Taking a deep breath, he walked up to the door and lifted the large, black knocker, bringing it down noisily on the brass plate. Lottie started barking immediately and he grinned at the familiar, reassuring noise. As expected, an immaculately dressed James opened the door, a happy looking Lottie not far behind him.

"Hi Eddie," James said amiably. "It's nice to see you again." He put out his hand and shook Eddie's vigorously. "Go through to the kitchen. Kate's in there."

Eddie's heart flipped when he saw Kate sitting on the sofa in the kitchen, a large white cup in her hand. He sat down beside her and placed a kiss on her cheek. She looked composed, relaxed even. He wasn't quite sure what he'd expected but it wasn't this, she looked like she'd popped by for a coffee with an old friend.

"Thanks." Eddie gratefully accepted the coffee James offered. "I have to say I'm surprised to see you James ... here especially." Eddie was relieved and surprised to hear the relative steadiness of his voice, James hadn't intimidated him yet.

"I don't doubt it." James said, pulling one of the chairs over from the kitchen table and sitting near Kate. "It's been a while, hasn't it?"

"It has. The last time I saw you was when you dropped Scooby off at our house. A dead Scooby."

"Ah yes." James' eyes clouded over slightly. "So sad. Although from something Molly said yesterday, it's possible you may have been misled about that incident."

"Misled?" Eddie looked from James to Kate, who shrugged her shoulders to indicate she was none the wiser.

"I didn't kill the dog, if that's what you think. Is that what Molly told you?" Kate nodded, her hand automatically reaching for Lottie's head. Both she and Eddie remained silent, waiting for clarification. "Look, Molly's your friend ... yours especially, Kate." James looked deeply into Kate's eyes thinking, just for a second, that she didn't look too well. Her blue eyes seemed to be masking something. "But she's a storyteller," he continued. "She tells fibs, white lies, call them what you want. She manipulates the truth to suit herself."

"But I was there James," Eddie interjected. "I saw that dog. Jesus, it's not a sight you forget. He was a complete mess. Those injuries, fatal injuries, were sustained when you threw him off the flyover."

"Is that what she said?" James barked. "That I threw him off?" Eddie nodded slowly. "Dear God." James' voice shook slightly. "What a fucking witch."

"Are you saying it's not true?" Kate asked quietly.

"For all my faults Kate, I'm not a murderer. I couldn't do that." James looked directly at her. "Scooby, the poor sod, got hit by a van when Molly dropped the lead. Jesus, what else has she lied about?"

"I don't know James. Why don't you tell us?" Kate asked bravely. "She didn't lie about the settlement problems, did she? The maintenance, the alimony? You haven't paid her a penny, have you? Do you know how hard that's been for her? She's had to live hand to mouth, had to pawn all that jewellery you bought her."

"No, she hasn't lied about any of that," James agreed unashamedly. "I didn't know she pawned the jewellery though. That's a shame. Some of it was good stuff, a couple of rings in particular." He stopped talking, he was gathering his thoughts. "She made a mug of me ... twice remember. And then she expected me to cough up ... just like that. Don't get me wrong, I could afford to pay her but it was more rewarding, from a purely selfish point of view, not to." He looked from Molly to Eddie and back again. "You've probably never been hurt like that. It destroys you." The strength had faded from his voice. He saw Kate exchange a look with Eddie. "Guys, you need a wake-up call. Seriously. What I did was small fry, compared to what Molly's done."

"James, how can you say that? Falling out of love isn't a crime. Sometimes it just happens, it's a fact of life," Kate tried to reason with him. "Having an affair and falling in love with someone else isn't a crime either.

OK, it's morally wrong, regrettable and sad. Especially for the families concerned but you've been very cruel. Unnecessarily cruel."

"I've been cruel?" James shook his head. "I'm not the guilty party." He glanced down for a second. "I've not done anything other than handle rejection badly. I put my hands up to that. And stalked her. Once I started ... well, I couldn't stop."

"James, what on earth are you talking about?" Eddie asked.

"I've kept an eye on Molly all these years. In a lot of ways, it's been my reward ... pulling her strings, playing with her, frightening her. I know I've taken it too far sometimes but that's because, believe it or not, I do still love her. And, most importantly, by being a constant thorn in her side, I've kept her out of trouble." He looked down at his hands. Kate followed his gaze, he was still wearing his wedding ring. "By and large she's complied. She's behaved. No-one's got hurt," he continued. "Which is a success in my book."

"Got hurt? What the hell do you mean?" Eddie felt anxious.

"It's been my mission to save her from herself," James explained. "It's a kind of reverse psychology, very different to tough love, you understand? If someone treats you like shit, you have to remember there's something wrong with them, don't you? That it's not you. It's not your fault. Normal people don't go around destroying other human beings, do they?"

"James, I have no idea what you're talking about," said a frustrated Kate. "Just what are you saying?"

"OK ... let me explain," James said, sighing a little. "In a relationship you get used to things, don't you? And it hurts when they're taken away. It hurts badly. I got used to Molly wanting me, loving me, but then she took those things from me ... just like that." He raised his hand and clicked his fingers. "She took it away overnight, like I had no right to it, like she'd given her love to me temporarily. Like she'd made a mistake."

"OK, I've had enough." Kate stood up. "You're making no sense at all. In fact, you're talking bollocks. I'd hoped you might have changed but that doesn't seem to be the case. Come on Eddie, let's go."

Eddie didn't move. "James, what did you mean when you said no-one got hurt? Does it have anything to do with what happened to Will?"

"Molly is used to getting what she wants." James let the words hang in the air for several seconds. "You know what happens if she doesn't get what she wants."

"For fuck's sake James. Stop with the games," Kate shouted. "Come on Eddie, let's go."

"Sorry Kate. I'm not intentionally trying to upset you," James apologised. "Please sit down. Let me see if I can put some meat on the bones … you might start to understand." He got up and walked over to the far end of the kitchen, returning with the cafetière of still warm coffee. He refilled their cups without asking.

"Let's look at some indisputable facts, shall we? Molly's parents. Stan, her father, spoilt her, really spoilt her. You know that, don't you?" Kate felt herself nodding. "Molly's every need was met. She was a pampered princess. Daddy indulged her every whim. Admittedly, some of it might have been guilt based. You remember the accident?"

Kate frowned. "I think you're stretching it. Sure, she was an indulged child but it wasn't because her father felt guilty. She was a much-wanted baby, she had a privileged life as a result. The accident was nothing. A couple of scars … for both of them. No other lasting damage."

"You reckon?" James seemed genuinely surprised. "Are you saying it wasn't a big drama? What about the flashbacks? She hated those scars." He walked back across the kitchen to return the cafetière.

"The scars weren't that bad … they faded." Kate hadn't given much thought to the accident in years. Molly had been involved in a car crash, Stan had been driving. "She never spoke of flashbacks."

"Are you suggesting that she lied to me? That she embellished the truth?" James asked sarcastically. "Funny that, eh?"

"James, you were going to put some meat on the bones?" Eddie cut in abruptly.

"Yes ... sorry Eddie. OK, so regardless of the reasons, we agree Molly was a spoilt child?" Kate nodded. "When we got married, she expected me to step into Daddy's shoes. Stupidly, I'm guilty of having done just that ... well I tried. Perhaps I should have done things differently. Maybe I should have tried to educate Molly, to open her eyes to reality. But, loving her as much as I did," he stopped to correct himself. "Loving her as much as I do, I went along with things. It seemed easier and I'm weak where she's concerned." He stopped speaking and looked out of the window. Kate followed his gaze, the garden looked different. "Did you know that a spoilt child becomes a helpless adult?" James asked. "Inflexible too. Molly expected the world to adjust to suit her, instead of her making any concessions to adjust to the ways of the world."

Kate pulled her gaze away from the garden and leant back on the sofa. "Where are you going with this James? I'm tired."

"Kate, there's so much you probably don't know. Molly refused to go back to work after Seth was born. Did you know that?" Kate shook her head. "She flatly refused, it was non-negotiable. That's why I had to take that first job in France. I had to earn more money, there was an extra mouth to feed ... I was hoping there would be even more. Seth could have been less lonely." He paused, thinking momentarily of the solitary child Seth had been. "I'm not denying that, in the long run, it wasn't a highly successful career move for me but, at the time, it wasn't what I wanted. One word from her and I'd have stayed ... done something else. I wanted to be around Seth, to have more children." Kate said nothing, James had given an accurate description of the young, selfish Molly but her refusal to work or have more children was news. She tried not to let it show.

"You didn't know that, did you?" James asked. "Bloody hell ... I'm surprised. I thought you two were as thick as thieves. What else don't you know, Kate? What about that ridiculous charade of renewing our marriage vows? What a joke that was. Did you know that was all her idea?" Kate was speechless, her head was swimming.

"Hang on," said Eddie. "Be careful Kate, don't be fooled, I've just remembered something." He moved forward on the sofa and looked directly at James. "What about the abuse? The bruises? When she came to our house after Scooby died, however he died, she was sporting a black eye. A black eye that you gave her. That doesn't sound like the dominant woman you're describing."

James held Eddie's gaze for a long time until a gentle, sad laugh escaped. "I only ever laid a finger on her once Eddie ... after Tim ... and I've had to live with the constant shame. I never, ever touched her again."

"So how come she had the black eye?" Eddie persisted.

"Make-up Eddie! Convincing make-up clearly ... if she had you fooled."

"Please! I'm not an idiot James." Eddie was offended. "There's no way Molly could have done that, that bruise was real."

James turned to Kate. "Tell him Kate ... remind him."

"Tell me what?" Eddie turned to his wife. "Kate?"

"It's possible," she said. "But why?"

"What are you talking about Kate?" Eddie asked gently, shocked to notice how tired she looked, sitting back against the big green sofa. More pale than usual, she looked frail. He put his hand on her knee, worried that she was having a relapse, upset that he hadn't noticed.

"What is the one thing Molly is trained to do? Have any qualifications in?" James asked slowly. "Come on Eddie ... she's a bloody make-up artist. A good one."

Eddie's phone pinged in his back pocket. It was a message from Seth.

Mum's not here. She's not answering her phone. Don't know where she's gone.

"Come on Kate, we've got to go, the kids are waiting for us." He got up and turned his back to James. Silently, he beseeched Kate to understand. She nodded and rose from the sofa without question.

"You probably need time to take this in, don't you Kate?" James asked. "You clearly don't know Molly very well, as it turns out. You have no idea what she's capable of ... really capable of. I'll leave it with you. Think about Seth, think about his problems. I'll be here for a few days ... if you want to talk."

Kate said nothing and followed Eddie to the front door. James was playing games, that's what he did. Or was he? So many terrible things had happened, she couldn't be sure any more. James had unsettled her but she wasn't going to give him the satisfaction of knowing it. Not yet.

***

Eddie and Kate walked quickly and silently down the drive with a reluctant Lottie trotting a few steps behind them. After crossing the road, Kate motioned for Eddie to slow down, Lottie was struggling with the pace.

"What was all that about?" Kate asked, breaking the silence.

Eddie reached out and took her hand. "I don't know. He's messed with my head ... just when I thought I was on to something."

"On to something?" Kate asked, surprised. "On to what?"

"It will sound weird but I've been thinking for a while that Will ... well that there was more to his death than we thought," Eddie said hesitantly. "I'd kind of convinced myself that James had something to do with it. But he's implying it might be Molly, isn't he?"

"Woah ... hang on!" Kate bent down to let Lottie off the lead. "Rewind! You thought James killed Will? And now you think Molly did? That's outrageous."

"That's not what I said," Eddie said defensively. "It's like I told Jack, hearing you relate Molly's past made me look at things differently ..."

"You mentioned this to Jack but not me?" Kate cut in.

Eddie looked suitably chastised. "Sorry ... but he's a copper, an ex-copper. I wanted to know if I was barking up the wrong tree."

"And what did he say?"

"Not a great deal really." Eddie sounded deflated. "But there's a lot he doesn't know."

"Like what?" She walked in front of him, as they crossed the wooden bridge.

"He doesn't know any more than we told him ... about Molly and James. And he doesn't know much about Will's suicide, apart from the fact that he drowned himself."

"What else does he need to know?"

"He died in the pool at Willow Hill, didn't he? In their pool." He pointed back up the hill to the house they had just left. "Isn't it possible that James, or even Molly, could have had something to do with it."

"Eddie! How can you even think that?" Kate retorted. "It was suicide."

"I know, I know," Eddie sighed. "And I never thought any different at the time." They said no more for a few minutes.

"He was a big man. Will ... a fit man," Kate said eventually. "I don't see how Molly could overpower him, let alone drown him. And don't forget about Seth. Seth was there. She wouldn't have done anything with Seth around." Darker thoughts were forming in her mind. Molly put herself first, Seth wouldn't have been a consideration.

"Will couldn't swim," Eddie reminded her. "It's not quite the same, is it?"

"Even so Eddie. Don't you think a non-swimmer could get out of that pool, if they really needed to? He was so fit."

"He nearly drowned as a kid ... when we were at school," Eddie said sadly. "He never went in the water again ... he'd have panicked."

"Were the police ever suspicious of Molly at the time? Or James?" Kate had no recollection. Her overriding memory was of Seth, a traumatised Seth.

"James wasn't seen again after the Scooby incident, was he?" Eddie replied. "We all thought he'd gone back to France. Don't you remember? He had a water-tight alibi. Sorry ... no pun intended." He giggled, a little hysterically.

"And Molly was staying with us," Kate added. She was trying to think back. Had there been anything odd about Molly's behaviour at the time? They walked along in silence.

"I've done a little bit of research," Eddie offered timidly.

"You have?" Kate was surprised. "What kind of research?"

"Nothing serious. I've just gone over what was published at the time. There's no mention of James."

"And Molly?" Kate asked.

"Nothing significant. Her name comes up because of Willow Hill. That's all."

"No mention of Seth?" Kate asked cautiously.

"No ... nothing ... fortunately."

"So just what is James saying?" Kate grabbed Lottie and quickly put her back on her lead. A group of people were having a picnic. Lottie, who could spot food at fifty paces, had invaded, and ruined, many picnics in her time.

"I don't know. I'm not sure," Eddie replied. "But he was convincing, wasn't he? Did you hear him say he wasn't a murderer? When he was talking about Scooby?" Eddie stopped suddenly. "Kate, do you believe him?"

Kate didn't respond. The notion that her best friend, the woman she'd have taken a bullet for, might be a vindictive liar, or something much worse, was too much to contemplate. She knew Molly inside out but, over the past few weeks, she had, reluctantly, been forced to re-evaluate their friendship. And now Eddie was asking her the unimaginable. "Who was your text message from?" she asked. She wanted to change the subject.

Eddie looked confused. "What message?"

"With James ... just now?"

"Oh ... that. It was Seth. Molly's gone AWOL."

"Oh God ... more drama. Where do you think she's gone? She's running out of options."

"Who knows?" Eddie replied. "Rita's?" It was a long shot. Even in the direst of situations, it was unlikely Molly would seek out her mother. He glanced at his wife, he didn't want to worry her but he needed to speak to Jack urgently. He had a suspicion. If he was right, the consequences didn't bear thinking about.

"Can you take Lottie home Ed? I'll be back in an hour or so ... there's somewhere I want to go."

"Of course." He took the dog's lead. "Is there anything you need me to do? For lunch? Don't forget Nicola's coming."

"No," she said. "There's plenty of time. Just get the kids up. I won't be long." She bent to stroke Lottie, planting a kiss on her husband's cheek as she straightened up. "See you in a while."

"Kate." He caught her arm and pulled her close. "Come home soon ... but say one for Molly. I've got a feeling she's going to need all the help she can get."

Slightly stunned, Kate watched as Eddie walked away, he never failed to amaze her. He'd known all along where she'd been going, what she'd been doing but he'd instinctively understood it was something she needed to do alone. She would say a prayer for Molly, as Eddie had requested, but the first prayer would be one of thanks for her husband. He was one of a kind.

Chapter Twenty-Seven

Jack and Annie were sitting at a picnic table in the pub garden, drinking strong, black coffee out of tall mugs. It was still early but a few cyclists had already gathered around a couple of the other tables. Jack usually found their upbeat demeanour infectious but this morning, waiting to hear back from Eddie, he was on edge. Once again, news about James had unsettled him.

"I've taken another look but I can't make out the number plate. The footage is poor," said Annie. "You should think of upgrading your CCTV."

"Yes Officer," Jack replied sarcastically. "Thanks for the advice."

"Sorry," Annie apologised. "We rely so heavily on good footage these days. I'm always telling people to upgrade."

"No, you're right ... I'm being grumpy." It was Jack's turn to apologise. "We're still using the system the previous owners installed. It's archaic. I'll get some quotes."

"So ... two cars ... two BMW's. Were we too quick to accept Seth's theory? Not very good detective work, eh?" Annie laughed gently.

"I'm ashamed to say, I let my feelings get in the way. It was too easy to think badly of her."

"Maybe ... maybe not." Annie thought Jack was being unduly critical. "She got in the car willingly. She just strolled over, on drunken legs I'll admit but no-one forced her to get in that car. Once we knew about Harry, there was no reason to doubt where she'd gone."

"I'm inclined to leave it all alone Annie," Jack sighed wearily. "There's something odd going on, people are playing games ... unhealthy games. It's hard to know what they get out of it, I'm not sure I want to know."

Annie drained the last of her coffee. "I was thinking the same thing. My heart goes out to Seth though. He's more damaged than he lets on."

"Why do you say that?" Jack asked.

"There's something lurking behind the eyes. I didn't spot it straight away but when he talks about his parents, it comes to the surface. I don't think he likes either of them." Annie pulled her sunglasses down from the top of her head, it promised to be another lovely day.

"With good reason," Jack said. "It sounds like he had a rubbish childhood."

"Yeah ... it does. But there's more to it than that. You and I both have a sixth sense, don't we? It comes with the job. I have a bad feeling about Seth."

Jack's phone pinged on the table and he picked it up. "Fuck! That's all we need. Molly's gone AWOL. No-one knows where she is."

"Was that Seth?" Annie asked.

Jack was typing. "No ... Eddie. He thinks she's gone looking for Harry."

"So? What's odd about that? They're having an affair."

Jack's phone pinged again. He stood up. "I'm going to find Harry."

"Why? What's going on?" Annie frowned. "Are you worried about Harry?"

"You're the detective, Annie."

"Oh my God." Annie scrambled out of her seat. "You think Harry's in danger, don't you? You think Eddie was right about Will? But you think Molly's the dangerous one? That she could have had something to do with Will's death? Jesus Christ."

"I honestly don't know." Jack handed the van keys to Annie. "But I can't stand by and do nothing. Can you get the van and meet me out front? I'll just let Sophie know."

"Where are we going Jack?" Annie asked, jumping up from the picnic table.

"To Harry's house," he said, holding up his phone. "Eddie sent me the address."

"Can't Eddie just call him? Check he's OK?"

"Weren't you just saying how bad our detective work has been? Don't you want to see for yourself?"

Annie, suitably chastised, nodded. "OK but then we leave it? Leave them to their games? Deal?"

Jack was already walking away. "Deal," he called over his shoulder.

In the kitchen, Sophie, helping Kim unload a crate of vegetables, wasn't impressed. "Shit Jack! It's Easter Sunday, we're going to be rammed. Why do you need to go? Can't Eddie go?"

"Eddie's with Kate ... they've just seen JP," he explained. "I need to do this Sophie. Call it my sixth sense."

"That old thing!" Sophie said sarcastically. "Hang on, did you say they've just seen JP?"

"It's a long story Sophie and I don't have time just now." Jack lowered his voice. "Please, trust me."

"What aren't you telling me, Jack?"

Jack studied his wife, even in scruffy work jeans and one of his old T-shirts, she looked beautiful. He reached out to push a strand of hair away from her face, he wasn't going to lie to her. "Eddie has doubts about how Will died. He doesn't think it was suicide," he whispered. "And something that JP, James ... whoever he bloody well is... something he's told Eddie this morning implicates Molly." He put his hands up, ready for the tongue lashing he was sure Sophie was about to give him but she surprised him and said nothing. He continued, uninterrupted. "I know it's hard to believe Sophie but I have to check. You get that, don't you?"

She reached up to kiss him on the cheek. "Yes, I do," she said softly. "It's one of the many things I love about you."

Jack pulled his wife close. "I'll be back as soon as I can," he whispered into her ear. "I love you."

"You owe me," she said, as he released his hold of her. "Big time."

"I do." Jack turned and walked out of the kitchen, the echo of his footsteps on the stone floor audible long after he'd disappeared from sight.

"What's going on?" asked Kim. "Are we going to be short staffed again today?"

"I'm going to ask Lucy to come in." Sophie picked her mobile phone up from the kitchen worktop and started typing a message. "I'm sure she'll do a shift ... and Jack will be back soon." She crossed her fingers and placed them in front of her lips, something she'd not done since Jack had retired. "I'll be back in a second Kim ... I'm just going to get Daniel sorted in the marquee."

"No need ... look who's here," Kim pointed to the kitchen door.

"Shit!" Sophie rushed to Molly's side. "We weren't expecting you."

"You asked me to do the lunch shift today, didn't you?" Molly asked, just failing to look Sophie in the eye.

"Yes ... I did," Sophie whispered. "But I didn't expect to see you ... after what happened. You don't have to work today."

"Jack's not opened the marquee. I'll do that first." Molly headed out to the garden.

Sophie, lost for words, called her husband. "Jack, she's here," she said to his voicemail. "She's just turned up. She's behaving oddly. Call me." Sophie followed Molly outside and watched as she set about opening the marquee. She weighed up her options. As the boss, she could insist that Molly go home but today wasn't the day to do that. Molly, even if it was Molly on automatic pilot, was a valuable member of the team. She decided to say nothing, she didn't need the drama.

***

"Men like that have no shame," Annie said suddenly. "Jeez. He was so fucking brazen."

Jack glanced at her and smiled. "I thought you were asleep."

"Nah ... just thinking."

"You're cross with Harry and I'm pissed off at Eddie for sending us down a blind alley." There was a hint of sarcastic laughter in Jack's words. "What a fucking waste of time."

"But we caught him red-handed," Annie continued. "And he couldn't have cared less. What a bastard! His poor wife, his poor kids. Shit! I even feel sorry for Molly."

They had indeed caught Harry red-handed but he hadn't behaved like a guilty man. Let down by Molly and determined to make the most of his free weekend, he'd quickly found a replacement. A tall, attractive, blond woman, sporting huge oval sunglasses, had been unloading shopping bags out of a shiny, black Audi, as Jack pulled the van off the private lane that led to Harry's house. Spotting Jack's van, the blond woman had put her phone to her ear and disappeared, quickly, behind the house. Harry, who had been helping his leggy companion unload the car, hadn't been fazed by the unexpected appearance of Jack and Annie. "Hello guys," he'd greeted them like old friends. "What brings you here?"

"Can I have a word? In private?" Jack had taken Harry by the elbow and guided him towards a double garage.

Annie had followed his glamourous friend and found her perched on a small, brick wall in the back garden. She'd seemed engrossed in her phone. "Hello. Lovely day, isn't it?" Annie had tried a friendly approach. The woman hadn't responded. "Doing anything nice this weekend?" Annie had tried again. The blond had forced an uninterested, bored smile, exposing perfectly straight, unnaturally bright, white teeth. American, Annie thought instantly, Harry's new friend is American. The designer, skin-tight jeans, the perfectly bleached hair, the beautifully manicured nails, the leggy blond couldn't be more different to Molly. "Just the two of you?" Annie had persisted, glancing up at the big family house and the well-tended garden, where a trampoline and a climbing frame stood side by side. Everything about the house pointed to family life. "And have you given any thought to what his wife and kids will be doing today? You know, while you indulge in your shag fest?" She'd regretted the words instantly but the open dishonesty of both Harry and the blond, riled her. Infuriatingly, the blond hadn't flinched. There had been no sign of remorse.

Like a child who'd failed to get her own way, Annie had stomped back to the van and been, uncharacteristically, quiet on the drive back. She was ashamed of her outburst. However upset she was with the blond woman's morals, it was Harry she was cross with and she hadn't given him a hard time. In Annie's book that wasn't fair.

"So Harry got fed up with waiting for Molly and found himself someone new to play with while his wife is away," Jack said, stating the obvious.

"He says he hasn't seen Molly or heard anything from her. We've drawn a blank."

"Storm in a fucking teacup," Annie said dejectedly. "A small-town drama. Leave them alone Jack, let them get on with it."

"That's not like you Annie," Jack glanced over at her. "You usually want to see things through to the bitter end. You hate unresolved cases."

"But that's just it," she countered. "It's not a case, is it? It's a stupid, little, provincial drama. One that you've been dragged into and it's going nowhere. A domestic dispute at best. God, I need to get back to London, to the real action."

Arriving back at the pub, Jack was alarmed. Bikes were stacked two abreast in the bike rack and, with no other available space, some cyclists had chained their bikes to anything that wouldn't move, including the small fence around the children's play area. He groaned, the Health and Safety brigade would have something to say about that. He was, however, relieved to spot Lucy walking through the garden with a tray of food. Sophie had obviously called in the cavalry.

"Shit! Jack ... look," Annie hissed. "That woman has the skin of a rhino!" She pointed to the marquee where Molly was serving.

"Fucking Eddie. Sorry Annie, can you go and help? And explain to Sophie? I need to have a quick word with Eddie. This has to stop ... for good."

***

For the second time, in just a few days, Seth approached the house that had once been his home. On this occasion, he did so slowly and with caution. He felt compelled to be here, he didn't know what else to do. Calling his father, to verify his whereabouts, would have been easier but it was an option he'd discounted. James would only delight in Molly's latest crisis. At first glance, the house looked empty, just as it had a few days ago. Of all the excuses his mother could have used, being here, with his father, was the most irrational. But did that therefore make it all the more plausible?

Coming here to check for himself was the only way to prove things, one way or the other.

The big gates were shut but not locked, just as they had been on his previous visit. Slipping through them, his eyes were immediately drawn to the garage. The trains, Bobby had reminded him about the trains. Glancing behind him, he pulled, tentatively, at the handle of the garage door. Badly in need of oiling, it squealed its objection as it moved. A brand-new BMW sat just inside. Seth touched the bonnet gently, it was cold. He felt strangely disappointed, there were no tracks, no miniature trains.

Approaching the house, he realised something was different. The curtains, pulled tightly shut on his last visit, were now open. He walked to the front door and lifted the knocker, it landed noisily on the brass plate. Silence, no footsteps, no sign of life. He lifted the knocker again, letting it drop twice on the brass plate. Still no answer. He stepped back and looked up to the first floor, to his old bedroom window.

A skinny, blond boy, dressed only in wet swimming trunks, lay on the bed. Shivering uncontrollably, he lay on his side, cradling a pillow, one corner of which was stuffed in his mouth. His eyes were open but glazed, the boy was in shock.

Seth pulled his eyes away from the bedroom window. Rational thoughts were telling him to go, to leave the past behind but his emotions were in control. He'd come this far, he had to have an answer. Once again, he followed the path that led to the back garden. This time he was prepared for the changes, there would be no surprises. He'd know what was missing, and he, more than anyone, would understand why.

A hand on his shoulder made him jump and he gasped; his father was standing behind him. "I thought I heard someone. Sorry Seth, I didn't mean to make you jump."

"Dad?" His mother had been the telling the truth. "What the fuck?"

"I'm popular today. First Kate, then Eddie ... now you." James was smiling. He was thrilled to see his son. "I suppose they told you I was here?"

Seth's head was swimming. "Kate? I don't know what you're talking about. Dad ... what have you done?"

James' dropped the smile. "Coffee?" he asked, walking towards the house. "Or maybe something stronger? Come on ... you look like you need it."

Seth took a step back, this was his chance to run. But if he ran now, he'd never know the truth. He walked forward slowly and stepped, gingerly, over the doorstep. Only one step in, he was struggling, he had no coping strategies for this situation.

"Take a seat Seth," James said. It sounded like an order. "Don't stand on ceremony, for God's sake ... this is your home." Seth walked slowly over to the green sofa and perched, awkwardly, on the edge. For a moment, he was a little boy again, sitting, waiting, always waiting. James placed two white mugs on the coffee table and poured a clear liquid into two shot glasses. "I take it she's told you she was here yesterday?" His tone was matter of fact, there was no hint of shame or remorse. Seth couldn't speak, images from his childhood were crashing, one after the other, into his head. "It's true she was here Seth but it wasn't against her will. She's concocted some story or other, hasn't she? Kate said as much."

Everything in the room was shockingly familiar, nothing had changed. A particularly disturbing memory wouldn't go away.

A tall, dark haired man was punching a small, blond woman. He had hold of her hair. She was screaming, she couldn't escape. The boy cowered behind the green sofa.

Seth shook involuntarily. "You never sold this? You've kept it all this time?" he asked, fighting hard to regain a degree of composure.

James looked around the room. "I couldn't sell it Seth. Like I said ... it's home."

"Home?" Seth struggled to speak. He grabbed the shot glass and downed the liquid, the alcohol tore at the back of his throat. "Home?" he repeated the word slowly. "You do remember what happened here, don't you Dad? All the incredibly bad things that happened here?" He got up and walked over to the door, he needed to get out before his head exploded. Coming here had been a bad idea.

"The pool's been filled in," James said, getting up and following his son. "Seth. Stop. It wasn't your fault. You were just a boy. Wrong place, wrong time."

Seth pushed the door open and stepped outside onto the terrace. He caught sight of the path that led nowhere. "Why did you leave the path? Why didn't you dig that up too?"

James followed his gaze. "No reason ... never got round to it. I've not been here."

The young boy was bare-chested, he was running across the grass in his bare feet, away from the path, away from the pool. He had his mouth open, he was screaming, a silent, shocked scream.

"What's the matter? Are you OK?" James touched Seth's arm.

Seth flinched. "I shouldn't have come here today ... shouldn't come here ever," he mumbled. "I've tried so hard to leave it behind ... to forget."

"You sound like your bloody mother. Man up for God's sake! You can't let what happened dictate who you are. You were just a kid ... you weren't meant to see. You shouldn't have been anywhere near the fucking pool."

"I have to go ... I shouldn't have come here." Tears ran down Seth's face. His father's words had triggered something, an unwelcome memory was trying to take hold.

Someone was in the pool. The boy, swimming towel tucked under his arm, could hear splashing noises as he made his way down the path towards the ivy trellis. The noises surprised him, he'd thought he was alone. He hesitated, he wasn't supposed to go to the pool on his own, his mother fretted. Afraid of being seen, the boy stopped at the ivy and poked his head, cautiously, round the edge of the trellis. The ivy tickled his chest.

"Seth ... Seth. Come back in ... let's talk." James was standing behind him; his voice was sharp. "I can't believe you're still so hung up, after all this bloody time. It's ridiculous."

Seth turned to his father. His pale, ashen face was twisted with rage. "What would you fucking know? You pissed off, didn't you? Like you always do. Left Mum to pick up the pieces. Left me alone. Shit Dad. What the holy fuck do you know?"

James was stunned. "Come back in … let's talk. You need help."

Seth's clenched fist shot out, connecting loudly with his father's chin. Caught off-guard, James staggered backwards, trying, in vain, to keep his balance. Seth watched, dispassionately, as his father put his arm out, in a futile attempt to break his fall. A sickening crack, the sound of a bone snapping, was followed by a scream, as James' head bounced off the terrace. Then there was silence. James lay, immobile, in a crumpled heap. Seth turned and walked away.

***

Eddie and Kate were sitting in the garden, enjoying the last dregs of their red wine. Bobby was in the kitchen with Nicola, clearing away the remains of their lunch and loading the dishwasher. Seth, who'd turned up uninvited, had gone to lie down on Bobby's bed.

"Well that worked out well … better than I imagined," said Kate. "She's a nice girl. Nothing like her mother."

Eddie smiled. "She is, isn't she? I think Bobby's quite taken."

"Your son is always on the prowl," laughed Kate. "I don't know where he gets it from."

Eddie laughed too, pleased to see Kate in better spirits. She was sitting in an old blue and white striped deckchair, a decrepit item that had once belonged to her mother. He'd love to throw it out, or put it on a bonfire but she wouldn't hear of it. It was a tangible link to her past, just like so many items scattered around their cluttered home.

"What do you think was eating Seth?" Kate asked, closing her eyes and turning her face to the sun. "He arrived in a bad mood and it got steadily worse, the more wine he drank."

"I have no idea," Eddie replied. "But a pound to a penny it will have something to do with Molly. Poor kid."

They both jumped as someone tried, unsuccessfully, to open the side gate. Lottie barked a warning.

"Hang on," called Eddie. "There's a knack to it." He walked briskly over to the gate, lifted it up and pulled it open. "Jack," he said, surprised. "Did you find Molly?"

"Yes Eddie." There was a heavy trace of sarcasm in Jack's voice. "I bloody well found her. She's where she's supposed to be. She's at work."

"What?" Eddie closed the gate. "I don't get it. She's working? After what happened yesterday?"

"Yep," said Jack. "Annie and I have been on a bloody wild goose chase, thanks to you. I'm not going to be popular with Sophie, leaving her to cope. It's Easter Sunday for God's sake."

"Sorry mate," Eddie apologised. "I didn't mean to waste your time. Would you like a beer? A glass of wine?" Jack shook his head, wasting more time wasn't an option. "So, Harry's OK?" Eddie asked, glancing at Kate.

"Oh, Harry's fine mate. More than fine, if you know what I mean." Jack winked. "Sorry Kate, I know he's family but the bloke is ...." He stopped, trying to recall the word Annie had used. "Brazen. Yep ... brazen. That's the word."

"Brazen?" Kate frowned. "What do you mean? What's going on?"

"Harry has another woman in tow," Jack said. He looked at the door that led to the kitchen and lowered his voice. "He's moved on from Molly already. It was very clear what was going on. Jesus, that guy must have the proverbial, little black book."

"Oh my God," Kate said. "Poor Patty."

"He's quite a character, isn't he?" Jack laughed. "I don't mean that as a compliment either. Has his wife never suspected?"

"I think she has but I'm a little ashamed to say we don't see a lot of each other. Harry's indiscretions are not something we talk about," Kate admitted. "Maybe I should work harder at that relationship."

"It takes two Kate," Eddie said quietly. "She's never been one to put herself out when it comes to staying in touch, has she?"

"Anyway, Harry's fine. He said he's going away for a few days. I don't know how he does it. The guy must be permanently knackered," Jack laughed. "Sorry Kate ... I keep forgetting he's family. He said Patty and the kids are away with friends?"

"Yes," said Kate. "That's what she told me. Cheshire, I think. Look ... I'm confused. How come you've seen Harry? And isn't it a good thing Molly's at work?"

"Kate, Eddie." It was Nicola. "Sorry to interrupt. I just wanted to say thank you for inviting me to lunch. I've had the best time."

"You're welcome Nicola," said Kate. "It's been lovely to see you."

"I've just had a text from Mum. She's on her way back ... earlier than I thought. I've asked her to pick me up. Is that OK?" The young girl smiled apologetically. "I can meet her somewhere else, if you'd rather."

"Of course it's OK. We don't bite," Eddie joked. It was high time some things were laid to rest.

"Thanks Eddie."

Kate noticed the small blush on Nicola's face. She smiled, she found this young girl endearing. With her height and her long, strawberry blond hair, she might resemble her mother, but Nicola had inherited her father's soft nature.

"Sorry guys ... I've got to go." Jack smiled at Nicola by way of an apology for butting in. He placed his hand on Eddie's shoulder. "You need to let this go mate. I get why it's important to you but drop it. It won't bring Will back." He caught the look of panic that Eddie and Kate exchanged. "What's the matter? What have I said?"

Kate scrambled out of her deckchair and put her arm around Nicola. "Sorry Jack. We should have introduced you. This is Nicola ... Will's daughter. Nicola ... this is Jack. An old friend of your dad's."

Nicola stretched out her hand. "Nice to meet you Jack. What won't bring Dad back?"

Never had Jack wanted the ground to open and swallow him more. "Nice to meet you too Nicola," he said, a little sheepishly. "Sorry. The reference to your dad ... I didn't mean anything. We ... me and Eddie ... we've been thinking about him a lot recently. We were all at school together."

Nicola nodded. "I didn't know that. What was he like?"

Bobby appeared at the back door. "Nicola," he called. "Your mum's here." He stepped aside to let Fiona pass.

"Hello everyone." Fiona removed her large, oval sunglasses. Dressed in skinny, white jeans and a strapless navy top, she looked fit and healthy. "Happy Easter. Not often we get weather like this on a holiday weekend, is it?" Kate and Eddie murmured appropriate responses. Fiona, the strong alpha woman, was taking control of the situation. "Thank you for looking after her." She linked her arm through her daughter's and pulled her forward. "Last place I expected to find her though, I have to say." Eddie and Kate laughed nervously. Jack remained silent.

"Are you leaving already Nicola?" Seth had been woken by the doorbell, the nap seemed to have done him some good. "Shame. I thought we could have gone for a beer." He nodded at Bobby. "The three of us. We could go and torment Lucy at work."

Nicola smiled. "I'd like that Seth," she said eagerly. "Another time perhaps?"

Fiona had replaced her sunglasses. "Come on Nicola. Hurry up ... we've got things to do." It was a command, one she clearly expected her daughter to obey. To reinforce it, she placed her perfectly manicured hands tightly on Nicola's shoulders and pushed her forcefully past the boys, exposing a vivid, uneven scar close to her tanned wrist. Seth noticed how her rings glinted in the sun. They reminded him of something but his head was fuzzy from the wine, the memory eluded him.

Jack let out a soft whistle as Nicola and her mother disappeared through the back door. "Holy shit," he whispered slowly. "Things just weirder and weirder."

"What do you mean?" Eddie heard the throaty roar of an engine out on the road. Fiona was keen to get away.

Jack sat down on the bench next to the shed. "This really is a small town, isn't it? In every sense of the word."

"What are you talking about Jack?" Kate took the space next to him. "Was it such a surprise to see Fiona? Haven't you met her before?"

"You guys are never going to believe this. Shit! I can hardly believe it myself." Jack had started to laugh.

"What's so funny?" Eddie found himself smiling. Jack's laughter was infectious.

"Molly's replacement. The other woman Annie and I saw with Harry this morning? It was her ... it was Fiona. Bloody hell fire!" Jack was shaking his head in wonder.

"No ..." Kate's voice shook. "No way! Are you sure?"

"Absolutely bloody sure. I knew it the moment she walked in. She's a very striking woman."

"Oh my God." Kate thought of her sister briefly, then of Molly.

"You couldn't write it, could you?" Jack's laughter had ebbed away. "Talk about playing with fire. Does Harry know? About Molly and Fiona? About Will?"

A low, sad, animal groan made them all jump. Kate's heart lurched; it sounded like Lottie, the old dog was in pain. The gut wrenching groan came again, it wasn't Lottie. Kate turned to look behind her. Curled up in a ball with his arms wrapped tightly around his knees and his face buried in his chest, Seth was lying, moaning, on the floor, just inside the back door. "Seth!" Kate screamed, as she ran to him.

"What is it? What's the matter with him?" Jack cried. "Is he having a fit?"

"No. Help me. Pick him up." Eddie prised Seth's hands from his knees. "We need to get him upstairs. Kate ... call for help."

Jack sprang into action. Taking most of the boy's weight, he half carried, half dragged Seth upstairs while Eddie followed, pushing from behind when necessary. Seth, still groaning, didn't offer any resistance. Jack glanced worriedly at the boy's pale face, his eyes were closed and tears streamed, silently, down his cheeks.

"Dr Mellor's one of the doctors on call. He's on his way ... ten minutes." Kate entered the bedroom as the two men lay Seth on Bobby's bed. She pulled a loose cover over him. "It's OK Seth," she said, softly taking his hand. "I've got you ... don't be frightened. We've done this before, haven't we? We can get through it again." Seth seemed to respond to the sound of her voice.

Eddie stood next to her. "Keep talking to him love. Keep talking."

"This has happened before?" Jack whispered. "What's the matter with him, Ed?"

Eddie was crying. There was so much he hadn't told Jack, so much he had never planned on sharing but Jack deserved to know the truth.

***

The boy slowly poked his head round the edge of the trellis. The soft ivy tickled his bare skin and he brushed it away. In the swimming pool, a dark-haired man was messing around, splashing and shouting. He was on his own. The boy was mesmerized. Young and naive, he didn't, instantly, understand. He crept to the edge of the pool and dropped his towel. The man saw him and screamed frantically. In that moment, the boy understood the jeopardy. He stepped forward but, as his right foot connected with the cold water, an unknown force pulled him back and a towel, his towel, was thrown over his head. Yelling out fiercely, the boy tried to pull free but a strong arm encircled him and a hand secured itself, firmly, over his mouth. He lashed out, wriggling frantically. For a split second, the towel dropped to his chin. Like a wild dog, he sank his teeth into the bare arm of his captor, gagging as a metallic taste, the taste of blood, filled his mouth. The towel slipped further to his shoulders affording him a brief glimpse of brightly painted nails and sparkling rings. Shocked, he released his teeth, the person holding him was female. Suddenly, he was off his feet and in the air. The water came up to meet him with a terrifying slap. Coughing and spluttering, he surfaced from the deep water. The towel, now soaking wet, stuck to his head. Struggling for air, he swam to the edge of the pool and removed the towel. Several seconds passed as his breathing settled. Knowing, without looking, what was behind him, he forced himself to turn around. Floating, face down, the man's lifeless body was just a few feet away. The boy started to scream. He was still screaming as he ran across the grass, back to the relative safety of the house.

Chapter Twenty-Eight

The church was cool, offering those sitting quietly in the pews, a welcome reprieve from the heat of the day. Few people spoke. Some of the men, uncomfortable in their suits, pulled at their tight collars and tried to loosen their ties. A couple of women fanned themselves, ineffectually, with the order of service they'd been handed at the church door. Jack and Sophie had arrived early and had chosen to sit, discreetly, near the back. Today, more than ever, they made a handsome couple. Suited and booted, Jack seemed leaner. His height, sculptured arms and wide chest were a designer's dream. Sophie, polished and elegant in a knee-length, black linen dress, which emphasised her toned arms and small waist, sat close to her husband, glancing up at him often. As more people wandered in, Jack squeezed his wife's hand, a touching act of reassurance and togetherness. Sophie bit her lip and brushed her eyes as a small tear threatened to fall. It was nothing new, tears had been falling for several weeks. Annie, sombrely dressed in black trousers and a grey, cotton shirt, sneaked quietly into the space beside them.

"Talk about cutting it fine," Jack whispered, a faint smile playing at the corner of his mouth.

"Trains," Annie whispered back. "Bloody trains."

All three looked up as a group of people came through the church doors to their left, sad faces and dark clothing the common denominator. Impassive, Jack watched as people he knew, regulars from the pub, slowly took their seats. Doris, dressed completely in black, slipped into the pew in front of them. Sophie reached out to touch her shoulder. The old woman smiled gratefully. Like Sophie, her eyes were moist.

Jack's heart raced as he spotted Lucy come slowly through the door. Head down, she was gently encouraging two scared looking children to walk in front of her. These were Lucy's cousins, Patty's children. It was an easy deduction, all three had inherited the red hair. Lucy glanced up and caught his eye momentarily. She inclined her head in his direction. Next to him, Sophie emitted a tiny, barely audible groan, a heartbroken cry of grief.

Sad, mournful music erupted and the congregation stood as one, their voices gradually growing in strength, as they sang a hymn Jack recognised but couldn't name. Sophie, her voice slightly too high, broke into song next to him. Annie remained silent. The coffin, laden with flowers, inched through the door, protruding slightly above the heads of the congregation, as it was carried slowly into the church by six pallbearers. Eddie, at the front, stared ahead, his face set firm, his jawline rigid. Only the sadness in his eyes hinted at his inner turmoil. Bobby, taller than his father, was at the rear. Unlike Eddie he was struggling to contain his emotions. Beside Jack, Sophie sniffed, she'd seen Bobby and the tears were in free-fall. He felt for her hand and gave it a squeeze, an expression of reassurance as much for his own benefit, as for his wife's.

Kate, her red hair hanging loosely to her shoulders, followed the coffin. Dressed head to toe in black, she walked, arm in arm, with another redheaded woman, a heavier, bulkier version of herself. It was Patty, Kate's sister. Jack, riddled with guilt, dropped his eyes. If he'd taken Eddie's concerns more seriously, if he hadn't made so many promises to Sophie, this wouldn't be happening. Bullying Kate for Molly's reference had been his first mistake, he should have let Molly speak for herself. Harry would be alive, if only he'd spoken to Molly. Spotting inconsistencies in tall stories was his field of expertise but laziness, coupled with a selfish desire to keep his wife happy, had ultimately let people down and now a man was dead. He glanced at the two small heads leaning in towards Lucy. Two children would be permanently scarred, nothing in their young lives would ever be the same again and he could have done something to prevent that. Shutting his eyes, he made a solemn vow. It was too late for Harry but never again would he take the easy option. He could have saved Harry, he should have saved Harry. Sophie could feel the tension in Jack. Annie, on the other side of her, was little better. They both felt some responsibility for Harry's death. Their misplaced guilt would, in time, become less painful but, for now, her husband and her good friend were consumed with remorse. Jack would never take the safe option again, no matter how many promises she extracted from him.

Sophie, Jack and Annie stayed in their seats as the coffin was carried out after the service. The three of them watched, surreptitiously, as Kate guided a distraught Patty back out into the warm sunshine. None of them felt inclined to follow.

"Are you going to the crematorium?" It was Seth. Like them he had placed himself discreetly near the back of the church.

"No Seth," Sophie said quietly. "We're holding the wake at the pub, we need to get back to see if Kim has everything ready."

"I could come with you if you want?" offered Annie.

"No, it's OK. I think it's best if we don't show our faces." He nodded to the pews near the far end of the church.

Sophie turned, a woman wearing a black scarf over blond hair, was sitting, head bent, near a huge, stone pillar. "Oh … OK." She didn't trust herself to say anything more.

"The crematorium is for family," said Jack tersely. He too had turned to look at the woman, he was incensed to see Molly.

"Seth, don't let this affect you. There's nothing you could have done." Sophie got up quickly and put her hand on his shoulder. Like Jack and Annie, she could sense Seth's remorse. It was all so unfair, none of them had done anything wrong. People old enough to know better had behaved outrageously for many years. Seth was a victim of their monstrous selfishness. "Things will get back to normal," she said softly. "Whatever normal is."

The four of them made their way out of the church. Seth noticed Annie glancing back at Molly. "Don't worry … she's promised to stay put until the coast is clear."

Annie nodded. "Wise move."

Several people were hovering around the entrance to the church, unsure what to do or where to go. Sophie, a natural leader, took control and people were soon making their way towards the pub.

"Shit! The Press are here ... look." Jack pointed to a group of scruffy men and women with cameras, standing near the church gates.

"Don't worry, I've got this, they'll be gone in two minutes ... or they'll regret it." Annie strode purposefully over to the small media contingent. Moments later they reluctantly moved away. Annie stood her ground and watched them go. A weak smile appeared, momentarily, on Jack's face. Annie wouldn't have minced her words and she wouldn't move until all the photographers had moved on.

Jack and Seth stood in silence for a few moments. "I want to apologise to you Jack ... to both of you." Seth glanced over at Sophie who was rounding up some stragglers. "I should have come clean, as soon as I knew what Mum was up to. Those scenes in the pub could have been avoided."

"There's nothing to apologise for." Jack said, as Sophie re-joined them. "You shouldn't feel responsible."

"Well I do," Seth replied quietly. "I think I always will. If I'd said something sooner maybe Harry would still be here." His voice caught on the last few words.

"I don't think it would have changed anything." Jack placed his hand on Seth's shoulder. "Harry led a double life and it backfired. He paid the price, maybe that was his destiny." He caught the look on Seth's face, the boy looked lost. "Life goes on Seth. Sorry, that sounds harsh. What I mean is, don't dwell on it ... and don't be a stranger. Kate regards you as one of her own and you have friends here ... us included."

Seth smiled and shook the hand Jack proffered. "Thanks Jack. That means a lot."

Jack watched Seth walk away. "What a fucking mess."

"Jack, the trial date is set ... she'll get her punishment." Sophie took his hand. "You can't turn the clock back."

"Yes ... she will." Jack's voice was deep with emotion. "I hope they throw the fucking book at her. Fuck it Sophie ... it's barbaric. A man with a peanut allergy is a vulnerable man at the best of times. Ordinary, everyday situations that most people, people like you and me, take for granted, are fraught with danger."

"But he knew that. His allergy dictated how he led his life," Sophie said gently. "He took all sorts of precautions to deal with it. I've already told the police about what he said to me. You know ... how much he appreciated the detail on our menus."

"I know ... I get it." Jack sounded tired. "But I don't get how someone can be so cold, so hell bent on revenge over something so trivial. It's evil."

Sophie sighed, they'd been over this so many times but Jack couldn't let it go. "You've seen worse Jack. It's your connection to the people in this town that's hurting you." She squeezed his hand gently. She felt useless, there was nothing she could do, or say, to make him feel better. "Come on. Let's go. Game face on ... we're needed."

Jack nodded his head slightly and fell into step with his wife. Sophie was right, he'd seen much worse. But in law enforcement he'd always been able to detach himself, it was his job. It didn't mean he didn't care. On the contrary, empathy and compassion came naturally to Jack. He'd worked on numerous murder cases; each and every one of them had been harrowing. Harry's murder was different though, Harry's murder was personal. "He was so cautious, he shouldn't have died that way."

"No. Of course he shouldn't." Sophie knew where the conversation was going, it was one they had daily. "But he was severely allergic Jack. It would have been relatively quick." She didn't know this for sure but she wanted to believe Harry hadn't suffered.

Jack kicked a loose stone off the pavement, they were nearly back at the pub. For weeks, he'd nursed a mental image of Fiona, as he'd seen her on Easter Sunday, in her tight jeans and huge sunglasses, intentionally adding peanut oil to Harry's food. He saw Harry contorted in pain, struggling to breath. Fiona, tall and tanned, stood over her victim with an EpiPen in her hand, the EpiPen that would have saved Harry's life.

"Woman scorned Jack," Sophie said gently. "Not quite accurate in this case but apt enough ... and it's what they're all saying in the pub."

"Yes ... I've heard it too," Jack replied. "It's so fucking unfair Sophie. One wrong text message. That's all it took. Can you believe it?" They were back at the pub. Sophie had taken off her coat and was on her way upstairs. "It's so fucking ordinary."

Sophie didn't reply, there was nothing she could say, everything had already been said. Harry had made a simple but catastrophic mistake. Sending a text message to the wrong person was such an easy, mundane thing to do. She'd done it herself more than once. Sometimes the consequences were embarrassing, sometimes funny, but never deadly. Harry had simply run out of patience, he thought Molly was playing hard to get. A serial womaniser, it had been easy for him to find another playmate at short notice. As Jack had joked, Harry had a little black book. But walking whilst texting had proved dangerous for Harry on more than one level. Jumping to avoid a car, as he left the pub after looking for Molly, he had inadvertently sent Fiona a message, a message meant for Molly. Fiona had played second fiddle to Molly Pope once before. Finding herself unexpectedly cast in that role again pushed her to the very edge. Harry didn't stand a chance.

Chapter Twenty-Nine

"They can't make a case out of it," Jack said. "They've tried ... believe me." He and Eddie were sitting on an old park bench whilst Lottie investigated something close to the river bank. It was four weeks since Harry's funeral. Life, for most people, was gradually returning to normal. "She'll only be tried for Harry's murder."

"Seth will be gutted," Eddie sighed. "It could have helped put some of his demons to bed."

"I know ... I wish there was more we could do." Jack leant back on the bench. "Seth didn't see her face ... he can't identify her. A glimpse of some rings and painted nails doesn't make Fiona guilty."

"But there's so much that adds up ... you know there is." Eddie spoke quietly. "She's even admitted to being there that day ... at Willow Hill."

"She has but she offered that information Eddie ... and the rest can't be proved either way."

"So, what else has she said?" Eddie asked.

Jack frowned. He and Annie had called in a few favours but he wasn't sure he should share all the detail with Eddie. "What I tell you stays between us, OK?" he asked. "It's not common knowledge."

Eddie nodded. "Of course. I'm not a gossip Jack."

Jack held his friend's gaze, he could trust Eddie. "Fiona admits going to the vicarage on the day Will died. She was looking for Molly, she wanted a confrontation. She was ready to fight for her marriage." He stopped speaking as Eddie let out a derisive laugh. "Provocative words, I agree," he continued. "But the sort of language a lot of people use. It doesn't prove intent to kill. She wanted to catch Molly off-guard. She's even admitted parking her car on the main road. She wanted to have the advantage of surprise."

"Why does that matter?" Eddie asked.

"It shows she's giving the police details Ed ... she's cooperating," Jack replied. "She's not trying to hide anything. She didn't find Molly at Willow

Hill but she did find Will. He was in the garden ... waiting for Molly." Jack stopped speaking as Lottie barked at a passing runner. The old dog might be slow but she still sounded like she meant business. It made Jack smile, he'd been thinking about getting a dog. "He was going to call it off Ed. Will was going back to his family ... back to Fiona."

"What? And you believe that?" Eddie asked incredulously.

"I don't know. Is it so hard to believe? Fiona's talked about walking around the garden with Will ... she insists they didn't go anywhere near the pool. She describes Will as being 'phobic' about water."

"An accurate description," Eddie agreed grudgingly. "Does she know that Seth thinks she killed Will? That she stopped him from saving Will? That she pushed him in the water?"

"I don't know," Jack sighed. "There's only so much we're being told ... by rights we shouldn't be privy to anything."

"Fiona's capable of murder. Look what she did to Harry." Eddie whispered dramatically. "Surely that's enough?"

"It's not that simple Ed." Jack put his hand on Eddie's shoulder. "There's no evidence."

"But Seth's evidence?" Eddie countered.

"Like I said ... painted nails, rings ... it's not enough." He didn't add that Seth's evidence could count against him. Some people were making noises about the possibility of the young boy being involved. Maybe Seth, aware of his mother's affair, had pushed Will into the pool. Others had got hold of the boy's fragile mental health history. Building a case, based on Seth's evidence, was doomed.

"The scar on her wrist?" Eddie insisted. "It's not just painted nails and rings. How many women have that kind of scar on their wrist?"

Jack shook his head. "Sorry Eddie ... it's not enough. Fiona claims hers is the result of a dog bite and ..." He stopped speaking.

"And what?" Eddie asked.

Jack sighed heavily. "Seth's not reliable." He hated saying these words, Seth deserved better.

"Not reliable?" Eddie hissed. "That lad's been traumatised for years about what happened that day. Have you any idea how hard his rehabilitation has been?" Jack held his gaze but said nothing. "If Fiona didn't do it, who did?"

"The suicide verdict remains," Jack said slowly. "Don't shoot the messenger Ed but what else do you expect? Seth was a troubled child. From all accounts, he became a troubled teenager. It's only recently that he's sought help and sorted himself out. Do you want to see that used against him? It's brutal but what happened to him makes him less credible."

"It stinks." Eddie stood up. "You can't tell me you're happy to accept that."

Jack looked up at his friend. "Until a few weeks ago you were convinced James was a killer. Jesus, there was even a moment when you believed Molly could have been responsible." He thought about the day he'd seen Fiona at Harry's house, she hadn't looked like she was about to kill anyone. Murderers came in all shapes and sizes.

"That was James … he made it look that way." Eddie sounded like a small child, churlish and resentful.

"Either way, don't you see? You want someone to be responsible so badly you're not looking at things logically." Jack stood up. "It won't bring Will back."

Eddie lowered his head. He was deflated and close to tears. Jack was right, he'd got carried away. Trying to prove Will was murdered had become a distraction. It had given him something to focus on, something other than Kate's declining health. Jack's arms pull him forward, the hug was just what he needed.

***

Late in the afternoon, on the anniversary of his death, Molly stood by Will's grave with a small bouquet of white lilies in her hand. Other fresh flowers lay under the grey headstone. Curious, she bent down to examine them. It reassured her a little to think that some people still remembered. She read the messages, something she'd religiously avoided in the past. Most were predictable, 'gone but not forgotten', 'in loving memory', 'with love and fond memories'. With the passage of time people had become lazy, had stopped trying to express their true feelings. It made her cross. Will had been worth more than that. A beautifully handwritten message attached to a small bunch of wild flowers brought a small lump to her throat. It was from Nicola. 'Daddy, loved and remembered every day.' Molly tried not to let herself think about Nicola too often. She'd played a pivotal role in the death of the young woman's father, as well as the incarceration of her mother. She didn't feel guilty about either but Nicola had, innocently, become the most injured party. She'd lost both her parents. A card attached to a small bunch of yellow roses caught her attention. It was Kate's handwriting, 'God has you in his keeping, we have you in our hearts.'

"Oh Kate." Molly whispered gently, as she picked up the roses and, head bowed, held them close to her chest. Kate had chosen these flowers, Kate had held them in her hands. They were a tenuous connection to her old friend and a sudden, stark reminder of what she'd lost. Kate had kept her word, their friendship was over, there was no way back.

Molly placed the roses back on the grave, thinking of all the good news she'd love to share with Kate. Her divorce from James had finally come through, the papers were signed and the settlement finalised. She was cash rich with more money in the bank than she knew what to do with and, thanks to the monthly alimony arrangement, her wealth kept growing. For the first time in her single life, money was, quite literally, no object.

Her tentative attempts at self-improvement would have impressed Kate more than her bank balance though. Kate would be pleased and impressed to hear about her sessions with a counsellor. Opening up to a stranger was bloody hard work and some parts of her history would, without a shadow of a doubt, go to her grave with her but, overall, Molly had to admit it was good to talk things through. She still had problems dealing with her mother but she tried harder now, Rita wasn't the enemy any more. Kate would approve.

She was also trying to adopt a positive lifestyle. With Kate in mind, she'd started taking yoga classes and she'd surprised herself. Not only did she enjoy the exercise but she was fitter than she'd ever been. Her energy levels had soared and, as a result, her body was toned and lean. Curvaceous Molly had been consigned to history. There were also other, more obvious, changes to her appearance. The make-up was still always perfect but it was more subtle, she'd learnt that less was more. The blond bob had also gone, replaced by a modern, short, elfin cut and the trademark shade of bright blond had been toned down to a more natural looking ash brown. Beauty salon treatments were, once again, part of her weekly routine. Facials and manicures ensured she felt good about life and about herself. Money in the bank had also put a stop to high-street shopping, Molly's wardrobe was now, exclusively, designer label. Nothing was ever too outlandish or sexy, she wasn't making any statements. As much as she still craved male attention, she didn't need to advertise the fact. Again, Kate would approve.

Molly was no saint though and some notable excesses might cause Kate to raise an eyebrow. Reverting to her maiden name, she'd bought a charming, if overpriced, cottage in a pretty, little village where no-one knew her. She'd commissioned a bespoke kitchen and bathroom and spent a small fortune on fixtures and fittings. A young man from the village took care of her garden. Both her lawn and her flowerbeds always looked immaculate. Seth, unsurprisingly, still refused to visit the new cottage but Molly lived in hope and a bedroom had been prepared and was ready and waiting for him. She was confident he would visit one day, he couldn't stay mad at her forever. She'd also bought a car. Unable to afford one for many years, Molly now drove a little, red convertible although she didn't venture far. There weren't many people to visit.

She'd made some investments too; investments Kate would probably consider frivolous. In an attempt to replace the jewellery she'd been forced to pawn when times were tough, she'd purchased several expensive items. Diamond necklaces with matching stud earrings were now wardrobe essentials, although more ornate pieces were also on hand for special occasions. Special occasions, however, were, sadly, still thin on the ground. New rings also adorned her fingers. Unattached romantically, she still liked to wear a large rock on her wedding finger. At her age, she preferred to appear attached, not married but attached. It allowed her to keep her options open. A big ring, coupled with superbly manicured nails, was a style she'd favoured in the past. It spoke volumes, it made her feel superior. Subconsciously, she knew she'd have to hide some of these items from Seth, if and when he visited, they wouldn't be good for his mental health.

Her most extravagant and her most recent purchase was her Rolex watch. For years she'd been forced to wear cheap imitations but just this morning, in an upmarket London jewellers, she had purchased the real thing. The watch with the oversized, diamond encrusted face and the extra wide, gold strap would be ready for her to collect in just over a week's time. The lead time for such items was usually several weeks but she had flirted outrageously with the young salesman, to ensure her order was given top priority. It had been a rewarding experience, flirting was still one of her best skills.

Sitting by Will's grave, in the fading light, wondering what Kate would make of her new life, Molly gently rubbed her left wrist. Bowled over by the display model in the Rolex shop, she'd taken a gamble and discarded her own tatty, old watch; it was out of character with her new image. She rubbed her naked wrist again; the dark red nails, the ones that complemented her new ruby ring, slowly traced the vicious, circular scar that sat near her wrist bone. Not particularly unsightly, it was however eye-catching, hence her penchant for large faced watches. It was a scar that would remain Molly's secret, a scar that no other human being would ever see; it was the scar left by the teeth of her own, young son. It was the tell-tale scar of a murderer.

Printed in Great Britain
by Amazon